THE SUMMER HOUSE

THE SUMMER HOUSE

Santa Montefiore

WINDSOR
PARAGON

First published 2012
by Simon & Schuster UK Ltd
This Large Print edition published 2013
by AudioGO Ltd
by arrangement with
Simon & Schuster UK Ltd

Hardcover   ISBN: 978 1 4713 3910 3
Softcover   ISBN: 978 1 4713 3911 0

British Library Cataloguing in Publication Data available

Printed and bound in Great Britain by
MPG Books Group Limited

To my children, Lily and Sasha, with love

Folly n. (pl. **follies**) **1** foolishness. **2** a foolish act or idea. **3** an ornamental building with no practical purpose. ORIGIN Old French *folie* 'madness'.

I call it a summer house . . .
(Author)

Chapter 1

Hampshire 2012

The beginning of March had been glorious. The earth had shaken off the early-morning frosts and little buds had emerged through the hardened bark to reveal lime-green shoots and pale-pink blossom. Daffodils had pushed their way up through the thawing ground to open into bright-yellow trumpets, and the sun had shone with renewed radiance. Birdsong filled the air and the branches were once again aquiver with the busy bustle of nest-building. It had been a triumphant start to spring.

Fairfield Park had never looked more beautiful. Built on swathes of fertile farmland, the Jacobean mansion was surrounded by sweeping lawns, ancient bluebell woods and fields of thriving crops and buttercups. There was a large ornamental lake where frogs made their homes among the bulrushes and goldfish swam about the lily pads. Towering beech trees protected the house from hostile winds in winter and gave shelter to hundreds of narcissi in spring. A nest of barn owls had set up residence in the hollow of an apple tree and fed off the mice and rats that dwelt on the farm and in the log barn, and high on the hill, surveying it all with the patience of a wise old man, a neglected stone folly was hidden away like a forgotten treasure.

Abandoned to the corrosion of time and weather, the pretty little folly remained benignly observant, confident that one day a great need would surely draw people to it as light to lost souls. Yet, today, no one below could even see those honey-coloured walls and fine, sturdy pillars, for the estate was submerged beneath a heavy mist that had settled upon it in a shroud of mourning. Today, even the birds were subdued. It was as if spring had suddenly lost her will.

The cause of this melancholy was the shiny black hearse that waited on the gravel in front of the house. Inside, the corpse of Lord Frampton, the house's patriarch, lay cold and vacant in a simple oak coffin. The fog swirled around the car like the greedy tentacles of death, impatient to pull his redundant body into the earth, and on the steps that led down from the entrance his two Great Danes lay as solemn and still as a pair of stone statues, their heads resting dolefully on their paws, their sad eyes fixed on the coffin; they knew intuitively that their master would not be coming home.

Inside the house, Lady Frampton stood before the hall mirror and placed a large black hat on her head. She sighed at her reflection, and her heart, already heavy with bereavement, grew heavier still at the sight of the eyes that stared back with the weary acquiescence of an old woman. Her face was blotchy where tears had fallen without respite ever since she had learned of her husband's sudden death in the Swiss Alps ten days before. The shock had blanched her skin and stolen her appetite so that her cheeks looked gaunt, even if her voluptuous body did not. She had been used to his absences while he had indulged his passion for climbing the great mountains of the world, but now the house reverberated with a different kind of silence: a loud, uncomfortable silence that echoed through the large rooms with a foreboding sense of permanence.

She straightened her coat as her eldest son, now the new Lord Frampton, stepped into the hall from the drawing room. 'What are they doing in there, David?' she asked, trying to contain her grief, at least until she got to the church. 'We're going to be late.'

David gazed down at her sadly. 'We can't be late, Mum,' he said, his dark eyes full of the same pain. 'Dad's . . . you know . . .' He looked to the window.

'No, you're right, of course.' She thought of George in the hearse outside and felt her throat constrict. She turned back to the mirror and began to fiddle with her hat again. 'Still, everyone will be waiting and it's frightfully cold.'

A moment later her middle son, Joshua, emerged from the drawing room with his chilly wife, Roberta. 'You OK, Mum?' he asked, finding the emotion of such an occasion embarrassing.

'Just keen to get on with it,' David interjected impatiently. Joshua thrust his hands into his pockets and hunched his shoulders. The house felt cold. He went to stand by the hall fire where large logs entwined with ivy crackled in the grate.

'What are they doing in there?' his mother asked again, glancing towards the drawing room. She could hear the low voice of her youngest son, Tom, and her mother-in-law's formidable consonants as she held forth, as usual unchallenged.

'Grandma's demanding that Tom show her how to use the mobile telephone he gave her,' Joshua replied.

'Now? Can't it wait till later?' Her chin trembled with anguish.

'They're finishing their drinks, Antoinette,' said Roberta with a disapproving sniff. 'Though I'm not sure Tom *should* be drinking with his history, should he?'

Antoinette bristled and walked over to the window. 'I think today of all days Tom is entitled to consume anything he wants,' she retorted tightly. Roberta pursed her lips and rolled her eyes at her husband, a gesture she wrongly assumed her mother-in-law couldn't see. Antoinette watched her arrange her pretentious feather fascinator in front of the mirror and wondered why her son had chosen to marry a woman whose cheekbones were sharp enough to slice through slate.

At last Tom sauntered into the hall with his grandmother, who was tucking the telephone into her handbag and clipping it shut. He smiled tenderly at his mother and Antoinette immediately felt a little better. Her youngest had always had the power to lift her high or pull her low, depending on his mood or state of health. A small glass of wine had left him none the worse and she ignored the niggling of her better judgement that knew he shouldn't consume any alcohol at all. Her thoughts sprang back to her husband and she recalled the time he had managed to telephone her from the Annapurna base camp just to find out how Tom was after a particularly bad week following a break-up. She felt her eyes welling with tears again and pulled her handkerchief out of her pocket. George had been a very *good* man.

'You haven't turned the heating off, have you?' exclaimed the Dowager Lady Frampton

4

accusingly. '*I* never let it get so frightfully cold!' In her long black dress, wide black hat and mink stole Margaret Frampton looked as if she were off to crash a Halloween party rather than attend her only son's funeral. Around her neck, wrist and dripping from her ears like elaborate icicles was the exquisite Frampton sapphire suite, acquired in India in 1868 by the first Lord Frampton for his wife, Theodora, and passed down the generations to George, who had loaned it to his mother because his wife refused to wear such an extravagant display of wealth. The Dowager Lady Frampton had no such reservations and wore the jewels whenever a suitable occasion arose. Antoinette wasn't sure Margaret's son's funeral was quite such an occasion.

'The heating *is* on, Margaret, and the fires are all lit. I think the house is in mourning, too,' she replied.

'What a ridiculous idea,' Margaret muttered.

'I think Mum's right,' interjected Tom, casting his gaze out of the window. 'Look at the fog. I think the whole estate is in mourning.'

'I've lost more people than I can count,' said Margaret, striding past Antoinette. 'But there's nothing worse than losing a son. An *only* son. I don't think I'll ever get over it. At the very least, one would expect the house to be warm!'

Harris, the old butler who had worked for the family for more than thirty years, opened the front door and the Dowager Lady Frampton stepped out into the mist, pulling her stole tighter across her chest. 'Goodness me, are we going to be able to get to church?' She stood at the top of the stone stair and surveyed the scene. 'It's as thick as

5

porridge.'

'Of course we will, Grandma,' Tom reassured her, taking her arm to guide her down. The Great Danes remained frozen beneath the weight of their sadness. Margaret settled her gaze on the coffin and thought how terribly lonely it looked through the glass of the hearse. For a moment the taut muscles in her jaw weakened and her chin trembled. She lifted her shoulders and stiffened, tearing her eyes away. Pain wasn't something one shared with other people.

The chauffeur stood to attention as Tom helped his grandmother into one of the Bentleys. Roberta followed dutifully after, but Antoinette hung back. 'You go, Josh,' she said. 'Tom and David will come with me.'

Joshua climbed into the front seat. One might have thought that his father's death would unite the two women, but it seemed they were still as hostile as ever. He listened to his wife and grandmother chatting in the back and wondered why his mother couldn't get along with Margaret as well as Roberta did.

'That woman is so trying,' Antoinette complained, dabbing her eyes carefully as the cars followed the hearse down the drive and through the iron gates adorned with the family crest of lion and rose. 'Do I look awfully blotchy?' she asked Tom.

'You look fine, Mum. It wouldn't be appropriate to look polished today.'

'I suppose not. Still, everyone's going to be there.'

'And everyone is going to be coming back,' grumbled David from the front seat. He didn't

6

relish the idea of having to socialize.

'I think we'll all need a stiff drink.' She patted Tom's hand, wishing she hadn't referred to alcohol. 'Even you. Today of all days.'

Tom laughed. 'Mum, you've got to stop worrying about me. A few drinks aren't going to kill me.'

'I know. I'm sorry, I shouldn't have mentioned it. I wonder who's come,' she said, changing the subject.

'Perish the thought of having to chat to Dad's dreadful aunts and all the boring relatives we've spent years avoiding,' David interjected. 'I'm not in the mood for a party.'

'It's not a party, darling,' his mother corrected. 'People just want to show their respect.'

David stared miserably out of the window. He could barely see the hedgerows as they drove down the lane towards the town of Fairfield. 'Can't everyone just bugger off and go home afterwards?'

'Absolutely not. It's polite to ask your father's friends and relatives home after the funeral. It'll cheer us all up.'

'Great,' David muttered glumly. 'I can't think of a better way of getting over Dad's death than having a knees-up with a bunch of old codgers.'

His mother began to cry again. 'Don't make this any harder for me, David.'

David peered around the seat and softened. 'I'm sorry, Mum. I didn't mean to upset you. I just don't feel like playing the glad game, that's all.'

'None of us do, darling.'

'Right now, I just want to be alone to wallow in my sorrow.'

'I could kill for a cigarette,' said Tom. 'Do you think I have time for a quick one round the back?'

7

The car drew up outside St Peter's medieval church. The chauffeur opened the passenger door and Antoinette waited for Tom to come round to help her out. Her legs felt weak and unsure. She could see her mother-in-law walking up the stony path towards the entrance of the church where two of George's cousins greeted her solemnly. *She* would never cry in public, Antoinette thought bitterly. Antoinette doubted whether she had ever cried in private. Margaret considered it very middle-class to show one's feelings and turned up her aristocratic nose at the generation of young people for whom it was normal to whine, shed tears and moan about their lot. She condemned them for their sense of entitlement and took great pleasure in telling her grandchildren that in her day people had had more dignity. Antoinette knew Margaret despised her for continuously sobbing, but she was unable to stop, even to satisfy her mother-in-law. But she dried her eyes before stepping out of the car, and took a deep breath; the Dowager Lady Frampton had no patience with public displays of emotion.

Antoinette walked up the path between her two sons and thought how proud George would be of his boys. Tom, who was so handsome and wild, with his father's thick blond hair and clear denim eyes, and David, who didn't look like his father at all, but was tall and magnetic and more than capable of bearing his title and running the estate. Up ahead, Joshua disappeared into the church with Roberta. Their middle son was clever and ambitious, making a name for himself in the City, as well as a great deal of money. George had respected his drive, even if he hadn't understood his unadventurous choice of career. George had been a man who loved natural, untamable landscapes; the concrete terrain of the Square Mile had turned his spirit to salt.

She swept her eyes over the flint walls of the church and remembered the many happy occasions they had enjoyed here. The boys' christenings, Joshua's marriage, his daughter Amber's christening only a year before—she hadn't expected to come for *this*. Not for at least another thirty years, anyway. George had been only fifty-eight.

She greeted George's cousins and, as she was the last to arrive, followed them into the church. Inside, the air was thick with body-heat and perfume. Candles flickered on the wide window ledges and lavish arrangements of spring flowers infused the church with the scent of lilies, freesias and narcissi. Reverend Morley greeted her with a sympathetic smile. He sandwiched her hand between his soft, doughy ones, and muttered words of consolation, although Antoinette didn't hear for the nerves buzzing in her ears like badly played violins. She blinked away tears and cast her mind back to his visit to the house just after she had heard the terrible news. If only she could rewind to before ...

It seemed that every moment of the last ten days had been leading up to this point. There had been so much to do. David and Tom had flown out to Switzerland to bring back their father's body. Joshua and Roberta had taken care of the funeral arrangements. Antoinette had organized the flowers herself, not trusting her daughter-in-law to know the difference between a lilac and a lily,

9

being a Londoner, and her sister, Rosamunde, had helped choose the hymns. Now the day was upon them Antoinette felt as if she were stepping into a different life; a life without George. She gripped Tom's arm and walked unsteadily up the aisle. She heard the congregation hush as she moved past and dared not catch anyone's eye for fear that their compassion would set her off again.

While Tom greeted their father's aunts, David settled his mother into the front pew. He glanced around the congregation. He recognized most of the faces—relations and friends dressed in black and looking uniformly sad. Then amidst all the grey, pallid faces, one bright, dewy one stood out like a ripe peach on a winter tree. She was staring straight at him, her astonishing grey eyes full of empathy. Transfixed, he gazed back. He took in the unruly cascade of blonde curls that tumbled over her shoulders, and the soft, creamy texture of her skin, and his heart stalled. It was as if a light had been switched on in the darkness of his soul. It didn't seem appropriate to smile, but David wanted to, very much. So he pulled a resigned smile and she did the same, silently imparting sympathy for his loss.

As David left the church again with his brothers and cousins to bear the coffin, he glanced back at the mystery blonde and wondered how she fitted into his father's life. Why had they never met before? He couldn't help the buoyant feeling that lifted him out of the quagmire of grief into a radiant and happy place. Was this what people called 'love at first sight'? Of all the days it should happen, his father's funeral was the most inappropriate.

10

Phaedra Chancellor knew who David Frampton was, for she had done her research. The eldest of three sons, he was twenty-nine, unmarried and lived in a house on the Fairfield estate where he managed the farm. He had studied at Cirencester Agricultural College, for while his father had found the life of a country squire unexciting, David was as comfortable in the land as a potato.

Phaedra had only seen photographs of George's sons. Tom was without doubt the most handsome. He had inherited his father's blue eyes and the mischievous curl of his lips. But David was better-looking in the flesh than she had imagined. He was less polished than Tom, with scruffy brown hair, dark eyes and a large aquiline nose that did not photograph well. In fact, his features were irregular and quirky and yet, somehow, together they were attractive—and he had inherited his father's charisma, that intangible magnetism that drew the eye. Joshua, on the other hand, was more conventional-looking, with a face that was generically handsome and consequently easy to forget.

She looked down at the service sheet and her vision blurred at the sight of George's face imprinted on the cover. He had been more beautiful than all his sons put together. She blinked away painful memories and stared at the man she had grown to love. She could see Tom and Joshua reflected in his features, but she couldn't see David; he looked like his mother.

She sniffed and wiped her nose with a Kleenex. Julius Beecher, George's lawyer, who sat beside her, patted her knee. 'You OK?' he whispered. She nodded. 'Nervous?'

'Yes.'

'Don't worry, you'll be fine.'

'I'm not sure this is the right day to drop the bombshell, Julius,' she hissed, as music began to fill the church.

'I'm afraid there's no avoiding it. They're going to find out sooner or later and besides, you wanted to be here.'

'I know. You're right. I wanted to be here very much. But I wish I didn't have to meet his family.'

The choir walked slowly down the aisle singing Mozart's 'Lacrimosa'. Their angelic voices echoed off the stone walls and reverberated into the vaulted ceiling as they rose in a rousing crescendo. The candle flames wavered at the sudden motion that stirred the air and an unexpected beam of sunlight shone in through the stained-glass windows and fell upon the coffin as it followed slowly behind.

Antoinette could barely contain her emotions; it was as if her heart would burst with grief. She glanced down the pew to where George's aunts Molly and Hester, one as thin as the other was fat, stood with the same icy poise as the Dowager Lady Frampton. Even Mozart was unable to penetrate their steely armour of self-control. Antoinette was grateful for her sister, Rosamunde, who howled with middle-class vigour in the pew behind.

Antoinette felt a sob catch in her chest. It was impossible to imagine that her vital, active husband was contained within those narrow oaken walls. That soon he'd be buried in the cold earth, all alone without anyone to comfort him, and that she'd never again feel the warmth of his skin and the tenderness of his touch. At that unbearable thought, the tears broke free. She glanced into the pew to see the flint-hard profile of her mother-in-law. But she no longer cared what the old woman thought of her. She had toed the line for George, but now he was gone, she'd cry her heart out if she wanted to.

When the service was over, the congregation stood while the family filed out. Antoinette walked with Tom, leaning heavily on his arm, while David escorted his grandmother. He passed the pew where the mysterious blonde was dabbing her eyes, but he didn't allow his gaze to linger. He desperately hoped she'd be coming back for tea.

Outside, the fog had lifted and patches of blue sky shone with renewed optimism. The grass glistened in fleeting pools of sunlight and birds chirped once again in the treetops.

'Who's the blonde?' asked Tom, sidling up to David.

'What blonde?' David replied nonchalantly.

Tom chuckled. 'The really hot blonde you couldn't have failed to notice about six pews behind. Very foxy. The day is suddenly looking up.'

'Come on, darling. Let's not linger outside the church,' said Antoinette, longing for the privacy of the car. The two brothers glanced behind them but the congregation was slow to come out.

Margaret sniffed her impatience. 'Take me to the car, David,' she commanded. 'I will greet people back at the house.' She strode forward and David was left no alternative but to escort her down the path. As she carefully lowered her large bottom onto the rear seat David's eyes strayed back to the church where the congregation was now spilling out onto the grass. He searched in

13

vain for the white curls in the sea of black. 'Come, come, don't dawdle. Good, here are Joshua and Roberta. Tell them to hurry up. I need a drink.'

'Beautiful service,' said Roberta, climbing in beside Margaret.

'Lovely,' Margaret agreed. 'Though Reverend Morley does go on, doesn't he?'

'They all love the sound of their own voices,' said Joshua.

'That's why they're vicars,' Roberta added.

'I thought what he said about Dad being every man's friend was spot on,' Joshua continued, getting into the front seat. 'He loved people.'

Roberta nodded. 'Oh, he was terrifically genial.'

'We certainly gave him a good send-off, didn't we, Grandma?'

'Yes, he would have enjoyed that,' said Margaret quietly, turning her face to the window.

David returned to Fairfield Park with his mother and Tom. The house was restored to its former splendour now that the sun had burnt away the fog. Bertie and Wooster, the Great Danes, were waiting for them on the steps. It seemed that the sun had lifted their spirits, too, for they leaped down to the car, wagging their tails.

Harris opened the door and Mary, who cleaned for Lady Frampton, stood in the hall with her daughter, Jane, bearing trays of wine. The fire had warmed the place at last and sunlight tumbled in through the large latticed windows. The house felt very different from the one they had left a couple of hours before, as if it had accepted its master's passing and was ready to embrace the new order.

David and Tom stood by the drawing-room fire. David had helped himself to a whisky while Tom

14

sipped a glass of Burgundy and smoked a sneaky cigarette—his mother and grandmother abhorred smoking inside, probably one of the only opinions they had in common. Little by little the room filled with guests and the air grew hot and stuffy. At first the atmosphere was heavy but after a glass or two of wine the conversations moved on from George and his untimely death, and they began to laugh again.

Both brothers looked out for the mysterious blonde. David had the advantage of being tall, so he could see over the herd, but, more dutiful than his brother, he found himself trapped in conversation first with Great Aunt Hester and then with Reverend Morley. Tom had thrown his cigarette butt into the fire and leaned against the mantelpiece, rudely looking over Great Aunt Molly's shoulder as she tried to ask him about the nightclub he ran in London.

At last the mystery guest drifted into view, like a swan among moorhens. Tom left Molly in mid conversation; David did his best to concentrate on Reverend Morley's long-winded story, while anxiously trying to extricate himself.

Phaedra suddenly felt very nervous. She took a big gulp of wine and stepped into the crowd. Julius cupped her elbow, determined not to lose her, and gently pushed her deeper into the throng. She swept her eyes about the room. What she could see of it was very beautiful. The ceilings were high, with grand mouldings and an impressive crystal chandelier that dominated the room and glittered like thousands of teardrops. Paintings hung on silk-lined walls in gilded frames, and expensive-looking objects clustered on tables. Tasselled shades glowed softly above Chinese porcelain lamps, and a magnificent display of purple orchids sat on the grand piano among family photographs in silver frames. It looked as if generations of Framptons had collected beautiful things from all over the world and laid them down regardless of colour or theme. The floor was a patchwork of rugs, cushions were heaped on sofas, pictures hung in tight collages, a library of books reached as high as the ceiling, and glass-topped cabinets containing collections of enamel pots and ivory combs gave the room a Victorian feel. Nothing matched and yet everything blended in harmony. George's life had been here, with his family, and she hadn't been a part of it. Just as she was about to cry again, Tom's grinning face appeared before her like the Cheshire Cat.

'Hello, I'm Tom,' he said, extending his hand. His eyes twinkled at her flirtatiously. 'I've been wondering who you are.'

She smiled, grateful for his friendliness. 'I'm Phaedra Chancellor,' she replied.

'American,' he said, raising an eyebrow in surprise.

'Canadian, actually.'

'Ah, Canadian.'

'Is that a bad thing?'

'No, I like Canadians, actually.'

She laughed at the languid way he dragged his vowels. 'That's lucky.'

'Hello, Tom,' interrupted Julius. The two men shook hands. 'Lovely service,' he said.

'Yes, it really was, very lovely,' Phaedra agreed. Tom didn't think he had ever seen such startlingly beautiful eyes. They were a clear grey-blue, almost

16

turquoise, framed by thick lashes and set wide apart, giving her face a charming innocence.

'So how did you know my father?' he asked.

Phaedra glanced anxiously at Julius. 'Well ...' she began.

Just as she was about to answer, David appeared, and her words caught in her throat. 'Ah, there you are, Tom,' said David, but his eyes fell on Phaedra and he smiled casually, as if he had chanced upon bumping into her. 'I'm David,' he said. His gaze lingered at last, drinking in her beauty as if it were ambrosia.

'Phaedra Chancellor,' she replied, putting out her hand. He took it, enjoying for an extended moment the warmth of her skin.

'Hello, David,' interrupted Julius, and reluctantly David let go of her hand. 'Where's Lady Frampton?'

'Oh, hello, Julius. I didn't see you there.'

'Well, I *am* here,' said Julius testily; he was very sensitive about being five foot seven and three-quarter inches short. 'I need to speak to her. You're tall, David. See if you can spot her from your lofty height.'

David looked down at Julius's shiny bald head and red, sweating brow, and thought how Dickensian he looked in his black suit and tie. 'She's not in here. Perhaps she's in the hall.'

'Then let's go and find her. I want her to meet Phaedra.'

Tom and David both wished Julius would go and find their mother on his own, but the portly lawyer put his arm around Phaedra's waist and escorted her out into the hall. Curious and furious, the two brothers followed after.

17

They finally found Antoinette in the library with her elder sister, Rosamunde. Wine glasses in hand, they were standing by George's desk, talking in low voices. 'Ah, you've found me hiding,' said Antoinette, composing herself. It was clear that she had been crying again.

'We came in here for a little peace. It's very busy out there,' Rosamunde explained in her deep, strident voice, hoping they'd take the hint and go away.

Antoinette saw the stranger in their midst and stiffened. 'Hello,' she said, dabbing her eyes. 'Have we met before?'

'No, we haven't,' Phaedra replied.

'Phaedra Chancellor,' David cut in, dazed by the force of her allure.

'Oh.' Antoinette smiled politely. 'And how ...' She frowned, not wanting to be rude.

Julius seized the moment. 'My dear Lady Frampton, I wasn't sure that this was the right time to introduce you. But I know that Lord Frampton was very keen that you should meet. In fact, he was planning it when ... well ...' He cleared his throat. 'I know this is what he'd want.'

'I don't understand.' Antoinette looked bewildered. 'How is Miss Chancellor connected to my husband?'

Phaedra looked to Julius for guidance. He nodded discreetly. She took a breath, knowing instinctively that her answer would neither be expected, nor welcomed. But she thought of her beloved George and plunged in.

'I'm his daughter,' she said, fighting the impulse to flee. 'George was my father.'

18

Chapter 2

Antoinette stared in horror at the strange blonde girl who stood before her, claiming to be her stepdaughter. Her first thought was how young she looked, possibly younger than David, which would mean that George had been unfaithful early on in their marriage. She wrung her hands anxiously, but was too shocked to cry.

'I really don't think this is the time or place ...' Rosamunde began, taking off her glasses, but Antoinette stopped her.

'How old are you, Phaedra?' she asked.

'I'm thirty-one,' the girl replied, dropping her eyes. She didn't look much older than *twenty*-one.

'I need to sit down.' Antoinette grabbed her sister's hand. The relief that George hadn't been unfaithful was overwhelming.

Rosamunde guided her to an armchair in front of the fire while Tom remained staring at his new sister with a mixture of surprise and amusement. David felt as if the world had just spun away from him. How could it be that a few simple words had put her forever out of his reach? 'Are you sure you're my father's daughter?' he asked, hoping there might be some mistake.

'Absolutely sure,' Julius replied firmly. 'Lord Frampton and Phaedra had their DNA tested before Lord Frampton changed his will.'

They all stared at him in astonishment. 'George changed his will?' Antoinette gasped. Rosamunde gave a disapproving snort. 'But he never told me anything about it.'

19

'He wanted to include his daughter, Lady Frampton.'

'But surely he would have told me.'

Tom strode over to the club fender and took his mother's hand. 'This is all very sudden. Was it really necessary to tell us the day of Dad's funeral? Can't you see Mother's upset?'

'Tom is right. I think it's unbelievably tactless to barge in like this,' Rosamunde agreed, putting her hands on her sturdy hips. 'I think you should go away and come back another time, when Lady Frampton is better disposed to speak to you.'

'I'm sorry. I've been very thoughtless ...' Phaedra began, looking pained. She caught David's eye but looked away sharply, as if she saw the longing in it and was afraid.

'Lord Frampton wanted Phaedra to become part of the family,' Julius explained with an air of authority. 'We talked about it at length. Phaedra has a right to be here today, but it would have been odd not to have introduced you, and natural for you to have wondered who she is and how she is connected to Lord Frampton. We were left with no choice but to tell you the truth.'

Antoinette gazed into the fire, fighting her distress. 'George always wanted a daughter.'

'How long have you known that George is your father, Phaedra?' Rosamunde demanded.

'About eighteen months,' the girl replied.

'Eighteen months?' Tom echoed. 'Dad kept you quiet that long?'

Phaedra sighed, finding it hard to explain. 'About two years ago the man who was my father for the first ten years of my life died. My Mom decided then to tell me that he wasn't my biological father,

20

as I had thought, and that my real father was George Frampton. So I decided to track him down, not knowing whether he'd want to meet me. I came to the UK and found him. At first he didn't believe me. It was a little awkward, to say the least. I left him my details and returned to Paris where I was living, thinking I'd never hear from him again. About three months later he called me back. We agreed to meet and, well, the rest is history.'

'I find it hard to believe that George kept such a big secret from me,' said Antoinette. 'And for so long. We had no secrets, or so I thought.'

Phaedra smiled and the sweetness in her face seemed to soften the tension in the room. 'He kept me secret because he was so frightened of hurting you. He was devoted to you.'

'Well, his fears were founded,' said Rosamunde.

Antoinette bit her bottom lip. 'Did your mother love him, too?'

'He was the love of her life.' Phaedra flushed and lowered her eyes. 'But she was not his.'

At that moment the door opened and Margaret strode in. 'I'm going home,' she announced, ignoring the fact that she might be interrupting. She swept her imperious gaze over the solemn faces and sucked in her cheeks. 'My goodness, has someone else died?'

'I think I'll go,' said Phaedra.

'Let me escort you out,' David suggested.

'*I'll* go with you,' interjected Julius.

'No, really, I can find my own way out. Thank you.' She turned to Antoinette. 'I'm sorry to have barged in like this. It's been very nice meeting you all, finally. I just want you to know that I loved him, too.' With that she strode past Margaret and

21

disappeared down the corridor.

'Who was that rude girl?' Margaret demanded.

'Your granddaughter,' Antoinette replied.

It was Margaret's turn to sink into the sofa. David handed her a glass of sherry and Tom opened a window. 'It's not true!'

'He was going to tell us, apparently,' said Antoinette numbly.

'It's absurd. A daughter we never knew about.'

'She's from America,' said Rosamunde.

'From Canada, actually,' Tom corrected.

Margaret looked horrified. 'She's American? Good God, I have an *American* granddaughter?' Her face hardened. 'I simply don't believe it.'

'It's been proven,' said Antoinette. 'Ask Mr Beecher.'

'Indeed it has, Lady Frampton,' Julius confirmed. 'A DNA test verified that Phaedra is Lord Frampton's biological daughter.'

'He's included her in his will,' Antoinette added.

'He's changed his will? Did *you* know about this?' Margaret rounded on her daughter-in-law.

'No one but Lord Frampton and I knew about the will,' interjected Julius pompously. 'As his lawyer it was my job to arrange it. Phaedra had no idea he was including her until I informed her at the time I informed her of his death.'

'So she lives in England, does she?' Margaret sniffed.

'For the time being she's staying at a friend's house in London,' Julius replied. 'Though I understand she'll be returning to Paris shortly.'

'What does she do?'

'She's a photographer.'

'Doesn't she have a *proper* job?' Margaret

22

snapped.

'Photography *is* a proper job, Grandma,' David interrupted.

'Does it make her any money?' Margaret persisted. 'Or was my son keeping her?' Julius hesitated.

Antoinette looked worried. 'Mr Beecher?'

'Lord Frampton was very keen to be a father to Phaedra,' he replied carefully. 'But it is fair to say that the girl is very independent. She never asked anything of him besides friendship.'

'Really, this is all very odd,' Margaret declared, taking a large swig of sherry.

'What are we going to do?' Antoinette asked.

'Do?' Margaret retorted. 'Why do we have to *do* anything?'

'Because she's family,' said David.

'And it's what Dad wanted,' Tom added, getting up to pace the room. He found it hard to remain still for very long.

'Well, I shan't be *doing* anything about it,' Margaret informed them resolutely. 'She can't just turn up here on the day of my son's funeral and expect us all to embrace her like the Prodigal Daughter. I don't *know* her and George never once mentioned her.'

'He had planned on mentioning her, Lady Frampton,' said Julius.

'That may well be, Mr Beecher, but as far as I am concerned the matter is of no consequence.'

The stubborn pursing of Margaret's lips aroused in Antoinette a desire to be contrary. She got to her feet. 'Well, the matter is of *great* consequence to me,' she said, feeling a sudden rush of empowerment as her mother-in-law let out a silent

23

gasp. 'If George accepted her as his daughter, then so shall I. I am willing to embrace her into the family. She's a part of George and therefore a part of me.'

'Good gracious, Antoinette, that's very noble, but is it prudent?' Margaret asked. 'You know nothing about her.'

'I'm with you, Mum,' said Tom in surprise. 'I rather like the idea of having a sister—and such a pretty one, too.'

'I'm in,' David agreed. 'If it's what Dad wanted. She's flesh and blood.'

'Blood is thicker than water,' added Rosamunde, standing by her sister like a loyal hound.

Antoinette turned to Julius. 'I'd like to meet as soon as possible to read the will, Mr Beecher.'

'At your convenience, Lady Frampton,' he replied. 'I shall call you when I'm back in my office on Monday and arrange a meeting. I will now leave you in peace. I'm glad you have decided to accept Phaedra as your stepdaughter.'

Margaret gave a disapproving sniff. 'I'm afraid I'm going to take a little longer to convince. It's more than I can absorb in one day. Burying my son has been quite enough, thank you very much. I'm going home. We'll talk about it tomorrow, when I'm feeling stronger. David, escort me to my car.'

David did as he was told and accompanied his grandmother down the corridor and into the hall. Guests parted to let her through. Harris helped her with her stole and she leaned on David as she descended the steps to where Lord Frampton's chauffeur waited to drive her to the pretty Queen Anne dower house positioned at the other end of the estate. 'Do you know what distresses me the

24

most?' she said, hesitating at the open door. 'That my son felt he couldn't confide in me.'

'He didn't confide in anyone,' David reassured her.

'But I'm his mother.'

'I think mothers are often the last to know.'

'Well, George and I were very close. I can't understand why he didn't tell me. How long had he known this girl?'

'Eighteen months.'

'Eighteen months! How could he have kept something so important from me for that long? I mean, I would have been surprised, certainly, but I wouldn't have thought any less of him.'

'He was probably biding his time, waiting for the right moment.'

'Of course he was. He could not have predicted this!'

David watched the car disappear down the drive and turn left up the farm track that cut through the estate. It irritated his mother that Margaret lived so close and visited so often. Fairfield House punctuated her daily walk through the park with Basil, her Yorkshire terrier. Being a woman ill at ease in her own company, she appeared unannounced most days and Antoinette felt compelled to entertain her while Bertie and Wooster chased Basil up and down the corridors. After all, the house had once belonged to her, before she and her late husband, Arthur, had moved out to accommodate their son and his growing family. Antoinette could hardly turn her away.

David did not want to go back inside. The sun now shone brightly and the damp grass glittered, beckoning him to walk over it. The countryside looked resplendent, as if the mist had given it a good polishing. He was still reeling from the disappointment of discovering that the first girl he had taken a shine to in years had turned out to be his half-sister. It was as if life had played a horrid practical joke at his expense.

He decided to wander around the gardens. Bertie and Wooster pricked their ears and watched him disappear through the gate in the hedge. Then they bounded down the steps to join him, eagerly expecting a long walk. He had to smile at their exuberance, although now he no longer felt like smiling at all. His soul was once more plunged into darkness and his heart felt heavy again, like a sack of ash.

His father had been such a dominant presence in his life; it was unimaginable that he would no longer be around. He gazed at the towering trees and gently undulating lawn, and remembered that nothing was forever. Not even the earth he was standing on. Eventually everything would pass away.

Life was quiet in the countryside. His father had advised him to settle down young, as *he* had, but David had failed to find the right girl. He had had relationships, but love had always eluded him. He had watched Joshua marry Roberta and knew that he didn't want a joyless marriage like theirs. He didn't want the rootless life that Tom had, either. A different girl every night so that in the end they all blurred into one soulless encounter.

He had really liked the look of Phaedra. In retrospect, perhaps it had been their common blood that had attracted him to her. Perhaps he

26

had sensed a bond, subconsciously. Whatever it was, the attraction was fruitless. When he saw her again, he'd have to suppress it.

She had been brave to come today, he thought, although misguided. His mother was understandably upset about the whole situation. He wasn't upset as much as surprised—suddenly to discover a half-sibling at twenty-nine was a very big surprise. He couldn't care less about his father changing his will. If he had wanted to include his daughter, that was his business. Tom wouldn't mind, either. He wasn't avaricious, just extravagant with what he had. Joshua and Roberta were a different matter altogether. He wondered how they would take the news. Not well, he concluded. If anyone was going to make a fuss about money, it was Roberta.

*   *   *

Phaedra drove her sky-blue Fiat Uno into a lay-by and turned off the engine. She dropped her head onto the steering wheel and squeezed her eyes shut. She had wanted more than anything to go to George's funeral, but she could see now that it had been a terrible mistake.

She winced as she recalled the look of horror on Antoinette's face and the way she had sunk into the armchair, her hands visibly shaking; the reproachful twist to her sister Rosamunde's mouth and the disbelief that had set the boys' cheeks aflame. Only Julius had remained resolute, as if he relished having dominance over them. She wished she had had the power to keep her name out of the will. She wished she hadn't come. If only she could

27

now disappear in a puff of smoke.

The trouble was that George had died without giving her time to say goodbye. She would have told him she loved him. She would have told him she had forgiven him. He didn't need to change his will to make it up to her. She didn't want his money. She didn't want his gifts. She wanted security of a different sort, and *that* he could no longer give her.

She had needed George, the man. The father figure of her early years had left her mother when Phaedra was ten and gone to live in New Zealand, eventually marrying again and starting a new family. Phaedra had been forgotten, or mislaid, in the murky past and she never saw him again. From then on her mother had jumped from unsuitable man to unsuitable man like a frog in a pond of lily pads, hoping that the next landing would make her happy. She didn't realize that with every hop she carried the source of her unhappiness within her, and she couldn't run away from herself. She resented Phaedra, for she was a living reminder of her husband's rejection and an unwanted responsibility. So, while her mother sank her sorrows into bottles of gin, Phaedra made her own way, relying on her friends and her dreams to carry her through the hard times. As soon as she was old enough she left home and her mother forever. She had no desire ever to go back. She had not only closed the chapter, but thrown away the book.

George had given her a lifeline that promised stability, permanence and love. She had grabbed it with both hands and held onto it with all her might. But it had broken and George had gone, leaving her alone and adrift once again. Nothing in

28

this life is permanent, she mused—only love. That thought made her howl for her own sorry predicament and the future that had died with him.

After a while she calmed down and wiped her nose and eyes on the sleeve of her black coat. She glanced in the rear-view mirror and recoiled. She had managed to put on a pretty good show at the funeral—she had wanted them all to see her looking her best. If they saw her now, with puffy red lizard eyes and blotchy skin, they'd be extremely underwhelmed.

She started the engine and turned on the radio. The music made her feel a little better. She wouldn't worry about the future but take every moment as it came, and as for the past—that lived only in her memory now, giving her pain whenever she dwelt on it. So she wouldn't dwell on it. She looked about her as she motored up the lane, the fresh green buds reminding her of renewal. If they could reawaken after winter, then so could she.

*   *   *

When David returned to the drawing room he found that most of the guests had gone. Only Molly and Hester remained with an old curmudgeonly cousin of his grandfather, drinking sherry out of small crystal glasses beside the fire. Julius had left, Antoinette had retired to her bedroom to lie down, while Rosamunde and Tom remained in the library with Joshua and Roberta who had just been told the news.

'It's unbelievable,' Roberta was saying from the sofa, her angular face ashen against her black

29

jacket.

'I suppose they've told you about Dad changing his will,' said David as he entered the room with Bertie and Wooster. A deep loathing of his sister-in-law propelled him to provoke her.

'I can't believe he'd do such a thing,' she continued, sitting back into the cushions and folding her arms. 'I mean, he's known her, what? A year and a half? Do you think she would have made an effort to be part of his life had he been a simple farmer?'

'Don't judge her by your own standards, Roberta—and don't presume she's after his money. She might be wealthy in her own right, for all you know.' David made for the drinks tray. 'Anyway, she only learned about the will after Dad had died.'

'You're being naïve, David. Of course she's after his money,' she retorted, giving a little sniff. 'To someone like her an English lord is synonymous with a large fortune.'

'By that you mean someone American?' said Tom, back on the club fender, smoking.

'Yes.'

'Then you should be ashamed of yourself,' he reproached her. 'She's not from some haystack in Kansas, you know. She's Canadian, anyway, which is very different. Canadians don't like to be mistaken for Americans.'

'Is she pretty?' she asked.

David poured himself a glass of whisky. 'Extremely pretty,' he replied, to torment her.

'She's hot,' Tom agreed, grinning. 'Though a little too wholesome for my tastes.'

'Oh really, Tom. You fancy anything in a skirt!'

Roberta retorted.

'I think I saw her,' said Joshua. 'Long blonde curly hair with very pale grey eyes.'

Roberta rounded on him. 'That's a lot of detail, darling, for someone who *thinks* he saw her.'

'She was the only person in the congregation under thirty,' he explained.

'She's thirty-one, actually,' David corrected.

'Blinded by her good looks: no wonder you boys can't see through her. Takes a woman to understand a woman, don't you think, Rosamunde?'

'I'm not sure I agree with you,' Rosamunde replied. She had always found Roberta a little overpowering.

'How much has he given her?' Roberta persisted.

'We don't know,' said Tom.

'When do we find out? I mean, we have to contest it, surely.'

'Why?' David asked, flopping onto the sofa and stretching out his long legs.

'Because it's not fair. The portion he gives her might be our daughter's inheritance.'

'I think we have enough,' said Joshua quietly, wishing his wife wouldn't make such a scene.

'That's not the point, darling. It's the principle,' she retorted.

'Antoinette has no intention of contesting it,' said Rosamunde authoritatively.

'She's tired and emotional. When she's had some rest, she'll change her mind,' Roberta assured her.

'I think you should go and talk it over with Grandma,' Tom suggested, smirking at the thought of the pair of them pecking away at poor Phaedra's remains after they had torn her to pieces.

31

'So Margaret agrees with me at least,' Roberta smiled.

'She didn't want to talk about it, actually,' David corrected. 'But I imagine she'll agree with you. Not that any of our opinions matter when it comes to the will. Dad had every right to change it. We can't undo it and Mum won't want us to. In spite of being tired and emotional, Roberta, she wants to honour Dad's request, and so do Tom and I.'

'Sure, whatever,' said Tom, flicking ash into the fire. 'But it is all rather odd, don't you think?'

David sank into the armchair and swirled the ice about in his tumbler, making a light tinkling sound. 'She's thirty-one, which means she was born in 1981. I was born two years later, so Dad slept with her mother a year before he married Mum.'

'That's cutting it pretty fine,' said Joshua. 'Considering he dated Mum for about a year before he proposed.'

'Perhaps it was a one-night stand,' said Roberta.

'Shhh, keep your voice down,' Joshua cautioned, thinking of his mother upstairs in her bedroom.

'Phaedra said Dad was her mother's "great love", so it must have been more than a one-night stand,' Tom recalled softly.

'But she was not your father's "great love",' Rosamunde was quick to add. 'I imagine it was a hasty fling for George that left the poor girl heartbroken. Happens all the time, though in this case he left a bun in the oven, which was very careless.'

'Why didn't she tell him he had got her pregnant?' Roberta asked. 'I mean, if she was so in love with him, might she not have thought he would do the decent thing and marry her?

32

Nowadays people have no sense of duty, but in those days—we're talking the 1980s—wasn't it a terrible blot on one's reputation to be pregnant outside marriage?'

'Depends what sort of family she came from,' said Rosamunde. 'In most respectable families, it wouldn't be considered proper even today.'

'Which leads me to suspect that she never told him,' said David. 'If she had, he would have looked after her. I'm not sure he would have married her, but Dad was a good man; he wouldn't have run off, leaving her to bring up his child alone. No, I believe she never told him.'

Roberta narrowed her eyes suspiciously. 'It all seems very fishy to me. She turns up the day of his funeral and declares herself his illegitimate daughter. It's a little too tidy.'

Tom blew smoke out of the side of his mouth. 'Not really. Mother brings daughter up on her own, tells daughter who her real father is, daughter goes looking for him, which is natural. Father feels guilty he wasn't around when she was growing up so includes her in his will. Nothing fishy about that.'

'It's just a feeling,' Roberta persisted. 'You're all much too trusting.'

'Look, Dad isn't around to answer our questions,' said David. 'The only person who knows the answers, and most likely not all of them, is Phaedra. I suggest we ask her when we next see her.'

'You're not thinking of seeing her again, are you?' Roberta looked horrified.

'Why not? Don't you want to know some answers?' David replied.

33

'God, you're going to invite her back, aren't you?'

'Perhaps,' David replied.

'With your mother's permission,' Rosamunde interrupted.

Roberta turned to her husband for support. 'Josh, aren't you going to say something?'

'I think you should calm down, darling, and wait until we know what's in the will,' he suggested. 'She might have been given so little it's not worth making a fuss.'

'Or she might have been given a great deal, in which case it is,' said Roberta firmly.

Chapter 3

Antoinette lay on her big brass bed and allowed her weary gaze to meander around the room. Her bedroom was her sanctuary—the only place in the house where she was safe from her mother-in-law. It was large and light with a high ceiling bordered in a bold fleur-de-lis cornice. Portraits of her sons as little boys hung on the pale-yellow-striped wallpaper, with paintings of dogs and eighteenth-century landscapes. Primrose-yellow curtains dropped from thick wooden poles where latticed windows looked out over the lawn and ancient woodland beyond. A wardrobe dominated one wall, a chest of drawers another, while a delicate dressing table stood in front of the window where Antoinette often sat before the Queen Anne mirror to brush her hair and apply her make-up. There had been little room for change when she had moved into the house just over twenty years ago, for the Framptons had traditionally been avid collectors of art and antiques from all over the world, and George liked it as it was. But she had decorated her bedroom exactly the way she wanted it.

It is the custom in great houses for the husband and wife to inhabit separate bedrooms, so George's dressing room was positioned the other side of the adjoining bathroom from Antoinette's. He had rarely slept in there—only when he had drunk too much or was coming home late—but all his clothes were kept there, along with sentimental trinkets and the customary ashtray full of loose change. He had always hated to throw anything away so the drawers were packed with old theatre tickets and ski passes, letters and postcards dating right back to before they married. The mantelpiece was adorned with trophies for ski-club races and tennis tournaments, and framed photographs of his school days. The biggest frame contained a black-and-white photograph of Antoinette as a young debutante in the early 1970s, with her dark hair drawn up into a beehive, her false eyelashes long and black. She had seldom entered that room, for she couldn't abide the chaos, but now she didn't dare because she was too scared. The appearance of George's illegitimate daughter raised the possibility that he might have kept other secrets from her. She had never mistrusted him in life, but in death a shadow had been cast over his integrity.

She pondered the unexpected appearance of Phaedra. It didn't surprise her that George had had girlfriends before he married—he had been a

35

handsome, sharp-witted and charming young man—but it *did* surprise her that he had never mentioned Phaedra's mother. She thought she knew all the names that related to his past; at least, all the important ones. And if Phaedra was thirty-one then she was only a year older than David. She and George had married the year before David was born but they had courted for eight months before that. Was there a chance that George had been unfaithful during that time? She wished George were alive to answer her questions and defend his honour. She wished he were there to put her mind at rest and reassure her that he had loved her, and only her.

But Phaedra's mother plagued her thoughts. In her imagination she conjured up a woman not unlike the daughter—slim and feminine, with pretty grey eyes and flawless skin—and envied her beauty. Antoinette was not beautiful. Her father had called her 'comely', which was the closest he had ever come to a compliment. Her mother had told her she had a 'sweet face' that reflected her 'gentle nature'. She knew she had unusual navy eyes and that her dark hair was thick and lustrous, but there was nothing remarkable about her features. She had only been beautiful in George's eyes, which was really all that mattered—but perhaps she hadn't been beautiful enough. Had Phaedra's mother caught his attention during their courtship and taken him to bed for one fateful night? Could her beloved George have betrayed her like that?

She must have drifted off to sleep, because when she woke up, Rosamunde was sitting on the armchair near the bed, doing her needlepoint. 'I'm glad you've had a good rest. You look much better,' she said when Antoinette opened her eyes.

Antoinette sighed. 'Waking up is hard. For a moment I think it's all a horrid dream. Then I realize it's not. He's gone, hasn't he?'

'Yes, Antoinette. He's in a better place.'

'If you believe that. I'm not sure I do.'

'It's a comfort.'

'I'd like it to be true. I hope there *is* a Heaven and that he's there. Goodness, to think he might be with our parents. I'm not sure Daddy wholly approved of George.'

'Only because he was suspicious of men who preferred to climb mountains rather than settle down to a proper job.'

'George was never going to be a banker or an accountant. He was an adventurer. He adored the wild unpredictability of nature and the challenge of those terrifyingly high peaks. God knows I hated him going off all the time, and I worried about his safety when he was incommunicado for weeks at a time, but I'd have loathed him to be chained to a desk. He'd have been miserable working in an office like Joshua. Anyway, he wasn't just a mountaineer, he was an entrepreneur. Do you remember how he imported cigars from Havana? And all those rugs from Nepal! He liked to support the communities he visited. He was such a free spirit.'

'Daddy knew that, but he wasn't flamboyant like George. I'm sure those things aren't important where they are.'

'What are you going to do about Phaedra?' Rosamunde asked, briefly halting her needlework. 'Roberta's adamant that you should contest the

37

will.'

Antoinette sat up. 'I bet she is, even though she doesn't know yet what's in it.'

'How do *you* feel about it?'

'On what grounds would I contest it? If George wanted to provide for his daughter, I support him. I'm sure he was planning to introduce us, and at some point he would have told me about the will. I don't believe he meant to keep a secret like that. He didn't expect to die, did he?'

Rosamunde saw the doubt in her sister's eyes and was quick to dispel it. 'Of course he would have told you,' she said firmly. 'Roberta's a greedy so-and-so.'

'I'm going to do what I think George would have wanted and ask Phaedra to stay the weekend. If she's a Frampton then we must welcome her into the family. I know Margaret will be horrified, and I can't say that doesn't give me a little pleasure, but I want to get to know her. I have so many questions. I think we need to talk.'

'You're very generous, Antoinette.'

'Well, it's not like George had an affair with her mother during our marriage, is it? I've worked it out, the dates, I mean. It happened *before* our courtship. Just before, but certainly not during. George wouldn't have been unfaithful, I know he wouldn't. He just wasn't that sort of man and he wouldn't have done it to me. I'm sure about that. He wouldn't have wanted to hurt me.'

'Of course he wouldn't.' Rosamunde paused in her sewing.

'I feel sorry for the poor girl. It must have been a short romance ...' Antoinette frowned, as if the effort to convince herself of her husband's fidelity

38

was suddenly too much.

'It must have been very brief and I suspect was over before she even discovered she was pregnant, which is why she never told him. She probably didn't know where to find him and in her heart she must have known that he didn't care for her at all.'

'But she *did* know where to find him, Rosamunde, otherwise Phaedra would never have tracked him down.' She blanched. 'Do you think they kept in touch? Do you think Phaedra's mother and George remained in contact all these years? What if he knew he had a daughter all along and kept her secret and only now decided to come clean?'

'Antoinette, you're letting your imagination run away with you,' Rosamunde said in a soothing voice. 'Listen, he changed his will just before he died. If he had known all along that he had a daughter he would have included her in his will years ago. No, I think Phaedra is telling the truth and that she came to London to find him.'

Antoinette was at once encouraged. 'Poor George. It must have been a shock to find out that he had fathered a child. I'm sure he kept her secret because he didn't want to hurt *me*. His love for his family was a priority. I know his intentions were good and honourable.'

'Oh, there's absolutely no doubt about that,' Rosamunde agreed. 'No one doubts his integrity, Antoinette.'

'What do the boys think?' Her face crumpled with anxiety. 'Do they doubt their father? I'd hate them to think badly of him ...'

'David and Tom want to honour his wishes, as you do. Josh ...'

39

'Well, he'll stand by his wife, of course. There's no doubt who wears the pants in that marriage!'

'I do hope David finds a nice girl to settle down with,' said Rosamunde, changing the subject. 'It would be nice to see the next generation of Framptons growing up here, now that David is Lord Frampton.'

'A title that carries great sorrow.'

'I can't see David taking his seat in the House of Lords, can you?'

Antoinette climbed out of bed. 'David just wants a simple life. How different my children all are from one another. David so laid-back, Josh so aspirational . . .'

'He wasn't, before he married Roberta.'

'Be that as it may, they're very social. Out all the time at parties; I dare say they see something of little Amber. Then there's Tom.' Her face softened and she smiled tenderly. 'Tom, so wild and so lost.'

'And now you have a stepdaughter,' Rosamunde added, rather enjoying the turn of events.

Antoinette reached for her trousers and sighed. 'The irony is that both George and I so wanted a daughter.'

That evening Joshua and Roberta departed for London. Roberta planted a cold little kiss on her mother-in-law's cheek before climbing into the front seat of the shiny black BMW 4×4 and crossly belting up. Joshua looked worn down.

'I'll let you know when we're meeting,' said Antoinette, kissing her son warmly.

'Yes, Mum, fine,' he replied, wishing the whole business of Phaedra and the will would just disappear. He knew he was going to get an earful all the way up to London.

'I'm going to ask Phaedra to come and stay one weekend. I'd very much like you and Roberta to be here.'

He shrugged helplessly. 'I'll do my best, Mum.'

'I know you will. Drive carefully.' She watched him climb into the driver's seat and start the engine with a roar. He waved solemnly and motored off into the dusk.

'Ridiculous woman,' said David, after they had gone.

'Ridiculous weak man,' Tom added mischievously.

'I agree with Tom,' said Rosamunde. 'I blame Josh for letting her get away with that sort of spoilt behaviour.'

'He should whip her into submission,' said Tom jovially.

'I wouldn't go quite that far,' Rosamunde replied with a chortle. 'But I do think she's being very mean-spirited. If Antoinette is big enough to accept Phaedra, then Roberta should just toe the line and keep her opinions to herself. She shouldn't forget she's a married-in.'

'She's never considered herself just that, Rosamunde,' Tom reminded her.

They settled down for supper in the kitchen, after which David would return to his house at the other side of the lake, and Tom would stay the night with his mother and leave for London in the morning. Rosamunde, being a spinster and having little to get home for besides her quartet of beagles, had set up residence with her sister for the foreseeable future. In her home town in Dorset there was little on offer besides Bible groups, bridge nights and the local Women's Institute

41

where ladies met to sew, bake and socialize. All to be avoided like measles, she thought resolutely. Here she felt needed and useful, two things she hadn't felt in a very long time.

'I confess I've dreaded reading the will,' said Antoinette, taking out of the Aga the cottage pie that Mrs Gunice had left for them. 'I put it off. But now the funeral is over I'm left no option but to face it.'

'It's very final, isn't it,' Rosamunde agreed sympathetically. 'But you've got nothing to be afraid of. It's only money.'

'I thought that if I avoided the whole thing, I could prevent it happening, somehow. I could pretend George was still here.' She put the pile of plates on top of the Aga and stood back to let everyone help themselves.

'Are you going to ask Phaedra to join us when we read the will?' David asked, digging the spoon into the steaming potato crust. Even the mention of Phaedra's name gave him a forbidden thrill.

Antoinette looked at her sister. 'I suppose I have to ask her, don't I?'

'You don't have to,' Rosamunde replied, sitting down at the table. 'But I think you should. If she's George's daughter it would be correct. I suspect Mr Beecher will insist upon it.'

'Ah, the oleaginous Julius Beecher, keeper of all Dad's secrets,' said Tom.

'If I'm not mistaken, Tom, there's only one,' said Antoinette, indulging him with a smile. Tom had always been prone to exaggeration.

'I don't know why Dad chose him to look after his affairs,' Tom continued. 'He makes my skin crawl. Something about his greedy little eyes.'

42

'Yes, but he worshipped Dad,' said David. 'He'd do anything for him. If you spend your time travelling, you want to be sure that the man looking after your businesses back at home is as loyal as a dog. Beecher is that dog.'

'He's a good lawyer,' Antoinette defended him. 'Your father trusted him with everything and he never let him down. And don't forget, your father was not an easy man to work for. He was so impulsive. One minute it was cigars, the next rugs, then herbal tea from Argentina and God knows what else. Your father would get a crush on something and toss it at Julius, knowing that he'd do all the hard work while George set off to climb another peak. Most lawyers would have thrown up their hands in exasperation, but not Julius. He rose to the challenge. He was more than a lawyer, he was George's right hand.'

'And I suspect he rather admired George's flamboyance,' Rosamunde added.

'Oh, he did,' Antoinette agreed. 'He thought the world of George.'

They began to eat, acutely aware of the empty seat at the head of the table.

'Mum, I want to go and spend some time out in Murenburg,' David began carefully. Antoinette's face darkened as she was confronted once again with the gritty reality of her husband's death. 'I want to go to where it happened. I don't think I can find peace until I've done that.'

'I'll go with you,' Tom suggested.

Antoinette lowered her eyes. 'I don't think I can ever go back,' she said quietly.

'Of course you can't,' Rosamunde agreed. 'It was never your cup of tea in the first place. George is

43

home now. There's absolutely no reason for you ever to return.'

'I never wanted to be in a position to say "I told you so",' Antoinette added.

Tom noticed his mother's shining eyes and reached across the table to touch her hand.

'Mum, you don't have to do anything you don't want to do,' he said.

Skiing had been one of George's passions that Antoinette had never understood. It was one thing to ski gently down pistes, but quite another to descend parts of the mountain where even chamois dared not tread. She hadn't grown up with the sport as he had, and found it hard to accept his infatuation and the risks it demanded. But George had laughed off her fears and told her that he was much more likely to die in a car on the M3 than on the mountain.

Soon after they married he had bought a chalet in Murenburg, a small, picturesque village a couple of hours from Zurich where he had skied all his life. He passed his enthusiasm on to his sons, who were all accomplished skiers by the age of ten. For Antoinette, besides enjoying the process of decorating a pretty home, skiing holidays were riddled with anxiety as she remained in the valley, gazing up at the mountains and trying not to imagine the worst.

At the end of the day they'd return with pink cheeks and sparkling eyes, wet clothes and cold noses, and Antoinette would hang everything over the radiators to dry and make them hot chocolate to drink in front of the fire. She'd listen to their stories without ever really understanding their language. It was impossible for her to appreciate the breathtaking views from the mountain peaks where they stood alone with nature, the thin, clean air burning their lungs and the bright snow glittering like a million diamonds, for she had little experience to draw on. They'd try to explain the thrill of hopping down narrow gullies where it was almost too tight to turn, and gliding over undulating meadows of untracked snow, but Antoinette had only ever skied on-piste and even that had terrified her.

'I'd be happier if you went together,' she said to her sons. 'Perhaps Josh will join you.'

'Roberta won't let him off the lead,' said Tom disdainfully. 'And we're absolutely not having *her*!'

'It would be nice to ask him, just the same,' their mother insisted.

'I have no reservations about telling him that we won't tolerate his wife,' said David. 'It's about time he stood up to her.'

'I don't think she'd want to go, anyway,' interjected Rosamunde. 'Doesn't she prefer to ski in Gstaad?'

'That's because she can't ski,' said Tom. 'Serious skiers don't go to Gstaad!'

'And because Murenburg isn't glamorous enough for her,' David added. 'No designer shops or celebrities.'

'It's understandable that she should want to carve her own niche. Murenburg is very much Frampton territory. I don't blame her for that,' said Antoinette, trying hard to keep the family united.

'But Josh is a serious skier, he must be bored rigid in Gstaad,' Tom mused. Then he laughed mischievously. 'But then again, he must be bored

45

rigid being married to Roberta.' David laughed with him while Antoinette and Rosamunde tried not to look amused.

'Shame on you, boys, you're too much!' Rosamunde exclaimed, her mouth twitching at the corners. She caught her sister's eye. 'But really, Antoinette, we do need something to laugh about!' Antoinette's face broke into a smile. She glanced at the head of the table and discovered that it was possible to laugh and cry at the same time.

After dinner, David walked across the garden to his house, positioned on the other side of the large ornamental lake his father had built for floating his collection of miniature boats. It was a pretty red-brick lodge, built in the same Jacobean style as the main house. Inside, the walls were lined with bookshelves, but many books lay piled on the floor for lack of space, and magazines were strewn across the surfaces. David loved to read, especially history, and spent many evenings in front of the fire with his dog, devouring books he had ordered on Amazon.

He opened the door and Rufus, his golden Labrador, bounded out of the kitchen to greet him. Trevor, the farm manager, had taken him off for the day, returning him home after a long walk at six. Rufus loved Trevor, who had two mongrels and a garden full of chickens, but he loved David most of all, and jumped up in his excitement to see him.

David let him out to stretch his legs, and the two of them walked briskly around the lake. The moon was bright, lighting up the water so that it shone like haematite. The air was damp and sweet with the smell of regeneration. He heard the mournful

46

hooting of a tawny owl calling to its mate, followed by the tinny cough of a pheasant as it was awoken by Rufus and driven into the sky in alarm. David loved the mystery of the night. He looked about him, at the thick shrubs and bushes, and wondered how many eyes were quietly watching him through the darkness. He enjoyed walking through their secret world and forgetting himself.

As he strode on, his mind wandered to Phaedra and the embarrassed look on her face when Julius had brought up the subject of his father's will. She was clearly aware she might appear money-grabbing and keen to show that she wasn't. Julius, on the other hand, had no shame. As executor of the will, he was only concerned with making sure that George's wishes were carried out. David wondered whether Phaedra would show up for the meeting—or indeed for the weekend his mother intended to invite her to stay. She had scurried out of the library like a frightened rabbit. He knew there was a good chance he'd never see her again.

He returned home and made himself a cup of tea. Content in his routine, Rufus curled up on his blankets in the corner of David's bedroom, closed his eyes and fell asleep instantly. David showered then climbed into bed to read his book. But his gaze meandered and he lost track more than once. It was no good. He was unable to concentrate. He put his book on the bedside table and turned off the light. A wave of apprehension washed over him. The world seemed so much bigger without his father in it.

*   *   *

47

On Monday morning Antoinette telephoned Julius to arrange the reading of the will. She told him to invite Phaedra, which seemed to make Julius very happy. 'You're doing the right thing, Lady Frampton,' he said cheerfully. 'Lord Frampton would be very pleased.' When she put down the telephone she felt an unexpected happiness fill her chest with the warm feeling of doing something good. She gazed out of the study window where Barry the gardener was cutting the winter grass into bright green stripes on his little tractor. There was something reassuring about the rumbling noise it made, and she realized that in spite of such a monumental change, life at Fairfield would continue as it always had.

She remained a moment at the window. She noticed the phosphorescent colour of the new grass and the promise of red tulips peeping through the earth in the lime walk. A pair of blue tits played about the viburnum. Spring had found her stride once more and the sun shone with a bright new radiance. Antoinette inhaled deeply and realized that she'd forgotten how soothing it was to observe the wondrous work of Nature.

Barry waved as he motored by. She waved back and smiled wistfully. It had been so long since she'd taken an interest in the gardens. Barry was always coming in to ask her this or that but her response was always the same: *Whatever you think, Barry*. She knew she disappointed him, because his feelings showed all over his face. But she hadn't had any surplus energy to put into the gardens. George had been very demanding, requiring her to be in London when he wasn't travelling, to entertain friends at the ballet or the opera or just for dinner, and at weekends the house had always been full. She gazed out onto the world with new eyes and couldn't help feeling that, in the ever-increasing whirl of her life, she'd overlooked something vitally important.

She moved away and turned her thoughts back to Phaedra. She was surprised by the strength of her desire to see her again. The girl was a hidden part of George. Something else he had left behind besides the family she knew. In a strange way she felt Phaedra was a gift, set aside to ease the shock of his departure, and she was eager to spend time with her—as if in some way it would enable her to hold onto George for a little longer.

'Antoinette, Dr Heyworth is in the hall,' Rosamunde hissed, peering around the door. 'Did you know he was coming?'

Antoinette's hand shot to her mouth. 'God, I forgot!' she exclaimed, flushing. 'I asked him to come and see me yesterday, at the funeral.'

'Why? Are you sick?'

'No, I just wanted to talk to someone.'

'You can talk to me,' said Rosamunde, put out.

'You're my sister. I wanted to talk to someone *outside* the family.'

Rosamunde pursed her lips. 'Very well,' she said tightly. 'There's a nice fire in the drawing room. I'll ask Harris to bring you both some tea.'

'Make that *three* cups of tea.'

Pleased to be included, Rosamunde smiled gratefully. 'Take your time, Antoinette. Leave everything to me. I'll entertain him.' She grinned and lowered her voice. 'He's very attractive.'

'Oh really, Rosamunde!'

'I might be old, but I can still admire.'

'He's been our family doctor for thirty years. I'd never look at him in that way.'

'Then don't deny me the pleasure.'

'He's all yours. Unmarried in his sixties: I'm not sure he's a very good bet, Rosamunde.'

'I'm unmarried at fifty-nine. I'm not a very good bet, either. I'll show him into the drawing room.' Rosamunde closed the door behind her.

The thought of Rosamunde flirting with Dr Heyworth made Antoinette smile. Rosamunde was an unlikely candidate for the handsome doctor. She was a sturdy, unfeminine woman who thought face cream and hair-dye were unnecessary indulgences. Consequently, her skin was carved with lines and marred with fine threads of broken veins embedded in her cheeks like minor roads on a map, and her grey hair was pulled back into a severe bun. As a younger woman she had devoted her time to horses and ridden out in all weather, but hip trouble had stopped her enjoying the sport she loved the most, so now she only watched it on the television and as a spectator at the races. Unlike Antoinette, who loved beautiful clothes, Rosamunde was happier in slacks, sensible shoes and cotton blouses, on her knees in the herbaceous border, or striding across the fields in gumboots with her pack of four energetic dogs. Antoinette had never asked her if she regretted not marrying and having children, she had always just assumed she hadn't desired either. In fact, she couldn't remember the last time she had heard her comment on a man's good looks. It was very out of character.

When she walked into the drawing room she found Dr Heyworth in the armchair beside the fire and Rosamunde settled contentedly into the sofa opposite, sipping cups of Earl Grey tea. Bertie lay sleeping at her sister's feet, while Wooster sat with his back straight, eyeballing Dr Heyworth, who tentatively patted his big head. When he saw Antoinette, he stood up to greet her. 'Hello, Dr Heyworth. Please don't get up,' she insisted. 'Wooster, leave the poor man alone!' Wooster didn't flinch and Dr Heyworth sat down again and resumed his hesitant patting.

'I think he likes you,' said Rosamunde.

'Oh yes, Wooster and I are old friends,' he replied.

Antoinette sat on the club fender near her sister. A hearty fire crackled in the grate as the flames lapped the logs with greedy tongues. 'Isn't this nice,' she said, feeling the heat on her back. 'A big house like this is hard to keep warm. Sometimes we even light fires in the summer.'

'It doesn't feel cold to me,' said Dr Heyworth.

'Me neither,' added Rosamunde. 'In fact, I'd go as far as saying I'm rather warm.'

'Then it must be my thin skin,' Antoinette declared, wrapping her cardigan tightly around her body.

Dr Heyworth smiled at her sympathetically, which made Antoinette's eyes well with tears. 'It's perfectly natural to feel the chill, Lady Frampton. Nothing at all to worry about.'

Antoinette had never really noticed how handsome Dr Heyworth was. If she had, she would have been a reluctant patient, unable to discuss intimate medical matters without embarrassment. But now her sister had mentioned the unmentionable, she realized that, in spite of his

51

glasses, he was indeed handsome. His face was long and kind, with intelligent green eyes and a strong nose that gave him an air of authority. His hair, which had once been dark, was now grey and thinning, but the generous shape of his head and the warm colour of his skin ensured that baldness would not diminish him. Although his visit was an informal one—he was now semi-retired and only saw private patients occasionally—he looked dignified and proper in a tweed jacket and tie.

'Thank you for coming to the funeral,' said Antoinette, wringing her hands to warm them.

'It was a beautiful service,' he replied. 'Lord Frampton was well loved and highly respected in the community. We shall all miss him.'

Antoinette felt the familiar tightening of her throat and the uncontrollable wobbling of her lower lip as her heart heaved with grief. She was grateful Margaret wasn't there to witness her crying in front of the doctor. 'I can't say I remember a great deal about the service. I was ...' When Antoinette's words trailed off, Rosamunde intervened to save her sister any embarrassment.

'The flowers were very pretty,' she said. 'You know Antoinette chose them all herself. The smell filled the whole church.'

'Indeed it did,' Dr Heyworth agreed. Then he settled his kind eyes on Antoinette. 'Did you get any sleep last night?' he asked softly, and the concern in his voice released a sob which Antoinette stifled with her handkerchief.

'A little,' she murmured.

'Would you like me to prescribe you some sleeping pills?'

'That would be nice, thank you.'

'Sleeping pills?' Rosamunde interjected as the doctor lifted his bag onto his knee to make out a prescription in small, illegible writing. 'Do you really need sleeping pills, Antoinette?' She turned to Dr Heyworth. 'Aren't they terribly bad for her?'

'They're very mild,' the doctor explained patiently. 'And it's only for a while. You see,' he continued, turning back to his patient and speaking in a slow, reassuring manner, 'if you are tired your heart cannot heal because all your energy goes into getting you through the day and not into tackling the core of the trouble. So you need to rest, eat well, take long walks in the country air, surround yourself with loved ones and give that battered heart of yours a chance to recover. If sleeping pills help you rest, then I can see no harm in taking them for a short period.' Antoinette listened attentively, wiping her eyes in an attempt to stem the flow of tears. It was very unusual that a doctor should talk about her emotional health with such understanding. For a moment she felt that he was a wise old friend and not a doctor at all. 'It's all right to cry, Lady Frampton,' he said. 'Tears are nature's way of healing.'

'Yes, Antoinette,' Rosamunde added. 'You must cry it all out, that's what our Mama would have said. It'll make you feel much better.'

Dr Heyworth handed Antoinette the prescription. 'It might be that your heart never completely heals, but that a patch metaphorically covers the wound to stave off the pain and enables you to pick yourself up, dust yourself down and go on. You have suffered a terrible shock and so you have to give yourself time and space to grieve. And

53

you mustn't feel guilty or that you are a burden to your family and friends, because if you don't let it all out, it will bury down deep and never go away. It will only find a moment later on in your life to come back and manifest as physical pain.' For a moment his eyes darkened, but he seemed to push through the sudden wave of sadness and continue with a compassionate smile. 'You must talk about it as much as you can, Lady Frampton. One day you'll discover that it doesn't hurt anything like as much as it does now.'

'Antoinette is certainly no burden to me, Dr Heyworth,' said Rosamunde firmly.

'Good. Do you live nearby?'

'In Dorset, about an hour away. But I'll stay here for as long as she wants me to.'

The doctor nodded his approval. 'I'm very pleased to hear it.'

By now Wooster had slid to the floor in a happy slumber with his head resting on Dr Heyworth's feet. Dr Heyworth bent down and stroked his ear. It twitched with pleasure. 'How are the boys?' he asked Antoinette.

She took a deep breath, calmer now. 'David is dealing with it in his own quiet way. Tom comes across as not really caring very much, but I know he's dreadfully sad. As you'll appreciate, he's not very good at coping with problems. So he puts his head under the carpet and pretends that everything is all right. I'd rather that than the alternative.'

'He's avoiding alcohol?'

Antoinette picked at the ragged cuticle on her thumb. 'He drank at the funeral, as one would expect. But generally he's being very careful. This

54

is a testing time for him, but he's being very strong.'

'And Joshua?'

'He's so uncomfortable with emotion he'd rather move on as swiftly as possible and get on with his life.'

'This has been very tough on you all. When death happens so unexpectedly, there's no time to prepare for it. It's a great shock. And an accident like Lord Frampton's seems unnecessary. It's natural to feel angry, too, Lady Frampton.'

Antoinette's face livened as the doctor articulated what she was too ashamed to admit: that she resented her husband's lack of caution as he had selfishly sought pleasure without any apparent concern for those who loved him.

Dr Heyworth knew he had touched a nerve. He stood up. 'You can come and see me any time,' he said to Antoinette. 'Sometimes it helps to talk to someone who is not in the family. I'm always here for you, Lady Frampton.'

Antoinette saw the sympathy in his eyes and knew that he meant it. In fact, he seemed to understand why she was cold all the time and how hard she was trying to act normally, when she just wanted to curl up into a ball and cry. He hadn't said a great deal, but she could sense in his expression the words left unspoken, and was grateful. 'I'd like that very much,' she replied.

'I'm not at my practice any more, but you're welcome to come to my home. I occasionally see patients there and it works very well. I've looked after your family for over thirty years. I hope you consider me a friend as well as a doctor. You can call me any time.'

He bade goodbye to Rosamunde, and Antoinette walked him through the hall. Harris helped the doctor into his coat and opened the door. 'Thank you so much for coming,' she said, folding her arms against the cold although the sun shone bright and warm. He waved and climbed into his Volvo.

As he departed she saw the formidable figure of her mother-in-law striding purposefully across the field beyond the drive with Basil, her Yorkshire terrier, scurrying around in the grass like a large mouse. She was wearing a long olive-green coat, headscarf and boots, and carrying a stick, although at the rate she was moving she clearly didn't need it for support. Antoinette dashed back inside to wipe her face and compose herself, but she knew there was no point running to hide. Margaret always knew where to find her.

Chapter 4

'Batten down the hatches, the Grand High Witch is coming to pay us a visit!' Antoinette announced, hurrying back into the drawing room. 'Oh, for some special Mouse-Maker to drop into her tea!'

'And a cat to catch her!' added Rosamunde. 'Roald Dahl was a genius!'

'Shame it's only fiction.'

'You could always put some sleeping pills in her sherry.'

'You are devious, Rosamunde!'

'Nothing fictitious about them.'

'But she's indestructible, like a cockroach,'

56

Antoinette replied. 'I don't think she'd notice even a packet of sleeping pills.'

'How does poor Dr Heyworth cope with having *her* as a patient?'

'She's one of those rare people who are never ill. I don't think she's been to a doctor since she gave birth, back in the Dark Ages. And even then, I wouldn't be at all surprised if George just popped out between her cocktail and dinner. But I must tell you that men love her.'

'Men have always been a mystery to me!' Rosamunde exclaimed.

'Yes, she's a man's woman and men think she's marvellous.' Antoinette sighed heavily. 'No one thought her more marvellous than George.'

At that moment a cold gust of wind swept through the hall and into the drawing room. Bertie and Wooster pricked their ears. The sound of little paws clattered across the marble floor as Harris closed the door with a loud bang, and Basil shot into the drawing room like a missile. The Great Danes jumped clumsily to their feet and chased him around the room before heading back into the hall and up the front stairs.

'Be off with you!' resounded through the house, then a few seconds later the large black-clad figure of the Dowager Lady Frampton filled the doorway like a docking ocean liner. She floated there a moment, catching her breath. 'Good, you're here,' she said to Antoinette. 'I need to talk to you urgently.'

'You look out of breath.'

'I've marched across the field.'

'Why don't you come and sit down. Would you like a glass of sherry?'

'Harris is going to bring me one.' She marched across the carpet and lowered herself gently into the armchair where Dr Heyworth had sat only minutes before. 'I haven't slept a wink for thinking of George's illegitimate daughter.'

'A sleeping pill might help,' Rosamunde suggested, sucking in her cheeks.

'Good Lord, I don't need medicine. I need peace of mind.' Rosamunde caught her sister's eye, but looked away instantly for fear of making her smile.

'I've been thinking about her, too,' Antoinette agreed.

'Good, I'm pleased you have come to your senses,' Margaret replied. 'You see, I'm not about to open my arms to some random girl who claims to be my granddaughter. My son is dead so there is absolutely no proof that she is who she says she is.'

Antoinette frowned. 'Mr Beecher supervised the DNA test.'

'DNA test, indeed! Have you seen it? Were you there when it was done? Codswallop, if you ask me!'

'She's your flesh and blood, Margaret, whether you like it or not.'

'She was conceived outside wedlock, brought up in Canada—I don't think a little bit of shared blood makes any difference at all. And I refuse to believe it. My son would have told me if he had fathered a child. I know he would. He told me everything.'

'Not if he was ashamed,' Antoinette offered.

'He had no reason to be ashamed. He was a very handsome man with a title and a large estate. It is clear to me that some ambitious girl seduced him and tried to extort money from him. Maybe she even wanted to marry him. Who knows? What we

58

do know, however, is that George accepted his daughter only very recently. Why didn't he accept her when she was a baby?' Margaret sniffed her satisfaction. 'Because he probably wasn't sure the child was his. Or because he didn't want any further dealings with her mother. He must have decided to change his will in a moment of madness, or guilt. You know how generous he was. When will it be read? I'd like to know how much he has given her.'

Harris walked in with a glass of sherry on a silver tray. Margaret took it without so much as a word of gratitude. Sensitive to the people who worked for her, Antoinette thanked him on her mother-in-law's behalf, although Harris was well accustomed to the Dowager Lady Frampton and would have been surprised to the point of shock to have received thanks.

'Mr Beecher is coming here tomorrow at midday' she informed Margaret.

'Good.'

'I have invited Phaedra to come, too,' Antoinette continued, in spite of the appalled expression on her mother-in-law's face. 'It's what George wanted. She's his daughter and he included her in his will. It's right that she should be here.'

Margaret's jaw stiffened. 'Then I most certainly won't attend.'

'As you wish.'

'I think you're very foolish, Antoinette.'

Rosamunde leapt to her sister's defence. 'Antoinette is simply honouring George's request.'

'You know nothing about the girl.'

'Except that my husband loved her.'

This silenced Margaret. Her mouth twitched

59

furiously, but there was nothing she could add. She took a long sip of sherry and swallowed with a loud gulp. 'If she has any decency, she will decline,' she said at last.

'I hope she won't,' Antoinette replied.

Margaret put down her glass and stood up. 'Well, as you're going to be unreasonable, I think I'll go home. If you change your mind, let me know and I'll pay you a friendlier visit. But until then I want nothing to do with the girl, do you understand?'

'You've made that very clear.'

'Good.' She stopped at the door and turned back. 'You can be very stubborn sometimes, Antoinette.'

'What can I do, Margaret? George chose to include her in his will. I'm only carrying out his wishes.'

'He didn't expect to die so young. He may well have thought better of it later. He only has one grandchild but in the years to come there will be more.'

'Are you expecting me to contest it?' Antoinette asked.

'Absolutely.'

'On what grounds? He was hardly insane or coerced into changing it.'

'There must be something you can do.'

'Well, if there is, I'm afraid I won't do it. George was in perfectly sound mind when he changed his will. I never dreamed of going against his wishes when he was alive and I most certainly won't now that he is dead.' Antoinette's chin began to wobble, but she clenched her jaw, determined not to cry again in front of her mother-in-law.

60

Margaret's face had folded into a discontented ball like a walnut, and her thin lips were clamped together as if she were struggling to hold her tongue. She was not used to being defied. She sniffed irately and disappeared into the hall.

'Basil! Basil!' A thunderous clamour could be heard in the upstairs corridor, then the three dogs exploded onto the stairs in an avalanche of fur. 'Bertie, Wooster! Enough! Come on, Basil, we're going home.' A few moments later another gust of wind swept in from the hall as Harris opened the front door. The house seemed to shudder as the Dowager Lady Frampton stepped outside, followed by all three dogs. Then a peaceful silence descended as the door closed behind them.

'So, it's war,' said Rosamunde, barely able to conceal the relish in her voice. Her life at home was so dreadfully dull, but here at Fairfield Park there was something new going on every minute.

Antoinette sighed and looked less pleased. 'Yes, I suppose one could say that it's come to that. Though in all honesty, it's been a *cold* war for years!'

*   *   *

The following day Julius Beecher's car drew up on the gravel at midday. He was a man who took pride in arriving on time. He also took pride in his appearance: the navy-blue Savile Row suit, the black lace-up shoes from Churchill's, the brown leather briefcase from Swaine Adeney Brigg in St James's, the Montblanc pen set that he still kept in

61

its velvet-lined box. His black BMW was as polished as the Franck Muller watch that hung loosely on his wrist. He deplored people who didn't take care of their belongings. Everything attached to Julius Beecher was shiny, clean and new. Working for Lord Frampton had afforded him great luxuries. One thing he didn't have, however, was a wife; he wasn't quite ready to share those hard-earned luxuries, unless his wife came with a fortune of her own.

Lady Frampton was waiting for him in the dining room. She was sitting at the long walnut table with her three sons, her daughter-in-law and her sister, Rosamunde. They were drinking tea and coffee, but no one had touched the shortbread biscuits arranged in a spiral on a plate in the middle.

The rich red velvet curtains were tied back to let in the light, but it was still dim due to the old-fashioned decoration and heavy upholstery. It didn't look as if the room had been changed for hundreds of years. The walls were papered in a deep crimson-and-gold pattern of exotic birds; a large gilt mirror hung above the marble fireplace, its glass stained with black spots caused by damp; and gloomy faces of the Frampton family ancestors stared down from oil-coated canvases. The ceiling was high, surrounded by a heavy, elaborate cornice, and in the centre a crystal chandelier dominated and glittered like diamonds. Julius Beecher found the atmosphere in the room as heavy as the upholstered chairs and carpeting.

'Good morning, Lady Frampton,' he said. He noticed her face cloud with anxiety as she realized he had come on his own, and was quick to explain. 'I'm afraid Miss Chancellor is unable to be with us today. I will act on her behalf.'

Antoinette was surprised by the depth of her disappointment. 'Did she say why?'

Julius took the chair left for him at the head of the table; the chair where George always used to sit. 'She was very grateful for your invitation, but she didn't feel it necessary to come down personally.' He opened his briefcase. 'To be frank, Lady Frampton, I think she's embarrassed.'

Roberta smirked and caught her husband's eye. David felt as disappointed as his mother did. He glanced at Tom who simply pulled a face and shrugged. It didn't matter to his younger brother one way or the other. To David, however, it mattered very much. He could safely assume that she wouldn't accept the invitation to stay the weekend, either. He wondered despondently whether he'd ever see her again.

'So, shall we proceed?' said Julius, pulling out the folder and placing it neatly in front of him.

'Would you like a cup of coffee?' Antoinette offered.

'Yes please, black, no sugar.' He opened the velvet-lined box and lifted out one of two Montblanc pens, then, closing it carefully, moved it to one side so that it lay exactly parallel to the folder. Julius Beecher liked everything to be orderly. As Antoinette pushed the cup and saucer across the table, he turned to the first page of the document. 'Dated March 5th 2012,' he read. 'This is Lord Frampton's last will and testament, witnessed by Mr Richard Headley of No. 8 Chester Square, London.' Julius raised his eyes and swept them over the expectant faces. 'He states he has a wife, Antoinette, and three children: David,

Joshua and Thomas.' Antoinette nodded, Roberta frowned. Why hadn't he mentioned his daughter? 'And one granddaughter, Amber Rose Elizabeth,' Julius continued. He inhaled through dilated nostrils and paused a moment while he ran his eyes over the words that were already familiar to him.

'Please go on, Mr Beecher,' said Antoinette, keen for the whole business to be over as soon as possible.

'In the event that he is outlived by his wife, he leaves Fairfield House and the estate to you, Lady Frampton, to be managed by your son David, who will inherit it upon your death.' There was no surprise about that. Everyone nodded their agreement. 'No. 5 Eaton Place shall remain yours, Lady Frampton, until Joshua inherits it upon your death. He leaves Chalet Marmot in Murenburg to Thomas.'

Tom registered Roberta's displeasure and smiled at her across the table. 'Why would you want Chalet Marmot, Roberta, when you and Josh never go there?'

Roberta blushed. 'You're quite wrong, Tom. It's right that you should have it,' she said in a tight voice, disguising her jealousy. 'Josh and I have so many friends in Gstaad, it would be wasted on us.'

Julius cleared his throat and continued. 'Now, he has left his share portfolio to you, Lady Frampton, with the wish that it should be distributed evenly between his three children in the event of your death.'

'What about Phaedra?' Roberta gasped. 'I thought she was his daughter? Doesn't she get a share?'

64

Julius ignored Roberta; only the subtle raising of one eyebrow betrayed his irritation. 'Until that time, he leaves a considerable annuity to all three of his children.'

'All *three* children!' Roberta echoed. 'Surely he had four children?' She turned to Joshua. 'Why, if he went to the trouble of changing his will, did he not give his daughter equal status to his sons?'

Joshua lowered his voice. 'I don't know, darling. Let's just listen to the rest of the will.'

Julius pushed on. 'A yearly income of the net sum of five hundred and fifty thousand pounds. To Miss Chancellor he leaves a yearly income of the same.'

Roberta was too shocked that George had settled the same amount of money on his illegitimate daughter to absorb the fact that she had just inherited a fortune. 'Has he provided for his granddaughter? What about the Frampton Sapphires? George made it very clear at Amber's christening that he was going to leave them to us.'

'No, darling, Dad said he looked forward to seeing Amber wear them on her twenty-first birthday.'

'The same thing,' Roberta hissed.

'I was just coming to that,' Julius replied testily. 'Lord Frampton has left the Frampton Sapphires to Miss Chancellor.'

A shocked silence fell upon the room. Roberta's eyes filled with tears of indignation. Joshua looked uncomfortable. David and Tom raised eyebrows, while Antoinette seemed to crumple beneath the weight of her daughter-in-law's disappointment. Rosamunde took a shortbread biscuit.

Julius inhaled importantly. 'We both felt that, as

Lord Frampton had only one granddaughter at the time of making his will, he should provide for his wife and children only, leaving you to provide for your own children.'

'I think he has been generous enough,' Antoinette muttered.

'Extremely generous,' Rosamunde echoed.

'I just can't believe he has given Phaedra the Sapphires,' Roberta wailed. 'They were meant to be ours.' She turned to her husband. 'Joshua, your father specifically said he'd leave them to you.'

Joshua looked uncomfortable. 'Dad changed his mind, obviously. There is precious little we can do about it.'

Roberta sat back in her chair with a huff and folded her arms.

'Shall we continue?' said Julius, clearing his throat and turning the page with deliberation.

'Yes, please, Mr Beecher,' Antoinette replied, embarrassed.

'Right, now where was I . . . ?'

Half an hour later Julius sped off in his BMW, but not before Bertie had cocked his leg on one of the tyres. Antoinette watched Julius go and hugged her body as a cold wind swept up the steps to chill her. She felt deeply disappointed that Phaedra hadn't turned up. She wanted to telephone her personally and tell her that George had provided for her in the same way as he had provided for his sons. She paced the step a while, deliberating what to do. If Phaedra hadn't appeared for the reading of the will, what were the chances of her coming to stay the weekend? They hadn't been very friendly. Perhaps she never wanted to see any of them again.

As she closed the front door behind her, she heard them all talking in the drawing room. Instead of returning to join them, she went upstairs to seek the solitude of her bedroom. She crept inside and leaned back against the door. Roberta's behaviour had severely upset her, but her son's inability to control his wife worried her more. Margaret's frequent visits were no consolation. George had held them all together; now he was dead, what was to become of them?

She sighed and wandered over to the window. The sun streamed through the glass, oblivious to the misery of her small world. How unimportant were the petty struggles of human beings when viewed from the great heights of Heaven. She wondered whether George was up there somewhere, basking in the light, free from such cares.

Galvanized by the sudden, overpowering desire to bring her husband back, she telephoned Julius's office and asked the secretary for Phaedra's number. The young girl was keen to please and swiftly found two: a mobile telephone and a landline. Antoinette dialled the mobile and waited. It seemed to ring for an achingly long time. She could almost hear her heart beating as she waited anxiously for the girl to respond. Finally, the gentle voice of her stepdaughter answered. 'Hello, Phaedra, it's Antoinette Frampton—' She was just about to explain who she was when Phaedra cut in.

'Oh, Lady Frampton. What a surprise. I wasn't expecting you to call.'

'Well, I wanted to apologize for the other day.'

'Listen, it's OK. I understand it must have come as a big shock. Please don't apologize. It is *I* who

67

should apologize to *you*.'

'Well, that's very kind of you. I'm sorry you couldn't make the reading of the will today. I just wanted to let you know that George has—'

'Please,' Phaedra interrupted swiftly. 'I really don't wish to know. It's all highly embarrassing.'

'Don't you want to know that he's taken care of you?'

'I'm trying not to think about him at all. It's simply too painful.'

Antoinette heard a sniff down the line and her heart swelled with compassion. 'I know how you feel, my dear. I'm drowning in memories too, all around me, all the time; I can barely breathe. I would love you to come and stay. Please don't say no. I know it's what George would have wanted. You're a Frampton, after all.' There was a lengthy pause. Antoinette began to chew her thumb where the skin was already raw. 'Maybe you need time to consider?'

'No, I don't need time,' Phaedra replied softly. 'I can't. I'm sorry. I really can't. Thank you for calling, Lady Frampton, it means a great deal to me.' And she hung up.

Antoinette was stunned. She remained on the bed, holding the receiver to her ear, unable to accept that the girl had refused her. If Antoinette had desired to see her before, she now longed with all her heart. It was as if Phaedra was a link to George, that if she could reach her, she'd reclaim a little of her husband. But she couldn't reach her; the more she stretched out, the further Phaedra pulled away. She replaced the receiver and put her head in her hands. What on earth was she to do now?

Chapter 5

Rosamunde found Antoinette on the bed, staring dejectedly into space. 'She won't come,' Antoinette exclaimed as soon as she saw her.

'Who won't come?'

'Phaedra. I called her and invited her to stay, but she won't come.'

'How unappreciative.' Rosamunde folded her arms across her sturdy bosom.

'I think we scared her off.'

'She should be thankful you're so kind, Antoinette. No one else would be that generous.' Antoinette lifted her eyes and Rosamunde saw the torment in them. 'Oh, Antoinette, this is all so bloody!' She sat beside her sister, her big heart filling with fury. 'Ungrateful girl! How dare she come down here, drop a bombshell and then disappear without so much as a backwards glance? It's unbelievably rude!'

There was a knock on the door, then Tom's concerned face appeared through the gap. 'Are you all right, Mum?'

'Phaedra has declined to come and stay,' Rosamunde informed him importantly. 'Your mother is very upset, quite understandably.' She patted her sister's kncc. 'You'll be all right, old girl. This will all go away, I promise.'

Antoinette shook her head. 'No, it won't. I can't rest knowing that a part of George is walking about the London streets and I'm not even able to talk to her.'

'She'll come round,' said Tom. 'Just leave her be
69

for a while. We weren't exactly friendly, were we?'

'No, we weren't,' Antoinette agreed. 'It was probably very hard for her, too.'

'What did she expect? You can't throw a grenade and expect a field of flowers to bloom,' Rosamunde added.

'Mum, can I drive Dad's Aston Martin back to London?' Tom asked.

'It's yours now, darling. You can do whatever you want with it.'

He grinned. 'Great!'

'Are you leaving now?'

'Got to get back, I'm afraid. Josh and Roberta have just gone. They didn't want to disturb you. Where are the keys?'

'In the drawer in the hall table.'

He bent down and kissed his mother's cheek. 'Are you going to be all right?'

'Of course she is,' Rosamunde replied briskly. 'I'm here to look after her and David's just across the garden.'

'Good. I'll be down on the weekend.'

'Drive carefully.'

'You bet.' He grinned again, imagining himself at the wheel of the gleaming Aston Martin, roaring up the motorway.

When David heard the news that Phaedra had refused to come and visit he was desperately disappointed. He drove the Land Rover around the farm with Rufus in the well of the passenger seat, mulling over the possibilities. Phaedra might change her mind. After all, she had braved the funeral and was obviously curious to meet them. His father had generously provided for her in his will; perhaps she would now feel more warmly

70

disposed towards his family. But the more he thought about it, the more convinced he became that Phaedra was unlikely to change her mind. They had made her feel uncomfortable and unwelcome. Why on earth would she wish to return to that unpleasant scene?

He hated to see his mother so upset. Losing her husband had been a colossal blow, but discovering he had an illegitimate daughter would have floored most grieving widows; not Antoinette. She considered Phaedra a living part of her dead husband. Perhaps she was even hoping that in some magical way the girl could bring a bit of him back. David knew his mother wouldn't find peace unless she made friends with her stepdaughter.

There was only one thing to do. He'd have to go to London and convince Phaedra to come down. The mere thought of seeing her again filled him with nervous excitement. He recalled the first time he had laid eyes on her in the church: the halo of blonde curls, the translucent skin, the pale innocence of her eyes, the compassionate way she had smiled. He mentally told himself to calm down, that she was his sister, his own flesh and blood, and he couldn't have her. But he brushed his reservations aside with a joyous toss of the head. He'd worry about that later.

He didn't tell his mother what he planned to do. He knew she'd advise against it. He confided in Julius instead. The lawyer was delighted to be part of his plan and gave him Phaedra's telephone numbers and address without hesitation, then took it upon himself to ring Phaedra to warn her.

Phaedra was horrified. 'He's coming here?' she exclaimed.

71

'I gave him your address,' Julius replied calmly.

'Why? I don't want to see any of them again. Ever. I'm moving back to Paris right away, Julius. I don't want to be entangled in this mess.'

'Don't be ridiculous. This is what we agreed, Phaedra. This is what you wanted, for George's sake.'

'Not any more. I felt such a beast, barging in on them the day of his funeral. It was so embarrassing. I can't face them again. Tell him not to come.'

'It's too late. He's probably already on his way.'

'Then I'll leave right now. I'm all packed up.'

'Phaedra, calm down,' he soothed. Julius took great pride in his people skills. 'Listen to me: George loved you—he proved that by leaving you those very valuable jewels in his will. He wanted to look after you forever. Besides, you said you didn't have a family. Well, now you do.'

'I want a family that wants me, Julius.'

'Why do you think David's driving all the way to London? Do you think he'd bother if they didn't want you? You told me that Lady Frampton telephoned you personally to invite you for the weekend. Do you think she would have done that if she didn't want to see you again? They're reaching out to you, Phaedra, which is astonishing, considering the circumstances. I think the very least you can do is graciously accept their invitation.'

'Tell them I've got cold feet.'

'Then have a hot bath.'

'Really, you're absurd!' She laughed in spite of herself.

'That's better. Now, take a deep breath and think

72

about what you're going to say. The least you can do is repay their generosity with gratitude.'

*   *   *

It was six o'clock in the evening when David rang the bell at number 19 Cheyne Row. The narrow street was hidden away like a secret, lost in a maze of one-way lanes and prettily painted town houses between the King's Road and Chelsea Embankment. In spite of the shadow cast by the Catholic church opposite, the setting sun found its way onto the damp pavements where a dog-walker was being dragged across the tarmac by a pack of five eager hounds.

Phaedra's residence was small and eccentric, having been converted into a home from an old fire station. The door was cut into a large wooden arch where the fire engine once used to drive in and out, and above, a wide window consumed the whole of the first-floor wall. The light was on inside, but no one answered. David pressed the bell again.

At last the door opened tentatively and Phaedra's pale face peered through. She feigned surprise. 'David, what are you doing here?'

The sight of her made his heart inflate with happiness. 'I need to talk to you.'

'Really? Well, you'd better come in, then.' She opened the door wide and David stepped into a small hallway dominated by a spiral staircase built around the original fire pole.

'This is a great house,' he said, taking it all in.

'Isn't it? It's so quirky. I love it.' She closed the door and showed him into a surprisingly spacious

73

kitchen/sitting room that led out into a little garden where a couple of finches were busily pecking at a bird feeder suspended from a tree. He noticed a large suitcase on the floor and a coat draped across the sofa.

'Are you going somewhere?' he asked.

'Paris. It's where I live. I've only been here for a month, house-sitting for a friend.'

'Oh, I thought you lived here.'

'No, home is Paris. I'm leaving tomorrow.'

David fought his disappointment. 'Then I'm intruding ...'

Phaedra felt bad. After all, he'd come all the way from Hampshire. 'Can I make you a cup of tea?' she offered. 'I know you Brits love tea.'

He smiled. 'We do, but I'd prefer coffee.'

'OK, I can do that, too. Cappuccino, espresso ...'

'Black, please.'

'Of course: this machine is genius.' She began to fuss about it with a little carton of coffee and a big blue cup. 'Why don't you sit down?' David pulled out a bright-red lacquered spindle-back chair. There were three others in blue, green and purple. A rose-scented candle burned in the centre of the table strewn with photographs. 'Excuse the mess, I've been going through my pictures.' As the cup filled with coffee, she lifted a box from the floor and hastily began to toss the photographs into it.

'Don't tidy up for my sake, you should see how I live.'

'Oh good, you're untidy too?'

'Very. Untidiness must run in the family, then,' said David, determined to cool his ardour by reminding himself that they were related.

She closed the box of photographs and placed

74

the cup of steaming coffee in front of him. 'I know why you've come,' she said, pulling out the purple chair and sitting down opposite him.

'Mother's very upset. She feels she treated you badly when you came to Dad's funeral. She wants to start again.'

'Look, I should never have introduced myself. I should have left straight after the service.'

'It probably wasn't the best time to make our acquaintance, but it is as it is. Let's try and move forward.'

She grinned at his pragmatism. 'That's a good idea.'

'I'm glad you agree.'

'I do. Now tell me if you like my coffee.'

He took a sip. 'Very good. Aren't you going to have some?'

'I've had a cup already. If I have another I'll be flying. Here, have a cookie. Cookies are my weakness.'

'You and Aunt Rosamunde.' He put his hand in the tin she held open for him and lifted out a circular black biscuit. 'Oreos.'

'A little tin of America in my London kitchen.' She watched him take it, then helped herself. 'Aren't they delicious?' They smiled at each other as they bit into their biscuits.

David tried as hard as he could to look upon Phaedra as a sibling, but it was useless. She sat opposite, her beautiful smile turning his stomach to jelly. The air was charged between them. He was sure she must feel it too, for it almost quivered over the table like heat above the desert. They laughed in unison and no quip or innuendo needed to be explained. It was as if they were

75

resuming an age-old friendship, and in spite of his efforts every fibre of his body yearned for her as no brother should.

David didn't relish the thought of leaving and driving back down to Hampshire. It was so comfortable in her kitchen, the allure of her presence so strong, that he wished he could stay. 'Have dinner with me?' he asked suddenly, without thinking it through.

'Dinner?'

'Yes, anywhere you want.'

'You're just like your father, always hungry.' She smiled at him a little sadly. 'He was always looking forward to the next meal, even in the middle of the current one.'

'Don't you think all men are like that?'

'Perhaps. It's just the way you said it. That spontaneous rush of enthusiasm. George was impulsive like that.' They both felt a cold wind sweep across the empty plains in their hearts.

David's gaze dropped onto the table. 'Maybe I should just drive home.'

'No, don't. I'll cook something here, then we don't need to go anywhere. Do you like pasta? George liked my spaghetti Napolitana.'

'I don't want you to go to any trouble.'

'Spaghetti Napolitana is no trouble. I like cooking. I find it relaxing.'

She got up and David watched her reach for the spaghetti in one of the cupboards above the sideboard. She wore a loose-fitting floral shirt over jeans and trainers, but he could tell she had a lovely, curvaceous body beneath. 'As you're staying for dinner, we might as well open a bottle of wine. There should be some Chardonnay in the fridge.

Would you mind?' He found the wine. She handed him a bottle opener and placed a couple of glasses on the table.

'Did you ever call my father "Dad"?' he asked, filling the glasses.

She hesitated a moment. 'No. It didn't feel right. I'm not a little girl any more. I called him George. It suited him.'

'I'm astonished that he managed to keep you to himself for such a long time.'

'Men are good at compartmentalization, don't you think? Besides, I was living in Paris. The time we spent together was in the Himalayas, not London.'

'So you're a climber too?'

'I'll do anything for a good photo.' She grinned at him. 'Even follow some mad Englishman up Mount Pumori!'

'My God, you really are his daughter.'

'We certainly shared a love of adventure and the outdoors.'

He handed her a glass and watched her take a sip. 'What did your mother think when you went in search of him?'

'I don't know. We don't get along.' Phaedra turned away to cut an onion.

'Did they meet again, Dad and your mother?'

'No. She didn't want to and neither did he. It was all in the past. They both decided to leave it there.'

'Very wise. Has your mother remarried?'

'No.' She turned around and grinned at him. 'You're a very inquisitive man, David Frampton. Why don't you make yourself useful and lay the table. Plates are in there,' she said, pointing to a dresser. 'Cutlery in the drawer. Glasses above and there's water in the fridge, assuming you're going to dilute your wine before you drive home.'

'I'd stay at Eaton Square if it wasn't for Rufus.'

'Rufus being a dog, I presume.'

'Right. A big, yellow dog who'd be very upset if I didn't come home tonight.'

'Have you left him all on his own?'

'The farm manager looks after him when I'm away. But he'll have brought him back and shut him in the kitchen at six.'

'Then you must drive home.' She looked at her watch. It was seven forty-five. 'I'll kick you out at nine thirty.'

When the spaghetti was ready they sat at the table to enjoy it. Phaedra had made a thick, sticky tomato and basil sauce, cooking the spaghetti in it for the last few minutes. 'You're a terrific cook,' David complimented her.

'Thank you.' He noticed her glass was empty and refilled it. 'Well, isn't this nice, having dinner with my brother.'

'I can't say this is something I ever imagined I'd be doing.'

'Did you ever wish for a sister when you were growing up?'

'Not really. Mother wished for a daughter, though. I think all women want a daughter, and my mother is very feminine. She would have loved a little girl to share girlie things with. Instead she got three rumbustious boys. Not a whiff of pink in the entire house.'

'I love pink.' She laughed bitterly. 'When I was little I had a blue bedroom because my mother loved blue. I wanted pink, like all little girls, but she insisted that blue was the best colour for me.

Actually, it was just the best colour for *her*. But she filled the room with soft toys and a ridiculously grown-up doll's house that was too fragile to play with.'

'It sounds like she tried her best.'

'Not at all. She gave me everything I could want materially, but not what I needed emotionally.'

'Why?'

'Because she never had time for me. She wasn't maternal. In fact, I'd go as far as saying that she was only interested in herself and the next man who could look after her. She was desperately insecure and I was in the way. The field of potential suitors is greatly reduced if you have a daughter in tow. So she'd pass me around her friends and throw money at me—anything to be rid of me.' She shrugged as if it didn't really matter.

'That's sad, Phaedra.'

'Oh, don't think I feel sorry for myself. By most people's standards, I had a privileged childhood. Anyway, I left as soon as I was old enough. Life got better as soon as I was in the driving seat. My mother's only a memory now.'

David drained his glass. 'Is there anyone special in your life?'

She grinned. 'By that you mean am I in a relationship?'

'I'd hate to think of you being lonely.'

She stared into her glass a moment. 'I'm far too self-sufficient to be lonely,' she replied boldly, but there was something about the way she dropped her shoulders that made him disbelieve her.

'So, do you have someone?' he persisted.

'No, I'm unattached.'

'That surprises me,' he said, but he felt his spirits lift.

'Why?'

'Because you're very beautiful. I'd imagine someone would have snapped you up by now.'

'Oh, someone did. For a brief time I was desperately, deliriously and overwhelmingly in love.'

David's inflated spirits were punctured with jealousy. 'Really?'

'Yes. But I lost him.' Her eyes glistened and she seemed to shrink with sorrow.

'I'm sorry. I shouldn't have asked.'

'You weren't to know.'

'What happened?'

She smiled at him in an attempt to brush off the sting that smarted constantly. 'I don't want to talk about it. But I'm not sure I can ever love like that again. I invested everything in it: my heart, my soul, my future. But there wasn't to be a future. I won't ever let anyone hurt me like that again.' She sighed deeply and took a gulp of wine. 'How about you? Have you ever been in a serious relationship?'

'I've never been in love, not as you describe— desperately, deliriously and overwhelmingly in love. I'm still holding out for that.'

'You've had girlfriends, surely?'

'Of course. But there's an ocean of difference between a girlfriend and someone you can't live without.'

Her eyes glittered again. 'I know what that's like.'

She bit her bottom lip. 'I feel so empty, David.'

'We all do.'

'It was so sudden. I keep expecting George to call me, but he never will. I thought I had a future, but he took it with him and now I'll never get it back. But you know what haunts me the most? The last time we spoke was in ...' She seemed to swallow the word, as if it was too painful to utter.

'Was in ...?'

She sighed in defeat and dropped her shoulders. 'It doesn't matter any more. I never said goodbye.'

Propelled by her stricken face, David moved to the chair beside her and put his arm around her shoulders. She dropped her head onto his chest and cried. David pulled her close, savouring the vanilla scent in her hair and the feeling of her body against his. He closed his eyes and felt his own heart slump with unexpressed grief. Unlike Phaedra, he found that tears didn't come so easily; they seemed to get stuck at the top of his throat, where the muscles contracted and ached from the effort of withholding.

'I'm sorry,' she muttered after a while. 'I'm just so devastated. I found him, then lost him.'

'Come and stay at Fairfield, Phaedra,' he pleaded. 'You'll find comfort in his family.'

'I can't.'

'I insist.'

'You know nothing about me. I'm a stranger. I can't impose.'

'I hardly think you're going to murder us all in the night.'

She sniffed. 'Of course not. But still, I don't feel comfortable accepting hospitality from your mother.'

'She wants you to come.'

'No, I've created enough trouble. I should really

81

go back to Paris.'

'Please. Don't run away. We've only just discovered you. Mother wants to get to know you. You're family. My father would like to think of you down at Fairfield. It's where you belong.'

There was a long silence. Phaedra had never belonged anywhere. The thought of having a family was very seductive. Perhaps Paris could wait. One weekend wouldn't hurt. She lifted her head. 'If you promise you'll look after me.'

'Of course I will.'

'OK, I'll come.' She wiped her eyes with the back of her hand, then, noticing the damp patch on David's shirt, attempted to wipe that too. 'Oh dear, looks like I've cried all over your shirt.'

'It's only a shirt.'

'I can dry it with my hairdryer.' She laughed at the expression on David's face. 'Or not.'

'What do you take me for? As if I care about a damp patch on my shirt.' They both laughed. 'It'll be dry before I get home, so it won't offend Rufus.'

She glanced at the clock on the wall. 'It's past nine thirty and I said I'd kick you out.'

'No need. I'll kick myself out. Must get back to my room-mate.'

She stood in the doorway as he stepped out onto the pavement. 'I've had a good time tonight. You really cheered me up,' she said.

'I'm not sure I cheered you up,' he replied, looking at her tear-stained face.

'Oh, you did. No doubt about that. It's good to talk about George with someone who knew him.'

'I'll see you Friday.' He put his hand in the small of her back and bent down to kiss her cheek. It was still damp.

82

'Friday it is,' she replied. 'Don't forget to look after me.'

She watched him walk beneath the street lamps to his muddy car. He turned and waved before climbing inside. She remained in the door frame as he pulled out and motored slowly down the street. So she was about to be embraced by George's family after all. She felt as wretched as a repentant thief.

Later, as she climbed into bed, her mobile telephone rang on the bedside table. She reached over and picked it up. She saw Julius Beecher's name displayed in the window. Reluctantly, she answered it.

'So, how did it go?' he asked.

Chapter 6

The following morning David strode across the fields with Rufus, his buoyant spirits giving his step a lively bounce. The sky was pale, a few pink clouds wafting across it, and the sun was already warm upon his face. He smiled, because today the thought of Phaedra coming to stay rendered everything more beautiful. Crops emerged through the earth, their green heads reaching up towards the light. Small birds danced and squabbled in the air and a wide-winged buzzard hovered high above in search of prey. He took pleasure in the emerging buds in the hedgerows and the green shoots of bluebells yet to flower in the woods. Rufus disappeared into the undergrowth where the curly green tentacles of bracken were already

83

beginning to unfurl. Suddenly the daily routine of his farming life didn't seem ordinary at all, but glorious. The trees reached out to embrace him, the sun beamed down to envelop him and the soft wind carried the scent of fertility and regeneration. His chest expanded with the sensual delight of it all.

When he reached his mother's house he found her in the kitchen, having breakfast with Rosamunde. 'I've got some news for you,' he announced, leaning back against the sideboard.

'I hope it's *good* news,' said Rosamunde.

'I think you'll be pleased.'

His mother looked at him anxiously. 'Well, don't keep us both in suspense.'

'Phaedra is coming to stay the weekend.'

Antoinette stared at him aghast. Small flourishes of pink broke onto her cheeks. 'How do you know? Did you call her?' she asked.

'I drove up to London to talk to her face to face,' he confessed.

His mother smiled gratefully. 'You did that for me?'

'Yes. I saw how upset you were. I wanted to help.'

'What did she say?'

'She was embarrassed at having barged in on us at Dad's funeral, but I convinced her we'd all forgive her for that.'

Rosamunde buttered a thick slice of toast. 'Good Lord, aren't you a dark horse, David!'

'Wasn't she surprised when you showed up?' Antoinette asked.

'Of course, but she invited me in and made me dinner.'

'She made you dinner?' Rosamunde repeated. 'Gracious, Antoinette, she made him dinner!'

'She's a rather good cook.'

'What did you have?' Rosamunde asked.

'Spaghetti Napolitana.'

'One of your father's favourites,' Antoinette added quietly.

'It was very good.' David grinned guiltily at the recollection, conscious that his growing feelings for Phaedra were inappropriate.

'How did you convince her to come down?' Antoinette asked.

'She misses Dad. I told her she'd find comfort here with us.'

'That's very sweet,' said Rosamunde.

'I'd better tell Tom the good news,' Antoinette said brightly. 'I wonder whether Josh and Roberta will come.'

'You're not going to tell them, are you?' David baulked.

'I think I should. They might not come, but it would be unkind not to include them. After all, Phaedra is Josh's sister, too.'

'If you want Phaedra to come again, I'd refrain. If anyone's going to scare her away, it's Roberta.'

Antoinette looked to her sister for support and Rosamunde was quick to show her allegiance. 'Antoinette is right, David. It wouldn't be fair to exclude them. Roberta's already feeling hard done by.'

'Then Phaedra must stay with you,' Antoinette suggested. 'That way she'll have somewhere to escape to when Roberta's insensitive.'

Rosamunde shook her head. 'I'm not sure that's proper, Antoinette.'

85

'She's my sister,' David reminded her.

'I suppose she is,' Rosamunde agreed.

'Your house is less intimidating than this one.'

David was overjoyed. He felt their dinner had somehow sealed his claim on her. 'If that's what you want, Mum.'

'I think she'd be more comfortable. After all, she knows you now.'

Rosamunde was still doubtful. 'I don't know. It doesn't feel right. She might be your sister, David, but you've only just met her.'

'We're not teenagers, Aunt Rosamunde,' David retorted with a chuckle.

'But you've never had a sister before.'

'Well, I have now and I intend to get to know her.' He grinned at his aunt, who was now anxiously buttering another slice of toast. 'There's Rufus, don't forget. We won't be alone.'

Rosamunde took a bite and chewed heartily. 'I suppose I'm rather old-fashioned.'

David grabbed an apple from the fruit bowl. 'Right, so that's settled. She's coming Friday. I suggest we all have dinner here. I must get on. See you later.' He almost skipped out into the sunshine where Rufus was playing with Bertie and Wooster on the grass.

That evening, when Joshua returned home from work, he told Roberta the news. She was horrified. 'What? That girl is going to stay the weekend? Has your mother gone mad?'

Joshua put down his briefcase in the hall and walked into the kitchen to get a snack from the fridge. 'No, she's just grieving, Roberta.'

'Then her grief has clouded her judgement.'

'Darling, calm down. She might be a very nice

girl. Don't you think it's a bit unfair to judge her before you've even met her?'

Roberta followed him into the kitchen and watched him take a slab of cheddar out of the fridge. 'I suppose we've been summoned.'

'Mum would like us to be there, of course.'

'I thought so.'

'She's my sister.'

'I'm not so sure. It's all very contrived. I smell a rat.'

Joshua dropped his shoulders wearily. 'You and your conspiracy theories. You read too much Patricia Cornwell.'

'Didn't you notice the relish in Beecher's voice when he declared that Phaedra had been left the Frampton Sapphires?'

'Not the bloody Sapphires again!'

'It matters, Joshua, if your family's being swindled. Antoinette is incredibly vulnerable at the moment. It's very easy for George's lawyer to pull the wool over her eyes.'

'Do we really have to talk about this all over again?'

He took the cheese and a tin of water biscuits to the table and sat down. 'What do you think we should do, Roberta?'

She sat opposite and folded her arms on the table. 'Firstly, I don't think Phaedra should be rewarded for breaking the news that she was George's illegitimate daughter on the day of his funeral, when his family was grieving. Secondly, I think it's devious of your father to have withheld that information for nearly two years. Thirdly, I think it's unforgivable to give her the Frampton Sapphires when they should be ours. Fourthly, he

87

should have come clean and told Antoinette everything. She's a good-natured woman, she was never going to kick up a fuss. He had no reason to doubt her.'

'That's the same as number two, but go on ...'

Roberta sighed impatiently. 'Forget the numbers, Josh. It's pretty clear to me that she's trying to inveigle her way into your family. It's a bit odd at her age. Doesn't she have family of her own?'

'Perhaps they're in Canada.'

'It's the twenty-first century, and with the money she's been given she can go back every week if she wishes!'

'Maybe she doesn't have family, then. Perhaps we are the only family she has.'

'It's still odd to adopt a family in your thirties. She should be concentrating on making a family of her own. You said she was pretty; funny she can't find a man to marry her.'

Joshua shook his head wearily. 'I don't know, Roberta, and I don't care. I'll go down at the weekend and meet her for Mum's sake. It would be nice if you came too, with Amber, but if you're going to make a scene I'd rather you stayed behind.'

She grinned wickedly. 'Oh no, I'm coming to observe, even though I gave Kathy the weekend off. I'll happily look after Amber all by myself in order to witness what would be a marvellous black comedy if it wasn't so tragic!'

The following afternoon Antoinette stood before her husband's grave and placed a posy of spring flowers against the temporary wooden headstone Barry had made. The sight of the dates 1954–2012 brought on a surge of anguish and she sank to her knees and put her head in her hands. It was hard to imagine that George lay buried beneath the ground, like the dogs buried at the top of their garden. Nothing remained of him but possessions, and they had no life without him. 'I'm so unhappy, George,' she whispered. 'I don't know how to be on my own any more. But more than that, I'm so cross. Yes, I'm furious with you for lying to me. Why didn't you tell me about Phaedra, when I would have supported you without question? Did you doubt me? Is that why you kept her secret? Did you think I'd be angry? How could you, when I never complained that you abandoned me all the time? You always went off on your travels and I let you go, because I loved you and wanted you to be happy. But whenever did you put *me* first, like I always put *you* first? Your climbing came before me and I didn't complain; surely you knew that I would never have complained about Phaedra. You were everything to me, George, but I was not everything to you. I realize that now and it makes me so cross. If I had been everything to you, you wouldn't have taken such risks. You wouldn't have died a young man and left me a widow. But you've abandoned me again, this time forever, and I can't accept it. I just can't.'

She wiped her cheeks with the back of her hand. The graveyard was littered with headstones, many inscribed with the Frampton name, dating back as far as the fourteenth century. Some were so old it was no longer possible to read the inscriptions on them. But each one of those graves bore witness to a life—a life that was once as vibrant as hers. One day she'd lie here beside George and her vibrant life would be over, too. Things that had seemed important would be reduced to nothing. Her existence would end like this, in a cold graveyard, and the years that had seemed so long would be reduced to a couple of inanimate dates carved into stone. How short life was—for what purpose?

A wave of fear washed over her and she caught her breath. Death was inevitable and it would come as surely as autumn follows summer. It wasn't just something that happened to everyone else, but something that would happen to *her*. There was no avoiding it.

She stood up and hurried into the church. There was no one inside. It was dim but for the afternoon light that streamed through the stained-glass windows and fell upon the pews, catching small particles of dust in the air and making them shine like tiny fireflies. She walked up the aisle and sat in the front pew, facing the altar. Kneeling in prayer, she clutched onto the traditions of her childhood like a shipwrecked sailor clinging to the small remains of his ship.

Please be there, God. Oh please be there, because I can't face nothing. I can't face all that I am being reduced to dust. I don't want to believe that George is in the ground. He's so much bigger than that. There has to be an immortal part of him that lives on somewhere. After all, he climbed mountains. He was a brave adventurer. I can't believe that the adventure is over and my larger-than-life George is rotting in a coffin beneath the ground. What was it all for? George was a good man, he deserves more than that. Please God, be up there somewhere. I want to believe in you, I really do. I want to think of George in Heaven. I want to believe there's a place for me too,

90

because I'm frightened of being left alone. Tears squeezed through her lashes and she pressed her clenched hands to her mouth. *Oh God, I'm frightened of being alone in the dark.*

She remained there on the hassock for a long while, listening to her breathing and the decelerating beats of her heart. At length the silence began to soothe her troubled soul and the soft vibrations that filled the church from many centuries of candlelight and prayer eased her distress. When she sat up, she felt strangely uplifted. Gone was the terrible fear. In its place there remained a strange sense of resignation—a feeling that someone stronger was going to take care of everything.

She walked outside and squinted in the brightness. She looked down at her watch; it was now just after 6 p.m. She had been in there for over an hour, so no wonder her eyes were taking time to adjust. As she set off down the path she noticed, to her horror, her mother-in-law chatting to Reverend Morley beneath the wooden gable of the church gate. They were so engrossed in conversation that they didn't notice her. Antoinette froze and frantically tried to think of another way out. The only exit was through the gate, where her car was parked on the verge, but there had to be an escape route behind the church.

She turned around slowly so as not to catch their attention, and walked as softly and swiftly as she could around to the back of the church. Once out of sight she strode faster, disappearing into shadow, and hurried across the grass to a high wall that bordered someone else's property. Cut into

91

the wall was a rusted iron gate. She peered through and marvelled at the sight of a lovingly tended garden. It was very big, with a well-mown lawn, borders of neatly trimmed perennials and burgeoning plants. Against the wall was a herbaceous border and along the right side clusters of daffodils and tulips were beginning to rise out of the compost and shine in the evening sunshine. The house at the far end was a pretty Georgian building with a red-tiled roof upon which a couple of pigeons perched together, as absorbed in each other as the Reverend Morley and Margaret Frampton.

Antoinette didn't know who lived there. She wasn't in the habit of socializing with the village, and many houses like this one were hidden down driveways and behind towering trees and shrubbery. It didn't look as if the owner was there, at least not outside, so she sneaked through the gate, which she found to her relief to be unlocked.

With her heart beating wildly she crept around the periphery of the garden. She felt like a criminal—though, on reflection, anything was better than having to stop and talk to her mother-in-law. As she made her way around she was arrested suddenly by the unmistakable smell of *Daphne odora*. She paused to inhale the sweet, jasmine-like scent of the shrub already in flower and her heart filled with pleasure. She took another luxurious breath, savouring the scent in her nostrils. Since George's death she hadn't been into her garden. She wasn't even sure whether hers was out yet, which was unusual for Antoinette because she considered *Daphne odora* spring's

92

greatest gift. As she stood with her eyes closed, sniffing the heady perfume, she slowly became aware that someone was watching her. She opened her eyes with a start, then a blush flowered on her cheeks and intensified when she realized that the man standing in the doorway of his conservatory was none other than Dr Heyworth.

She wrung her hands and smiled apologetically. 'Oh dear, you must be wondering what I'm doing in your garden?' she mumbled, hurrying across the lawn to explain herself.

'You like my daphne?' he said with a grin.

'Oh, I love your daphne. You know, I'm not sure whether ours is out yet, I must check. It's my favourite shrub and the first thing to come into flower.' She realized she was talking very fast, trying desperately to act as if her unexpected appearance in his garden was the most natural thing in the world.

'I should think yours is out now.' He frowned apprehensively as she reached him, and Antoinette realized that her face must betray her earlier tears in the church. 'Are you all right, Lady Frampton?'

'I've just been to see George,' she replied, shoulders dropping.

'Ah.'

'Then I sat in church for a while. It's very peaceful in there. It made me feel a lot better. It's good for the soul to reflect quietly in a place like that, when no one else is there. Well, they were about to come inside . . .'

Dr Heyworth raised his eyebrows. 'They?'

'Reverend Morley and my mother-in-law,' she replied hastily. 'I didn't want to face them on the path so I sneaked around the back and managed to

93

get away without being seen. At least I'm pretty sure they didn't see me. That's why I'm in your garden.'

Dr Heyworth chuckled in amusement and she knew she wasn't making any sense at all. 'You know, most people use the front drive,' he said.

She stared at him, not knowing what to say. Then he laughed so hard his whole face creased and she felt the laughter bubble up from her belly too, taking her by surprise because she hadn't laughed like that in a very long time. 'Oh dear, you must think me very odd,' she said, holding her stomach.

'Well, as you're here, would you like to come in for a cup of tea?' It was quite possible that Reverend Morley and Margaret were still chatting at the church gate, so it would be difficult to get to her car without being seen.

'I'd love to,' she replied, following him inside.

'Good. Let's go and put the kettle on.'

*   *   *

Rosamunde was by now very worried about Antoinette. She had been gone for hours and it was getting dark. How long did it take to put flowers on your husband's grave? She put down her needlepoint and looked at her watch. It was after seven o'clock. She strained her ears for the sound of the car drawing up on the gravel, but only a few late roosters were twittering in the lime trees.

Harris appeared in the doorway and asked whether she'd like a drink. 'Yes, please, sherry, and make it a large one. What do you think Lady Frampton is up to, Harris?'

94

'I suspect she'll be back soon. I wouldn't worry. In my experience, no news is good news.'

'Well, that's certainly true. I think—' At that moment the lights of a car flashed in through the window. 'Oh good, that must be her now.' Rosamunde got up and hurried into the hall, feeling greatly relieved. Harris went ahead to open the door. However, it wasn't Antoinette who climbed the steps with such haste, but Margaret.

'Good evening, Lady Frampton,' said Harris, not looking at all surprised.

Margaret gave a snort. 'Where's Antoinette?' she demanded.

Rosamunde looked anxiously past her for her sister's car. 'She's not here,' she replied, perplexed.

'Her car is outside the church but she's nowhere to be seen. I thought she might have walked back, forgetting that she had left her car on the verge. You know, grief can do funny things to the mind. I hate to drive, as you know, but I felt compelled to come over and find out what the devil is going on.'

'She went to lay flowers on George's grave ...'

'What's the good of that? He's not going to see them.' She marched through the hall and into the drawing room. 'Will you bring me a glass of sherry, Harris. Ah, good, the fire is lit. Well, that's something, at least.'

Rosamunde did not relish the prospect of sitting alone with her sister's strident mother-in-law, especially as she wasn't able to tell her where Antoinette was. Rosamunde liked to be in the know about things. Margaret sat down in the armchair. 'I want to talk to her about this girl.'

'You mean Phaedra,' Rosamunde replied, pleased that she knew all about *her*.

95

'I hear she's coming to stay the weekend?'

'Yes, Antoinette invited her.'

'No one told me about it. Was I to be kept in the dark?'

'I'm sure she was going to tell you. She telephoned Joshua and Tom. Of course David knew because it was he who drove up to London to invite her and they had dinner.'

'I had to hear it from Roberta. She wants to borrow the Frampton Sapphires for a charity ball at Buckingham Palace in the presence of the Prince of Wales and the Duchess of Cornwall. Lovely to think of them being worn in such splendid company. Antoinette has never cared for jewellery, but Roberta loves to sparkle and I must say she does look very fine in them.' Rosamunde realized that Roberta had failed to tell her that Phaedra had been left those precious family jewels. Margaret sniffed her annoyance. 'At least there's someone in the family prepared to fill me in with the goings-on down here.'

Harris entered with a tray holding two glasses of sherry and a bowl of pistachio nuts. 'Where do you think she's gone?' Margaret asked.

'I imagine she's found a friend and is having a drink,' said Rosamunde, determined not to show how worried she was.

Margaret looked at her watch. 'Well, I have nothing else to do, so I'll wait.' She sipped her sherry and watched Rosamunde through hooded eyes. Rosamunde sipped hers and stared back. It seemed a long while before the sound of Antoinette's car was at last heard on the gravel outside.

'Ah, good,' Margaret sighed. 'Now she can tell us

96

where she's been.'

Rosamunde smiled knowingly. 'Or not. I'm sure she'll feel no compulsion to tell us anything.'

Chapter 7

Margaret and Rosamunde remained in the drawing room as Harris opened the door and Antoinette hastened into the hall. They listened as she patted her dogs and exchanged a few words with the butler. Then she appeared in the doorway suppressing a smile, because there in the armchair was the Dowager Lady Frampton whom she had gone to such great lengths to avoid.

'Well, you look like the cat that's got the cream,' said Margaret. 'Where have you been? I saw your car parked outside the church, but you were nowhere to be seen.'

'I assumed you'd found a friend and gone to have a drink,' Rosamunde added, not to be outdone.

'I went to see Dr Heyworth,' Antoinette replied casually, taking a seat beside her sister on the sofa.

'Are you ill?' Margaret asked.

'No, it was a social call.'

Margaret raised her eyebrows. 'A social call? With Dr Heyworth?'

'Yes.' Antoinette was not prepared to disclose any more than that, although it was clear that Margaret expected something of an explanation. There followed a lengthy silence but Antoinette did not rush to fill it.

'We've been waiting for you to come home,' said

97

Margaret.

'If I'd known you were coming I would have made sure I was back in time,' Antoinette replied. 'Perhaps you should call next time.'

'I've just been talking to Rosamunde about that girl coming to stay the weekend,' Margaret began.

'Phaedra,' said Rosamunde.

'*Roberta* told me,' Margaret added then inhaled through her nostrils to show that she resented being informed by her grandson's wife.

'I told Margaret you were going to tell her—' Rosamunde began, but Antoinette cut her off briskly.

'I most certainly wasn't, Rosamunde.' She turned to her mother-in-law. 'You made it very clear that you didn't want anything to do with her, Margaret, and I took you at your word.'

For a moment Margaret didn't know what to say. She took a long sip of sherry before replying. 'You're right, I don't want anything to do with her, but if she is my son's daughter I think I should at least meet her.'

Antoinette's heart sank at the thought of Margaret and Roberta cornering Phaedra. 'I don't think that's a good idea. I'm anxious for her stay to be pleasant.'

'Oh, I insist. I have many questions I wish to ask her.'

'I don't think it's fair to launch an inquisition.'

'I'm not going to launch an inquisition, Antoinette. I'm sure you're as curious as I am. It's very distressing to think of George keeping such a secret. We need answers.'

'I don't need any answers at all,' said Antoinette, just to be contrary. 'I only want to get to know my

98

stepdaughter. If, in time, she chooses to share things with me, I'll be happy to listen. But I'm not going to pin her against a wall and demand answers.'

Margaret's face hardened and she narrowed her eyes. 'My son has left her a fortune in his will—an income which ensures that she never has to work again ...'

'And the Frampton Sapphires,' Antoinette added. 'Don't forget *them*.'

Margaret nearly spilled her sherry. 'What did you say?'

'The Frampton Sapphires. George left them to Phaedra.'

'He can't have done! Are you certain? Those jewels must stay in the family!'

'Phaedra *is* family,' Antoinette insisted.

'I don't believe it!' The old lady's face reddened to the colour of a beetroot.

'It's true, Margaret. Roberta's very upset about it.'

'I should think so! George was going to leave them to David.'

'Roberta was under the impression that he was going to leave them to Joshua,' said Antoinette.

'Rubbish!' Margaret snapped. 'They go to the eldest son, everyone knows that. Roberta likes to borrow them, which is perfectly fine, but there's no question of them being given to anyone but David.'

'Well, he's left them to Phaedra.'

'It's outrageous. I wonder why Roberta never mentioned it to me. We had a long talk this morning.'

'I don't suppose she mentioned her appalling

99

behaviour at the reading of the will, either?'

Margaret frowned. 'No, she didn't mention that.'

'She behaved very badly, Margaret. I was embarrassed.'

The old lady drained her glass and put it down on the sofa table beside her chair. She suddenly looked defeated. 'What was George thinking?'

Antoinette couldn't answer that. She didn't know, either.

'Oh dear, how are you going to prevent Margaret from muscling in this weekend?' Rosamunde asked once she had gone.

'I don't think I can. She's never waited for an invitation to come here, but barges in whenever she feels like it. I'm afraid there's no keeping her away. Phaedra will just have to deal with it.'

'Well, the girl has nothing to hide. It's all out in the open now, isn't it?'

'Exactly. Perhaps she'll want to share the details of how she found him and how they built their relationship after so many years. We're probably fussing about nothing.'

Rosamunde grinned. 'Margaret *is* the girl's grandmother.'

'Poor child. One can't pick one's relations.'

'I bet she didn't anticipate *her* when she went in search of her father.'

'Goodness no, one simply couldn't conjure up a woman like Margaret, even if one strained one's imagination.'

'Oh, I don't think one has to strain one's imagination too much. It's all there in folklore and fiction: *The Wizard of Oz, Cinderella, 101 Dalmatians, Hansel and Gretel*, to name just a few.'

'You are wicked,' Antoinette laughed.

'Oh yes, there are Margarets everywhere,' said Rosamunde.

*   *   *

On Friday morning Phaedra packed her weekend bag with some trepidation. She laid a light floral dress on the bed and teamed it up with a pair of scarlet pumps and black tights, in case she needed to be elegant on Saturday night. She wasn't exactly sure what was expected, never having been to stay in a grand English country house before. She rummaged through the suitcase she had already packed for her return to Paris and pulled out a bright-green cardigan, black lace-up ankle boots, a flowery blouse and burgundy woollen tights. She suspected her attire would be unsuitable, but she had nothing of the country tweeds and corduroy she'd seen in magazines and movies.

Since meeting David she felt somewhat reassured. She imagined the rest of his family must be as nice as him. Antoinette had sounded very warm on the telephone, quite different from the woman she had encountered at the funeral. But that wasn't a surprise; Phaedra had just hit her with the most terrible revelation at the worst possible time. She still cringed at the thought. It would be nice to meet them under less stressful circumstances.

However, she hoped no one would bring up the subject of George's will. It was incredibly embarrassing that he had given her so much, not to mention the Frampton Sapphires. When Julius had informed her they were now hers she had nearly fainted with shame, for she knew why he

101

had given them to her, and she didn't want them. Besides the fact that she wasn't the type to wear jewellery, they were somehow tainted, wrapped as they were in guilt. Had he really thought it through she was sure he would never have been so impulsive.

Julius had told her that the sapphires had been bought in India by the first Lord Frampton who was Governor General in 1838, and handed down from generation to generation. There was a large portrait of his wife Theodora, the first Lady Frampton, in the hall at Fairfield Park, dazzling in the exquisitely crafted diamond and sapphire necklace, earrings and bracelet. Julius had gone quite puce in the face when he had described them. Phaedra didn't care much for jewellery but Julius had insisted that no woman, however modest, could resist them.

That evening she heaved her bag onto the back seat of her car and drove west out of London, stopping at a boutique on the King's Road to buy Antoinette a small present. There was a lot of traffic on the Talgarth Road but she listened to Capital Radio and soon she was driving down the M3, her small Fiat cruising smoothly at 70 mph.

The skies were heavy with thick grey cloud, but to the west, where the sun was setting, the golden light was shining through and turning them pink. She began to get nervous when she came off the motorway and headed into the countryside. The hedgerows were already beginning to bud and a green smoke appeared to be wafting through the woodlands as the branches revealed their first lime-coloured leaves. Spring had lifted the land out of the bleak brownness of winter and breathed new life onto the fields, turning them a lively, phosphorescent green. She took pleasure in the little birds that darted in and out of the hedges, and opened the window to expel the city pollution from her lungs and inhale the fresh, clean air. She felt uplifted in spite of her apprehension.

At last she drove through the old market town of Fairfield. The high street was very wide and lined with cherry trees, yet to flower. She motored up the hill, admiring the colour-washed rainbow of Georgian houses and little shops that she had been too nervous to notice when she came for the funeral. It was like stepping back in time to another age, and if it hadn't been for the cars parked beneath the fruit trees she could have imagined what it must have been like two hundred years before when King George sat on the throne.

She slowed down when she drove past the church. Somewhere in that yard George lay buried and for a moment she felt the urge to park the car and go and find his grave, but she didn't want to be late and it was already seven o'clock. So she drove on and up the narrow lane that led to Fairfield Park, situated a mile outside the town. She shuddered as she motored past the little white cottages and through the iron gates, remembering the last time she had been there and how desperate she was to leave. She recalled how she had vowed never to return, but here she was now, once again making her way up the drive beneath the plane trees.

Harris heard the car on the gravel and walked hastily to the drawing room to inform Lady Frampton. Antoinette hurried out into the hall with David, while Joshua and Roberta remained on the sofas with Rosamunde. Tom hadn't yet arrived, which wasn't unusual. As Antoinette prepared herself in the hall, anxious for everything to go smoothly and for Phaedra to like her, Roberta swept across the room to sneak a peek through the curtains. She saw the car draw up and halt. She saw the girl inside turn off the engine and open the door. Then she saw Phaedra climb out, and her body stiffened with jealousy, for even in the semi-darkness she could see that she was a beauty. Roberta withdrew as if the curtain had scalded her.

Harris descended the steps to help Phaedra with her suitcase. David followed after, a wide smile swallowing up his face. When Phaedra saw him, her shoulders relaxed and she smiled back gratefully. He said he'd look after her and he'd been true to his word. She felt a warm sense of relief just seeing him there.

'You got here in good time,' he said, bending down to kiss her cheek.

'There wasn't much traffic. It was fine.'

He could tell she was nervous. 'I thought you'd prefer to stay in my cottage,' he whispered in her ear. 'Then you can leave when my family gets too much.'

She laughed, pleasantly surprised. 'Was that your idea?'

'No, Mother's actually.'

'That's very thoughtful of her. May we go now?'

He looked at her askance. 'That's a joke, right?'

'Only half.'

He put his hand in the small of her back and led her up the steps. 'Don't worry, they don't bite. And the one that does, isn't here,' he added, referring

104

to his grandmother.

Antoinette was at the top of the steps, ready to welcome her. 'Phaedra, I'm so pleased you agreed to come.'

'Hello, Lady Frampton.'

'Please, call me Antoinette. You're my stepdaughter, after all.' She smiled warmly and Phaedra's fears began to slip away. 'Don't mind the dogs, they're very friendly.'

'They're big, aren't they? I suppose they must eat you out of house and home.'

'They don't eat as much as you'd imagine. Come on in. The others are in the drawing room. Tom hasn't arrived yet, but that's no surprise, he's never on time for anything.'

Phaedra followed Antoinette through the hall. It looked so much larger now that it wasn't full of people. A big fire danced boisterously in the grate, beneath a large black canopy to catch the smoke. She inhaled the smell of burning logs and sighed with pleasure; there was something very comforting about that woody scent. She stepped over the Persian rugs, noticing everything, from the vast display of lilies on the hall table to the line of silver trophies on the mantelpiece above the fire, presumably George's. This was *his* home, *his* family, *his* intimate life—and she had never been a part of any of it.

As she walked through to the drawing room the big portrait of Theodora caught her attention. It hung at the bottom of the stairs where the light from the hall seemed to catch the sapphires and diamonds around her neck and on her ears and wrist, making them glitter as if they were real. Quite apart from the serene beauty of the woman, the Frampton suite blazed with a magnificence of its own. Phaedra didn't have time to linger, but Julius had been right; no woman, however modest, could fail to be impressed by them.

She walked into the drawing room where Rosamunde and Joshua stood to greet her. 'Technically we've met before,' said Rosamunde. 'But I don't count that.' She extended her hand. 'I'm Rosamunde, Antoinette's sister.'

'Yes, hello again.' Phaedra shook her hand, relieved to see that the rather severe-looking woman she had met in the library was quite friendly when she smiled.

'This is Josh,' said Antoinette, then she introduced Roberta and there was nothing in her demeanour to suggest that she wasn't entirely fond of her daughter-in-law.

Phaedra shook Joshua's hand; unlike his brother's it was as soft and bland as dough. His features were pleasant enough, in fact he should have been very handsome, but there was no character in his face to give it the individuality and strength that David's possessed. He had something of the lame duck about him, a slight stoop of the shoulders and a detachment in the eyes, as if he had wilfully disengaged. She was surprised by his wife's coolness. She remained solemn, her sharp jaw taut, looking down at Phaedra with an imperious gaze, making Phaedra feel small in every way.

Just as Roberta was about to speak, David stepped in to rescue her. 'Let's sit down,' he suggested. There was a moment of awkwardness as David moved his hand towards the small of her back to direct her to the sofa. Thinking better of it,

106

he pulled away at the last moment. 'Harris will get you a drink,' he said, putting his errant hand in his pocket. 'What would you like?'

'Lime and soda?'

'Are you sure you don't need more fortification?' he grinned down at her.

'Maybe later.'

'I would apologize for them,' he whispered once they had sat down. 'But they're your family, too.' They both laughed and Antoinette thought how already they appeared like siblings.

Harris brought drinks and they chatted around the fire. Roberta perched on the window seat, some distance from the rest of the family, listening but not taking part. Antoinette didn't bother to beckon her forward. If she wants to be stand-offish, she thought, that's *her* problem. She hoped Phaedra didn't notice the girl's rudeness.

Phaedra noticed everything and wasn't in the least surprised by Roberta's hostility, although it hurt. She was grateful that everyone else treated her kindly. Julius had said that George's family would embrace her as a long-lost daughter, but Phaedra hadn't been so sure. It seemed a lot to ask of a family still in mourning. But the gamble appeared to have paid off. Antoinette was ready to welcome her, and David, especially, was going to great lengths to make her feel she belonged. Joshua's eyes brightened every time he looked at her, and Rosamunde, clearly keen to please her sister, was very gracious indeed. To Phaedra, however, blood was of little importance—their shared love for George bonded them in a way that DNA never could.

As Antoinette talked about her dogs Phaedra

noticed the pain behind her eyes. The woman smiled and laughed occasionally at David's jokes, but Phaedra guessed that inside, her heart was a brick. She stood alone at the beginning of an uncharted and solitary road. She had her sons to comfort her and her sister to give her strength, and yet her widowhood rendered her isolated and forlorn. Phaedra wanted to reach out to her, but she knew that no amount of carefully chosen words could bring George back. Anything less than that fell desperately short.

Tom still hadn't turned up by the time they moved into the dining room for dinner. Antoinette looked anxiously at her watch. 'Don't worry about him, Mum. He's probably forgotten,' said David, pulling the chair out for Phaedra.

'I'm not worrying,' she replied, smiling unconvincingly.

'I'm sure he hasn't forgotten,' Rosamunde reassured her.

'Has Tom ever been on time for anything?' said Joshua, sitting down.

'Oh, I think that's a little unfair,' Antoinette replied, her hackles rising as she prepared to defend him.

'He'll be down,' Roberta added. 'He certainly won't miss this weekend. There's nothing he enjoys more than a good drama.' Phaedra wanted to respond to the suggestion that *she* was the drama, but refrained. There was no point prodding the tail of the tigress, she'd only get bitten.

'Any excuse to drive Dad's car,' David added.

Joshua chuckled. 'Yes, he's like Toad of Toad Hall at the wheel of the Aston Martin.'

Phaedra laughed and Joshua's eyes flickered a

moment with pleasure. 'I'm not sure he'd be too pleased with that description,' she said. 'No one would like to be compared with Toad!'

'He'd be the first to see the parallel; there's a lot of Toad in Tom,' Joshua continued, delighted that Phaedra found him amusing.

Roberta sat directly opposite Phaedra and watched as David and her husband placed themselves either side of her. 'So, you're a Kenneth Grahame fan,' she said.

'Of course. *The Wind in the Willows* is one of my all-time favourites.'

'Where were you educated?'

'In Vancouver,' Phaedra replied with a shrug. 'I hated school.'

'But you went to university?'

'No, I worked from the age of sixteen. I left home as soon as I could.'

Roberta crinkled her nose. 'Really, why would you do that?'

'Long story,' Phaedra replied dismissively. She'd never share it with Roberta.

'Such a shame not to finish your education. I bet you regret it now.' Roberta pulled a saccharine smile.

'Not at all. Life has been a great educator.'

'You know, my favourite character was always Ratty,' said Joshua.

'Oh, me too,' enthused Phaedra, happy to turn away from Roberta. 'Steady old Ratty.'

'I think David's a little like Ratty,' said Joshua.

'I'd rather be Badger. He's more charismatic,' David interjected dryly.

'David's much more like Badger than Ratty!' Phaedra exclaimed.

109

Roberta stiffened and tapped her fingers on the table impatiently. 'Tell us about you and George, Phaedra. We're all dying to know.'

There followed an uncomfortable silence. Joshua glared at his wife, but Roberta smiled the smile of a wily crocodile. Antoinette struggled to find something to say. It was inevitable that the subject would swing around to George at some stage of the evening, but she hadn't expected it to turn so early on. Roberta was unforgivably rude. But Phaedra seemed not to mind. Harris filled her glass with white wine and she took a slow sip. David would have liked to change the subject to save Phaedra any embarrassment, but he was as curious as everyone else.

'What exactly are you wanting to know, Roberta?' she asked.

'Everything, from the very beginning. Let's start with your mother.'

Phaedra frowned. 'My mother's memories are her own. She never confided in me.'

'Roberta, this isn't the Spanish Inquisition,' said Rosamunde, repeating what she had heard her sister say to Margaret.

'Don't pretend you're not interested, Rosamunde. George's illegitimate daughter suddenly appears at his funeral and inherits a fortune, not to mention the Frampton Sapphires.' At the mention of the jewels Roberta's voice thinned with emotion. 'I think it's our right, as his family, to know how it all came about.'

'Phaedra must tell us only what she wants to tell us,' said Antoinette diplomatically.

'You don't have any objection, do you?' Roberta asked Phaedra.

110

'She's not in the dock, Roberta,' said Joshua.

Roberta rounded on her husband. 'Well, I'm obviously the only one here who is honest enough to admit that I find the whole situation deeply shocking.'

'Roberta!' David exclaimed, his face hardening with fury.

Phaedra forced a smile and raised her hand. 'Please, let's not start a war. I'm very happy to answer for myself. Of course you're shocked, Roberta, *I* would be in the same situation. The man you thought you knew had a big secret, one he didn't share with anyone. But aren't we all multi-faceted? Don't we all harbour secrets in one way or another? Isn't that natural? He kept me secret to avoid hurting all of you, and, as you can see from Roberta's reaction, he was right to do so. Had he not died, you'd all be none the wiser.'

'But apparently he was going to tell us?' said Antoinette keenly.

'That's what he told me, too. But maybe he never would have.' She shrugged. 'I mean, he talked about it and he certainly made his intentions very clear to Julius. But it's one thing *saying* you're going to do something and quite another actually *doing* it.'

'And we all know how impulsive George was,' Roberta interjected. 'He developed short crushes on things, didn't he? Remember those cigars from Havana? How long did those last? A year at the most. Then he decided to import llamas from Peru. His crushes extended to people, too.'

'But he loved his family constantly,' Antoinette cut in.

'That's true,' Roberta agreed. She examined

111

Phaedra's face, trying to find traces of George in her features. 'You don't look anything like him.'

Phaedra felt the chill of her scrutiny. 'True, I look like my mother.'

David leapt to her defence. '*I* don't look anything like Dad, either.'

'But you share many characteristics,' Roberta added. 'What characteristics do *you* share with George, Phaedra?'

At that question, Phaedra's face lit up. 'We had so much in common. We loved all the same things: the mountains, climbing in wild places, travelling, sport.'

'You don't ski, do you?' David asked, excitedly.

'Absolutely. I grew up in Vancouver.'

'Did you ski with Dad?'

'Yes, he was a beautiful skier.'

'Did he take you to Murenburg?' Antoinette asked, fighting a sudden sense of betrayal. How was it that they had done all these things together without her knowledge? Climbing, travelling, skiing ... She swallowed back tears as the secret suddenly became so much bigger.

'No, he took me to Whistler in Canada for my birthday. We also played cards. He was a wicked bridge player.' Antoinette recalled the various times George had tried, and failed, to teach her bridge. She watched Phaedra across the table and wondered whether George had found a soulmate in his daughter, someone who loved all the same things that he loved; all the things *she* hated.

'Was he very surprised when you appeared, claiming to be his daughter?' Roberta probed deeper. 'I mean, did your mother really keep your birth secret from him? I find that very unlikely.'

112

Phaedra couldn't help but admire the girl's perseverance, although she didn't relish having to answer her questions. Her heart was thumping wildly and her hands had begun to sweat. Everyone was staring at her, which was daunting. 'My mother didn't want anything from George, Roberta. It was a brief love affair that ended. Telling him she was carrying his child would not have resurrected it. Besides, she soon married Jack and we became a family for a while. I grew up believing Jack was my father.'

'Why did she leave it so late to tell you the truth?' Roberta asked.

Phaedra lowered her eyes and seemed to wilt for a moment beneath the pressure of Roberta's questioning. 'Jack died. She wanted me to know then that he wasn't my real father.'

'Dear girl, how ghastly for you to lose two fathers in such a short space of time,' said Rosamunde.

'Jack was a father to me for the first ten years of my life, and I felt bereft and betrayed when he left. He settled in New Zealand and raised a family there. He didn't keep in touch. When he died I felt nothing. I barely remember him now.'

David noticed that Phaedra's eyes had begun to glitter and pushed back his chair. 'Right, let's eat. I'm ravenous!' Harris had brought in the food on large china dishes and placed them on the sideboard at the end of the room. 'Phaedra, why don't you come and help yourself,' he suggested quietly.

But Roberta wasn't finished. 'Did you see a lot of George over the eighteen months that you knew him?' she persisted.

'Yes. He was a busy man but he made time for

113

me. We skied and trekked together. I lived in Paris but spent a lot of time travelling in Asia, which is where he loved to be, too. I've been working on a big photographic book of the Himalayan communities, you see. George was helping me. He knew the area well. I only moved to London very recently to see more of him.' She lowered her eyes and fingered her fork nervously. 'I'll be moving back to Paris now as I have to finish my book and there's no reason for me to stay.'

'Why Paris?'

'I've lived all over, Roberta, but Paris is the city I feel most at home in,' Phaedra replied, trying to remain composed as Roberta fired one question after another. 'I speak French and have many friends there.'

'Did George introduce you to people? How did he keep you secret for all that time?'

'He didn't have to. We were climbing mostly. Just us and a few sherpas and porters. It was irrelevant.'

'But when you were skiing in Whistler, for example? How did he keep you secret there?'

'He didn't. He kept the fact that I was his *daughter* secret.'

Roberta crinkled her nose. 'So, how did he introduce you?'

'As a photographer,' Phaedra replied simply, placing her napkin on the table and standing up. 'He didn't feel the need to explain to anyone.'

Just then the door swung open and Tom stood in the doorway, his hair standing on end like a monkey. 'Sorry I'm late. I came all the way down from London with the roof off. Fast as I could. Mmmm, what's for dinner?'

Chapter 8

Phaedra was relieved that Tom had arrived in time to deflect the conversation from her. She was uncomfortable talking about George. She felt exposed having to field questions about their relationship. As far as she was concerned, they all missed him—and that was all that mattered.

She wished she hadn't got involved with his family, but she had been determined to attend the funeral. Julius did warn her of the consequences, but she had insisted. Now she understood why he had advised her to act with caution. The sooner she could return to Paris and put this all behind her, the better.

Antoinette was relieved to see Tom. The constant churning of anxious thoughts in her head was momentarily stilled as her son bent down to kiss her. 'Sorry, Mum. I overslept.'

'That's OK, darling. I'm just glad you're here.' She watched him greet Phaedra, happy that Roberta's badgering had come to a halt. Perhaps they could all enjoy a nice family dinner now.

'And I'm glad *you're* here, sis,' he said with a chuckle. 'I'm loving the sound of that—sis—it has a nice, cosy kind of ring to it.' Roberta rolled her eyes and sighed heavily.

David glowered at her from the sideboard. 'If you don't tell your wife to back off, I'm going to,' he hissed at Joshua, who was now helping himself to roast potatoes.

'She's suspicious, that's all,' Joshua replied.

'Well, she can keep her conspiracy theories to

herself.'

'Go and get some dinner, darling, or it'll get cold,' said Antoinette to Tom, noticing how tired he looked around the eyes. His lifestyle was dreadfully unhealthy, but apart from a general weariness, he looked well. Tom helped himself to a large portion of salmon crêpes then sat beside his mother. He entertained the table with the latest drama from his nightclub. An employee had been selling stories about their celebrity clients and they had trapped him by giving him an invented piece of gossip then waiting to see whether it came out in the papers. He was full of excitement because it had appeared in the *Daily Mail* the following morning.

'I fired him,' said Tom. 'We can't have that sort of thing going on in the Red Lizard!'

Phaedra chatted to Joshua. He didn't ask her about George; what interested him was the person she was, not her relationship with his father. It seemed that only Roberta needed to know details, as if she suspected her of lying and was intent on catching her out. Phaedra felt very safe sandwiched between Joshua and David. She felt the same sense of security as when she'd been in their father's company, and she relaxed and enjoyed the dinner because she was now part of something stronger than herself.

After dinner she played bridge with Tom, David and Joshua at a small table set up near the large bay window at the other end of the drawing room. Roberta disappeared upstairs to check on Amber, but Phaedra suspected she didn't want to remain in her company and was using her daughter as an excuse to get away. Antoinette sat beside the fire

116

with her sister and watched the four siblings interact. 'This is what it might have been like if I'd had another child,' she said softly to Rosamunde. 'George so wanted a little girl.'

'Yes, it would have been nice to have had a daughter. There's not a hint of pink anywhere in the house.'

'I was worried that Roberta was going to frighten her away, but judging by the sight of the four of them now, playing bridge so happily together, I think my fears are unfounded. Phaedra is made of sterner stuff.'

'Roberta is unforgivably rude,' Rosamunde agreed. 'I don't know why she's taken it upon herself to be the family sheriff. The jewels were never going to belong to her, but to David. Margaret would know.'

'Yes, she would, of course, but George has changed all that now. I really don't care about them at all. In fact, I'd say they're very ostentatious; the sort of thing Margaret likes to wear. But they're a part of our family history. It would be a shame to watch them vanish down another family line.' She thought of Phaedra disappearing to Paris with the sapphire suite, never to be seen again, and her chest grew tight. 'However, you're right, it's not Roberta's place to represent the family,' she added. 'Whatever anyone thinks, George's wishes must be honoured.'

'She should remember that she's a married-in, not blood.'

'She's just jealous, Rosamunde. Phaedra's far more beautiful and charming than she is.'

'*And* she's blood.'

117

'Yes, she's blood. I still find it hard to get my head around that. It's astonishing to think that all those years she grew up not knowing that George was her father. And George never knew he had a daughter.'

'It's not a surprise that he loved her instantly. There's something vulnerable about her, don't you think?'

'Yes, she rather makes me want to mother her. I could have killed Roberta when she started firing questions at her. It's as if she's desperate to expose her as a fraud.'

'A DNA test has been done and that's final. Roberta's not going to find anything there.'

'It's all about money, I'm afraid,' said Antoinette with a sigh. 'She came into the family with nothing and was suddenly very rich. She's lucky we're not questioning *her* motives for marrying Josh.'

'Perhaps her suspicions about Phaedra reveal more about herself than she realizes.'

'Yes, I hadn't thought of that.'

Antoinette watched Harris place the tray of coffee on the low table in front of her. 'Now, I wonder whether Roberta will come down again, or whether we've seen the last of her for tonight.'

Phaedra was a gifted bridge player. Tom was happy to partner her when he realized how cunning she was. They won without any difficulty and laughed all the way through the post-mortem. Phaedra sipped peppermint tea and recalled wistfully how it was George who had taught her to play during a three-day stopover at Annapurna base camp when they were held back due to bad weather. Climbing would never be the same now that George was dead. That chapter of her life had

118

closed forever.

David watched Phaedra across the table. The more he got to know her the more he admired her, and every now and then, when those astonishing grey eyes locked into his, he sensed that she admired him too. There was something intimate in the way she looked at him, as if their dinner in London was a secret they shared. He wanted her all to himself, but she was Joshua and Tom's sister too. By the nature of her birth she belonged to the three of them equally. However, David couldn't help but feel superior, for she was coming back to *his* house that night and he would take her off and show her around the estate in the morning. She had asked him to look after her and he was going to do everything in his power to do exactly that.

Roberta did not appear again. Joshua retired upstairs soon after their bridge game had ended and Antoinette and Rosamunde went to bed a little later. Tom, David and Phaedra sat around the fire sharing stories, laughing at jokes, and Tom opened another bottle of claret.

It was well past one when David drove Phaedra through the park to his home. It was only a ten-minute walk from the main house, but it was too dark to walk across the field. Phaedra stared out of the window as they drove along the farm tracks and savoured the intensity of the country night. The moon was a bright crescent, the sky as black as ink, the stars twinkling like tiny chips of broken glass. In the city the stars were barely visible and the sky never turned this deep velvet colour. 'Oh, I do love the countryside,' she said with a yawn.

'You're ready for bed.'

'I know. It's been a lovely evening, David. I've

really enjoyed hanging out with your family.'

'*Our* family,' he reminded her.

'It's going to take a while for me to feel that I really belong.'

'I'm sorry about Roberta.'

'Don't be. She's unhappy about me suddenly horning in.'

'You're not horning in, Phaedra. You're a Frampton.'

'Thank you. You're very kind.'

'I know, like Ratty.' They both laughed. Then David grew serious again. 'Roberta can be very mean-spirited.'

'It's understandable that she's suspicious. She thinks I'm a opportunist, slipping into your family to steal all your money.' She looked at him steadily. 'I'm not interested in George's money, David. I'm not going to touch it.'

'Don't be silly. It's yours.'

'No, it isn't. You're very kind and I'm grateful for your support. But really, I don't want the money. I earn my own living and I'm happy with my life. I'm not acquisitive. I have simple tastes. George was way too rash, including me in his will out of guilt ...' She paused and stared out of the window. 'He shouldn't have done it ... and perhaps, had he lived, he might have changed it back.'

'Well, we'll never know. Just accept things as they are, Phaedra. Whatever you feel about it, you're a Frampton. There's no changing that.'

The car pulled up in front of the picturesque little house. 'Home sweet home,' he said, switching off the engine.

'It's divine!' she enthused, running her eyes over the old weathered brick and gently sagging roof. It

120

was as if the building had grown tired of sitting up straight and had dropped its shoulders to rest. They both climbed out. 'Your house looks almost sleepy, don't you think?'

'I can't say I do,' he replied, glancing up at it.

'Oh yes, it does. I imagine it's hundreds of years old. Poor old thing, having to remain strong for all that time, resisting winds and rain. No wonder it wants to droop a little.'

'Are you telling me my house is drooping?'

She laughed at the bewildered look on his face. 'Well, it is, in a kind of sleepy way. It's adorable, David.' She made for the door. 'I'm looking forward to meeting Rufus.'

David opened the boot and lifted out her bag. 'He'll love you. He has an eye for the ladies.'

'Does that mean if he doesn't like me, I'm no lady?'

'Trust me, he'll like you.' He carried her bag to the door and unlocked it. A very excited Rufus bounded out of the kitchen and leapt up at Phaedra. 'Hey, steady on, Rufus!'

But Phaedra was delighted. 'He's gorgeous,' she gushed, wrapping her arms around him. 'Hello there, Rufus!'

'You see, he likes you.'

'So I *am* a lady,' she said. 'I'm so relieved!'

David showed her into the kitchen. It was immaculate. 'Mary came especially,' he explained, feeling like a fraud. 'It's not usually so tidy.'

She ran her eyes over the shiny granite worktops and pretty blue cupboards. 'Do you like chocolate cake?'

'What do *you* think?'

'I take that as a yes, then. Let's make a cake

121

tomorrow. I'm very good at chocolate cake. No one can resist it.'

'I believe you.'

'I'm so excited. Your kitchen is charming.'

'I'll show you to your room.' Rufus trotted up the stairs ahead of them. 'Or rather, Rufus will show you to your room. I hope you will find that equally charming.'

They walked down a narrow corridor. David had to stoop because of the low beams. 'Lucky I'm short,' she said with a laugh.

'It's a miracle I haven't developed a stoop,' he replied. 'Right, I'm at the end and you're down here.' She cast her eyes into his room and saw the corner of the bed and a chest of drawers covered in books and magazines in haphazard piles. The place smelt of dog and man.

'Where does Rufus sleep?'

'He should sleep in the kitchen, but in winter he sleeps with me. When it's too hot, he goes back downstairs.'

'How lovely to have a friend to share your nights with.' Then she laughed because she realized how provocative that sounded.

'It's OK, you're my sister,' he replied, laughing with her when inside he wanted to curse the God who made it so.

Her bedroom was very pretty, with a big brass bed, a quilt decorated with red poppies, and matching curtains. 'I'd like to take credit for the decoration, but Mother did it all for me.'

She smiled. 'I figured.'

'Any excuse for her to decorate and she's in like a shot.'

'Because you're unmarried. If you had a wife,

122

she'd probably leave her to look after you.'

'I wouldn't say she exactly looks after me. Gone are the days when I used to carry over my dirty-clothes basket. She buzzes around Tom, though. He makes her feel needed. She'll be buzzing around him all the more now Dad is gone.'

'I'd like to go and visit George's grave tomorrow,' Phaedra said softly. 'I passed the church today but I didn't have time to stop.'

'Of course. I'll take you.'

'Thank you.'

'Barry made a temporary headstone out of wood. The real one won't be ready for another month. I rather like the one Barry made, but Mum wants him to have one made out of marble. I suppose it'll last longer.'

'Who's Barry?'

'The gardener. He loved Dad.' David sighed. 'Everyone did. Well, your bathroom is next door. I hope you sleep well. Don't worry if you hear an odd screeching, that's just Boris the barn owl.'

'Does he answer to that?'

'You can try. If you hold out a dead mouse, you'll get an instant reaction.'

Phaedra laughed. 'Goodnight, David, and thank you for having me. You were right, this cottage suits me perfectly. I feel very safe here. The main house is extremely big, isn't it?'

'Not so big once you're used to it. I'm pleased you like my house, though. Don't wake early, but if you do, there's plenty to eat in the fridge. I didn't know what you'd like so I bought everything, even pancakes.'

'Pancakes? I shall cook you *fresh* pancakes,' she said with a grin.

123

'Are all sisters so nice?'

'I wouldn't know, I grew up alone.'

David put the suitcase on the luggage rack. 'Then I've just struck lucky.'

She smiled back at him warmly. 'And so have I.'

Phaedra lay in bed listening to the sounds of the night. She heard Boris screeching from a tree near the house, and the wind whistling through the branches. In George she had finally found the potential for the security she'd looked for all her life, as if she were a little boat anchored to a big, sturdy rock. She had never expected that rock to disappear. The feeling of drifting again was intolerable. Now she felt as though she had once again found a rock to set her anchor against. She curled up, the weight of the blanket and quilt pleasantly heavy on her body. She felt a frisson of happiness ripple through her being and closed her eyes. The country sounds soon lulled her to sleep.

The following morning different country sounds woke her at nine. Birds clamoured in the trees, pigeons cooed on the roof just outside her window, and the distant rumble of a tractor rattling up the farm track reminded her where she was. She lay on her back and enjoyed the sunshine breaking through the gap in the curtains and flooding the end of the bed with light. The day was full of promise.

She found a man's dressing gown on the back of the door and slipped it over her pyjamas. When she appeared in the kitchen David was already dressed, drinking coffee and reading the Saturday papers. 'Good morning,' he said, taking in the sight of her in his old school dressing gown, her tousled hair falling over her shoulders in a pretty

124

mess. 'Did you sleep well?'

'Oh yes, Boris was very tuneful.'

'Can I offer you a cup of coffee? I'm afraid my coffee is not quite as sophisticated as yours.'

'Coffee would be lovely. I see you have a cafetière, you can't do much better than that.'

'I hate instant.'

'So do I. Horrible stuff.' She opened the fridge. 'Wow, you certainly know how to shop.'

'I told you, I bought everything.'

'What have you had?'

'Nothing yet. I was waiting for you.'

'That's very gallant. I promised to make you pancakes, remember?'

'That's an offer I can't refuse.'

'OK, so you have flour, eggs and milk?'

'I do.'

'And an Aga. You know those are such wonderful things. I learned how to make pancakes from an expert and she had an Aga. Watch and learn, Mr Frampton.' Then she put her hand over her mouth and laughed. 'Oh, you're *Lord* Frampton now, aren't you?'

'I'm afraid I am.'

'Very classy. Right, *milord*, to work.'

While David made coffee, Phaedra whisked up the pancake batter with the bright-red mixer his mother had bought but which David had never used. It was still in its box. Then she squeezed some lemons into a jug and placed it on the table with the sugar pot and a couple of plates, knives and forks.

David watched her bustle about his kitchen and felt a surge of pleasure. She looked adorable in his old dressing gown and every now and then he got a glimpse of smooth leg peeping through. Once the mixture was ready, she poured a little straight onto the Aga.

'I do have a pan, you know,' he said.

'I don't need one.'

'Really? I've never seen anyone do that before.'

'That's the genius of an Aga. Watch how well it cooks. You'll never buy ready-made pancakes again.'

'I will, because you won't be here to make them for me.'

'Then I'll just have to come and stay very often.'

He laughed. 'I'd like that.' She used the spatula to scrape the pancake off the ring and turn it over. It was golden-brown and smelt delicious. David's stomach ached with hunger. 'Bring me your plate.' He did as he was told and Phaedra placed the hot pancake on it for him to sprinkle with lemon and sugar. Then she made one for herself.

'Oh, this *is* good. *Very* good,' David enthused, chewing with his eyes closed to savour the taste. 'I don't think I'm going to let you leave,' he added.

'That's fine by me. I'll pay rent with pancakes.'

'I'd say you don't have to, as you're family—but I won't turn down the offer of pancakes.' She sat at the end of the table and began to eat hers. He glanced at the jug of mix. 'Are there any more?'

'As many as you can eat.'

'I have a big appetite.'

'I know. You're a big man. I accounted for that.'

'A cook who can ski—is there anything you can't do, Phaedra?'

'There's lots I can't do. I'm just showing off the things I *can* do.'

'I'm yet to believe it.'

'Let me endear myself further by making you another pancake.'

After breakfast Phaedra took a long, luxurious bath before walking with David and Rufus to the big house. They took a route through the woods, where the sunshine fell onto the track in glimmering puddles of light and the cheerful twittering of birds resounded in the branches of ancient oak and beech trees. A trio of roe deer leaped nimbly over the bracken and blackberry bushes, disappearing into the hazel, and Rufus gamely chased hares and pheasants out of the undergrowth. Phaedra was enchanted and smiled contentedly as she listened to David telling her about the farm and his childhood growing up on such a magnificent estate.

They emerged into the open countryside where fields of growing crops rustled in the breeze and climbed a small hill to where a classically proportioned stone folly stood alone and neglected amid overgrown shrubs and piles of wind-blown brown leaves. From up there they could see the lake to the left and the chimneys of Fairfield Park, partially obscured by trees.

'Your home is very beautiful,' said Phaedra. 'What's this little house for? It's adorable but so forlorn.' She let her gaze wander over the soft honey-coloured walls and sensed a gentle tugging somewhere deep inside her, as if the building was whispering to her to step inside.

'It's called a folly,' David informed her.

'Is it just ornamental?'

'Perhaps, or it was built as a tea house,' said David. 'I don't really know.'

'A tea house? All the way up here?'

127

'Yes, they used to build follies for afternoon tea.'

'Who are *they*?'

'I have no idea.'

'Have you ever asked?'

'No.'

She frowned. 'It looks forgotten. But how could anyone forget such a magical little house?'

'We used to play in it as boys, but besides that no one ever bothers with it. I agree with you, it's very pretty.'

'It's *more* than pretty. It's warm and alluring. Don't you feel the urge to go inside and curl up on a sofa? Perhaps there's a fireplace in there? Look, there are chimneys. It must have been very special to someone once because it's beautifully designed and built with real care. I mean, the view is spectacular. If it were mine I'd restore it to its former glory and sit up here to watch the sunsets. It's very romantic.'

'Perhaps Amber will play in it when she's a little bigger.'

'Oh, it's more than a child's playhouse. That's a waste: I mean, a child wouldn't appreciate it. It needs to be loved, David. Shame on you all for leaving it to the mercy of ivy and moss and Lord knows what else.' She sighed and ran a hand over one of the pillars holding up the pediment.

'I'd love to have grown up in a place like this. It's full of enchantment,' she continued softly.

'Do you think so?'

'You have no idea because you know no different. This is straight out of Enid Blyton and C. S. Lewis.' She grinned. 'I bet if you walk inside you'll enter a whole different world.'

'What world did you grow up in?' He looked at

128

her quizzically.

'A concrete one. My mother didn't much like the countryside. She said it was boring. She was very sociable, out all the time, full hair and make-up, always.'

'What did she do?'

'She didn't do anything. Her father had brought her up to think she was a prize. Women like that don't work; they find men to do that for them.' She smiled bashfully. 'I left home at sixteen and went to work in Whistler. At last I was in the mountains: you know, high peaks and big skies and loads of climbing and skiing. I worked as a rep for a ski company. I loved it so much I stayed three years.'

'Why did you leave?'

'Well, you can't live your whole life in a place like that. I got restless and wanted to see the world.'

'Is that when you learned to be a photographer?'

'Yes, I had a relationship with a photographer in Rome and he inspired me. It didn't work out but I left with my camera and the knowledge I'd acquired and went back to Canada.'

'How did you end up in Paris?'

'Long story, another time, perhaps.' She turned away. The wind caught a curl and tossed it against her cheek. David sensed she didn't want to talk about that part of her life.

'Do you mind if I take some photos up here? It's really magical, David.'

'Did you bring your camera?'

'Only a little one. A photographer is never without a camera.'

'Sure, you snap away.'

'Do you mind if I take you?'

129

'I'm not photogenic.'

'That's because you haven't had your photograph taken by a professional.' She smiled and pulled a small Canon out of her pocket. 'Allow me!'

*   *   *

A while later Phaedra reluctantly left the folly and followed David down the hill. At last they approached the steps of the house. 'One thing I want to ask you, Phaedra,' he said, stopping on the gravel.

'Sure.'

'When you hung out with Dad and he introduced you to people as a photographer, didn't they think it a little odd?'

She shrugged. 'No one thought it odd in Paris.'

'When you moved to London?'

Her face darkened and she grew suddenly solemn. 'It got complicated.' She put her hands in her coat pockets.

'But no one gossiped?'

'Not that I know of. I wasn't here long enough.'

'That's quite astonishing.'

'I disagree. If you really want to keep something quiet, you can,' she said with a shrug. 'If he hadn't included me in his will and I hadn't turned up at the funeral, none of you would ever have known.'

He sensed her discomfort and wanted to put her back at ease. 'Speaking for myself, I can say for certain that I'd be the worse off.'

'That's sweet.' She gave a small smile and David felt happy again.

'Come on, let's go and find Mother.'

130

Chapter 9

Antoinette was in the drawing room with Roberta, Joshua and Rosamunde when they saw David and Phaedra appear in the doorway. Antoinette's eyes lit up, Joshua's grey cheeks flushed pink and Roberta scowled. She swept her eyes over Phaedra's bright floral dress, apple-green cardigan, black tights and ankle boots and thought how inappropriately dressed she was for the countryside. Phaedra noticed her contempt and wished she'd worn jeans instead.

'I was wondering when you'd appear,' said Antoinette.

'Did you sleep well over there?' Rosamunde asked.

'Very well, thank you. The country sounds sent me right off,' Phaedra replied.

'She made me pancakes for breakfast,' said David, noticing the pink in Joshua's cheeks turn a little green.

'Lucky you,' Rosamunde gushed. 'I *love* pancakes!'

'Much easier to buy the ready-made sort,' said Roberta with a sniff.

'Easier, yes, but not nearly as tasty,' Phaedra replied.

'I can attest to that,' David agreed.

'I thought we could go into Fairfield,' Antoinette suggested. 'There are some lovely little boutiques Phaedra might enjoy.'

'I'd like to see where George is buried, if that's all right with you,' Phaedra replied.

131

'Of course it is. We can take some daffodils from the garden if you like.'

Phaedra smiled. 'That would be lovely.'

David was distracted by his mobile telephone. He walked over to the window to answer it.

'Josh, would you like to come?' Antoinette asked.

Joshua glanced at his wife. 'We're going to take Amber for a walk,' he replied, trying to look enthusiastic.

'I'll go with you,' said Rosamunde. 'That way Antoinette can get to know her stepdaughter.'

Antoinette turned to Phaedra and smiled. 'It's just us and David, then. Tom is still in bed. That's what he does, stays up all week then flops the minute he gets home.'

'Does he bring his washing with him as well?' Phaedra asked with a grin.

'How did you know?' Antoinette laughed.

'David confessed that he'd done that in the past.'

'Well, you're right. If Tom didn't bring it home, it simply wouldn't get done.'

'You're a good mother,' said Phaedra. She could feel Roberta's disdainful stare burning through her skin. 'Where's Amber? I'd love to meet her,' she added, making an effort to include Roberta.

'She's asleep upstairs,' Roberta replied frostily.

'Well, I look forward to seeing her when she wakes up. I love children.'

'She's adorable,' said Joshua. 'Very pretty, like her mother.'

Roberta rolled her eyes. 'He has to say that,' she retorted.

'I'd say she's very lucky if she looks like you, Roberta. You have the most wonderful bone structure. I'd give my right arm for cheekbones like yours.'

Roberta was much too shrewd to fall for flattery. 'Thank you,' she replied with cool politeness.

Joshua grinned at his wife. 'Yes, Amber will be very lucky to look like Roberta.'

'I'm afraid I have to go up to the farm,' David sighed. 'Broken drill.'

'Oh dear!' Phaedra looked alarmed.

'I'll come and join you later,' he reassured her.

'Oh, do. We're going to the church, then down the high street, right, Antoinette?'

'If you like.'

'So come and find us. You will, won't you?'

David was flattered. 'As soon as I manage to extricate myself.'

'Do you think it'll take you long?'

'I'll make sure it doesn't,' he said. 'But Mother will look after you. I'm not good in shops. I lose my patience and become rude.'

Antoinette shook her head. 'We'll buy him an ice cream and he can sit on the pavement while we visit the boutiques!'

*   *   *

Antoinette and Phaedra disappeared down the drive in Antoinette's car while David walked back across the field towards the farm, situated up the back drive a quarter of a mile from the house. Rosamunde remained in the drawing room with Roberta and Joshua. 'She's a very nice girl,' said Rosamunde firmly. 'Very like George, don't you think?'

'In what way?' Roberta asked. She saw no

133

similarity whatsoever.

'The charisma. They both have that unique quality that draws one's attention. I call people like that "halo people", because they're surrounded by a brilliant light that makes you want to go on looking at them.'

'Well, I'm afraid I don't see her halo.'

'I agree, Rosamunde, she's very compelling,' Joshua said. 'She likes *you*, Roberta.'

'No, she doesn't,' Roberta retorted, appalled at the thought. 'She's just trying to win me over. She knows I smell a rat.'

'You're being unkind, Roberta,' said Rosamunde stridently. 'You've been nothing but unfriendly since she arrived.'

Roberta gave a little sniff. 'I'm not a gusher,' she explained. 'I can't pretend if I don't feel it.'

'Do you still think she's a usurper who's penetrated the family to steal all our money?' said Joshua.

'I'm not sure. I don't believe her story. Something doesn't add up, but I can't work out what it is. Call it intuition, but I've got a strong feeling that she's not telling us the truth.'

Suddenly Margaret's formidable presence filled the doorway. Basil came scurrying across the floor in search of Bertie and Wooster, then shot out again when he didn't find them. 'So, where is our guest?' she demanded, scanning the room with her incisive gaze.

Rosamunde caught Joshua's eye. 'David's taken her back to his house,' she lied.

Margaret inhaled through dilated nostrils. 'For goodness sake, why didn't somebody tell me? I've walked all the way across the fields.' She strode in

134

and sat down in the armchair.

Harris brought in a cup of coffee on a tray. Margaret lifted it down and took a little sip. 'Goodness me, that's very strong, Harris. I'm going to be buzzing for the rest of the day.'

'Mrs Gunice made it, ma'am.'

'I suggest *you* make it next time, Harris. You know how I like it.'

'Yes, I do, ma'am.'

'Good, that's settled, then. Will you make sure Basil gets some water? He's run miles, he must be dreadfully thirsty.'

She turned back to the room. 'So, Roberta, what's she like?'

'She's very nice,' Roberta replied tightly.

'You know, at school we were told never to describe anything as "nice". You can do better than that.'

'All right, she's sugary-sweet and charming.'

'Is she, indeed?'

'Well, she's won everyone over.'

'Except you.' Margaret narrowed her eyes and scrutinized her granddaughter-in-law.

'She's doing her best,' Roberta added, a small smile momentarily brushing her face.

'Is she anything like George?'

'I think she's her mother's daughter,' said Roberta.

'You mean, she's nothing like him at all?'

Rosamunde took it upon herself to rectify the situation. 'She's got George's charisma.'

'Oh yes, he did have the most dazzling charisma. *That* he inherited from me.'

'She's undoubtedly clever like you, too,' Rosamunde added, knowing how easily Margaret was taken in by flattery.

'Is she? How interesting.'

'And she's very beautiful,' Joshua put in.

'In a chocolate-boxy way,' interjected Roberta meanly. 'And she has an extraordinary sense of fashion—or should I say, she has no fashion sense at all!'

'I disagree,' said Rosamunde. 'I love her quirky dressing and she's got the most unusual eyes. There's nothing chocolate-boxy about her eyes at all. What I think you mean, Roberta, is that she's blonde and a little unconventional.'

'Like Tom,' said Margaret with a smile. 'Beautiful, clever and blonde. That sounds like a Frampton to me. George had white-blond hair when he was a little boy. When are they coming back?'

'Not for a while,' Joshua replied hastily.

'Then you must drive me to David's.'

'Now?'

'Of course now. You don't expect me to walk all the way over there, do you?'

'Don't worry, darling,' said Roberta. 'I'll take Amber out with Rosamunde.'

'You see,' said Margaret, getting up. 'You've been let off the hook. Come on. Let's go and find them.'

*   *   *

Antoinette and Phaedra walked slowly towards George's grave. The churchyard was quiet but for a pair of blackbirds playing noisily on the grass. The sun shone merrily but seemed unable to penetrate the shadow of sadness that hung over

136

the place. Antoinette and Phaedra stood in silence, staring at the rectangle of fresh earth that covered his coffin, buried deep down beneath. Barry's wooden headstone was simple and understated, and the sight of it unleashed Phaedra's sorrow so that tears spilled over her cheeks, dropping off her chin onto her shirt. 'I can't believe his life has been reduced to those few words and that sad group of numbers,' she said softly. Antoinette instinctively took the girl's hand. 'It's the last four numbers that look so menacing. Don't you think? It's like a nightmare to see them there. 2012. It shouldn't be. I expect to open my eyes and wake up to find it's all a bad dream.'

Phaedra's words struck a chord in Antoinette's heart because she expected to wake up too, but the wakening never came. 'Every day is the same, Phaedra. I feel I'm masquerading because I can't go on boring my family with my pain. I laugh and pretend I'm OK then cry when I'm alone in bed and no one can hear me.'

'Oh, Antoinette, that's awful. You should be allowed to grieve.'

'I know and I do, but I don't want them to worry about me. It's bad enough that they've lost their father.'

'They'll heal and move on with their lives. Joshua with Roberta and Amber, Tom with his club and the possibility of a wife and family one day, David with the farm and the soulmate he hopes to meet. Their lives are opening like flowers, filled with all sorts of possibilities. But George *was* your life and the flower of endless possibilities seems forever closed. I understand that, Antoinette. You see no future without George.'

Antoinette stared at Phaedra and through her tears she saw the compassion in her face. 'For such a young woman you understand a great deal.'

Phaedra squeezed her hand. 'It sounds silly, but George was my future, too.' She wiped her cheek on her sleeve. 'Before him I belonged nowhere and I had no one. I was drifting, trying to make sense of my life, trying to find a Phaedra-shaped place that I could slot into. George gave me that shape and it fitted perfectly. He gave me a sense of belonging and a sense of purpose. Now he's gone I feel I'm nothing.'

'You're not nothing, Phaedra. I'm your stepmother and you belong at Fairfield with us.'

Phaedra smiled. 'You're so generous, but I couldn't possibly ...'

'No, you don't understand.' Antoinette felt a rush of adrenalin. '*I* need *you*.'

'You do?'

'Yes, you're a part of George. A part of the man I loved.'

Phaedra dropped her gaze to the earth at her feet. 'You know he's not in there, don't you?'

'Sorry?'

'Oh, his body's in there, of course. Like the shell of a tortoise or the skin of a snake. But George, his essence, his soul, the person who looked out at us through his eyes, he's somewhere else.' She looked about her. 'He could be here, right now.'

Antoinette let her eyes wander, hoping for a flicker of light, a shimmer of shadow, a vague outline ... anything. 'Do you think he's here?' she asked.

'I *know* he is.' Phaedra's voice was now a whisper. 'He lives on, Antoinette. Don't think he

138

doesn't. You have to believe he's with you.'

'I want to. I so desperately want to.'

'Then close your eyes and feel him.'

Antoinette closed her eyes and felt the breeze brush her cheek and the sunlight warm her skin. Perhaps George was in the wind and in the sunshine. She felt the tears squeeze between her lashes and slide down her face. As much as she tried, she felt nothing extraordinary at all. She opened her eyes. Phaedra was still standing with hers closed, a beatific smile giving her beauty an unearthly sheen. Antoinette felt the stirring of something deep inside her, something that had died when, as a teenager, she had discovered that all things come to an end eventually: moments, friendships, life. Nothing was forever. Father Christmas was just her father, and the Easter Bunny her Uncle Douglas with a basket of chocolate eggs. God was not a friendly bearded man in the clouds but a primitive invention, like totem poles and ceramic idols. But now, the little nugget of faith buried in the dark recesses of her soul began to glow with life and fill her chest with something warm and sweet. What if Phaedra was right and George lived on? She closed her eyes again and smiled at the wonderful possibility.

*　　　*　　　*

'Well, she's not here!' Margaret announced, stalking back to the car. 'I've knocked several times and no one answers. The door is locked. No one's home. Where do you think they went?'

'Maybe they've gone for a walk?' Joshua suggested.

'Well, where's Antoinette?'

'Gone to the garden centre,' he lied.

'Are they all coming back for lunch or am I going to have to race about the countryside in search of them?'

'They'll be back for lunch.'

Margaret sniffed, dissatisfied. 'Let's go and have a look in town. Antoinette has taken to disappearing lately; perhaps they're at George's graveside. Come on, Basil, back in the car.'

Joshua motored down the narrow lane into Fairfield. Margaret sat with her jaw set in a grimace, unmoved by the wondrous display of nature bursting into spring. She didn't see the blue tits darting in and out of the hedgerows, or the lime-green colour of the fields and emerging buds. She ignored the primroses and pansies planted in people's gardens as they drove down the street towards the centre of town, and she was impervious to the charm of the multi-coloured Georgian houses, having lived among them for so much of her life. In fact, she noticed nothing at all except the incessant whirring of her brain as she focused on trying to track down George's elusive daughter.

At last they reached the church. Margaret smiled triumphantly at the sight of Antoinette's car parked on the verge. 'Ah, you see, I was right. They must be here. Now we'll find them.'

Joshua drew up beside it. 'They've probably gone shopping,' he suggested lamely.

'No, they haven't. They'll be here in the churchyard. Mark my words.' She waited for her grandson to open her door and help her out.

'Good God!' Antoinette exclaimed, spotting

140

Joshua and his grandmother down by the church gate. 'That woman is a curse. Come on, Phaedra. We have to get out of here.'

'Who is she?' Phaedra caught sight of a stout old woman in a navy-blue dress and long cardigan being escorted up the path by Joshua.

'I'll explain in a minute. Come, I know the escape route now. It's really very simple and I'm sure Dr Heyworth won't mind me barging in again.' She hurried off around the back of the church with Phaedra following behind, wondering who could have sent Antoinette into such a panic.

* * *

Margaret put her hands on her hips. 'Right, you look in the church, I'll wander around the graveyard, though it's not a place I'm keen to linger. I might never leave!'

Joshua did as he was told and went to look inside the church. Margaret walked hesitantly over the grass. All those dead people beneath her feet made her feel decidedly anxious. It wouldn't be long before she joined them and that was a most unsavoury thought. She cast her eyes about the graves, sure that Antoinette and her granddaughter would be among them.

She was distracted a moment by a bunch of bright-yellow daffodils leaning against a makeshift headstone. She paused a moment to read the inscription. Then her cheeks flushed as she realized the grave belonged to her son. A wave of shame washed over her, for she hadn't even visited it. Not because she didn't care: she cared with all her heart, but because she was afraid. She hadn't

141

wanted to see it. She hadn't wanted to believe that her beloved George was dead and buried. The sight of the loose earth and those final words roughly carved were too much to bear. Better to bury her pain where she couldn't find it and push on, as she had done when her husband died. Grief was not something to be chewed on like a pining dog with a bone, for it did nothing to bring back the deceased and everything to prolong the agony. But now she crouched down and placed her hand on the earth. It was warm where the sun had kissed it. A ball of fire began to roll up from her belly to her chest and she inhaled sharply. The feeling was overwhelming, as if her insides were being scorched. She gripped her heart, fearing she was suffering an attack.

'She's not in the church,' said Joshua, walking up behind her. 'Ah, they've been here,' he added, noticing the flowers on his father's grave. 'Good of Barry to make a headstone, though it's a little primitive.' As soon as Margaret heard her grandson's voice, the ball of fire was extinguished—gone as if it had never been there. She took a deep, frightened breath and put out her arm. Joshua helped her up, noticing at once that his grandmother had gone very pale. 'Are you all right, Grandma?'

She nodded, taking a moment to find her voice. 'Yes, I'm fine.'

'You don't look well.'

'I'm as fit as a fiddle.' She pulled her arm away and smoothed down her dress.

'Do you want to look on the high street?'

'Take me home.'

'To the dower house?'

142

'No, the main house. I shall wait for them there.' She tried to walk but her legs felt heavy and numb. 'Give me your arm, Joshua. There, that's better. My legs are a little stiff from crouching down.' She began to step slowly towards the path. Joshua tried to pretend he hadn't noticed that her movements were laboured and her breath staggered. Margaret wondered what would have happened if Joshua hadn't appeared. Was she having a heart attack? What *was* that burning pain making its way up through her body? But instead of dwelling on it, she switched off her emotions as she had done all her life when things got too painful to endure, and focused instead on getting safely back to the car.

*　　　*　　　*

Antoinette closed the gate behind her. 'Safe at last!' she said, putting her hand on her chest and feeling her racing heart decelerate to a less alarming rate.

Phaedra looked around the beautiful garden. 'What a stunning place!' she exclaimed. 'It's like we've just stepped into paradise.'

'It belongs to Dr Heyworth. The last time I hid from my mother-in-law I stumbled upon it, and upon Dr Heyworth, who thankfully has a good sense of humour and asked me in for tea.'

'Oh, so that was George's mother.'

'Frightful woman. She wants to meet you. I'm not sure it's such a good idea.'

'Is she so awful?'

'Yes, she really is. I think we should avoid her as much as possible. Though she'll find you in the end. She's a very persistent woman.'

143

'She must be devastated to lose her only son.'

'You would think, wouldn't you. However, she's so English you'd never know she was in mourning. She's had a face like a boot for as long as I've known her.'

'Oh dear, how sad.'

At that moment Dr Heyworth appeared at his conservatory door. 'Ah, Lady Frampton, what a pleasure to see you at my garden gate.' He grinned at her knowingly. 'I'm assuming you're running away again?'

'Oh dear,' she hissed to Phaedra. 'This is becoming something of a habit. He must think I'm mad!' She strode across the lawn. 'Well, as it happens, I *am* running away again,' she replied.

'If you're seeking refuge why don't you both come in for a drink?' He turned his eyes on Phaedra.

'This is George's daughter,' she explained.

Dr Heyworth raised his eyebrows. 'Ah.'

'Hello, I'm Phaedra.' They shook hands.

'Lady Frampton was just telling me about you the other day. I'm so pleased you came down. Come on in. How long do you need?'

Antoinette walked through the door he held open for her. 'As long as it takes my mother-in-law to scour the town.'

'A good half-hour, then,' he replied with a chuckle. 'Good, that gives us a nice amount of time to enjoy a little aperitif.'

Chapter 10

Margaret sat in Antoinette's drawing room, a glass of sherry in her hand, her face as white as death. Rosamunde noticed she was trembling. She didn't look quite herself. Joshua made conversation so that his grandmother didn't have to. She hadn't said a word all the way back in the car.

'They had been to Dad's grave because Mum's car was parked outside the church and they'd put daffodils by Barry's headstone,' Joshua explained.

'I suspect they'd gone up the high street to do a little window-shopping,' said Rosamunde.

'Do women ever really window-shop?' Joshua asked provocatively, hoping to rouse his grandmother out of her trance. It was unlike her to be so quiet.

'Those who don't have the money to spend do a lot of window-shopping. I don't think Antoinette and Phaedra will come away empty-handed, though, do you?' said Rosamunde. She glanced at Margaret and frowned. 'George has enabled them to buy whatever they want.' This last comment caused Margaret's eyes to flicker a moment, and she glanced at Rosamunde. 'Are you all right, Margaret? Can we get you anything?'

'I'm cold,' Margaret replied softly. 'I'm dreadfully cold.'

Joshua leaped up and put a few more logs on the fire. The flames licked them hungrily, spitting out little sparks. 'That's better,' he said, feeling the heat intensify. 'They should be back soon. After all, how much shopping can they do in Fairfield?'

145

'More than you can imagine, I dare say,' said Rosamunde.

Roberta walked into the room with Amber in her arms. 'Did you find them?' she asked.

Joshua shook his head. 'No, but they'll be back for lunch.'

Roberta sensed the tension in the room and glanced at Margaret. She noticed at once that something was wrong. It was very uncharacteristic of Basil to lie so quietly at her feet. 'Hi, Margaret. Look, Amber, it's your great-grandmother.'

'Here, let me take her,' Joshua cut in, pulling a face at his wife to alert her to his grandmother's odd behaviour. She handed over the child and sat down beside him on the sofa.

'It's a beautiful spring day,' Roberta continued, trying not to stare at Margaret who was now the colour of putty. 'Lovely. We should all go for another walk after lunch.'

'Amber's got very rosy cheeks,' Rosamunde exclaimed. 'She certainly benefits from being out in the country air, doesn't she?'

'Not only her, I feel revived, too.'

Joshua looked at his watch. 'It's nearly lunchtime. They should be back by now.'

Suddenly Margaret put her head in her hand. 'I think I need to go and lie down,' she said feebly. 'I'm not well.'

Rosamunde stood up in alarm. Margaret had never been ill the entire time she had known her. 'Of course you must, Margaret. You're just having a turn. A lie-down will make you feel so much better.' Joshua helped his grandmother to her feet. 'Which room do you think, Joshua?'

'The blue room,' he replied, expecting Margaret

146

to insist upon another, but she remained quiet and unsteady. They escorted her up the stairs while Roberta remained in the drawing room with Amber and Basil, wondering what had happened while she had been in the kitchen, feeding her daughter.

Once Margaret was settled on the bed, Rosamunde covered her with the quilt and closed the curtains. She noticed how old she looked when her eyes were closed. Her face sagged like a deflated ball left abandoned on a wintry beach. Without a word Rosamunde made for the door. Just as she was about to leave, Margaret spoke. 'Bring Phaedra to me when I wake up. I'm sure I'll feel better by then.'

'Of course I will, Margaret. Now you get some rest and don't worry about anything. It's probably something you ate.' Margaret didn't reply. She let go and allowed her body to drift into sleep where there was no pain, just sunny memories of happier times.

As Rosamunde came down the stairs David, Phaedra and Antoinette were stepping into the hall with Rufus and the Great Danes. They were animated, laughing together as if they had all shared an adventure. 'Is she here?' Antoinette hissed to Harris.

'I'm afraid she took a turn, Lady Frampton,' Harris replied solemnly.

Antoinette saw her sister descending the stairs. 'Where's Margaret?'

'She's lying on the bed in the blue room. She wasn't feeling well,' Rosamunde replied importantly. 'She came back with Joshua and she wasn't herself. Her hands were trembling and her

147

face was deathly pale. I don't know what happened.'

'Where's Josh?'

'In the drawing room with Roberta.'

Antoinette hurried past her.

'Looks like you've got away with it,' said David to Phaedra.

'I'd *like* to meet George's mother,' Phaedra replied.

'Trust me, you really wouldn't.'

Phaedra tapped him playfully. 'You're just being mean. There's goodness everywhere if you look for it.'

'I've looked and found nothing close to goodness.'

'Then maybe a fresh eye will find it.'

'What happened to Margaret?' Antoinette asked Joshua as she perched anxiously on the club fender.

'She was determined to find you,' he explained. 'I took her to David's to play for time. Then she insisted we look at the church. She saw your car on the verge and went to find you. I went inside, but you weren't there. When I came out, she was crouching by Dad's grave. She was clutching her heart.'

'Oh Lord, how dreadful,' Antoinette gasped.

'I helped her up and she insisted she was OK, but she didn't talk all the way back in the car. She just stared out of the window. Then she sat in here shivering with cold, so I put a few more logs on the fire.'

'Then she asked to go and lie down,' Rosamunde continued, striding into the room. 'She's lying on the bed under the quilt. She really doesn't look well.'

'Oh dear. What if she's had a stroke? Do you think we should call Dr Heyworth?' Antoinette asked. 'Phaedra and I escaped through the gate behind the church into his garden. We were having a drink, that's all. It was mean of us to run away. I feel terrible.'

'I found them sneaking about the town like a pair of fugitives,' David added, wandering in with Phaedra. 'At least she won't have to meet her now.'

'You're wrong,' Rosamunde exclaimed. 'She specifically asked for Phaedra to be brought to her after lunch. I'm sure she'll feel better by then.'

'So I won't call the doctor until we see how she is when she wakes up,' said Antoinette.

'The sacrificial lamb,' said David, raising an eyebrow at Phaedra.

'The virgin offering to appease the beast,' said Tom, standing sleepily in the doorway. He frowned. 'What's going on?'

'Tom, darling,' Antoinette gushed. 'You've missed all the drama.'

'What a shame, I love drama.' Tom swept a hand through his tousled blond hair. 'So, grandma has taken a turn, has she?'

'She's asleep in the blue room,' said Rosamunde.

'Is she on her way out?' he hissed.

Antoinette flushed. 'You can't say that sort of thing, Tom.'

'She's just lost her son,' Roberta cut in. 'As a mother I can only imagine how devastating that must be.'

'Really, Roberta, she's barely shed a tear,' David retorted.

'Not on the outside.' She looked at him steadily.

149

'She's as tough as an old rhino,' Tom added with a snigger. 'She's never felt a thing.'

Roberta rolled her eyes. 'Oh, shallow, heartless boys, you understand nothing.'

'Let's eat,' said Antoinette, getting up. 'Tom, darling, go and check on your grandmother.'

Tom pulled a face. 'Why me?'

'I'll go,' Roberta volunteered, taking her child out of Joshua's arms. 'I should put her down for her sleep.'

'Not before I've met her,' said Phaedra, rushing across the room. 'Oh, she's beautiful,' she admired. 'May I?'

Roberta flinched. 'She's rather tired. I don't think she'll like being picked up by a stranger.'

'Oh, please. She's delicious.' Phaedra wound her hands around the baby's body and lifted her out of her mother's arms. Roberta grimaced, but Amber smiled contentedly. 'She looks just like you, Roberta. She's got your eyes. She's going to be a real knock-out.' Phaedra nuzzled the child affectionately. Roberta saw the tender look on Antoinette's face and her heart hardened with irritation. Amber grabbed Phaedra's hair and tried to pull it, and Phaedra laughed as Roberta gently unwound her little fingers to set it free.

'Well, you've won another friend,' said Roberta dryly.

'Oh, I do hope so.'

'I'd better take her upstairs before she lets herself down and cries.'

'Small children are meant to cry, aren't they?'

'Preferably not in public.'

Phaedra lowered her voice. 'I disagree: it's important that she cries in public so they all know

150

who's boss.'

Roberta fought against the sudden softening of her resolve. It was easy to see how weaker people were seduced by the girl's charm. 'You wouldn't say that if you'd heard her wail,' she replied coolly and wandered into the hall.

As she made for the stairs she noticed what must surely be Phaedra's stripy canvas handbag left carelessly on the sofa. She looked about, like a thief with an opportunity to steal. She was alone. It would take only a moment to rifle through it. Struck by the intense desire to expose her, Roberta sat on the sofa, placed Amber on her knee, and thrust her hand into the bag. She rummaged about a set of keys, diary, lipstick, papers, sweet wrapper and goodness knows what else until her fingers felt the hard surface of an iPhone. Hastily she pulled it out and pressed the button at the bottom. The light went on and Roberta gasped. There, to her delight, one clear sentence shone out: Missed call: Julius Beecher. Hearing voices from the drawing room, she hurriedly slipped it back in the bag and set off up the stairs. It wasn't proof, but it was a lead. Julius Beecher and Phaedra were up to no good together, and Roberta was determined to find out what.

A moment later David escorted Phaedra into the dining room where roast beef and Yorkshire pudding was waiting on the sideboard. 'You need to gather your strength if you're to be summoned,' he said mischievously.

Phaedra laughed. 'Don't you think you're being a little unkind? Roberta's right. She's just lost her son. She might not cry in public, but she'd be superhuman if she wasn't howling inside.'

He frowned at her. 'I've never thought . . .'

'Sometimes people are aggressive to hide their true feelings, not only from others but from themselves. I'll bet she sweeps it all under the carpet so she doesn't have to suffer. The trouble is, she suffers all the more because she holds it all in.'

David pulled a face. 'I hate to think of Roberta being right about anything.'

'You don't like her, do you?'

'Is it that obvious?'

'The atmosphere in this house when you're all together is shocking.'

'She rubs me up the wrong way.'

'Probably because she thinks no one ever listens to her.'

'We would, if what she said was sensible.'

'Don't make her feel like an outsider.' She sat down and draped her napkin over her knees. 'I tell you what, the next time you have the urge to say something squashing, do the opposite. I find that usually works.'

He pulled out the chair beside her and sat down. 'You mean, say something nice?'

'Yes, let's see what happens.'

'You're asking a great deal of me, Phaedra.'

'To whom much is given, much is expected.'

'I'll give it a go,' he said. 'But only for you.' Her smile filled his heart with effervescence.

'Thank you.'

Roberta returned with the baby monitor and reported that Margaret was still asleep.

'Is she snoring?' Tom asked.

Roberta shook her head impatiently. 'She's as quiet as a mouse.'

'That's a contradiction in terms,' Tom laughed.

152

Roberta bent down to plug the monitor into the wall and gave a long-suffering sigh. 'God, I do hate it when Kathy has the weekend off.'

'Is Kathy your nanny?' Phaedra asked.

'Yes, I don't know how I manage without her.'

'Looks like you manage very well from where I'm sitting.'

'It's full-on, not a moment to myself.'

'She's a very good little girl,' said Phaedra.

'That's true,' Roberta agreed. 'She rarely cries.'

'She knows there's no point because her mother will just leave her,' said Tom.

'Which is exactly what a mother should do,' David interjected, winking at Phaedra.

'How do *you* know so much about childcare all of a sudden?' Roberta replied, taking a seat at the table.

'I don't, but I assume you're doing the right thing. Amber's a happy child. That speaks volumes,' David continued.

Roberta poured herself a glass of water. 'Well, I don't know whether or not I'm doing the right thing, but I can safely say I do my best.'

'Your best is good enough,' David added cheerfully.

'Are you mocking me, David?'

'No.' He shrugged innocently.

David's enthusiasm made Roberta feel uneasy, so she changed the subject. 'What do you think of Fairfield, Phaedra?' she asked.

'It's an adorable town. Antoinette and I went to the church and then wandered around the shops.'

'You've yet to see the farm,' said David.

'I don't think she'd want to see the farm,' Roberta argued. 'I can't believe a girl like Phaedra

153

would be interested in tractors and grain barns.'

'A girl like me?' Phaedra repeated. 'What *is* a girl like me?'

'Well, you just don't look like the type, in those urban boots and tights.'

'Ah, the country type, you mean?'

'Yes, that's exactly what I mean.'

'Perhaps I should have worn a tweed suit.'

'I wouldn't say you have to go that far.' Roberta sniffed. 'But dressed like that you'll scare the pheasants.'

'Are *you* a country type?'

'No.' Roberta laughed as if the idea was preposterous. 'I'm a city girl.'

'Then you're judging me by your own standards. Which is fine; most people are quick to assume everyone else is like them. But I must correct you, I love the country and am happier here than in any town or city. I'd love to be shown around the farm.' She turned to David. 'I absolutely insist that you take me this afternoon.'

'If you insist, I can't refuse you,' he replied. Then, remembering the deal he had made with Phaedra, he added, 'Roberta, you might not consider yourself a country girl, because you're very sophisticated and urbane, but you adapt very well. Never a piece of clothing out of place, always perfectly pitched.'

'David, I feel you're making fun of me,' Roberta said tightly.

'Not at all. I'm speaking the truth. You're one of those people who looks the part wherever you are. Don't you agree?'

'I take trouble, certainly.'

'There, you see? I'm not making fun of you. Josh

154

is lucky to have a wife he can take anywhere and know she won't let him down. Appearances are important to Josh.'

'What's that about me?' Joshua cut in.

'I'm just saying you're lucky to be married to Roberta.' Tom suppressed a chortle, Antoinette looked baffled, Rosamunde watched Roberta's mouth twist into a small smile. Phaedra was pleased to see that David didn't flinch.

'You're right,' said Joshua. 'I *am* lucky to have her.'

Roberta looked embarrassed. 'Thank you, Josh. That's very sweet. Now let's talk about something else; I'm not used to getting so much positive attention! I could get used to it and then demand it all the time.' The whole table laughed, and for once, Roberta laughed with them.

After lunch Antoinette went upstairs to check on her mother-in-law. She tiptoed to the door and opened it a crack. It was dark and there was no noise coming from within. She peered inside but Margaret was facing the other way so she couldn't see whether or not she was breathing. For a dreadful moment she feared she might be dead. Quietly, she trod across the carpet and around the bed. Margaret lay on her side with her eyes closed, but Antoinette could tell from the rhythmic expansion of her chest that she was breathing.

She was about to leave the room when the old woman woke up. 'Is that you, George?'

Antoinette's heart buckled. 'Margaret, it's me, Antoinette,' she said, returning to the bedside.

'I thought you were George.'

'No, I'm sorry. Just me.'

'George is dead, isn't he? I quite forgot.'

155

'I do that, too. I wake up and think that everything is as it should be. Then, as I slowly come to my senses, I realize that nothing is right any more and never will be.'

'But Phaedra is here?'

'Yes, she's downstairs.'

'Bring her to me. I want to meet her.'

'Are you sure?'

'Of course I'm sure. I'm the only one in the family who hasn't met her and by rights, *I* should have been the first.'

Antoinette left the room, relieved not to be needed. Margaret had seemed so benign while she slept that Antoinette had almost felt sorry for her. But the old dragon was as fierce as ever when awake. Poor Phaedra, she hoped David had prepared her.

'She's herself again,' said Antoinette, entering the drawing room.

'I'm so relieved,' Rosamunde replied. 'I was very worried. It really was unlike her to be so quiet.'

'Well, she's not quiet now and you might regret being relieved,' Antoinette added. 'Phaedra, she wants to see you.'

'Sure.' Phaedra got up good-naturedly.

'Into the witch's cavern,' said Tom.

'Don't listen to Tom, Phaedra. She's a little brisk, but her heart is in the right place,' said Roberta.

'I'm not worried. Of course she should want to meet me. I'm very happy, actually.'

'Shouldn't I go with her?' David asked his mother.

'She didn't demand your presence as well,' Antoinette replied.

156

'What are you, her shadow?' said Tom.

'I feel responsible,' David replied. 'It was I who convinced Phaedra to come and stay. I'll feel very bad if she gets a mauling from Grandma.'

'Why would she?' Roberta asked.

'You're right, why would she?' David replied. 'You and she get on extremely well, there's no reason Phaedra won't, too.' He smiled at Roberta who gazed back suspiciously.

'She's really very sweet underneath,' Roberta added.

'I don't doubt it,' said David. 'None of us has ever tried to look underneath.'

'Now would be a good time to start. She needs her family more than ever.'

David listened as Phaedra had told him to do, and to his surprise he found that on this occasion, at least, Roberta did make sense.

Phaedra followed Antoinette up the stairs. She gazed at the wall where the Frampton suite of sapphires and diamonds shone out from its oily canvas. 'You have a beautiful house,' she said.

'When I married George we lived in the dower house where Margaret lives now. It's a very pretty Queen Anne house, light and airy with big windows and high ceilings. There are none of these dusty old portraits and knick-knacks collected over generations. I have to admit that I preferred living there. I felt it belonged to me. I don't feel this house belongs to me. I'm the caretaker, making sure that all these exquisite things last for future generations of Framptons. When we moved in I wasn't allowed to change anything. I would have loved to change the dining room and redecorate the drawing room. The only room in the house

157

that I redecorated was our bedroom. I think it's important to make a house your home. You can't live in a museum. But George was aware of his heritage and insisted that it remain the same. Now he's gone I could do whatever I like with it, but I won't. George wouldn't like it.' She laughed sadly. 'I'll keep it like this to honour him.'

'You have to think of yourself, Antoinette.'

'I can't change the habit of a lifetime.'

'You can change a habit any time you want.' Phaedra smiled at her. 'You only have to overcome your fears, and that's not really very hard if you put your mind to it.'

'I've never thought …'

'You lived for George, but now he's no longer here, you have to live for yourself. You have to do all the things you wanted to do when you were married, but couldn't because you were being a good wife and mother. But you're neither. You're *you*. This is the perfect time to do something for your own selfish pleasure, otherwise you'll get lost in memories and duty and you might never find yourself again.'

'I'm not sure Margaret would be happy for me to change the place.'

'Have you ever asked her?'

'No. But she didn't change a single thing when she lived here.'

'But it's *your* place and *you* have to live in it. I think George will think very differently now he's in spirit. Things that seemed so terribly important while he was down here will no longer hold any importance at all, because material things only have value in our material world. I'm sure he'll be delighted with whatever you choose to do, so long

158

as it makes you happy and doesn't hurt anyone.'

'You're very sure he's in ... in *spirit*.' That word felt strange to Antoinette.

'Oh, I *know* he is.' There was no quiver of doubt in Phaedra's voice.

Antoinette stopped just outside Margaret's bedroom door and sighed. 'I wish I had your conviction.'

'It'll come if you want it to. Just focus on something beautiful, like a flower or the stars at night, and you'll feel a sense of something greater than yourself.'

'Really? Is it that easy?'

Phaedra nodded. 'It really is.' She was so convincing, Antoinette found herself ready to try.

Chapter 11

Phaedra knocked on the door. 'Come in,' Margaret called out. Antoinette hesitated as Phaedra entered and closed the door behind her. She felt a wave of apprehension, as if by allowing Phaedra into Margaret's clutches she might lose her. Antoinette stood a moment, listening through the wood, but the voices were so low she heard nothing but the thumping of her own fretful heart.

Margaret had turned on the bedside lamp but the curtains were still closed. 'Open them, will you, then I can get a good look at you,' Margaret demanded, propping herself up with pillows. Phaedra did as she was told. The light spilled into the room, transmuting the heavy atmosphere into sunshine. She turned to the old woman in the bed.

159

Margaret Frampton was round and ruffled like a fat hen on her nest. Grief pulled her mouth down at the corners and her pale-grey eyes were glassy and bloodshot. Phaedra was struck by an unexpected wave of compassion, for it was plain to see that George's mother was a hard knot of unhappiness.

Margaret's formidable gaze scrutinized her, but Phaedra didn't avert her eyes. This small act of defiance won Margaret's admiration, for she was used to people shrinking in her presence. 'Ah, now *that* you have inherited from me,' she said triumphantly. 'Come closer.' She patted the bed. Phaedra sat down. 'Yes, I was a beauty in my day, just like you. It's all in the eyes, you know. You have lovely eyes.'

'Thank you.'

'No, you inherited them from me, of course.' Margaret smiled and Phaedra laughed, more out of relief than joy.

'Are you feeling better?' she asked.

'I just needed to lie down. I suppose Antoinette thought I was dying.'

'Well, she was very worried.'

'Sometimes I think she'd rather like me out of the way.'

'I'm sure she wouldn't, not in her heart.'

'Oh, I'm an irritation, you know. When George was alive I used to come over all the time. He was my only child and we were very close. My husband died a long time ago, so for years it was just me and George. But now he's gone, I find I still need that diversion. Fairfield Park has been my home for most of my life, you see. It's a frightful bore for Antoinette as I pop in daily. I'm a bit like a

160

homing pigeon. I came for George, but now . . . I don't know.' She looked confused and her voice trailed off. 'I'm drawn here . . .'

'This is a very pretty room,' Phaedra mused, sweeping her eyes over the blue floral wallpaper and bedspread.

'I like the colour blue. It's very restful, don't you think?'

'Blue can be a cold colour, but it feels warm in here. Not cold at all.'

'This house is a nuisance to keep warm because it's so big. I didn't feel the cold when I lived here. When George was a boy he used to run about in short sleeves even in winter. But I feel the cold now. It's age, I'm afraid. One can't fight it. I don't think I have the energy to fight anything any more.' She sighed and for a moment she looked a little lost, as if her mind were being pulled in an unfamiliar direction.

'Resistance only brings unhappiness,' Phaedra said wisely. 'It's through acceptance and letting go that one finds peace.' Margaret's gaze fell away. 'I miss George terribly, all the time, but I have to let him go, because holding onto pain will only make me miserable and it won't bring him back.' Phaedra noticed the old woman's mouth twitch, like the minute cracking of a great dam. 'I went to his grave today and we laid daffodils. I know he's not in there, but it felt good to pay my respects and to feel I was *doing* something. I don't need to visit his grave to feel close to him. He's around us all the time, I'm sure. But I needed to see where his body was laid to rest, for my own peace of mind, and to give me a sense of closure. I have to accept that he's gone—and to let him go.'

161

The twitching of Margaret's mouth grew more intense. Suddenly she grabbed Phaedra's arm and stared at her with large, frightened eyes. 'It's my heart again. I think I'm having a heart attack,' she gasped. But the fire that had once again started in the pit of her belly rose past her heart and into her throat where it rolled about as if desperately trying to find a way out. Margaret resisted, tightening the muscles there, holding it in for fear of what might happen if she let it escape. Phaedra stared back in alarm as Margaret's face turned the colour of a pepper. Then, just as she was about to leap up and raise the alarm, Margaret let out a loud wail and her whole body heaved as her grief was ejected in one giant sob.

Phaedra recognized her anguish and put her arms around her. Margaret didn't pull away. The crack in the dam was now a gaping hole and the old woman's grief poured out like water. She sobbed and sighed and tears tumbled down the lines in her skin. She looked appalled, as if such a release of emotion was an unwelcome novelty, and quite horrifying. 'It's OK to cry,' said Phaedra, feeling the tears stinging her own eyes. 'You're going to set me off, too. But it's OK. We'll cry together.' She smiled as Margaret slowly calmed down, leaving her body trembling with the aftershock. Phaedra pulled away, but kept a reassuring hand on her arm.

'Good God!' Margaret exclaimed, finding a space between shuddering breaths. 'I don't know what's come over me today.'

'Lady Frampton ...'

'After that shameful display I think you should call me Margaret.'

162

'Margaret, you mustn't be ashamed. You're a mother who has lost her only child. I know it's very British to hold it all in, but it's unhealthy. And it's not natural. We're given tears and the ability to cry for a reason. It releases the tension and allows us to heal. How can we possibly heal if we don't acknowledge we're hurt?'

She stared at Phaedra in surprise. 'My dear child, I don't know from whom you inherited your wisdom, because George was never wise like you.'

'I'm not wise, Margaret, I just know a little about unhappiness.'

Margaret narrowed her eyes. 'You know, I feel I can confide in you, Phaedra.' Her face tightened and she dropped her gaze into her hands. 'I saw George's grave today for the first time. I hadn't dared go before. I couldn't bear to see it. I couldn't face the loose ground and the thought of his coffin . . . it was all too much.'

'It's good that you went. You said goodbye. You can now take the first step out of your grief.'

'It cuts me to the quick.' She put her hand on her heart.

'I know it does.'

'Antoinette cries all the time. It makes me so cross because I can't.'

'You can now,' Phaedra replied, watching the knotted woman slowly untangle and feeling a sense of pride that she had helped her do it.

'Tell me, Phaedra, do you have a grandmother?'

'No. I have no one.'

'What about your mama?'

'She's in Canada. We're not close.'

'So George was the only family you had?'

'You can imagine how happy I was to find him

163

and that we got along so well.' Margaret smiled as Phaedra's face lit up. 'He gave me such wonderful opportunities. I wouldn't have had the courage to do my book if he hadn't taken me trekking with him.'

'Yes, you're a photographer, aren't you?'

'Yes, I love to photograph life from a distance— you know, observing it the way it is, without manipulating it. I started photographing families and children, mostly, because that paid the bills. But then I decided to do something more adventurous. George inspired the idea.'

'Did he?'

'I'd like to take your photograph, if you'll let me.'

Margaret pulled a face. 'I'm not photogenic, though in my day the camera loved me.'

'You have a strong face. Such an interesting face, full of contradiction. I think you'll take a very good photograph.'

'Well, if you insist, although at my age there's no point in being vain, one would be so disappointed.'

Phaedra laughed. 'You're not so old, Margaret, and you're plump, *that* makes you look a lot younger than your years. Skinny old ladies look half dead, if you ask me.'

'I'll take that as a compliment.'

'It was certainly meant that way.'

'Well, I suppose we should go downstairs. If I keep you much longer they'll think I've eaten you for lunch!' Margaret threw back the bedclothes. 'You're a good girl, Phaedra. I'm happy you found us. Though I don't like that Julius Beecher one bit. Frightfully arrogant man, up to no good, I fancy. I always told George to watch out for him, but he wouldn't hear a word against him. I suppose Julius

164

did a good job, running George's businesses while he was off somewhere, pleasing himself. So you be careful, Phaedra. He's not a man to be trusted.'

'Julius has been very good to me.'

'I'm sure he has, my dear. But as your grandmother, I feel I must warn you. He's not an honourable man and money is his god.'

'I'll take your advice on board.'

'Now, I'm going to freshen up. Why don't you go downstairs and show them that you're still in one piece. I know I can trust you to keep our conversation private.'

'What happens in Vegas stays in Vegas,' Phaedra replied.

Margaret frowned. 'I suppose that's how they say "yes" in America.'

Phaedra wandered downstairs feeling a little light-headed. One thing life had taught her was that mean people are unhappy people. She had yet to find a genuinely contented person who was unkind. So, according to that rule, Margaret was simply miserable. She walked across the hall where Bertie and Wooster lay sleeping on the rugs with Basil, a warm sense of achievement giving her step a gentle bounce. It felt wonderful to have done something good.

'Ah, Phaedra!' Rosamunde exclaimed when she saw her.

'Are you OK?' Antoinette asked, pleased to see that she was smiling.

'Margaret's feeling better,' Phaedra announced.

'How are *you* feeling?' Tom asked from the club fender.

'Fine, thank you. She's a lovely woman.'

They all stared at her in astonishment. 'Are you

sure we're talking about the same person?' said David.

'Look, I don't know her like you do, but she was very charming to me.' She went and sat down beside David on the sofa.

'They make a lot of fuss,' said Roberta. 'Personally, I find she has a very soft centre.'

'She's just unhappy,' Phaedra continued. 'Anyway, she's coming down, so you can see for yourselves. She's perfectly well.'

'I *am* relieved,' said Antoinette.

'I suggest we all go for a walk,' said Joshua. 'Are you going to get Amber up?' he asked his wife, glancing at his watch.

'You can take her on your back,' said Roberta.

'Great, let's escape before Grandma comes down,' said Tom, jumping to his feet.

'Really, darling, I think that's a little unkind,' Antoinette reproached him, but she smiled as if his face was made of sunshine.

When Margaret appeared she still looked pale, but her fighting spirit was restored. 'Joshua, will you drive me home? I'm not feeling strong enough to walk.'

'Are you rested?' Antoinette asked.

'Phaedra has cheered me up enormously.' She turned to her newly found granddaughter and smiled warmly, which was a revelation to Antoinette.

'I'm so pleased,' Phaedra replied, feeling the eyes of the whole room upon her.

'I hope you will make this your home,' Margaret continued. 'You are certainly very welcome at the dower house whenever you need a break from London.' Roberta felt a stab of jealousy; she and

166

Margaret had always had a special relationship.

'Thank you so much. I'd love to see it,' Phaedra replied.

'Then you shall. David will bring you tomorrow morning and I will show you photographs of George as a little boy. He was very dear. Now I'd like to go home. Joshua?'

'We'll wait for you,' said Roberta.

'Don't fret, my dear, I shan't keep him.' And she left the room, calling for Basil.

When Joshua returned, the family set off up the farm track that led to the woods. The sky had clouded over and it looked as if it might rain. A chilly wind blew through the trees where birds frolicked in the branches and squirrels chased their own tails. Bertie, Wooster and Rufus ran free now that the shooting season was over, and the odd fat pheasant flew out of the undergrowth, his wings creaking like rusty hinges as he took to the skies.

Phaedra walked beside David. She liked him very much. He didn't look like his father, but he had the same charisma that filled the space around him and made her feel invigorated. She was drawn to him, like a chilly traveller to a hotel fire. As with George, David made her feel safe.

After a while she recognized the landscape and knew that David's house was near. 'Are we going to bake a cake this afternoon?' she asked him.

'Isn't that a bit like hard work?' he replied, grinning down at her.

'It's not hard work for me, I love baking. All you have to do is taste the mixture. If you're very good you can lick the bowl.'

'And eat the cake.'

'We'll share it with the rest of your family. I bet Tom likes chocolate cake.' She called back to Tom, who walked between Rosamunde and his mother. 'Tom, do you like chocolate cake?'

'Does anyone *not* like chocolate cake?' he called back.

'I don't,' said Roberta, who walked beside her husband with Amber strapped into a harness on his back.

'Then we'll make you a lemon cupcake,' said Phaedra.

'Oh, don't worry about me,' said Roberta.

'But you do like lemon cupcakes?' Phaedra asked.

'Yes, I do.'

'Do you think she looks like a woman who eats cake?' David hissed.

Phaedra ignored him. 'Then we won't leave you out, will we, David?'

'No, we won't leave Roberta out,' David replied dutifully.

'You can share it with Amber,' Phaedra suggested. Roberta forced a smile.

'She's trying to be nice,' said Joshua, lowering his voice. 'Give her a break, darling.'

'I don't want her cake!' Roberta huffed. Joshua shook his head wearily.

'Can I please lick the lemon mix bowl as well?' David asked Phaedra.

Phaedra smiled up at him. 'Yes, David, you most certainly can.' It felt good to be part of his family.

Once back in David's kitchen, Phaedra set about clearing the kitchen table. She laid out scales, bowls, a spatula, two wooden spoons, a teaspoon for David and the ingredients Harris had brought

168

down from the main house in the car: eggs, extra butter, flour, cocoa and baking powder—things that David would never have in his store cupboard. David sat at the table with a cup of tea, watching her bustle about as if she had always cooked in his kitchen. She wore his mother's green apron and a purposeful expression on her face. He decided that women must all think alike, for his mother had arranged his cutlery, utensils and crockery and Phaedra seemed to know instinctively where she had put everything.

She had tied her hair back into a ponytail so now he could see her face more clearly. Her beauty was arresting, especially as the balls of her cheeks blushed like sweet plums. A part of him was elated that she had walked into his life and set it aflame with her enthusiasm and joy, but the other part lamented the fact that he could never have her. He realized that, in spite of all the obstacles, he was falling in love with her.

'Instead of staring at me as if I'm an alien, why don't you mix some butter and icing sugar together for the filling?' She passed him a bowl and wooden spoon. 'And no licking until I give you permission.'

'You're not an alien, Phaedra,' he replied seriously. 'You're a beautiful woman. I still can't quite get my head around the fact that you're my half-sister.'

She cracked an egg on the side of her bowl and dropped the contents into the flour and sugar mixture with a gentle puff. 'Neither can I. One moment I have no one and then suddenly, I have a family.'

'Can't you delay your return to Paris?' he suggested.

She began to stir the mixture. 'It's only across the Channel, David.'

'I know, but we've only just found you.'

'London isn't home to me.'

'Fairfield can be your home. We're your family now. Wouldn't you like to be part of a big family?'

She stopped stirring for a moment and smiled wistfully. 'I used to watch my friends with their families and wish that I had a family like them. You know, the old cliché: mother, father, a dog or two. I always felt different. Middle-class families are very conventional where I come from. I longed to be like everyone else.' She began to beat the mixture with vigour. 'I'm happy now, though. I like my life.'

'Aren't you lonely?'

'Of course not.'

David didn't believe her. 'Everyone needs a family,' he persisted.

'I'm a grown-up now.'

'It makes no difference what age you are. You've just learned to suppress your longing. Delay Paris and give us a chance. I think you'll be happy you stayed.'

She grinned at him and he knew he had won her over. 'Put a little more muscle into that stirring and I'll think about it.' She swapped her spoon for an electric whisk and the room grew noisy with the sound of whirring.

Once the cakes were in the oven Phaedra disappeared upstairs to her room. She closed the door and sat on the edge of the bed, staring uneasily into the half-distance. She hadn't imagined she would feel attracted to any of George's sons. She hadn't even listed it as a

170

possibility. But she couldn't deny that she had liked the look of David right from the moment she had laid eyes on him in the church. Then when he had driven up to London to persuade her to come to Fairfield Park for the weekend, she had relished the fizzy feeling he gave her in the pit of her belly and how that feeling had carried her through the week, along with the eager anticipation of seeing him again on the Friday. Dear God, what would George say? If he was watching her now, what was he thinking?

David had been very persuasive. She did find the idea of having a family seductive. All her life she'd felt alone—a burden to her mother, dislocated from society because she was 'that poor Chancellor girl', passed around her mother's friends for sleepovers when she wanted to go off with her suitors, or worse, dragged along on vacation when her mother had no alternative but to take her with them. Phaedra remembered those lonely summers on windy beaches, sent off to play by herself because her mother wanted time alone with her man. How she'd longed for a family then. Now she had the chance of having a big family, she'd be mad to let it go.

When she came back downstairs, the sweet aroma of cake filled the kitchen. David remained at the table, reading the Saturday papers. 'They smell ready,' she said, grabbing the oven gloves and opening the Aga door. A hot blast of sponge-scented air enveloped them. She pulled the tray of lemon cupcakes out first, then bent down again to pull out the cake tins.

'The filling is perfect, I think you'll agree,' said David, lifting the *Telegraph* to reveal his bowl.

171

'They have to cool before we ice them.'

'Then what shall we do in the meantime?'

Phaedra dipped her finger into the butter-and-sugar filling that David had beaten to a rich, creamy texture. 'Mmmm, this is good. Do you want some?' She handed him his teaspoon.

He scooped up a dollop of mixture and put it in his mouth. 'Really good,' he enthused. 'So, what would you like to do while the cakes cool?'

'Play cards?'

'All right.'

She began to clear the table. 'I warn you, I'm a fierce opponent.'

'I witnessed your ferocity at the bridge table, remember?'

'Oh, I was just warming up.'

'Good, because I'm not a bridge player. I hold the family title for Racing Demon.'

'Only *one* family title?' she said with a laugh.

'There are many more, but I won't bore you with my achievements. For now, let's get the cards out, make another pot of tea . . .'

'A pot of tea: my, you *do* mean business!'

'I do indeed. Tea to an Englishman is as spinach to Popeye.'

'Then let's see if you have as much brain as you have brawn! Deal the cards, my friend, I am ready.'

Chapter 12

Antoinette felt better. Ever since Phaedra had arrived on Friday night, Fairfield had been infused with a buoyancy that hadn't been there before. Since George's death a murky miasma had lingered in all the rooms like fog, and Antoinette had constantly felt cold. But now she no longer felt the chill and the dark mist had been relegated to the corners, banished by Phaedra's optimistic and enthusiastic nature. She was like a beautiful angel, and Antoinette felt blessed that although George had been taken with one hand, Phaedra had been given with the other.

The girl was a miracle. She had won over Margaret. Joshua, Tom and David were clearly bedazzled by her. She lifted the vibration whenever she entered the room and their three expectant faces turned towards her like sunflowers facing the sun. No one was immune to her charm, except Roberta, who was being unreasonable; Antoinette only wished George hadn't kept Phaedra a secret all that time, because they could have enjoyed her together.

Even Dr Heyworth had found her delightful. He had taken great trouble to make them tea. He had put biscuits and some fruitcake a grateful patient had given him on the table, along with napkins. He might not have been so amused to see Antoinette in his garden again had it not been for Phaedra. Antoinette didn't imagine there was a man alive who wouldn't leap for joy at the sight of her. They had remained chatting and time had seemed unimportant. Dr Heyworth was certainly in no hurry for them to be gone, persuading them to stay longer with fresh cups of tea and more slices of cake. It was a very good cake and Antoinette had found it hard to resist. She had never been slim, but not for want of trying. Dr Heyworth's enthusiasm had been infectious and she had foolishly allowed him to cut her a second slice. She'd regret it, even though she no longer had a man to slim down for.

George had always liked her the way she was. She had been 'comely' when they met and he had never asked her to change. That's not to say he didn't have an eye for the ladies. He loved beautiful women and flirted with all the attractive females he came into contact with. But Antoinette had been secure in the knowledge that he loved her the most. A little flirting gave him pleasure and what pleased him, pleased her. It pleased him that she gave him three sons and it pleased him that she dedicated her time to their upbringing. When they grew into men and flew the nest it pleased him that she dedicated her time to him and their home, so that he always had a charming wife on his arm and a warm welcome to come back to.

Antoinette knew he wouldn't have been happy sitting around at home, he was far too restless and eager for experience, and she had accepted that life without question. She was so used to it, she hadn't been aware that there were questions to be raised until Phaedra had told her it was time to think of herself. She hadn't considered herself in so long, she wasn't sure what she really thought about anything. But the possibility of doing

174

something entirely selfish gave her a little frisson of excitement. A sense of doing something very wicked, like skipping class at school, or stealing a packet of sweets in the sweet shop. Phaedra had inspired her to be positive about the future. More than anything, being positive gave her a welcome sense of control.

* * *

'Tom and I are going to Murenburg next week,' David announced to his family at Sunday lunch. 'Just for a few days. I need to see where Dad died, you know, in order to move on.'

Margaret looked at him wearily. 'Do you really want to perpetuate the tragedy?'

'The trouble is, Grandma, if I don't go there'll be no end to it,' he explained, looking anguished.

'I agree with Margaret,' said Antoinette in a quiet voice. 'Wouldn't it be better if we all let him go?'

Margaret straightened in surprise. 'Well, I think that's a first, you and me agreeing on something, Antoinette.' She gave a small smile. The room fell quiet. She raised her voice. 'Antoinette and I are in agreement that we should all move on now and let George rest in peace.' Antoinette almost strained the muscles in her face as she struggled to hold back her tears. The thought of letting George go was dreadful.

'It's the only way I'll find peace,' David persisted. Then his gaze fell upon Phaedra. 'As you're our sister, would you like to come as well?'

Phaedra looked embarrassed. 'Me? Are you sure?'

175

'Why wouldn't I be sure?' David asked. 'You have as much right as the rest of us. He was your father, too.'

She lowered her eyes. 'If you're certain I wouldn't be intrusive, I'd really like to come.'

'I can't imagine how you'd be intrusive, Phaedra,' Margaret cut in, as Harris returned with her glass of sherry. 'The boys will be jolly lucky to have you. Though I don't think much of their plan.'

'Then that's settled,' said Tom happily, holding his wine glass out to Harris for a refill. 'Josh, are you in? Roberta?' It was clear from his tone of voice that he very much hoped they would decline. Antoinette very much hoped Harris wouldn't top up his glass.

'I've got a lot on next week,' Joshua replied. 'I couldn't possibly drop everything, and Roberta's the same, aren't you, darling?'

'Yes, my diary is very full, I'm afraid,' Roberta confirmed. 'People book one months in advance.'

'Then that's settled. I wonder what the snow conditions are. Shall I check on the Internet? Wouldn't it be great if it's just dumped a whole heap of snow?' Tom pulled his iPhone out of his breast pocket.

'After lunch, Tom,' said Antoinette, noticing Harris nodding in the doorway. 'Let's go through.'

Tom jumped to his feet, still holding his replenished glass of wine. 'What's for lunch?'

'Leg of lamb,' Harris replied solemnly.

'Great, my favourite. I hope Mrs Gunice has made enough Yorkshire puddings. I'm as hungry as a horse.' And he was the first to make his way across the hall to the dining room.

176

Lunch was a surprisingly jolly affair. Margaret had recovered from her turn the day before and seemed enlivened by her morning with Phaedra. Her cheeks were flushed with sherry and the pleasure of listening to Phaedra's funny imitations of her schoolteachers. The girl certainly knew how to turn unpleasant situations into entertaining anecdotes. This inspired the boys to recount their own schooldays, recalling tutors with halitosis, and nights stealing into the grub cupboard. Even Roberta joined in and laughed at their stories. In that rare moment of family harmony Antoinette truly believed that everything would be all right.

After lunch Antoinette asked Phaedra to accompany her up to George's bedroom. 'I haven't had the courage to go in, until now. I think I'll cope better going through all his things if we do it together,' she explained.

Phaedra immediately felt nervous. 'You don't think it's something you should do by yourself, or with your boys? I mean, you need time to remember him without having to worry about someone else.'

'No, I want you to be there. I need the moral support.'

Phaedra smiled weakly. 'Well, if you insist.'

Antoinette looked at her with motherly affection. 'I know you're a little afraid, too. It's OK. We'll do it together.' Phaedra took a deep breath and followed her up the stairs. 'George kept everything. He never liked to chuck anything away. I'm a real chucker. I hate mess and accumulated nonsense. But George has drawers of sentimental things he's kept over the years. I simply can't go through it all on my own. Half of

177

me wants to take a great big bin liner and throw it all away so I don't have to look at it, but the other half worries that I might miss something important. The truth is I can't really believe he's not coming back. Going through his things is so final, like accepting he's gone. I don't feel ready to do that.'

'Then leave it, Antoinette, until you feel stronger.'

'No, I have to do it now. George isn't coming back. I have to accept that, otherwise I'll be stuck in a horrible sort of limbo.'

They stood a moment outside his dressing-room door, fighting the sudden sense of loss that no amount of humour or stoicism could hold off. Antoinette inhaled through her nose as if mustering courage, then she lifted the latch and pushed it open. Inside it smelt manly: a little spicy, like sandalwood, yet uniquely George. The very air vibrated with his presence as if he were there with them, filling the space around him with his powerful charisma. And yet the room was empty but for his clothes, tossed carelessly onto the big double bed, over chairs, and on the divan beneath one window. Silver dishes were placed haphazardly on the table at the end of the bed and on the tall cherrywood chest of drawers in front of the other window, full of loose change and paperclips, nails, stubs from boarding cards, and other useless things that were once part of something important. The little drawers under the Queen Anne mirror were brimming with old tickets from the opera, ballet, cinema, theatre and even the London Underground.

There was also a musty smell, for no one had

been in to clean since George died, and the old house accumulated a great deal of dust. Phaedra walked over to the window that looked out onto the front lawn and was startled to find clusters of ladybirds basking in the sunshine in the corner against the glass.

'I think I should set these small creatures free, don't you?' she said, lifting the stiff leaden latch to open it. She noticed that her hands were shaking. She flicked the ladybirds out with her fingers and allowed the fresh air to rush into the room. The light, tinkling sound of birdsong was carried on the breeze and Phaedra breathed it in, restored a little by the beauty of the sun-drenched gardens. 'Come, Antoinette. Have a look out of here,' she said. Antoinette joined her at the window. 'It's so lovely I just want to stay here a moment and enjoy it.'

Antoinette let her gaze wander over the view. 'It's a beautiful day, isn't it?'

'George would have looked out, perhaps every morning when he opened the curtains. He would have taken a long breath, savouring the sights. He must have loved it here.'

'He did. Fairfield was always home. But in a funny way, he ran from it, too.'

Phaedra looked at her quizzically. 'Do you think?'

'I'm sure of it. He never spent more than a couple of days in a row down here, then he was shooting back up to London, or off to do something silly like climbing Everest or skiing.'

'Yes, he seemed a restless man, always having to push himself to the edge,' Phaedra agreed.

'Until he fell off,' Antoinette added sadly.

'He didn't mean to fall off.'

'Of course not. But if you always push your limits, you're bound to break.'

They drew away from the window. 'Now, where to begin?' said Antoinette with a sigh. The quantity of belongings was overwhelming.

'Let's start with the drawers,' Phaedra suggested, pointing to the bedside tables.

'Let's take them out and put them in the middle of the room. Then we can go through them methodically. We'll have a pile for rubbish and a pile for things too sentimental to chuck out—and darling, if you want to keep anything, please don't hesitate to ask.'

Phaedra suddenly felt nauseous. She wished she was anywhere but here, about to go through all George's private things. 'Thank you. I shall,' she replied weakly. She pulled out the top drawer of the right-hand cabinet and put it down on the rug. It was filled to the brim with papers, photographs, shooting cards and itineraries. One by one, the two women lifted out the contents, both nervous of what they might find. If he was capable of keeping Phaedra a secret, what else might he have hidden?

'Ah, now I remember *this*,' said Antoinette, showing Phaedra a handwritten dinner menu, decorated elaborately in gold, pale pinks and blues. 'This was for George's fiftieth birthday in Paris at Le Moulin Rouge.' Her eyes glittered at the memory. 'We had tremendous fun. I think I'll keep that.' And she put it to one side with notes for a speech and a diary he wrote on safari a few years before.

'He's kept a record of everything. It's incredible,' Phaedra mused, pulling out old black-and-white photographs of his school friends at Eton. Each one had written a personal message on the back. 'I wonder what's happened to all of these young men. I wonder how many he kept in touch with.'

Antoinette glanced over their young faces. 'I recognize a couple. Goodness, wasn't Henry Patterson handsome then.'

'What became of Henry Patterson?'

'He married twice and divorced twice and grew red-faced and as fat as a toad. I haven't seen him in years.'

Phaedra laughed, feeling a little better. 'Life is wonderful, isn't it? So many different chapters, like lives in themselves.'

'Look at this!' Antoinette exclaimed. 'Talking about chapters. *This* is a chapter I knew nothing about. Wasn't George a dark horse!' She studied a photograph closely, a deep frown lining her brow.

She handed Phaedra a pile of photographs of George standing by what looked like ruined forts and castles in the desert. He was grinning raffishly, clearly playing the fool. 'They look recent, don't they? I mean, this must have been taken in the last year. Where do you think he was?'

Phaedra looked carefully at each one. For a while she said nothing. Antoinette noticed her blanch and her own eyes welled again with tears. It was the first photograph of George they had come across, and he looked so happy, with everything to live for. Antoinette was grateful for her stepdaughter's company. It made it easier having someone with whom to share her grief. 'They're old Crusader castles,' said Phaedra at last. 'Probably in Syria or Jordan.'

Antoinette was impressed. 'How on earth do you know about Crusader castles?'

181

'I love ruins, though Irish ones are my favourites. Probably because we don't have much history in Canada.' She leafed through them with haste and Antoinette wondered whether she found it too painful to take her time. After she'd gone through them once, she looked at them again, this time more slowly. The colour returned to her cheeks and her hands stopped trembling. 'They're breathtaking, aren't they? To think people lived in these nine hundred years ago. I think this one is Shobak in Jordan.' She handed them back to Antoinette. 'Shobak is famous and incredibly beautiful.'

'Why don't you keep one or two?'

'May I?'

'Of course. I have so many. It's strange, but sometimes I think that George had a whole other life besides the one we shared. He never even told me he went to Jordan. Do you think that's odd?' She shrugged. 'I mean, you think you know someone.'

'I don't think we ever really *know* anyone,' Phaedra replied. 'I'm not sure we even know ourselves.'

'I understood that he needed time on his own, you see,' Antoinette continued.

'You don't think he ever got lonely?'

'No, he made friends wherever he went, and he was a bit of a lone wolf. He needed his time by himself.'

'You never felt marginalized?'

'Not at all. I was so busy down here and in London. Frankly, he was so demanding, I needed the rest.' But her face crumpled into a frown. 'Well, perhaps a little marginalized, now you mention it.' She wiped her nose with her handkerchief. 'I think sometimes one gets so used to a certain routine that one doesn't question how one feels about it. George and I were like that. I never questioned the way we lived.'

Phaedra smiled at her kindly. 'But you are now.'

'I am now.' She put the photographs in her 'to keep' pile. 'He kept you secret; it's made me question his integrity.'

'Oh, Antoinette ...'

'No, it's not that I think ill of him, it's just that I feel less secure about us as a couple. I can confide in you, I know you won't tell the boys. I'd hate them to feel I'm in any way criticizing their father. I'm not, really I'm not. I just wonder what else he might have kept from me, that's all, and I ask myself, didn't he trust me enough to share?'

'He was only trying to protect you ...'

'Yes, yes, but he knew me better than that. It's very out of character for him not to confide in me, you see. Perhaps he was hiding you for another reason ... I don't know what that was, but I can't believe it was simply because he was afraid I would disapprove or be hurt. He knew I would have supported him.'

'Had he lived I'm sure he would have introduced me to you in time,' Phaedra suggested gently.

'Perhaps. He just wasn't given time.' She dismissed those thoughts and returned to her task. Little by little they made their way through George's drawers and cupboards.

*   *   *

'Phaedra, will you come back soon?' Antoinette

183

asked when they felt they had done enough for one afternoon. 'I really need you. There's still so much to do and I feel comfortable doing it with you.' Antoinette smiled bashfully. 'You really understood George, even though you knew him such a short time.'

'I'll come whenever you need me. I like going through his things, it makes me feel close to him.'

'You know you said he wasn't in the ground, but around us in spirit?'

'Yes.'

'Do you think he's here now?'

Phaedra let her eyes float about the room. 'I'm sure he is. Perhaps that's why we both felt him so strongly when we came in.'

'It's a comforting thought.'

'I have no doubt.'

'I envy you. It must be nice not to doubt. What must he think, watching us going through all his accumulated rubbish?'

'Just that, I imagine. That it's all rubbish. Things that seemed very important in life are suddenly worthless to him in death. These sentimental keepsakes only matter to *us* now. He's probably laughing at the importance we're giving them.'

'Like the Frampton Sapphires,' Antoinette said with a chuckle. 'I've never really cared for jewellery, not like Roberta who's a magpie.'

'Me neither. I'm flattered that George left them to me, but I can't imagine I'll ever wear them. I don't have that kind of life.'

'You'll look beautiful in them. The Sapphires will bring out the blue in your eyes.'

'I'll feel like a Christmas tree.'

Antoinette laughed. 'I know what you mean.

184

Jewellery never suited me, either. I've always been too ordinary for diamonds! But you're not ordinary. You just shine all on your own.'

'What will George think, seeing us together discussing the Frampton Sapphires?'

'He'll be pleased that we're friends, I think,' Antoinette said softly.

Phaedra picked up one of the photographs from her pile and studied his face pensively. 'I think nothing matters in Heaven but love. If a person's actions are motivated by love, it has to be good. I came here with a big heart, Antoinette. I know it hasn't been easy for any of you. But I hope you now realize I don't want anything from you.'

Antoinette laughed. 'Oh, Phaedra, darling, you've brought a breath of fresh air into the family. If George is looking down on us all, he can only be happy.'

'I hope so,' Phaedra replied with a shudder.

Chapter 13

Phaedra arrived back at Cheyne Row at seven o'clock in the evening with a heavy heart. Saying goodbye to her new family had been tempered by the promise of four days in Murenburg with David and Tom and the open invitation to return to Fairfield whenever she wanted, and yet she had hated leaving George's home, as if his spirit lingered *there* and it was *him* she was leaving . . . or was it David that she hated leaving the most?

They had all waved her off on the steps. Even Margaret had come for tea and stayed until five

185

thirty when Phaedra had reluctantly stood up to leave. They had accompanied her outside where David had hugged her affectionately, wrapping his strong arms around her and squeezing her a little too hard. She had caught her breath and pulled away, conscious of the blush in her cheeks. The sudden frisson of attraction had taken her by surprise and she had felt dizzy with uncertainty.

Antoinette, her eyes full of anxiety, had advised her to take care in Murenburg, and Rosamunde had suggested she wear a helmet, which indicated how little she knew of modern skiing because nowadays *everyone* wore helmets as a matter of course. But Phaedra had barely heard them. She was aware only of David standing on the second step, watching her with a strange look on his face. Confused by the unexpected dawning of desire she had hastily kissed Roberta's cold cheek, feeling her sharp bone like metal against her skin, and said goodbye to Joshua, who had beamed with pleasure as she reached up to kiss him too. She didn't dare look at David again, but in her peripheral vision she could see that he was still watching her, hands in pockets, his face now long and serious.

Tom had decided to leave at the same time. His Aston Martin had roared out of sight as soon as they hit the open road, and Phaedra had been left with the wistful sound of Sarah McLachlan and her own muddled thoughts.

Back at home she carried her weekend bag up to her bedroom and turned on her mobile telephone. Just as she went to run the bath, it rang with an incoming call. For a moment she thought it might be David and her heart gave a little flutter of anticipation, but when she looked she saw to her

186

disappointment that it was Julius's name displayed in the glass.

'Are you home?' he asked, without even saying 'hello'.

'Yes,' she replied.

'How did it go?'

She sat on the bed. 'It was great,' she replied.

'Roberta didn't eat you alive, then?'

'Not quite, but she was very unfriendly.'

'Remember she has only one thing in mind: the Frampton Sapphires.'

'Oh, I'll give them to her,' said Phaedra wearily. 'I really couldn't care less about jewellery.'

'You will do no such thing, Phaedra. They're yours. George gave them to you and if you respect his wishes, you will keep them.'

'Of course I respect his wishes. But if they're going to drive a wedge between us, I'd rather not have them.'

'Don't be silly, she'll get over it.'

'I feel such a fraud.'

'Don't let me ever hear you say that again. George wanted to take care of you. He was very aware that he would die before you and was anxious for you to be looked after.'

'They're a very nice family,' she said dreamily.

'So are you still planning on returning to Paris?'

'Of course. This changes nothing, Julius. It just delays it a little.'

'Shame. Sounds like you all got on very well.'

'We did.'

'Then they'll invite you again.' He chuckled. 'Don't pretend you didn't enjoy being part of their family.'

'I won't pretend. I did enjoy being a Frampton,'

187

she confessed.

'You *are* a Frampton, my dear,' he exclaimed triumphantly.

'Don't kid yourself, Julius. I'm a Chancellor.'

'It'll take a bit of getting used to, but in time you'll feel like a Frampton, trust me.'

'I'm going to Murenburg next week with David and Tom.'

'Good. A bit of family bonding.'

'We're going to see where George died.'

'Then you can put him behind you and move on.'

'I don't think I'll ever be able to put George behind me, Julius.' She felt a swell of unhappiness in her chest. 'I'm so confused.'

'How about dinner?'

'Dinner?'

'You sound down. I'll cheer you up. Tomorrow night?'

'Well, I ...' But she couldn't think of an excuse.

'I'll get my secretary to book the Ivy. I'll pick you up around eight? How does that sound?'

'OK, thank you.'

'We're a good team, you and I. George would be very happy to know that I am taking care of you.'

'I really don't need taking care of, Julius. I've spent most of my life taking care of myself and I've got along just fine.'

'Not in the way that George wanted to take care of you.'

'Money isn't everything, Julius.'

'That's where you're wrong. Now you're rich, you'll discover that money is the key to happiness.'

Phaedra hung up and remained on the bed, staring into the half-distance. She felt ashamed. George had left her a fortune as well as a very valuable suite of jewellery she didn't even want. Before he had died, he had spoiled her, but his gifts were easier to accept when given with warm hands. Now he was dead, it seemed somehow avaricious to accept them. It wasn't right that she should own the Frampton Sapphires, and yet Julius had made her feel ungrateful when she had suggested she give them to Roberta. Why all the fuss about a few pieces of gold, diamonds and sapphires? Julius *wasn't* right: in the grand scheme of things, money had no real value; she had learned that from watching her mother. Only love had any value—and she missed George with all her heart.

However, it wasn't long before her thoughts sprang back to David. She stood up and wandered into the bathroom to run a bath. While it ran she flicked through the photographs she'd taken at the folly on her digital camera. She paused on David's face and felt the familiar warmth spread across her chest, followed by a gnawing sense of shame that induced her hastily to put him away like a forbidden toy. George was barely cold in his grave and she was already feeling an inappropriate desire for his eldest son. She undressed and stepped into the bubbly water, allowing it to wash over her. Perhaps she shouldn't go to Murenburg. Maybe it would be better if she didn't see them all again. Spending time with David might just lead her into terrible trouble—and she'd only have herself to blame. She should return to Paris and forget about Fairfield and the Framptons. She closed her eyes and sank her head beneath the water.

Antoinette was sorry to see Phaedra go, but happy that they had become friends. In one weekend, they had achieved more than she could possibly have hoped for. Not only had they spent time together, but they had really enjoyed each other's company. If she had been blessed with a daughter, she would have liked her to be just like Phaedra.

She wandered into George's room and looked out of the window. The sky was cloudy, but for a few clear patches where the stars were able to shine through. She remembered Phaedra's advice to focus on the stars in order to sense a higher power, so she gazed up through an opening and lost herself a moment in the eternal space beyond. She felt very small, and yet at the same time, somewhere in the region of her chest, she felt a part of that mysterious expanse, as if she were more than just skin and bone; part of the everlasting current of Life.

That moment of consciousness was brief. Afterwards, her attention was distracted by the garden. Although it was dark, she could make out the pair of apple trees and the tops of the avenue of lime trees where they were silhouetted against the sky. She listened to the breeze sweeping through the branches and remembered how Phaedra had imagined George looking out onto that view every morning when he drew the curtains. It was true, George had loved Fairfield, and like a homing pigeon he had punctuated his life with weekends here whenever he had been able to. And yet he had been restless, as if he had expected more from his home and been disappointed. As if, perhaps, the *thought* of home had exceeded the reality.

Antoinette considered Margaret and the type of mother she had made. She hadn't been affectionate, but Antoinette was certain she had thought the world of George—he had been her only son. Yet he had married a very different woman. In fact, the more Antoinette pondered on their differences, the more she realized that he had chosen to spend his life with the total antithesis of his mother. Perhaps he had married a woman whose affection was assured because his mother's was hard to win. With Antoinette he had been a hero right from the moment she had met him; Margaret was less forthcoming in her praise, which didn't mean she hadn't been proud of him, just that she had found it hard to express. But George had been a man who needed both verbal and physical confirmation of his value. Antoinette wasn't sure that Margaret had ever fulfilled that need.

Phaedra had had a soothing effect on Margaret, too. From the moment the old lady had come down from her rest, she had been restored. Phaedra hadn't elaborated on their conversation, but whatever they had said to each other had lifted Margaret out of the quagmire of her suppressed grief and she had smiled at Phaedra in a way that Antoinette had rarely seen her smile. Only Roberta had remained cold and suspicious. She knew in her heart that Roberta was highly protective of her family, but she also knew how materialistic her daughter-in-law was. Would she have accepted Phaedra if George hadn't left her the Frampton Sapphires?

191

She thought of Tom and David taking Phaedra to stay at Chalet Marmot, and then she turned her thoughts to herself. What was *she* going to do now that George was no longer around to need her? She had money, she could do anything she wanted ... but what? The idea of embarking on an adventure of her own was very daunting. She was safe down here at Fairfield. Part of her just wanted to hide away and lick her wounds. She didn't feel up to seeing anyone outside the family—except Dr Heyworth.

She didn't mind seeing *him*. He had been so kind and understanding when he had found her in his garden, the *first* time. He had listened to her as she unburdened herself of her anger towards George, and her resentment of him throwing all caution to the wind and taking unnecessary risks. Dr Heyworth hadn't disapproved, in fact he had told her that it was 'perfectly natural' to feel that way and a good thing to talk it through. After her escape to his garden a *second* time, they were now firm friends. Margaret would highly disapprove, she thought with a smile. But Rosamunde might be a little put out—after all, she had clearly taken a shine to him. She decided she'd ask him up to the house again, for Rosamunde. She pulled away from the window, feeling suddenly more positive. Perhaps she'd ask him for dinner.

The following evening Julius's black BMW drew up outside Phaedra's little house on Cheyne Row and Julius stepped out with a large bouquet of red roses. He straightened his tie as he stood at the door, about to ring the bell. Phaedra had watched him from the window above and her heart sank at the sight of the flowers. She consoled herself with the thought of flying to Zurich in a couple of days, grabbed her handbag from the bed and went down the stairs to open the door.

'Ah, Phaedra,' said Julius, running his eyes up and down her body appreciatively. 'You look very pretty.'

'Thank you,' she replied, hoping she wasn't sending out the wrong signals by wearing a dress.

'I've brought you roses. I know girls love flowers and I thought you sounded rather sad on the telephone last night.'

'I miss him, Julius.'

'Of course you do. But time is a great healer; so are distractions. I'm going to give you a nice dinner and try to take your mind off it all.' He handed her the flowers and followed her into the little hall.

'I'll just go and put these in water. They're beautiful, thank you.'

Julius's BMW was the latest model and immaculately clean. Fine leather seats, shiny wooden dashboard, not a fleck of dust to be seen anywhere. The interior smelt of polish and Julius's heavy-handed use of cologne. He started the engine and classical music at once filled the car. Phaedra belted up and Julius swung out into the street and sped down towards the Embankment at high speed. It was dusk. The sky was a gentle, muted pink, the light turning the wheeling seagulls into small flamingos. As the car swept across the city Phaedra felt uplifted by the swathes of crocuses and daffodils in Hyde Park. Candy-coloured blossom floated on the breeze and flocks of pigeons gathered on the pavements and around bins where there was food to be scavenged. 'I like

London at this time of year,' she said.

'Very pretty,' Julius agreed, but it was clear that he didn't really notice.

'Fairfield was so beautiful. The leaves just beginning to unfurl, the blossom flowering on the apple trees, hundreds of tulips peeping out of the earth. It's a very special place.'

'Did you see the paintings? They have some very valuable works of art.'

'I saw them, but I wouldn't know their value.'

'Did Antoinette show you the portrait of Theodora in the Frampton Sapphires?'

'No,' she lied; she didn't want to look like she'd been snooping.

'Really? It's hanging on the stairs. You know, beside the big one of Algernon Frampton. Check it out next time you go. That one must be worth a small fortune.'

'I might have seen it and not realized. I haven't been shown the sapphires.'

'They're as big as sweets.'

'I'm sure they're lovely.'

'You'll be wearing them soon enough.'

Phaedra laughed. 'I don't think so! When am I ever going to have the opportunity to wear jewels? You know I don't lead that kind of life.'

'You could do, if you wanted to.'

'But I don't want to. I'm very happy with my life just as it is. I'm a jeans and T-shirt kind of girl.'

He gave her a sideways glance and grinned, as if to indicate that he knew better.

The Ivy was warm, dimly lit and packed with diners. Julius was made a great fuss of by fawning staff, which he clearly enjoyed, having been a frequent guest of George's. The manager offered his condolences as they were escorted to George's regular table in the centre of the room, and Julius looked suitably solemn as he accepted them. Phaedra sat on the red leather banquette and glanced around at the other guests. By the time Julius sat down she had already spotted three famous actors and one celebrity chef.

'We're in good company,' said Julius happily.

'It's a lovely restaurant.'

'George's favourite. He used to come at least three times a week.'

'No wonder they treat you like royalty.'

'We had our lunch meetings in here, dinner meetings at Mark's Club. George was set in his ways in that respect.' He ordered a bottle of wine without looking at the menu. 'We'll start with white then we'll see.'

'I'm happy with white.'

'Depends what you have for dinner.'

'I'm not fussy. What would you recommend?'

'I'll order for you.'

She watched Julius as he scanned the menu with his incisive gaze. He had small eyes, the colour of gunmetal, but she guessed they missed nothing. It didn't take him long to decide and he summoned the waiter with a snap of his fingers. 'I think you'll be pleased,' he said once the waiter had moved away. 'I know you better than you think.'

'We'll see about that,' she said with a smile, certain that he didn't know her at all.

'Now you're a rich woman, what do you plan to do?'

'I'll do exactly the same as I have always done. Return to Paris, finish my book ...'

'Your photography's a charming hobby, Phaedra,

195

but don't you think you could better use your time on the board of charities? I know some key people who would happily put you forward.'

'You mean charities that were close to George's heart, like Tibetan children . . .'

'No, I mean high-profile London charities.'

'Why would I want to do that? I mean, I'm happy to help if I have an interest in the charity, but I don't want to get involved for the sake of social climbing.'

'I'm not suggesting you social climb, just that charity is the classic way foreigners like you meet the right people.'

'I know enough people in Paris.'

'That's Paris. I mean London and the *right* people in London. You're a wealthy young woman now. It's time you mixed with other wealthy people.'

'Julius, let me stop you right here. I don't want the money.'

Julius looked horrified. 'You're being ridiculous.'

'I'm being serious. I don't want it. I won't touch a penny.'

'You will when it's winking at you in a bank account with your name on it.'

'I haven't given you my bank details, and I won't. I told you, I don't want the money. It's tainted.'

He laughed and patted her hand. 'You'll see sense in the end and embark on a whole new life. New friends, new . . .'

She cut him off. 'I know my friends and I trust them. I don't need to start making new ones. Besides, I feel more comfortable lying low. I'm not a party girl.'

'Don't tell me you're going to decline my

196

invitation to Annabel's after dinner.'

'You want to go dancing?' She was appalled.

'Absolutely. I have a beautiful girl on my arm tonight. I want to show her off.'

'Oh, Julius, I'm tired. I don't think I have the energy to go dancing.'

'Wait until you've had a few glasses of wine. You might feel differently.'

But at the end of dinner Phaedra still felt the same. Julius was disappointed, but he didn't try to change her mind. She congratulated him on the choices he had made for her dinner; the fish was tender and light and the lamb perfectly pink. Then he drove her back home, hitting the Embankment as early as possible so that she could see the Thames at night. He knew girls liked the romance of the lights reflected on the water. By the time they reached Cheyne Row it was eleven thirty.

'You're looking a lot perkier now,' he said as he opened the passenger door and watched her step out.

'I've had a really nice evening, thank you.'

'I'm happy, because I know George would approve of me keeping an eye on you, and I owe him everything.' Phaedra imagined it must have been very lucrative being George's lawyer. 'So, you're off on Wednesday.'

'Yes.'

'Chalet Marmot is ravishing. Antoinette has beautiful taste; shame she can't ski.'

'Did you ever go and stay with George?'

'Yes. I'm an excellent skier. The off-piste in Murenburg is phenomenal. You know, I have some good footage of George and me skiing together.' He grinned. 'One of the best days we had was the

197

week before he died.'

Phaedra paled. 'You were with him the week before he was killed?'

'I had to return to London to sort out a few things for him. George couldn't resist the fresh snow and stayed on. I'm sure if I'd been there I'd have dissuaded him from going off-piste that day.'

'Why?'

'It was way too warm. The conditions were dangerous. But George thought he could do anything. He thought he was immortal.' He shook his head dolefully. '*I* thought he was immortal.'

Phaedra suddenly felt sorry for him and put a hand on his shoulder. 'We all did, Julius.'

He looked at her seriously. 'I hope those boys are going to look after you.'

'I'm sure they will.'

'I don't hold out much hope for Tom. If he manages to organize himself to wake up in time to ski, I'll be very surprised.'

'It doesn't really matter. David's very reliable.'

Julius pulled a face. 'None of them have George's drive, though, do they?'

Phaedra put the key in the lock. 'I'm not sure that's a bad thing. I mean, George had something to prove. He was more complicated. David's happy in his skin.'

'Joshua would be the one to watch, he's making good money in the City, but he's dominated by his greedy wife. George wasn't weak. Tom runs a nightclub: what sort of a job is that? I don't think he makes much at all and he drinks too much ever to make a success of anything. What a family!'

Phaedra was shocked and withdrew her hand. 'I thought you liked them.'

198

'It paid well to like them.' He laughed at her expression. 'Don't look so alarmed. Of course I *like* them. As families go, they're not bad. It's just not usual that apples fall so far from the tree, and I had enormous admiration for George.' He sighed heavily. 'None of them are a patch on him.'

Phaedra pushed open the door and stepped into the hall. 'Thank you for dinner, Julius. And I'm sorry I didn't go dancing with you.'

'Next time. Call me.'

She frowned as an uneasy feeling crept over her. 'Listen, Julius, you've been wonderful. You've helped me get through a really tough time; I don't know what I would have done without you. But you can let me go now. I promise I can manage on my own.'

She winced as he put his hands on her waist and leant across to kiss her cheek. 'Don't be silly, Phaedra. We're in this together, you and I—and you know you *need* me. I'll call you when you're in Murenburg just to make sure you're all right.'

'Oh, I will be. I'll be with my brothers.' It sounded absurd.

'Brothers are only good up to a point. You need a *man*.'

'I had one.'

'So, you need another. Broken hearts mend, Phaedra, and life is more fun as a pair. Now go to bed and have a good night's sleep.'

She closed the door, her heart beating frantically behind her ribcage like a frightened monkey. She could smell his cologne on her skin and she recoiled. *Oh, George, look at the mess you've got me into!*

A couple of days later Phaedra, David and Tom met at Heathrow Airport to fly to Zurich. There was an air of excitement about their trip in spite of the solemnity of the mission. The boys had small suitcases, for their ski clothes were already in Murenburg, while Phaedra had a very large and heavy one. 'Are you planning on staying there until summer?' Tom quipped when he saw it.

'I know, I'm sorry; it's ridiculously large, but my helmet takes up half of it.'

'Aunt Rosamunde will be happy to know you packed it,' said David, pulling it across the floor towards check-in.

'She's a character, your aunt Rosamunde,' Phaedra laughed.

'Is she ever going to leave?' Tom wondered.

'She's thrilled to be of use,' David replied. 'Mum will get fed up with her in the end.'

'You know what they say about guests, that like fish they begin to smell after a few days,' said Phaedra.

'Well, Aunt Rosamunde has been there for a couple of weeks now: she must be really stinky!' said Tom.

'Oh really, Tom, that's very unfair.' Phaedra smacked him playfully on the wrist. 'Why has she never married, do you think?'

'Bad timing, bad choices,' David began.

'If you were a man, would you want to marry her?' said Tom.

'She might have been pretty as a young woman,' Phaedra mused.

'She's never been pretty and she's always been

200

keener on horses than men.'

'Ah, well, there's the flaw,' Phaedra said.

Tom snorted with laughter. 'No man can compete with a horse!'

They reached the front of the queue and David lifted Phaedra's suitcase onto the conveyor belt. 'Passports,' he said, holding out his hand. 'I can see I'm going to have to organize the two of you,' he added, watching Phaedra delve into her handbag and Tom reach into every pocket. At last Tom found his in the back of his jeans and Phaedra fished hers out from the clutter.

'You have a British passport?' he said when he saw Phaedra's.

'Yes, I'm a British citizen,' she replied proudly.

'How come?'

'Well, you might as well know: I was married to a Brit.'

Tom and David stared at her. 'You were married?' David exclaimed.

'You're a hot divorcee,' said Tom with a smirk.

'Will you behave, Tom—and do hand them over, David, the poor lady has been waiting patiently and there's a queue behind us.'

David gave the Swissair attendant the passports then turned back to Phaedra. 'Was he the one who broke your heart?' he asked quietly.

'Now isn't the time or place to discuss my ex-husband,' she replied, and an invisible but tangible gate closed out her past.

'Your bag is like the Tardis,' said Tom, peering inside.

'It's like a bucket,' she replied. The attendant handed the passports back to David and while Phaedra was talking to Tom about her handbag, he

201

stole a peek at her photograph. It was a good representation. His eyes wandered to the right where her birthday shot out at him like a bullet. February 9th 1984. He stared at it in astonishment. If she was thirty-one, as she claimed, she would have been born in 1981. This meant she was really twenty-eight, a year younger than him.

'Hey, you're not looking at my photograph, are you?' she laughed, grabbing it out of his hand.

'You look exactly the same,' he replied, covering his confusion with nonchalance.

'Let me see,' said Tom.

'No.' She dropped it into her bag. 'It's a horrible photograph. Now, I need a cup of coffee. Shall we go through and find a nice café on the other side?'

The three of them walked through the airport. David felt uneasy. If Phaedra was a year younger than him, then her mother must have been sleeping with his father during his marriage to Antoinette, which would mean that his father had been unfaithful right at the very start of his marriage. Had Phaedra lied to protect him? Had she lied to protect *them*? He took a deep breath and tried to brush it off: after all, it had all happened twenty-eight years ago and his parents had been very happy since. He considered his mother and how devastated she'd be if she knew the truth. He resolved to try and forget it.

Chapter 14

Chalet Marmot was as picturesque as a traditional Swiss chalet could possibly be. It was built high up on the meadows above the village, its wide balconies surveying the magnificent Gotschna mountain opposite and the Prättigau valley gently falling away to the right. The chalet had a pretty snow-capped roof, wooden walls darkened to a rich brown and red shutters into which large hearts had been skilfully carved.

It was four in the afternoon when they arrived. The sky was a deep, startling blue and the sunlight dazzling, causing the snow crystals to glitter like pavé diamonds. David carried the bags inside while Tom paced up and down outside with his iPhone clamped to his ear and a cigarette hanging from the corner of his mouth. Phaedra stepped into the hall and inhaled the reassuring smell of pine. She swept her eyes over the interior, her delight growing as she walked on through into the sitting room where a traditional Swiss fireplace dominated the far wall, ready-prepared with a neat pile of logs. The walls and ceilings were panelled in antique pine stripped from Prättigau farmhouses two or three hundred years old, and carved in the Swiss tradition with flowers and italic inscriptions. Impressionist paintings hung alongside old masters, and the sofas were big and inviting and scattered with cushions. Outside it was white and snowy, but inside the wood panelling and enormous red Persian rug gave it a cosy feel.

'Your mother has extremely good taste,' she said,

wandering through an archway into the dining room. 'She has a good eye for fabrics. Blues and reds look really good in the mountains.'

'I don't know.' David shrugged. 'It's certainly comfortable.'

'She should have been an interior decorator. She has such style.'

He followed her into the dining room where old pewter beer mugs were lined across the windowsills and pine walls and beams gave it the feel of a traditional farmhouse. 'Maybe she would have been, had she not married my father,' he said.

'She's still young.'

'Hard to start something new at her age,' David argued.

'Perhaps she'll give Fairfield an overhaul.'

'Dad never let her touch a thing, except the bedrooms.'

'You know, it could do with the odd lick of paint here and there. Now George isn't around to stop her ...'

'I agree with you. A house should be a home. But I think she's too aware of the heritage to mess around with it. And my grandmother is still ever-present to keep a beady eye on what goes on in there.'

'I think she should do as she pleases. She's spent the last thirty years of her life pleasing other people. Don't you think it's time she pleased herself? Perhaps she should travel.'

'She'd never go on her own and Aunt Rosamunde would drive her mad pretty quickly.'

'She needs to get out of the house and out of her head. When we're in familiar surroundings we

204

dwell in our minds, with all those rubbishy thoughts we don't really need. When we go abroad we live in our senses, taking in all the new and wonderful sights, smells and sounds. We rise above the useless prattle of our thoughts and fully exist in the present, like I'm doing now. I'm taking in these marvellous new sights and I feel so uplifted.' She grinned diffidently, aware of sounding quaint. 'It was such a good idea of yours to come out. I feel better already.'

It was clear from David's affectionate gaze that he didn't think her at all quaint. 'So do I,' he agreed. 'But then the very sight of you is enough to make me feel uplifted!' She turned away, embarrassed. His flirtatious comment had taken her by surprise. He laughed it off, as it had taken him by surprise too and he was regretting having said it. 'Come, let me show you where you're going to sleep.'

If the downstairs had delighted her, the upstairs would please her even more. Her bedroom was decorated entirely in battened blue toile de Jouy with a bed so high she'd have to climb to get into it. She walked over to the window and gazed down into the valley. No wonder George had loved Murenburg so much; it had the charm of an advent calendar.

The boys didn't give Phaedra time to unpack. They were keen for her to hire skis and boots so that they could set off early the following morning. They drove down to the village in George's Jeep and parked opposite the Co-op to buy supplies. Phaedra relished the thought of cooking in that beautiful chalet, but David and Tom both insisted that they'd be going out every night for dinner at the Wynegg and Chesa Grishuna.

She hired an impressive pair of Core skis at Gotschna Sport and David made sure she got a bleeper for skiing off-piste. The staff offered their sincere condolences. George had been a much loved and ubiquitous figure in Murenburg. Ever since his death the village had talked of little else and mourned him as one of their own.

David secured her skis onto the roof rack and they drove slowly through the village pointing out the sights and waving at the locals, who recognized the car and greeted them enthusiastically.

Phaedra was enchanted. Murenburg had the air of a lost age of elegance and the charm of a box of Lindt chocolates. Two Bernese Mountain Dogs enthusiastically greeted their fur-coated mistress as she emerged from the gift shop; a pair of horses harnessed to a sleigh outside the Alpina hotel set their bells ringing every time they tossed their heads; and the driver, in his traditional blue embroidered smock, smoked a pipe, cheerily chatting to passers-by as they stopped to stroke the animals. Opposite, on the station platform, a weatherbeaten local in a beret sold hot chestnuts behind a stand as he had for the past forty years, his voice resounding across the street as he cried: 'Heisse maroni, heisse maroni.' The primrose-coloured hotel Vereina gleamed in the sunshine with palatial grandeur while the more discreet Chesa, a little further down the street, exuded an old-world allure.

Tom pointed out the only nightclub, the Casa Antica, then elaborated with a few stories of his adventures there. David drew up outside the bread shop where only a few remaining plaited loaves lingered on the shelves. Phaedra accompanied him inside and listened as he chatted good-naturedly in broken Swiss-German to the old lady behind the counter. 'I'm afraid I'm not a linguist,' he said to Phaedra as the shopkeeper lifted a loaf with a pair of tongs and dropped it into a paper bag.

'You did well, from what I heard,' she replied.

'What you heard is about all I can say.'

'The whole point of speaking another language is to communicate, isn't it? In which case you achieved your aim.'

'Tom speaks far better than me. He spent a year working here after he left school.' David looked out of the window to see his brother striding around the car talking on his iPhone. 'Languages come easily to Tom.'

'I suspect he's one of those gifted people who is rather lazy. Am I right?'

David laughed. 'Got it in one. He could turn his hand to anything he wants, but he chooses to run a nightclub.'

'Nothing wrong with that, so long as he's happy.'

'I'm not sure that he is.' David frowned. 'He's an avoider . . .'

The old lady put out her hand and David delved into his pocket of loose change to pay her. Phaedra watched Tom as he guffawed into his telephone and wondered whether he had really mourned his father's death, or whether, as David suggested, he had simply pushed the pain to one side. She realized that while this trip was important for her and David, it was *very* important for Tom.

That evening the three of them dined at the Chesa, where David and Tom were greeted like

207

family. They seemed to know most people there and it took a while to get to their table through the enthusiastic handshaking and chatting. David introduced Phaedra to everyone, but he never mentioned that she was his half-sister. Phaedra was relieved. She didn't feel ready to share her story with strangers. It would be better for them all if it remained a family secret.

As she was made a great fuss of, it dawned on her that people assumed she was David's girlfriend. They looked from her to David and smiled in that knowing way, and it was clear from their admiring glances that they considered them a good match. David put his hand in the small of Phaedra's back and ushered her to their table in the corner. But she could feel people watching them and talking about them in low voices. To her surprise she liked the way it made her feel; she liked being linked to David.

The table was in the perfect position to survey the room. The restaurant was almost full and the waitresses wove between the tables wearing pretty dirndls with tidy white aprons. Phaedra ran her eyes over the alpine designs carved into the wooden beams, absorbed the warm atmosphere of the room and sighed with pleasure. She was pleased that Julius had persuaded her to accept David's original invitation to stay at Fairfield. She now felt part of their family—and she hadn't *ever* felt part of a real family.

They drank wine, ate the delicious dishes and laughed at Tom's stories. Then when Tom went out to smoke a cigarette, David and Phaedra were left together and once again the electricity between them quivered with such force that

Phaedra was certain the whole dining room would notice. David smiled across the table. He was unable to hide his feelings. They were growing so fast he wasn't sure he'd be able to control them, and were it not for the word 'sibling' that hung between them like prison bars, it would have been the most natural thing in the world to have held her hand.

David paid the bill—Phaedra noticed that Tom didn't even offer—then they drove back up the narrow lane to Chalet Marmot. The sky glittered with stars, and the moon lit up the mountains in a phosphorescent silver light so that every tree and rock on the Gotschna could be seen with clarity.

'It's magnificent, isn't it?' said Phaedra as she and David stood on the balcony a little later, hugging mugs of hot chocolate. 'The mountain really leaps out at you and the sky looks so deep. So very far away.' She watched her breath turn to mist on the cold air.

'It's hard to imagine that Dad died up there,' said David, his face creasing into a frown.

'From here it looks so benign.'

'Terrible to think that something so beautiful can cause so much harm.'

'It was written in the Book of Life, David.'

'I know.'

'It was his destiny to go.'

'Still, it's tough on all of us.' He took a swig of hot chocolate and swallowed hard.

'It's those left behind who suffer the most. Your father probably knew very little about it when the avalanche hit him. He probably didn't feel any pain at all. But we feel it constantly.'

David put his arm around her shoulders and

209

drew her close. 'I'm glad you're here, Phaedra.'

'So am I,' she replied, blinking away tears. 'We're in this together and it makes it so much easier to bear.'

David wanted to ask her why she had lied about her age. The question dangled on the tip of his tongue. But fear overcame his curiosity and he managed to restrain himself. He didn't want to risk losing her trust by admitting that he'd snooped, or that he had caught her lying. It was obvious that she had only lied to protect them all from the truth: that his father had been unfaithful right at the start of his marriage. Surely he didn't really need to ask. However, it bothered him like an unsightly plastic bag left lying in a beautiful woodland. As long as he knew it was there, he was unable wholly to enjoy the view. In the end he would have to ask her—but not while she rested against him.

Later, when he lay in bed, he thought about his parents' marriage. As far as he could see they had been very happy. His mother had worshipped his father in a kind of childlike way, never questioning his actions and allowing him to dominate with the submissive acceptance of a geisha. George, in turn, had always treated her with the greatest respect and defended her with the ferocity of a lion if anyone had ever hurt her. They had never argued or fought and he remembered tender moments between them, when his father had held her hand or bent down to kiss her cheek. The loving look on his mother's face was an image he had never forgotten. So if his father had been unfaithful, did it matter? As far as David knew, it hadn't affected their marriage. It was morally wrong but it hadn't harmed anyone. What the eye doesn't see the heart doesn't grieve for, which was a cliché because it was true. He rolled over and closed his eyes. He knew one thing for sure: if his father had gone to such great lengths to avoid hurting Antoinette, then so would he.

The following morning they breakfasted early and were up at the top of the Gotschna by nine. The air was crisp and cold, the sky a bright, enthusiastic blue against which the mountain shone brightly. However, the mood between the three of them was sombre. Today they'd visit the place where George had died. The anticipation hung over them like a thundercloud.

Phaedra was nervous. Only her gloves prevented her from biting her nails. Apart from a couple of lame jokes in the cable car, Tom was very quiet. David masked his anxiety with efficiency, telling Phaedra the plan for the day and pointing out the famous Wang, which was one of the steepest slopes in Murenburg. 'With every turn you fall a few feet,' he explained. 'Beautiful in powder but also phenomenally dangerous.' Phaedra looked down at the wide avenue of burgeoning trees that cut through the forest below and realized that this was prime avalanche territory.

Once at the top, Tom smoked a quick cigarette as they clicked into their skis and surveyed the magnificent view of the valley and south-facing Madrisa mountain opposite, bathed in sunshine. Phaedra wore a pair of white trousers and a navy jacket that emphasized her small waist and feminine hips. She shivered, not from cold, and watched Tom throw his cigarette butt into the snow. They caught eyes and for the first time she could see the apprehension on his face. She smiled with empathy and Tom did his best to smile back. He looked like a boy and she wanted to rush up and wrap her arms around him. All of a sudden the gravity of what they were about to do hit them like a gust of cold wind. After that, they said nothing. David pushed off and Phaedra followed, her heart heavy with sorrow, for George must have skied this mountain a thousand times.

That first run together should have filled them with pleasure because they all skied fast and skilfully. David was impressed with Phaedra's ability as she carved her turns like a racer, nimbly shifting her weight from side to side, her skis slicing the snow with sharp whooshing sounds. She was elegant and powerful, but above all she was speedy, and the Framptons were well known for being fast. However, they were all too aware of their purpose to give way to the fun, and George's death remained at the forefront of their minds.

Tom took the T-bar alone, leaving David and Phaedra to go up together. 'He's quiet,' said Phaedra.

'Tom's an avoider but there's no avoiding Dad here.'

'It's hitting him, isn't it?'

'It was always going to hit him sooner or later.'

'Poor Tom,' she sighed sympathetically.

'He looks tough ...'

'No, he doesn't,' Phaedra interrupted.

'Resilient, then.'

'No, David, he looks like an avoider.'

'He's used to drowning his issues in alcohol. Now he's got nowhere to hide.'

'Which is healthier. He'll grieve, then let it go

212

and get on with his life. That's what we all have to do.'

David looked down at her. 'You ski well, Phaedra.'

She grinned up at him. 'So do you, David.'

'Where did you learn to ski like that?'

'I grew up in Vancouver, remember.'

'I don't know many women who can ski as fast as you.'

'I'll take that as a compliment, not as a chauvinistic comment.'

'I'm stating a fact, not being provocative. Most women I know aren't as brave as you. Are you as good off the piste as you are on it?'

'Sure.' She shrugged modestly. 'I'll take anything I'm given.'

'You're going to be tested. Dad died extreme skiing. It's what he loved to do, pushing the boundaries. He always skied like that and most of the time he got away with it. I think he was just unlucky.'

'We'll go carefully.'

'I doubt bad luck will strike twice.'

Phaedra shook her head. 'Never say never. I can be reckless, too, but George has made me rein myself in a little.'

'You've turned on your bleeper?' he asked, referring to the electronic device used to find one another in the event of an avalanche.

'Of course. Please tell me you know how to use it!'

David grew serious and looked up at the sharp peaks of the Weissfluhgipfel. 'I do. But let's hope I don't need to.'

They regrouped at the top of the Mahder lift

then set off to the Furka, from where they traversed into the Gaudergrat then clicked out of their skis to climb Alp Duranna for the rest of the morning. The sun grew hotter and Phaedra tied her jacket and helmet around her waist and climbed with her sweater rolled up to her elbows and the zip pulled down to expose her chest. The snow sparkled around her and the mountains rose into jagged peaks and sheer precipices.

At last they reached the top. They stuck their skis into the snow and sat down to share a bar of chocolate and David's hip flask of sloe gin. 'This is stunning,' Phaedra enthused, gazing at the sea of pale-blue peaks.

'We're on top of the world,' said David.

'It's an incredible feeling,' she continued. 'Like we're part of eternity. It makes me feel so small and yet so connected to everything.' She filled her lungs with a deep, luxurious breath.

'Dad would have sat here after his climb,' said David solemnly. 'He would have been looking forward to the descent. He would have been excited with all the new snow. I wonder whether he had looked out over those peaks as we're doing now and felt a connection with something bigger than himself? I never asked him what he felt about God.'

Tom took a deep breath and stared out at the vast expanse that seemed to have no end. Miles away, on the far horizon, the mountains melted into mist. Beyond was infinity. As he stared into it, he sensed something profound stir within him. For the first time in his life he became aware of the eternal current, and in some extraordinary way he felt part of it. He hadn't dared imagine where his

214

father was now. He hadn't wanted to face the fact that he had gone. Pretending everything was fine was the only form of self-defence he knew. But now, suddenly, his chest expanded with unexpressed emotion and he gasped in horror as it welled into his throat and on up until he let out a deep, shuddering groan. He had no control, as if a strange entity had taken possession of his body and he could only observe, powerless, as it raged through him, making him convulse and tremble.

David stared in horror as his brother's face contorted with pain and he struggled to breathe. Phaedra crawled across the snow and wrapped her arms around him. He yielded without hesitation, burying his face in her jacket. They all sat very still while Tom allowed his grief to pass through him.

'This is good,' Phaedra said once Tom had grown quiet. 'It will make you feel so much better. You can't hold it in forever. That's the very worst thing you can do. You have to acknowledge it, then release it. Pretending it isn't there will only make it stronger.'

Tom reached for his rucksack but David was quick to unzip it and delve inside for his brother's cigarettes. With shaking hands Tom popped one into his mouth and lit it with the lighter David held out for him. The first drag filled his lungs and he felt instantly calmed. 'I'm sorry,' he said at last. 'I don't know what came over me.'

'It's OK,' said David. 'Your reaction was just a little delayed, that's all.'

Tom gazed down the mountain to where his father had skied to his death. 'I miss him,' he said in a small voice. 'I miss him very much.'

'I know you do,' David replied. His eyes followed

his brother's and he, too, gazed down the mountainside. 'Somewhere down there is the avalanche.'

'Are you ready to face it, Tom?' Phaedra asked.

'I don't think I'll ever be ready,' he replied with a sigh, then took another long drag.

'But we have to,' Phaedra continued. 'None of us will be able to move on until we've paid our respects there.' She pushed herself up. 'Come on, boys. The longer we wait the harder it will be.'

Chapter 15

It had recently snowed and only a few tracks marred the perfection of the mountainside. Tom couldn't help but feel reinvigorated as he bounced through powder as light as goose down, and David discovered to his delight that Phaedra was as adept off the piste as on.

Phaedra felt the sun on her face and the wind against her chest where her sweater was still open, and her heart grew wistful at the beauty of it all, because there among the glittering crystals and undulating slopes was surely George, watching the people he loved in the place he had loved so deeply.

After a while and a few breaks to catch their breath, they stopped. Below, the slope disappeared into a very long and steep incline. At that moment the wind seemed to drop and Tom and David grew quiet. A few rogue clouds had blown in over the peak and now cast them in shadow. Phaedra sensed that they had arrived.

216

'Let's ski this one at a time,' said David. 'Keep to the right and don't stop. I'll go first.' As he launched himself over the lip and on down the slope, he could see to his left the remains of the avalanche that had taken half the mountainside with it. Knowing it was too risky to stop, he continued on until he reached the bottom. The avalanche had started right at the top, leaving a wide ridge about six feet high where the snow had simply broken away like a slice of wedding cake. It must have gathered momentum as it tumbled down, gaining speed and strength as it went, until it reached the bottom where the terrain flattened out into a little valley before falling once again. There it had heaped itself into a mound of big icy boulders, now covered in a thick layer of snow. It looked so innocuous, like a beast lying asleep beneath a white quilt. It was hard to imagine that it had once had the ferocity to sweep their father to his death.

Phaedra skied down second, trying not to look to her left in case she lost her balance and fell, thus putting herself in danger. So she skied on until she reached David, then stood beside him and gazed at the sight they had all come so far to see. Only the sound of her heart racing and her panting breath broke the silence that weighed so heavily upon them.

Tom arrived next. He clicked out of his skis and trudged through the deep snow to climb up onto the avalanche. He stood at the top and put his hands on his hips, looking up at the denuded slope, as if trying to work out how exactly it had managed to fell his seemingly indomitable father.

'Let's go and join him,' David suggested, clicking

217

out of his skis and spearing them into the ground. Phaedra followed, but when she stepped onto the snow she sank right up to her knees.

'Let me help you,' he offered, extending his hand. Phaedra took it and together they waded through.

'It's hard to believe that this killed Dad,' said Tom quietly when the others reached him on the mound. 'It doesn't look much, does it?'

'It doesn't *take* much,' David replied.

'It was meant to happen,' said Phaedra philosophically, feeling her throat tighten with all the things she never got the chance to tell George. 'I think when your time is up, it's up and there's no avoiding it. He died doing what he loved.'

'That's what Mum said,' David mused.

'Hard for us, but he just skied on up to Heaven.'

'You make it sound so easy, Phaedra,' said Tom.

'I think it *is* easy when you eventually leave the world.'

'No, I don't mean that. I mean easy to accept.'

'No, that's not at all easy. It's very hard to accept that he's gone and will no longer be a part of my life. However, I have no choice but to accept it. Fighting it won't bring him back, nor will it make me feel better; it'll just make me miserable and fill me with resentment. I'll end up hating life for taking him away from me. But you can't go about hitting your head against a brick wall. At some stage you have to realize that it's not going to change and your rage won't make any difference— you'll just get a sore head.'

'So, how do I accept it like you?' Tom asked.

'We say goodbye, Tom.'

Tom stared at her forlornly. 'How do I say

218

goodbye?'

Phaedra noticed his eyes were sparkling and his cheeks were coloured a ruddy red. Once again, he was a small boy in his desolation, and she reached across and took his hand. To her surprise David took her other one. She smiled at him gratefully then closed her eyes. 'We imagine him alive and well in a better place,' she said softly. 'We see him smiling, radiant and full of joy, and we wish him well with all our hearts. Then, when you're ready, you say goodbye any way you like, knowing that he'll always be around and that one day, when it's your time to go, he'll be waiting to welcome you home.'

The three of them stood together in the place where George had died, and said goodbye. The breeze swept across their faces, a bird cried high in the sky and the clouds moved away, allowing the sun to drench the mountain in light once more. When they opened their eyes the world looked the same and yet something had shifted within them. They felt different; had a sense of closure.

They skied on down the mountain, leaving the avalanche far behind them. Before, it had seemed disrespectful to enjoy themselves, but now they felt at liberty to do so. They came upon a village of wooden cowsheds and chalets shut up for the winter, nestled in the nape of the mountain, then skied on into the trees and down the Serneus meadows into the valley. The conditions couldn't have been better for off-piste skiing and they took their pleasure greedily.

When they returned home at the end of the day their bodies were tired and aching but they felt lighter in their hearts. 'I feel like a sauna and a swim,' said David, sitting on the wooden bench and unclipping his boots.

'Good idea,' Tom agreed.

'Where do we go for that treat?' Phaedra asked David.

'To the basement,' he replied nonchalantly.

Phaedra looked surprised. 'You have a pool, in here?'

'Of course.'

'No, *I* have a pool in here,' Tom corrected. 'Remember, Dad left this place to me.'

'So we have to butter you up now for the rest of our lives if we want to enjoy it?' David laughed.

'Naturally.' Tom padded down the corridor from the boot room to the kitchen. 'Is it too early for a glass of wine?'

'After the day we've had, I'd say a glass of wine is essential,' said Phaedra. David frowned apprehensively and watched Tom disappear into the kitchen.

Phaedra found a navy-blue dressing gown on the back of her bedroom door. She stripped off her clothes and shrugged it on. David led her down a flight of narrow stairs to the basement. It was warm in the belly of the chalet and smelt of a mixture of chlorine and pine. They continued along a sandy-coloured tunnel, over long rugs Antoinette had thrown down to soften the ground for bare feet, until one wall soon became large glass windows through which they could see the swimming pool. It was luxurious and inviting, as were the teak loungers placed in a row of six, upholstered in navy and white stripes. The electric light reflected off the water and threw zany displays across the walls and ceiling. The limestone

220

floor was heated from beneath.

David led her into the pool area and on into the changing rooms. A cartoon hippo in a 1920s swimming costume was displayed on the boys' changing-room door, while a girl hippo in a pink bikini appeared on the girls'. 'Steam or sauna?' he asked.

'Steam, if I have a choice.'

'You most certainly do.' And he opened the door to switch it on.

Phaedra went into the changing room, where she found white towels stacked in a neat pile and bathing suits hanging on hooks. Displayed in a row behind the two basins were a whole range of Clarins body products. It was like a spa. Phaedra couldn't imagine why Antoinette didn't like it here. If *she* hadn't been a skier, she'd be perfectly content beautifying herself in this underground paradise. She slipped out of her dressing gown and chose a pretty blue-and-white bathing suit. Then she wrapped herself in a towel and went to join David in the steam room.

He sat on the top shelf, a towel around his waist, as the steam began to billow about him in a hot mist. Phaedra climbed up to join him, choosing the adjacent wall so she could face him. 'This is wonderful,' she said with a sigh, leaning back against the stone. 'Just what the doctor ordered.'

'It's a great way of loosening up after all that exercise,' said David.

'It smells of eucalyptus.'

'Good for clearing the airways.'

Phaedra laughed. 'Did you put that in?'

'Oh yes, I like my aromatherapy,' he said in a tone heavy with sarcasm.

221

'Then who does?'

'I don't know. Probably one of Tom's girlfriends. He's always bringing them here.'

'Then I've got one of his girlfriends' bathing suits on.'

'No, they don't belong to anyone. Mum bought some for the chalet. She thought of everything.'

'She certainly did. It's like a five-star hotel.'

'I'm glad you like it.'

'Oh, I love it, David. It's beautiful. It's going to be difficult leaving it tomorrow to go skiing, knowing the joys down here!'

They both began to feel hot and sleepy. The little room filled with steam so that they could only just make each other out. 'How long do we have to stay in here?'

'About fifteen minutes will do.'

'How long has it been?'

'About eight.'

'Good Lord, I'm not sure I'll survive another seven minutes.'

'Just think of the good it's doing you.'

'I'll try not to pass out.'

'I'll keep an eye on you.'

She laughed. 'Thank you.'

But David was serious. Keeping an eye on Phaedra was the easiest thing in the world. He watched her close her eyes and lean her head back. She had a lovely smooth neck, he thought, running his gaze down her collarbone and chest. Thick, milky skin and long, slim limbs. He shuffled, trying to subdue the aching in his loins. The more time he spent with her the harder it was for him to fight his increasing ardour. He had never felt like this about any woman in his life. It wasn't simply the fact that he couldn't have her that rendered her so desirable. She had qualities he had never found in anyone else, qualities he admired.

David had been touched by the way she had comforted Tom on the mountain and how she had chosen to find the best in his famously difficult grandmother. Phaedra was a *good* person. He allowed his mind to wander because he didn't have the strength to rein it in. She'd make a gentle mother, he thought indulgently, remembering the tender way she had taken Amber into her arms and kissed her. She'd make a sensual lover, he guessed, releasing his mind to wander across the most forbidden territory. He didn't believe there was another woman on earth who'd make such a perfect wife. He pulled back, his daydream suddenly causing him more pain than pleasure. He couldn't have her. A drop of sweat ran over his temple. There was no way he could possibly have her.

'Time's up,' he said.

Phaedra opened her eyes. 'Thank the Lord!' She climbed down.

David followed after. 'I'm going to jump straight into the pool.'

'Me too! It'll sizzle when I put my hot body into it!' She watched David drop his towel by the side of the pool and dive in. He had a strong, athletic physique, the body of a man who's constantly on the move, lifting, sweeping, heaping and carrying. His shoulders were wide and muscular, his waist lean, his legs long and strong. His farmer's life ensured that he was at the peak of fitness.

He swam a few strokes of front crawl and then swivelled round to face her. When he caught her watching him, he grinned. Phaedra felt the blood rush to her already scarlet face. It was no use trying to pretend they didn't fancy each other. The attraction was as strong as summer sunshine. A kiss might defuse the tension, but a kiss could never be. The tension would continue to mount, and then what?

'You can't stand there all evening,' David laughed when he reached the edge. 'You need to cool down.' He was right about that, Phaedra thought. She noticed the rich olive colour of his skin and couldn't help but imagine her pale body lying next to it, as white as a lily.

'All right. Go swim another length,' she demanded. He smiled mischievously and swam off. Phaedra dived in. The water was cold against her burning skin. She could almost feel herself hiss like a boiling hot pan in the sink. It felt good to wet her hair and wash off the sweat. She trod water, aware of every move David made. He had the ability to make a big room feel small just by being in it.

David swam back towards her. 'Bet that feels good?' he said.

'It sure does.'

She laughed nervously as she felt the pull of a magnet beneath the water, drawing her towards him. He laughed with her, but he really wanted to press her up against the side of the pool and kiss her. He could see her body beneath the water. He tried to keep his eyes trained on her face.

'I think I'll get out now,' she said suddenly.

'You've only just got in.'

'Which is a great achievement. But now I want to get out and take a bath.'

'I'm going to swim a few more lengths.' She

watched him go then swam to the steps. She glanced up the pool to make sure he was still swimming, then climbed out and hurried across to her towel. David leant back against the far wall and watched her walk back into the changing area. He wondered how on earth this was going to resolve itself and wished with all his heart that it was a Hollywood movie with a happy ending. But how could it end, other than in disappointment and frustration? He recoiled at the thought of incest, and yet he'd sacrifice everything to have her. He was doing his best, but it was useless trying to think of her as his sister. His *half*-sister, even. He felt no fraternal instinct whatsoever.

That evening they dined at the Wynegg, a small alpine restaurant in the heart of the village, and played cards until late with a few friends who were dining in one of the wooden alcoves at the back. David ordered a large jug of Fendant, the local wine, but most of it was consumed by Tom, who had already drunk half a bottle of Burgundy before they left the chalet. Once again Phaedra was introduced as a family friend and once again it was assumed that she was David's new girlfriend. Neither attempted to correct this, and Tom was too inebriated to notice. When at last they drove home, Tom went very quiet, sitting on the back seat, staring out of the window at the stars as if they were moving across the sky in a hypnotic dance.

They arrived back home and helped Tom out of the car. 'I think I drank too much,' he slurred as they frogmarched him into the chalet.

'You sure did,' said David.

'I might have a cigarette.'

225

'No time for that. Let's get you up to bed.'

He resisted weakly before allowing them to half carry him up the stairs and into his bedroom. Phaedra took off his shoes and helped him out of his sweater and shirt, then she left David to do the rest.

When he came downstairs David found Phaedra wrapped in her coat, sitting out on the balcony on one of the teak loungers used for sunbathing in the summer. 'At times like these I'd like to smoke,' she said as he stepped out to join her. 'It would be nice to sit here in the cold with a cigarette.'

'How about a mug of hot chocolate?'

'That'll do.'

'Leave it to me.' And he withdrew back inside.

Phaedra was left alone with her thoughts. She loved the mountains and the silence. Surrounded by such magnificence it was hard not to think about the big questions. In the face of such beauty it was hard not to feel romantic. When life was reduced to its essence love was the only thing that remained.

David returned a few minutes later with two steaming mugs of hot chocolate. He handed one to Phaedra then sat down beside her on the other wooden lounger. She took a sip. 'Mmm, that's good. What have you put in it?'

'A little fortification,' he replied, grinning playfully.

'Is that another Swiss tradition?'

'A *Frampton* tradition.'

She hugged the mug and took another sip, feeling the chocolate burn its way down to her stomach. 'I highly approve of it.'

'I thought you would.'

226

'I liked dinner tonight, though I'm sure I'll be sweating garlic out of every pore for the next week.'

'At least we all ate garlic.'

'So we can kiss each other,' she said with a laugh.

David looked across at her through the darkness. Her hair was pulled off her face and the fur collar of her coat drawn up to her chin. Her skin looked milky in the moonlight, her lips as red as holly berries, her blue eyes as pale as moonstones—she was more beautiful tonight than he had ever seen her, and he longed to kiss her with every aching muscle in his body. 'Tell me about your ex-husband, Phaedra,' he asked in order to distract himself.

'Well, I was very young, just twenty. He was called Shane Connelly, Irish of course, with an English mother. Did you know that Connelly means as fierce as a hound in Gaelic? Well, that was what he told me and he was, well, fierce, from time to time. We met in Whistler. He came out to ski with a group of friends and we fell in love. It all happened very quickly. He was much older than me and very together. I was rather chaotic. Well, I still am, really.'

'You don't look at all chaotic.'

'I hide it well. In truth, I'm very forgetful and disorganized.'

'You remembered everything today.'

She laughed. 'That's because I took the trouble of laying everything out on my chair last night so that I wouldn't forget anything! It would be typical of me to reach the top of the mountain with only one glove. I wanted to give you a good impression.'

'You certainly did that. So, what happened?'

227

David was curious to know about her past, even though the thought of her and Shane Connelly filled him with jealousy.

'He worked in Geneva for Franck Muller, you know, the watch designer. He was crazy about watches. Unfortunately, I didn't pick up on the signals. He was a good skier and very handsome; it didn't occur to me that we had nothing in common, or that his obsessive nature would destroy us in the end.'

'In what ways was he obsessive?'

'Everything had to be immaculate. He'd get angry when I forgot things. He could be very cruel and he was very possessive. He didn't let me have male friends; he got mad when another man chatted me up.'

'I hate this Shane Connelly!' he exclaimed with passion.

Phaedra laughed. 'You're too wonderful, David. I love you for your support.'

'You have no idea,' he said, gazing at her affectionately. 'How long were you married?'

'Five years.'

'Was it he who broke your heart?'

She sighed heavily and looked up at the lights of the Gotschna lift station that twinkled on the mountain pinnacle like big stars. 'No. I broke his. I had loved a mirage. Once I realized that, I knew that I hadn't been in love at all. It had just been wish-fulfilment. My love disappeared like mist in sunshine and there was nothing left but disappointment. I walked away.'

'To Paris?'

'Yes, I went to work in Paris. Your father wanted me to move to London.' She dropped her gaze into

228

her mug and sighed. 'I don't think he'd thought it through. He was very impulsive ...'

They sat in silence for a long moment. David felt her awkwardness, as if the air between them had somehow knotted. Just then, the whooshing sound of the red train could be heard sweeping up the valley. A moment later it whistled and they watched the little square window lights as it snaked on into the village, disappearing behind the chalets.

'Phaedra,' he said softly. 'I know the truth about Dad.'

She stared at him, stunned. The pink hue on her cheeks drained away, leaving an ashen pallor. 'You do?'

'It's OK. I understand why you lied.' She looked horrified, as if she were staring down the barrel of a gun.

'Let me explain. It's such a long story ...'

David interrupted. 'I know you did it to protect Dad.'

'Oh my God!' she gasped.

'And to protect Mum, too, because it would break her heart if she knew that Dad had been unfaithful.'

'I'm so sorry.' She put her hand over her mouth to stifle a cry.

'It's OK, Phaedra.'

'I didn't know. I swear I didn't know.'

'Look, I don't think the worse of you. In fact, you've been very tactful.' She was so upset, he wished he hadn't mentioned it. 'You know, you don't look thirty-two.'

'What?'

'Well, it makes sense now. You're younger than

229

me. So Dad had a relationship with your mother when he was married to mine. It doesn't matter. It makes no difference.' She stopped crying and gazed at him, frowning. 'I thought about it long and hard and I wasn't going to let on that I know. But I can't go on pretending I don't know the truth. I can't lie to you, Phaedra.'

'How did you find out?'

'I saw your passport at the airport.'

In a sudden flurry of relief, she threw herself at him. David had not expected her reaction to be so extreme. 'Oh, thank you, David,' she gasped. 'Thank you for your forgiveness.'

He wrapped his arms around her and felt her clutch the sides of his coat as if her life depended on him. 'Of course I forgive you,' he laughed incredulously.

'I'm so sorry.'

'Don't be silly, it's not your fault. And it happened a long time ago. But listen, it must be our secret. We must never tell anyone else, do you understand? It would break Mother's heart if she were to ever find out.'

'Yes.'

'Then that's settled. We'll speak no more about it.'

But Phaedra didn't pull away and David didn't want her to.

Chapter 16

That night when she went to bed, Phaedra received a text from Julius asking how it was all going and suggesting a date for dinner once she was back. She read it with a rising feeling of resentment. It was Julius who had got her into this mess and now she couldn't get out of it. As George's lawyer he should have counselled him against changing his will so rashly. If she hadn't been mentioned she could have simply disappeared and no one would have known she had lied. She didn't want George's money or the Frampton Sapphires. If George had been so determined for her to have them, why didn't he simply give them to her? Why did he have to change his will? Surely he could have anticipated the problems that would create. She had been put in a very awkward position. And to add fuel to the fire, she was falling in love with David.

She lay awake, her head throbbing with unmanageable thoughts. Julius and George were tossed about in her mind like stones in a concrete mixer. But right at the very centre of it all was David. She had never anticipated falling in love with George's son. The idea was inconceivable and wrong. She couldn't have him, not ever—if her heart ached with regret she had only herself to blame.

The following morning it was snowing. Big fluffy flakes like balls of cotton wool fell outside her window, and only the blurred outline of the fir tree could be distinguished through the fog. It was quiet and still and she lay a while, watching the ballet of dancing snow, wishing that David was beside her, holding her close. Once again she thought of George and wondered what he'd think of her growing infatuation for his son.

Tom was too hungover to ski, so David and Phaedra set off on their own. Barely anyone was at the Gotschna. As usual, only the British were foolhardy enough to want to spend the day in a blizzard. But David took her skiing in the trees where the visibility was better. The snow had fallen sufficiently in the night for a thick layer to have formed on top of yesterday's tracks, so they had a morning of flawless white glades and undulating meadows all the way down to the village of Saas.

By lunchtime white beams of sunshine were breaking through the cloud, causing the last fragile snowflakes to sparkle like tinsel. They lunched at the top of the Weissfluhjoch, the highest point in Murenburg, and gazed over the panorama of serrated peaks emerging out of the evaporating fog. They were aware that their time together in Murenburg was short and a melancholy feeling fell upon them like the patches of mist the sun failed to reach. As David sipped his coffee and Phaedra her hot chocolate, they both sensed their mutual attraction as animals do, wordlessly, instinctively— and both knew it was too horrendous to speak of.

Phaedra loved skiing with David. Being alone together in the mountains had a romance beyond anything else. They chased each other at high speed down the pistes and dodged the fir trees in light powder. They stood together watching a small group of chamois in a glade nuzzling the snow for grass. The mountains were silent and magnificent and they both felt a sense of awe and privilege that they were there, on such a glorious day, amidst such beauty.

Neither wanted the day to end. They had come out for George, but had found each other. It was a discovery that left them both frustrated and confounded.

When they returned to the chalet they found Tom still in his pyjamas, watching a DVD. There was an empty bottle of wine on the table beside the armchair and a half-eaten plate of bundnerfleisch, the local air-dried beef. David caught Phaedra's eye. He shrugged in defeat. 'I suppose it was inevitable, considering the circumstances,' he whispered to her.

'Let me go talk to him.'

'Do you feel like a steam?'

'I'll meet you down there.'

'Don't be too long or I'll overcook.'

Phaedra padded up to the armchair. Tom was slumped in a daze, watching *The Sopranos*. She took the bottle, which alerted him to the fact that he wasn't alone. 'Oh, hi,' he said, grinning up at her. 'Good day?'

'A perfect day,' she replied. 'But we missed you.'

'I wasn't in any state to ski this morning.'

'What time did you get up?'

'I don't know. About midday.'

'Have you eaten?' She picked up the plate of bundnerfleisch. 'This isn't enough for a growing boy.'

'I had some bread too.'

'Good, but you should have eaten properly, you know. How about we all eat in tonight and I cook?'

'David says you cook a mean pasta.'

'I do. It's so mean, it's wicked.'

'You're on.'

'Come down and have a steam with us.' She smiled at him kindly. 'You might sweat out some of that alcohol.'

'I haven't had much, just a drop,' he replied quickly.

'It always starts with a drop.' His face clouded and she knew he was about to get defensive. 'My mother is an alcoholic,' she added and watched his guilt turn to interest.

'Really?'

'Yes. She's been in denial for years.'

'Why?'

'Because life has disappointed her at every turn. Everyone has their own reason and they're all good—but you have to somehow find the strength to rise above your sense of inadequacy or fear.' He pursed his lips and let his gaze wander over the rug at his feet. Phaedra continued. 'I grew up without siblings, but you know what? I'm really enjoying having brothers. I missed out. It's fun having people to care about. I care about you, Tom. The thing is, I couldn't help my mother. She didn't listen and her problems ran too deep. We never really connected. I always felt I was an alien who somehow fell into her lap at birth. We've always been strangers. But I feel I connect with you. I understand that this is a difficult time and the easiest way to deal with it is to avoid the pain by dulling it with alcohol. You feel much better when you've had something to drink. We all do. But that's just cutting corners. You'll never be satisfied unless you go the long way around.'

'I hear you,' he said. He gazed out of the

window. 'You know, Dad was this great hero, climbing the insurmountable, trekking to remote places, one with nature.' He chuckled resentfully. 'Everyone loved Dad. But he wasn't there for *us*. Mum won't agree with me, of course, because she worshipped him without question, like a sweet dog. But it's true. He was never around for sports day or weekends out from school. I don't think Joshua and David minded so much. I did. I wanted him to take an interest in me, but he was more interested in himself.' He sighed, as if a great burden had fallen off his shoulders. 'I shouldn't have said that. I feel bad exploding the myth.'

She reached out and touched his arm. 'That's OK. You're entitled to your point of view. But Tom, you can't carry this bitterness around with you. You have to let it go. The past doesn't exist any more, it's only thought. It's your story but it's not who you are now.'

He looked at her, his eyes glassy, and smiled. 'You sound like a self-help book!'

She laughed. 'I've read a few.'

'I can tell.'

'Come and have a steam, then we'll have dinner by the fire. We can all watch *The Sopranos* together. There's nothing better than a good American drama.'

He sighed and switched off the television. 'OK, I'll come and sweat it out. I like having you around, Phaedra,' he said, getting up. 'There's something about you that makes me feel better about myself.'

'I hate to see someone I care about pressing the self-destruct button.'

'It also helps talking to someone outside the

235

family. Well, you *are* family, of course, but you know what I mean.'

'I certainly do.'

'I don't feel so ashamed talking to you about Dad.'

'You shouldn't feel ashamed at all, Tom. We all have our battles: even those who don't seem to have any, have a few. We're all finding our way in the dark.' She grinned affectionately.

With that, he threw back his head and laughed. 'Come on, then, Wise One. To the steam room. Where's David?'

'Already cooking.'

'Does he know we have a guru in the family?'

She grinned at him bashfully. 'I don't know. Perhaps you should tell him.'

'No, I think I'm going to keep you as my *secret* guru.'

'That's perfectly fine.'

'You're going to help me, right?'

'If you like.'

'Only because you're a pretty guru. If you were a big hairy *man*-guru I'd decline. But you're pretty and wise, so yes please, share your wisdom and make me a better man.'

That night they sat around the fire playing cards. Phaedra had cooked pasta with George's favourite tomato sauce. The boys had eaten two helpings each and Tom had resorted to scraping the bottom of the pan with a spatula. None of them consumed wine and Tom didn't ask for any. He had sweated out so much alcohol in the steam room, he had promised himself he would never drink another drop. With Phaedra's support he was convinced he could do it.

236

The whistle of the train echoed across the valley and David caught Phaedra's eye. She blushed as she recalled their conversation the night before. He didn't look away and the longing in his gaze touched her deeply, because she felt it too. For a long moment they stared at each other, wordlessly confessing their desire, until Phaedra found the strength to avert her eyes.

She could accept George's death and she could accept that she now had to get on with her life. But she couldn't bear the thought of accepting that David was a man she could never love. George had put him forever out of her reach.

*   *   *

Back at Fairfield Antoinette and Rosamunde returned home after a couple of days in London, shopping for spring clothes. They had enjoyed lunch with friends at Lucio's on the Fulham Road, and trawled the racks in Harvey Nichols and Harrods until their legs grew so tired they had to stop for a cup of Earl Grey in the Harrods tea room. Rosamunde wasn't very interested in fashion, but the thought of bumping into Dr Heyworth inspired her to buy a new blouse in a pretty floral pattern and a pair of slacks to match. Antoinette had no one to dress for, but she returned home with a boot full of carrier bags and felt infinitely better for them.

'We should do that more often,' she said to Rosamunde as they sipped cups of tea in the drawing room. 'I feel rejuvenated.'

'So do I,' Rosamunde agreed. 'Frightfully extravagant buying that silk blouse, but I'm rather looking forward to wearing it. Silk isn't a fabric I'd usually buy.'

'One never regrets what one does, only what one doesn't do. Do you think that applies to shopping?'

'I think so.'

'I'm going to start spending more time in town,' Antoinette declared. 'I can't mope about here all day, and it's good to leave home every now and then, it makes one appreciate it so much more.' She smiled, pausing her little teacup before her lips. 'Maybe Phaedra and I can have lunch. Do you think she might accept an invitation from me?'

'I don't see why not. She made it very clear that she likes you.'

'It would be nice, don't you think? Perhaps we could nip into Peter Jones and she could advise me on make-up. She's jolly pretty.'

'You look fine just the way you are.' Rosamunde thought a little rouge was all a woman needed to enhance her looks.

'She might advise me on my hair.'

'What's wrong with your hair?'

'Oh, nothing's wrong. I'm just rather bored with it, that's all.'

'You've had it like that for thirty years, why change it now?'

'I don't know. I'm just being silly, really.' She put down her cup and sat back into the sofa. 'George is gone, my life has taken an unexpected turn. I feel I want to change with it.'

'And change is good. But I like your hair. It's you,' Rosamunde insisted.

'But who am I?'

'What do you mean, who are you? You're

238

Antoinette Frampton.' Rosamunde looked confused.

'Yes, I'm Antoinette Frampton. I've been Antoinette Frampton for over thirty years. But who is Antoinette?'

Now Rosamunde looked worried. 'I'm not sure what you mean. Do you think Harris could dig out some of Mrs Gunice's shortbread biscuits?'

'Of course.' Antoinette got up and pulled a tasselled cord to the right of the fireplace. A moment later Harris appeared in the doorway. 'Ah, Harris, would you bring us some of Mrs Gunice's shortbreads?'

'Certainly, Lady Frampton,' he replied.

Rosamunde smiled in anticipation. 'They really are delish!' she enthused.

'What were we talking about?' Antoinette asked.

'You were looking for Antoinette,' Rosamunde replied ironically.

'Yes, Phaedra got me thinking. I've been a wife and mother for so long I've lost myself along the way. I know it sounds silly, but I'm a people-pleaser. I always have been. I've always sacrificed my own desires to put George first. Now he's not here, it's like the scaffolding's come down and I'm left with nothing but me. What do *I* want? I'm not sure I know.'

'I think you do.'

'No, Rosamunde, you don't understand. I really don't. I wake up in the morning and I don't know what to do with myself. I don't know what the day is going to hold. When George was alive, I knew where I stood. I could plan. Now I have no structure. No one to tell me when we're having dinner, or when we're going to the ballet, or when

I'm expected to be in London for a cocktail party. I'm not filling the house with his friends at weekends, or taking his suits to the cleaners. I'm free, but my freedom makes me feel lost. Do you see?'

'Yes, I think I do.'

'I can't drift forever.'

'You'll sort yourself out.'

'I've got to do something constructive.'

'Like what?'

'Exactly.' Antoinette looked defeated. 'Like what?'

At that moment Harris entered with a tray of shortbread biscuits. He bent down and offered them to Rosamunde first, for he had noticed the way she had polished off the lot during the meeting with Julius Beecher. Rosamunde took a bite. The sweet, buttery taste melted on her tongue and she let out a little moan. 'Oh, these really are terribly good. Thank you, Harris. You can leave the plate here.' He put it down on the coffee table and left the room.

Rosamunde's shoulders dropped and she no longer felt so tense. Antoinette was simply reacting in the way all recently widowed women react when suddenly faced with an uncertain future. 'Why don't you learn to play bridge?'

'Gracious, no. George tried to teach me to play bridge but I never got it. I don't like it, either.'

'You could get involved in charity.'

'I already support charities, but if you mean sitting on committees, think again. I'm not suited to it. I'm too reserved. Charities are full of women like Margaret.'

'I do see.' Rosamunde reached for another

240

biscuit. 'They need dynamic, formidable women to doggedly raise funds. You are very well connected, though.'

'I'd rather give discreetly and not pester my friends.' Antoinette smiled wistfully. 'When I was young, I wanted to have a boutique.'

'My dear, you can't be a shopkeeper. You're a lady.'

'Isn't it every little girl's dream to have a shop?'

'You're no longer a little girl. And yes, it's an old cliché.' Rosamunde laughed. 'What would you sell in your shop?'

'I don't know. It's just fantasy.'

'You could get involved in the church.'

'Margaret is already there. I could redecorate the house,' she suggested, brightening.

'That would send Margaret to an early grave, wouldn't it?'

'A house is for living in. It's not a museum.'

'Try telling that to your mother-in-law.'

Antoinette shrugged helplessly. 'Then I don't know what to do with myself.'

'Give it time,' said Rosamunde. 'And have a biscuit. They're marvellous.'

The following day, Rosamunde returned home to Dorset to see her dogs. Antoinette put on her boots and coat and took Bertie and Wooster out into the garden. The days were longer now, the sunshine warm upon her face and so bright she needed to wear sunglasses. The light uplifted her and she inhaled the sweet scent of regeneration that rose up from the compost in the herbaceous border along with awakening shrubs and emerging bulbs. Puddles of blue windflowers glistened beneath the chestnut trees and daffodils lifted

241

their yellow skirts to the sun. Blue tits flew in and out of the bushes and the trees were ringing with birdsong. The earth was reawakening and she hadn't even noticed.

She found Barry pottering around the borders. 'Good morning, Lady Frampton,' he said. Beneath his cap, his head was a mass of tight white curls, like a sheep.

'Barry, I'm sorry I've been very disinterested in the garden lately . . .'

'That's understandable, Lady Frampton.'

'I know, but the garden is a healing place. It will do me good to spend more time in it.' She smiled at the unassuming man who had looked after the grounds for as long as she had lived at Fairfield, and felt a sudden impulse to get her hands dirty as she had in the early days when she'd been young and full of enthusiasm. 'Let's walk around and you can show me what you're doing. Now spring is here I'd like to be involved.'

'Very good, ma'am,' he replied jovially, unable to conceal his delight. 'Well, let's start in the walled garden, then. You won't be wanting for greens this summer. Oh no, I'm planning a bumper harvest.' And he accompanied her across the grounds to the vegetable garden, contained within an ancient red-brick wall. The weatherbeaten oak gate opened with a groan and they stepped beneath the archway into a low maze of neatly trimmed plots and gravel pathways bordered with lavender or box. In the centre was a circular stone shelter to sit in and admire the garden, but Antoinette had never had time for that. It looked peaceful and tempting in the sunshine.

Barry proudly showed her around each section,

pointing to the first signs of emerging asparagus and artichoke, the neatly planted rows of beetroots, carrots and beans and the heaped mounds where the potatoes would appear before long. There were iron frames arching over the pathways where sweet peas would bloom, later scrambling up the climbing roses and clematis. 'I know deep purple is your favourite sweet pea,' he told her with a grin. 'I'll make sure we have plenty of them this summer.'

As Barry chatted on, Antoinette's enthusiasm began to grow. When George was alive she had been so busy in the house she hadn't had the time to take much of an interest in the gardens. Barry, with the help of his small band of local lads, kept the estate looking beautiful and visitors had always admired the immaculate borders and potted plants, but Antoinette had never presumed to take credit for any of it. Barry had been head gardener for over forty years and knew better than anyone how best to look after the gardens.

When she'd moved in as the young Mrs George Frampton the gardens had been the only part of Fairfield she'd been able to affect. She'd taken such pleasure in planting with Barry. They'd gone to the garden centre together and bought hundreds of tulips, then spent an entire week pressing them into the ground either side of the lime walk. When they'd shot up that first spring she felt she'd performed a miracle. It looked like the parting of the Red Sea. She smiled now at the memory. How quickly her life had changed. The children had arrived, George had grown more demanding and somehow the gardens had been forgotten, along with that almost divine sense of joy.

'Let's go to the garden centre, Barry,' she said, riding the sudden wave of excitement.

'Right now?'

'Yes. No time to lose.'

'What do you want to buy?'

'I don't know. Anything, everything, whatever catches my eye.'

'Very good.'

'Oh, do you remember the fun we had, Barry?'

'I do, indeed, ma'am.'

'I want to do it again. I want to get my hands dirty and watch things grow.' She laughed at the sight of his bewildered face. 'I must sound very silly, Barry. I'm not a young woman any more. But I think the gardens are going to make me feel very happy.'

'Oh, they'll do that all right,' he replied.

'I'm not treading on your toes, am I?' she asked, at once apprehensive. 'I don't want you to think I'm going to take over.'

He chuckled. 'Treading on my toes, Lady Frampton? Why, I've waited years for you to come home,' he added softly.

Chapter 17

The following day Rosamunde returned to Fairfield to find her sister on her knees in the orchard, planting new fruit trees. It had taken a full fifteen minutes to find her, shouting at the top of her lungs until the dogs had rushed out through the hedge and barked as if she were an intruder.

244

'Good gracious, Antoinette! What on earth are you doing?' Rosamunde exclaimed when she saw her muddy knees and ruddy cheeks.

'I'm planting,' Antoinette replied proudly. 'Barry and I went off to the garden centre, not the small one in Fairfield, but the really big one at Bristlemere. They had to deliver because we bought too much to fit into the car. Look at this darling peach tree. Can you imagine, Rosamunde, we're going to have peaches!'

'Does Barry need an extra pair of hands? I thought he had an army of young men to help him!'

Antoinette laughed. 'I *want* to do it, silly.'

'Look at the state of you! You're covered in mud.'

Antoinette grinned up at her. 'You should see your face.'

'I'm just surprised, that's all.'

'I haven't had so much fun in years!' She picked up the young tree and pulled it gently out of its pot. 'In it goes.' Rosamunde watched as she loosened the roots then placed it carefully in the hole she had dug. 'There, a nice new home for you, Mr Peach Tree.' She sat back on her haunches and wiped her brow with the back of her hand, smearing a streak of mud across her skin. 'Do you remember, when we were children, planting pots of hyacinths with Mother?'

'Of course. I love hyacinths.'

'And you'd always dig up the garden and come in top-to-toe in mud.'

'Yes, and you were always very prissy and clean, if I remember rightly.'

'Well, I think you had more fun than I did.'

245

'Most certainly. Children love playing in mud.'

'So, I'm making up for lost time. Barry's gone off to fetch another one. They're all lined up at the back of the house. Ten of them.'

'All peaches?'

'No, we have two plums, two apples, two pears, two cherries and of course two peaches.'

'If it wasn't for my stiff hip I'd get down on my knees and help you.'

'I know you would. But you can talk to me instead and keep me company. Isn't it a glorious day? Listen to the birds. Why is it that I can hear them in the trees but I can't see them? Have you ever wondered why? Listen! The branches are alive with them, *hundreds* of them, yet can you spot a single bird?'

Rosamunde laughed, because it was so uplifting to see her sister happy again. 'Perhaps Barry can bring me a chair when he comes back.'

'Yes, one of the garden chairs, it's about time they came out again and shook off the winter cobwebs. By the way, guess who's coming for dinner tonight?'

'Margaret.'

'No, not Margaret, though I dare say we'll be seeing her sometime today.' She grinned up at Rosamunde. 'You can wear your new blouse and trousers.'

Rosamunde's face lit up. 'Oh, Dr Heyworth.'

'Yes, I thought it would be nice to see him and thank him for harbouring me in his garden not once but twice, when I was hiding from Margaret.'

'Quite right, he's a knight in shining armour.'

'I thought you'd be pleased.'

'I'm just enjoying a mild flirtation. Really, it's

246

nothing more than that.'

'Are you sure you're telling the truth? It's me you're talking to, remember.'

'Good gracious, I'm too old for anything more—and set in my ways, too. But a little flirting is good for one's morale.'

Antoinette began to fill the hole with a mixture of earth and compost. 'It's been over thirty years since I last enjoyed a flirtation. I wouldn't know how to do it.'

'Isn't it like riding a bicycle?'

'I'm not sure I could do that, either.' She flattened the earth with her hands. 'I can't imagine ever being with anyone but George.'

'You're still young.'

'Widow is a horrid word, I think.'

'You don't have to remain single for the rest of your life.'

Antoinette stood up and stretched her legs. 'Look at me, Rosamunde. I'm not fit for anyone.'

'Well, not with a splodge of mud on your face.'

'And I'm not sure I'll ever *want* anyone.'

'Oh, that may change in the years to come.'

'No, Rosamunde,' Antoinette insisted firmly. 'I'll always belong to George.'

By the end of the day Antoinette had successfully planted all ten fruit trees. Barry had dug the holes and she had done the rest. Rosamunde had sat on a garden chair and kept her sister company, while the sun moved slowly above them in a cloudless sky and Bertie and Wooster slept lazily at her feet.

Antoinette bathed and changed for dinner. She felt lighter in her heart and she hummed as she moved about the bedroom, choosing her clothes

247

and drying her hair. The garden had restored her spirit and given her cheeks a healthy radiance. Gone was the grey pallor in her skin and her eyes sparkled with happiness—she never thought she'd feel happy ever again. She had assumed George had taken it with him; after all, hadn't her happiness been tied into his?

Today she had tasted freedom—freedom from cares, from schedules, from plans and commitments. Today she had ambled about the gardens, savouring the wind that stirred her hair and brushed her face with gentle fingers, the delightful clamour of birds and the warm sunshine that was so full of love it penetrated her disconsolate heart and filled it up until it was ready to burst. Nature had restored her faith in her own abilities. Today she realized she'd manage on her own after all.

Antoinette went downstairs to find Rosamunde already in the drawing room sitting in one of the armchairs, doing her needlepoint. She was wearing her new slacks and floral silk blouse tied at the neck in a loose bow. 'You look lovely,' said Antoinette.

'And you look a lot better without that muddy smear across your face.'

Antoinette smiled broadly. 'I had such a nice day today. Really, it was a *perfect* day.'

'And no sight of Margaret. Very unusual not to get a visit.'

'I hope she's all right.'

'Of course she's all right.'

'It's just rather strange not to see her. She tends to come up daily. And she did have that strange turn the other day.'

'Do you want to call her?'

Antoinette brushed her worries aside. 'No, I'll call her tomorrow. Dr Heyworth will be here any minute.'

Harris appeared in the doorway. 'Can I get you a drink, Lady Frampton?'

'Yes, that would be very nice. I'll have a vodka tonic, thank you.'

'A vodka tonic?' Rosamunde repeated in surprise.

'I'm living dangerously,' Antoinette replied.

'You certainly are. Well, if you're going to have one, then so will I.' Harris walked across the room to the drinks table. George had always insisted it should be well stocked, with all the spirits in pretty crystal decanters, each clearly labelled with a little chained dog tag. 'It's been years since I had a cocktail.'

'I never liked vodka,' said Antoinette.

'Then why are you having some now?'

'Because I'm a new person, Rosamunde.'

By the time Dr Heyworth arrived, both women were halfway through their cocktails. Harris opened the door and showed the doctor into the hall, taking his coat and hanging it over his arm before accompanying him into the drawing room. 'Lady Frampton, Dr Heyworth is here.' Antoinette stood up to greet him as Bertie and Wooster rushed over, nearly knocking him down in the doorway.

'What an enthusiastic welcome,' said Dr Heyworth, patting Wooster's head.

'Dogs like you, Dr Heyworth,' said Rosamunde, striding across the carpet to rescue him. 'You know, that says a great deal about you.'

'All good, I hope,' he replied, shaking Rosamunde's hand. She pulled the dogs off him and the doctor managed to squeeze past them into the room. He turned his attention to Antoinette, who remained by the armchair, and his face broke into a wide smile. 'You look well, Lady Frampton.'

'I feel very well today,' she replied. 'I've been in the garden all day, planting trees.'

'It's done you a lot of good. You've got your colour back.'

'That could be the cocktail.' She arched an eyebrow.

He laughed. 'Ah, yes, that might have something to do with it.'

'What would you like to drink, Dr Heyworth?' she asked, as Harris returned, having put the doctor's coat away.

'I'd love a glass of wine.'

'White or red?'

'White would be nice.' Harris nodded and walked across the rugs to fetch a bottle from the drinks fridge, hidden behind a concealed door built into the bookcase at the far end of the room.

'Isn't red better for you?' Rosamunde asked.

'Yes, but I'm off duty, and besides, I believe the odd small vice is essential for one's good health.'

'Lovely,' Antoinette sighed, sinking back into the armchair. 'You're my kind of doctor.'

The three of them sat around the fire, which Harris had lit every evening since Lord Frampton had died because the house had felt so cold. Antoinette and Rosamunde drained their glasses, Dr Heyworth sipped his wine more abstemiously. 'What is your Christian name?' asked Rosamunde. 'Dr Heyworth does seem very formal, considering

250

we're all friends having dinner together.'
Antoinette frowned. She wasn't sure she wanted to
be on first-name terms with her doctor.

'William,' he replied, looking a little
embarrassed.

'William,' Rosamunde repeated, as if the name
was sweeter than any other. 'Now you must call me
Rosamunde, William. Doesn't that sound better?'

He took another sip of wine. Antoinette thought
she could detect the hint of a light blush on his
cheeks.

'You know David, Tom and Phaedra have all
gone to Murenburg together,' she said, changing
the subject.

'How is it going?' he asked.

'I haven't heard a squeak. I hope it's going well. I
always think no news is good news.'

'I'm sure you're right.'

'Do you ski, William?' Rosamunde asked. The
vodka had made her feel wonderfully confident.

'No, I'm afraid not.'

'Well, neither do I. Isn't that grand?'

'It looks great fun, but sadly my parents were not
sporty types,' he continued.

'Was your father a doctor, too?' Antoinette
asked.

'Yes, he was. He's retired now.'

'How old is he?'

'Eighty-nine, and my mother is eighty-three.
They are both very healthy, thank God.'

'Lovely to reach old age in one piece,'
Rosamunde agreed. 'I hope you've inherited their
genes, William.'

'So do I,' he replied. 'All one needs in life is good
health and good luck.'

251

'Neither of which is in our hands,' said Antoinette.

'Which is why we have to seize the day.' He smiled at her. 'Like you did today, Lady Frampton.'

She smiled back. 'I certainly did, Dr Heyworth, and I am so much the better for it.' She noticed Harris at the door again. 'Dinner is ready. Shall we go through?'

Harris had set a round table in the small sitting room the other side of the hall. There was a fire in the grate and a pot of blue hyacinths in the middle of the table. The room was cosy, with hand-painted floral wallpaper in purple and green, Persian rugs spread over the carpet and one entire wall completely lined with antiquarian books. The curtains were closed and the scented candles that were arranged on the sofa table flickered hospitably. It was a friendlier room than the big drawing room and the three of them settled down to tuck into the dinner of home-made watercress soup followed by duck *à l'orange*. Rosamunde buttered a large wholegrain bread roll and took a bite, chewing in wonder at Mrs Gunice's culinary talents. The bread was always home-baked, the vegetables fresh and seasonal, straight out of the garden, and the meat was always tender and well hung by the butcher in Fairfield. She hoped the time to move back home would never come.

Harris poured a light Sauvignon to start, followed by a Bordeaux to accompany the duck. Antoinette had felt a little light-headed after the vodka, so she took care not to drink too much wine and asked Harris to refill her water glass for the second time. Rosamunde, however, was far too excited by the presence of Dr Heyworth to notice that the wine was now going to her head. She drank heartily and savoured every morsel of red cabbage, new Jersey potato and tender duck breast. The small sitting room had an air of informality and the three of them laughed and talked, at ease in each other's company.

Rosamunde discovered that she and William had much in common. Besides not skiing, they both loved gardening, although Rosamunde was unable to be actively involved any more in the planting. Antoinette praised the doctor's garden enthusiastically and told Rosamunde about the sweet-smelling *Daphne odora* that had quite literally stopped her in her tracks the first time she had sneaked into his garden. He also liked horses and used to ride as a young man. Rosamunde took great pleasure in telling him how she had competed as a girl and hunted with the Beaufort. 'Antoinette can't go near horses because of an allergy to them,' she said. 'But I lived and breathed them for years, until my hip started to give me trouble. There's nothing like the feeling of galloping at high speed with the wind in your face and the sight of rolling green fields in front of you. I do miss it.' She sighed and scraped the last bit of duck onto her fork. 'Gracious, Mrs Gunice is a wonder. This is as good a meal as I've ever had!'

For pudding Mrs Gunice had made the lightest, sweetest, stickiest chocolate mousse Rosamunde had ever tasted. Her senses heightened by the wine, she rolled the first spoonful around her tongue, relishing the slight tang of orange. The taste was so sensual she felt herself swell with the pleasure it gave her. Antoinette noticed her sister's cheeks flush the colour of raspberry jam and her eyes sparkle like a dreamy teenager. She wanted to move her wine glass away but felt it would be humiliating to do so in front of Dr Heyworth, and there was no way she could do it without being seen. Instead, she could only watch helplessly as Rosamunde became as loose as a slackly wound ball of wool. She laughed with her jaw lax and her body floppy, and her usually stiff posture slouched over her mousse so that her generous bosom rested on the table like a parcel wrapped in silk and tied with a bow.

When she began to slur her words Antoinette decided it was time to adjourn to the drawing room for coffee. Perhaps the more formal atmosphere in there would sober her sister up a little. They walked out into the hall where Harris waited with a tray of tea and coffee. 'We'll have it in the drawing room, Harris,' said Antoinette.

'I think I'll go up and powder my snose,' Rosamunde giggled. 'I mean my *nose*.' And she set off up the stairs.

Antoinette and Dr Heyworth's conversation was abruptly halted as they watched Rosamunde reach halfway then falter. She teetered on the step for what felt like a dreadfully long moment, struggling to regain her balance. She waved her arms, shifted her weight and wobbled alarmingly but to no avail. Very slowly, as if the world had suddenly gone into slow motion, she fell backwards. By some miracle, she managed to turn her body around to fall on her bottom, rather than her back, and rolled down the stairs like a barrel. Dr Heyworth hurried to catch her as she tumbled onto the floor. Antoinette gasped in horror and found herself unable to move for terror.

Rosamunde groaned as the pain shot up her left leg and into her lower back. She blinked up at Dr Heyworth. 'God, am I alive?' she mumbled. The room was spinning around her.

'You're going to be fine,' he said in a reassuring voice. 'Now lie still while I make sure that everything is where it should be.'

'My left leg hurts,' she murmured. 'And ... well ... I think I hurt all over.'

Gently he removed her shoes and touched her toes. 'Can you feel your toes, Rosamunde?'

She wiggled them. 'Yes.'

'Can you see them moving?'

'I can see *hundreds* of toes moving. They're very busy.'

'Can you feel your legs?' She was able to move them, too.

Antoinette stepped closer. 'Is anything broken?' she asked in a small voice. She watched the doctor test Rosamunde's shoulders, arms and neck.

'You've given yourself a terrible shock and some serious bruising. Let's get you up to bed,' he said at last.

Rosamunde was surprised that she could get up so easily. Her body hurt but nothing like as badly as she had imagined. 'You were very floppy when you fell, which is why you haven't sustained any serious damage,' Dr Heyworth continued as he helped her climb the stairs.

'I think I drank too much.' She began to tremble all over in shock. 'I feel very unsteady.'

'You'll feel better when you're lying down,' he reassured her.

'Shall I bring some painkillers?' Antoinette

255

asked, wanting to be useful.

'Yes please, and some arnica,' the doctor replied, and Antoinette hurried past them to look in the bathroom cabinet. She returned a moment later armed with half the contents of her medicine cupboard.

Together they settled Rosamunde into bed. She felt very foolish. The evening had started off so well but now her body was hurt and her pride dented. She let the doctor tuck her in and closed her eyes, hoping the painkillers would kick in soon, but before she could dwell any further on her bruises, or on the dizzy sensation of spinning, the voices receded and the world went dark. She sank deep into that comforting darkness until she was no longer aware of herself.

'She'll be very black-and-blue in the morning,' said Dr Heyworth, softly closing the door to Rosamunde's bedroom.

'In spite of all that arnica?'

'I'm afraid she's taken a nasty bang to her side. I wouldn't be at all surprised if it's the colour of the worst sort of English sky tomorrow.'

'Oh dear, poor Rosamunde.'

'How long is she staying with you?'

'As long as I need her.'

'Well, she's going to need *you* now. I don't think she'll be able to go home for at least a week.'

'Really, that long?'

'She'll need looking after. The older we get, the longer we take to heal. I'd hate to think of her having to go out and buy the groceries. Here, she'll be taken care of and she can rest. That's the only thing I can prescribe: a lot of rest.'

'If you say so, doctor.'

256

'I do.'

'Oh dear, what a drama. I do apologize.'

'What for? I'm glad I was here.'

'I'm not sure it would have happened if you hadn't been here,' she said, sighing heavily. 'Let's go and have some coffee. I wonder whether Mrs Gunice has any fudge. I think I need a lump of fudge.'

They sat in the drawing room once again while Harris filled their cups with coffee then went off to the kitchen in search of fudge. 'I'll come up tomorrow to check on your sister, Lady Frampton.'

'Oh, you don't have to go to such trouble.'

'I'd like to, if you don't mind. I'd like to make sure that she's all right and perhaps bring some ointment for the bruising. She might need some stronger painkillers.'

'Well, if you don't mind. I know Rosamunde would be very grateful.'

'If it's a nice day, maybe you'd show me your planting.'

Antoinette's face opened into an enthusiastic smile. 'I'd love to. It's my new thing, gardening. It was heavenly to be out in the sunshine today, with my hands in the soil, listening to the birdsong. It made me feel so good. Barry says there's so much to do at the moment, what with all the tidying up in preparation for summer. He says he could do with the extra pair of hands.'

'I'm sure he's very grateful for your help.'

'I think he's just indulging me, to be honest. After all, he's managed without me for years! But I'm just happy to be outside. Everything is coming up now, and the green is such a pretty shade.'

'You must have quite a magnificent vegetable

257

garden, judging by dinner.'

'We do. In fact, Barry and I were discussing it just this morning. All the things we're going to plant once it gets a little bit warmer. We have the space to feed an army, but it's only me and David here now, and Josh and Tom when they come for weekends. When George was alive we used to fill the house with guests every weekend. He loved to entertain. He never stopped, even on bank holidays! It's rather quiet now, by comparison, but I'm enjoying it. I can hear myself think. I have time, suddenly. What a luxury time is, don't you think?'

'One of the greatest luxuries of all, if you know how to use it.'

'What do you do in your spare time besides gardening, Dr Heyworth?'

'I play the piano.'

'Really?'

'Yes, I find it very relaxing.'

'Will you play something for me now?' He appeared to be reluctant. 'Don't, if you'd rather not. I'd hate to put you under pressure.'

'Of course I will. What do you like, classical? Jazz?'

'Whatever you feel like playing.'

He got up and went over to the grand piano. 'It's a Steinway,' he said, impressed. He sat on the stool and opened the lid.

'I dabble,' said Antoinette, remaining in the armchair. 'I was a good player as a child. While Rosamunde gallivanted about the countryside on her horse, I was made to practise the piano. How I resented it. Now, of course, I wish I'd practised a little more. It's a lovely thing to do, creating music.

258

You start whenever you're ready and I'll shut up.'

'I'll play you my favourite piece,' he said and rested his fingers above the keys.

He began to play and Antoinette sat quietly and listened. She had never heard the piece before. It was lovely, evoking a sense of tranquillity and wonder. She imagined a flock of geese flying through a pale-pink sky on their way to roost beside a limpid river. She thought of evening, the melancholy of the dying day and the sense of transience that always comes when we are faced with something beautiful. She thought of George's grave in that quiet spot in the churchyard and then she thought of his spirit, free and unencumbered by the heavy weight of his physical body, and her mind turned to Phaedra and her unwavering belief in life after death. The music touched her deeply and unexpectedly. As Dr Heyworth played, she felt an awareness opening inside her mind, like the unwrapping of a crocus in the glare of the sun. She closed her eyes and let the music fill her.

As he touched the final note, Antoinette opened her eyes and smiled at him. 'That was beautiful,' she said. 'What is it?'

'My mother wrote it.'

'Your mother is a composer?'

'An *amateur* composer. She makes light of it, but I think she writes very well.'

'I think she writes *more* than well. I'm astonished. It transported me.'

'It makes me think of the end of the day,' he said, closing the lid of the piano.

'Me too. That's exactly what I was thinking.'

He laughed, pleased. 'You were supposed to. It's called *Sunset*.'

259

'How amazing that a piece of music can make us all think of the same thing.'

'It has a wonderful serenity to it and a sense of winding down. It's a very sad piece, really.'

'Sunset is sad, because it's so magnificent and so fleeting.' She watched him walk back to the sofa. 'You play beautifully, Dr Heyworth.'

'I'm glad you liked it.'

'Will you play again sometime?'

'On one condition.'

'What might that be?'

'That you give me a guided tour of your garden tomorrow.'

She smiled. 'That's a good deal. And you've inspired me. It's been years since I've touched those keys. I'm going to take it up again.'

'That's a very good idea.'

'Will you recommend me something to play?'

'I'll bring some sheet music tomorrow when I come for the tour and to visit your sister.'

'Will you bring me *Sunset*? Would your mother mind?'

'She'd be honoured, Lady Frampton, and so would I.'

Antoinette sat back in the armchair and smiled at Dr Heyworth. She wasn't sure if it was her day in the garden, the wine, or the lovely piece of music she had just heard, but her heart felt full of optimism, as if the future were a bright, alluring place full of wondrous possibilities. If it hadn't been for Rosamunde's fall, it would have been a perfect ending to a perfect day.

Chapter 18

The following morning Rosamunde awoke with a throbbing headache and a dull pain down her left side. She got up to use the bathroom and staggered painfully across the carpet. When she lifted her nightie and saw the extent of the bruising she was horrified. Her left thigh looked like a hunk of raw meat. She couldn't possibly let William see her like this.

Antoinette had left the packet of painkillers on her bedside table with a glass of water. She took four and climbed back into bed. She must have drifted off to sleep again because when she next opened her eyes, Antoinette was standing over her.

'Good morning, Rosamunde,' she said, smiling sympathetically. 'How are you feeling?'

Rosamunde blinked up at her sister and mentally assessed her body. The headache had passed, or been killed by the pills, and her thigh only hurt if she moved it. 'Terrible,' she replied. 'Just terrible. What happened last night? I don't remember a thing.'

'You fell down the stairs.'

'Oh, yes. I do remember that, now you come to mention it. What a bump it was. I can barely move without pain.'

'Dr Heyworth is here to see you.'

Rosamunde blanched. 'Here? Now? How do I look? I haven't even brushed my teeth. Tell him to wait. I'm not ready to see him just yet.'

'I'm not sure you should get out of bed,'

261

Antoinette muttered as Rosamunde threw back the bedclothes and hobbled into the bathroom, groaning with each step. Antoinette heard the sound of the toothbrush and the running of the tap. Conscious that the doctor was waiting outside the door, she opened it a crack and spoke through it. 'She won't be a minute, Dr Heyworth.'

'That's all right,' he replied. 'I'm in no hurry.'

A moment later Rosamunde was back in bed and Dr Heyworth was admitted to her bedside. 'How's the patient this morning?' he asked, putting his bag on the floor. Rosamunde immediately felt reassured; he had a very comforting voice and a kind manner. She felt foolish that she had baulked at the thought of showing him her bruises. He must have seen far worse in his time.

'I had a horrible headache when I awoke this morning so I took four pills and went back to sleep again.'

He frowned. 'Now that's a little excessive, Rosamunde.'

'It hurt very much. I didn't think two would do the job.'

'I've brought you something a little stronger, but you must only take two at a time, all right?'

'As long as they do the trick.'

'How's your leg?'

'It looks very ugly.'

'May I see it?'

'If you have to. It's not a sight for sore eyes.'

'My eyes are perfectly well this morning.' He lifted her nightdress to reveal her purple hip and thigh. 'Yes, I thought you'd sustain a little bruising. Don't worry, Rosamunde, it's perfectly natural. You took quite a fall. I have some ointment to put

262

on and some pills for you to take. However, I'm afraid we must leave the healing to rest and Mother Nature.'

'What a bore. I hate sitting in bed.'

'I'm sure Lady Frampton can bring you up a few books from her wonderful library.'

'I'm not a reader, William. I suppose I shall finish my needlepoint now.' She sighed heavily. 'May I sit downstairs and watch the television?'

'Of course, but I suggest you get some help walking down the stairs. We don't want another fall.'

'Gracious, no. I shall go very carefully.' She was cheered by the thought of spending a restful week in the sitting room in front of the fire, watching television and sewing.

'I'll pop in tomorrow to see how you're recovering.'

'That would be very kind, thank you.' She noticed his green eyes smiling down at her compassionately. They were a very gentle green, like aventurine.

'Lady Frampton has promised me a tour of the gardens,' he told her.

'I suppose she'll be rolling up her sleeves again today.'

'It's doing her the world of good.'

'I know. I'm beginning to wonder whether George didn't diminish her in many ways.'

'Now she's discovering there's a life for her after all.'

'It's a good thing, too. She's given more than thirty years to her children and her husband. I'm very pleased she's finding time for herself at last.'

'There is always a silver lining.'

'One can't always see it at the time. When God closes one door, He opens another.' Dr Heyworth left the room and Rosamunde grinned at the thought of the silver lining to her own bad luck— William was going to pop by and see her again, perhaps every day for an entire week. The thought was enough to put her on the fast track to recovery.

Dr Heyworth found Antoinette waiting for him in the drawing room. He had brought some music scores for her to play and his mother's own composition, *Sunset*. She was overjoyed and placed them on the piano, ready. 'Thank you so much,' she exclaimed happily. 'This is all so thrilling. I never thought I'd play the piano again.'

'You can do anything you want once you set your mind to it,' Dr Heyworth replied.

'Then come and see the gardens. I have so many ideas. Barry and I are cooking up some wonderful plans.'

Dr Heyworth followed her out into the light. The morning mist had now evaporated in the warm spring sunshine and the sky was a serene blue. A fine haze still lingered here and there but it wouldn't be long before that too was burnt away, leaving the heavens clear and bright. Were it not for the budding trees it could almost have been summer.

They wandered across the lawn to the walled vegetable garden and Antoinette explained what grew there and what was yet to be planted. Dr Heyworth pulled off a sprig of rosemary and pressed it to his nose. 'I love the smell of herbs, don't you?' he said.

'I do, very much,' Antoinette replied. 'Thyme is

264

my favourite. In the summer all these little paths are covered with it and the smell is just delicious as you tread.'

'It reminds me of Italy.'

'Does it? Well, that's nice. Italy is beautiful.' They walked through to the orchard where Antoinette had planted the fruit trees the day before. As she opened the gate they disturbed a flock of pigeons who took to the sky, flapping their creaking wings loudly. 'They're so fat, it's a wonder they take off,' she said.

'Do you feed them?'

'Not intentionally. Barry puts out food for the little ones: robins and thrushes and of course the charming little blue tits. The finches love nyjer seed so Barry puts out feeders especially for them. Of course the pigeons try to hog the feeders. George had a shoot, so the keeper always put down feed for the pheasants and partridges. I'm not sure what's going to happen now. It all depends on David and I'm not sure he really enjoys it. He doesn't like killing things.'

'Fair enough,' said Dr Heyworth. 'It's a brutal sport.'

She proudly showed him the trees she had planted at the end of the orchard. Some of them already displayed a little pink blossom. 'I can't tell you the fun I had yesterday. It was so liberating to sit out here and work. I felt I had real purpose. It was peaceful and warm.' She inhaled and smiled contentedly. 'Really, I can't think why I didn't do more gardening when George was alive. Busy, I suppose. But one should make the effort to do things one enjoys. Don't you agree, Dr Heyworth?'

He was looking at her indulgently, clearly

charmed by her enthusiasm. 'I think you've found the key to happiness, Lady Frampton.'

She laughed dismissively. 'You flatter me.'

'Not at all. I think people spend their lives running around so fast they never have time to just *be*. You were just *being* yesterday, out here in this lovely garden with the flora and fauna. You were enjoying the moment and I think that is the key to real happiness.'

'Well, I did feel very happy.' She glanced at him anxiously. 'Should I feel this happy so soon after George's death?'

'I don't think Lord Frampton would want you to mourn him indefinitely.'

'But it's only been a few weeks.'

'You'll have your ups and downs, Lady Frampton. But whenever you feel down you must come out into the garden because it makes you feel better. That can only be a good thing.'

She smiled again. 'Then I shall and I shan't feel guilty about it. Come on, there's lots more to see. Check out our bird feeders, you'll be astonished by the amount of birds we have here at Fairfield.'

They continued to wander around the grounds, chatting together contentedly. Dr Heyworth admired the ancient trees. He knew the names of every one of them. He recognized the plants emerging through the ground after the long winter and made suggestions for one or two new shrubs that would work well in her garden. At one point he suggested it was time to leave, but Antoinette persuaded him to see the folly. 'It's only a few minutes' walk up the hill. A charming little place and quite run to ruin now,' she explained. 'I hadn't thought about it in years until yesterday, when I was pottering in the garden. You see, it's all alone up there on the hill. Neglected and forgotten, which is a crime as it's so pretty. As I'm getting involved in the garden now, I thought I might restore it. It's part of Fairfield Park, after all, and someone quite clearly built it with love. It's only right that we should look after it.'

The folly was very charming, in spite of the mildew that discoloured the windows and the ivy that grew up the pillars supporting the pediment. It was classically proportioned and harmonious, the stone giving it a warm allure. 'How very interesting,' said Dr Heyworth, studying it closely. 'It's made of Bath stone. I recognize it from a house I used to stay in as a child in Wiltshire.'

'What's Bath stone doing all the way over here in Hampshire?' said Antoinette.

'I can't imagine.'

'It's romantic, isn't it?'

'Very.'

'What shall I do with it? I mean, it's hidden away here and overgrown with plants. Nature does take over if you let it, doesn't it?'

'It certainly does.' He rubbed his chin thoughtfully. 'I think it just needs a bit of cleaning, inside and out. It was obviously built up here because of the view of the house and the lake.' They both surveyed the grounds that spread out before them, making a spectacular view. The lake shone a deep navy and a few wild ducks moved smoothly across the water like little boats.

'I've always thought this was a place to come and picnic,' Antoinette mused.

'Perhaps. It's south-facing so it gets the sun as it rises in the east and sets in the west. It's very peaceful up here. Of course it might have been built to observe from the house, in which case it was merely ornamental.'

'A waste, if that's the case.'

'Yes, I agree with you. It's a place that must be enjoyed.'

'I'm going to do it. I'm going to make it beautiful again.' Her voice rose with excitement. 'And I'm going to try and find out why it was built in Bath stone. I mean, it would have been easier to build in Hampshire brick.'

'But not nearly so pretty,' said Dr Heyworth.

She sighed. 'To think, it's been up here for all the years I've lived in the house and never once have I asked myself why, or even spent time up here. It never crossed my mind. It's as if my eyes have opened to a world within my familiar world. Does that sound silly?'

'Not at all.'

'It's really very strange. I feel quite different.'

'Consider a tree, Lady Frampton. Growing in its shadow is a smaller tree. That small tree can only see the branches of the big tree that grow over it. One day that big tree is felled and the little tree thinks it cannot possibly survive without the shelter the big tree gave it. But then the little tree opens its eyes and sees the sky, the sun, the stars at night and the birds flying across it. They were always there, only it couldn't see for the branches of the big tree. While it mourns the loss of the big tree, it celebrates the new world that has opened up right above its head.'

'And I'm the small tree,' she said, smiling wistfully, recalling how George had always dominated because of his bigger personality.

'It's true. You will all miss George but a new chapter is beginning for you now.'

'I think it's going to be an exciting new chapter.'

They walked back down the hill to the house. 'I shall go home now,' Dr Heyworth said, pulling his car keys out of his pocket.

'Thank you for coming on a Saturday.'

'No, thank *you* for inviting me for dinner last night. I'm only sorry your sister suffered such a nasty fall. I'll pop by and see her tomorrow.'

'But it's Sunday. You don't want to come here on a Sunday, do you?'

'Weekends are pretty much the same as weekdays to me, as I only work part time. I'd very much like to see Rosamunde, just to check that she's recovering as she should.'

Antoinette gave a knowing smile. 'Well, if you insist.'

'Make sure she gets lots of rest. No walking about unnecessarily.'

'I will.'

'Call me if you're worried.'

She watched him climb into his car and put the key in the ignition. 'Rosamunde is a strong girl, she'll recover fast. I'm going to go and find Barry and tell him about my plans for the folly.'

'I look forward to seeing it in all its glory.'

She laughed. 'You shall. I'll get David to help me when he comes back tomorrow. I hope they're having a good time. I haven't heard a squeak.'

'See you tomorrow, Lady Frampton. Oh, and by the way . . .'

'Yes?'

'You have a very fine garden!'

She waved him off and he disappeared down the

269

drive. Just as he vanished, the ubiquitous figure of Margaret Frampton came into view, striding across the field with Basil. Antoinette stood on the steps and waved. Margaret waved back. Antoinette wondered what her mother-in-law had been up to these past few days. It was unusual for her to keep such a low profile.

She watched her open the little gate at the edge of the field and wait impatiently for Basil to scurry through. The dog found a trace of something appealing and scuttled off in the opposite direction. Margaret barked at him, slapping her thigh, until he was forced to abandon his hunt and do as he was told. He came darting through the gate like a terrified guinea pig. Margaret closed the gate behind her and strode across the gravel towards the front of the house.

'Hello, Antoinette,' she exclaimed.

'Hello, Margaret. I was going to call you this morning,' said Antoinette.

'Oh, really. Why?'

'I hadn't seen you for a couple of days. I wanted to check that you were all right.'

'Perfectly well, thank you.' She climbed the steps then stood a moment at the top, catching her breath. Her large bosom heaved up and down like bellows. 'I hear Rosamunde took a fall last night.'

Antoinette was astonished that news had travelled so fast. 'Yes, she did. Who told you?'

'Reverend Morley,' Margaret replied casually.

'Reverend Morley? How on earth did he know?'

'He knows everything,' Margaret said, a secretive smile spreading around her eyes and the corners of her mouth. 'Don't forget he has a direct line to God.'

Antoinette didn't know which was more surprising, the humour on the woman's face or the fact that she was making a quip about God. 'Let's go inside,' she said, turning and walking back into the hall. There was something different about her mother-in-law today.

They went into the drawing room and sat down on the sofa next to the unlit fire. It was a warm day and Antoinette had told Harris to light a fire in the small sitting room instead, so that Rosamunde would be warm should she want to come downstairs and watch television. 'So you invited Dr Heyworth for dinner,' said Margaret.

Antoinette wondered whether the spy had also told her that Rosamunde was drunk. 'Yes, he's been very good to me these last few weeks,' she replied.

'Really, that's beyond the call of duty, Antoinette. Still, very generous of you to have him.' Her tone was patronizing and Antoinette knew she felt it was beneath her to entertain the local doctor.

'He came this morning to see Rosamunde.'

'How is she? Was it a very nasty fall?'

'Yes, it was. She's badly bruised.'

'Oh dear, poor thing.' She seemed genuinely sympathetic. 'I do hope she stays in bed and gives her body time to recover. No gallivanting about the fields with the dogs.'

'No, she's going to take it very easy.'

'Good.'

Margaret's face softened as a pleasant thought popped into her head. 'So, when's that delightful girl coming back to Fairfield?'

'You mean Phaedra?'

'Of course I mean Phaedra. There isn't another delightful girl that I'm not aware of, is there?'

'They're back from Murenburg tomorrow,' Antoinette replied.

'Next weekend, then. That would be nice. You will ask her, won't you?'

'Of course I will. I'd like to see more of her, too.'

'You know, she's very wise for her years.'

'Yes, she's a deep person,' Antoinette agreed.

'Yes, that's a good word,' said Margaret with satisfaction. 'She has depth, *real* depth.'

'It sounds like she had a rather tough upbringing.'

'Unhappiness drives a person deeper, so Reverend Morley tells me. That's meant to be a good thing. Apparently it teaches us wisdom and compassion. Phaedra seems to have a good deal of both. Unusual in a young person, don't you think? Young people these days are awfully selfish.'

'I think the boys were rather disappointed that she turned out to be their half-sister,' Antoinette confided.

'Well, I do see why. She's a very pretty girl. She'd have been too good for Tom, anyhow, and I wouldn't have wished David on her. He's not a good bet. As siblings they'll always be in each other's lives.'

Antoinette leapt to her son's defence. 'I don't think David's a bad bet, Margaret. He just hasn't found the right girl. He's very discerning.'

'He should get out more. Perhaps Phaedra can take him out a bit in London. He's not going to meet many potential wives down here, is he?'

'That's very true. Maybe Phaedra has a nice friend she can introduce him to.'

272

'I'd imagine she has plenty. Birds of a feather flock together.'

'You're so right, they do. I'll take her aside when I next see her and ask her to take David in hand.' The idea gave Antoinette a rush of confidence.

'If he's going to inherit this place one day, he's going to have to fill it with children. He can't be rattling around all on his own.'

'Rather like me,' said Antoinette with a sigh. 'I'm rattling around in it now.'

'But you've had years of filling it up with a family. That's very different from starting on your own. When David marries then you can think about passing it on to him as Arthur and I did when George married you. It's a house that needs to be full of people. But don't ever feel bad that you're rattling, Antoinette. You can rattle in your own home as much as you like.'

Antoinette was disarmed by her mother-in-law's response. In fact, they had pretty much agreed on everything, which was extraordinary. 'You know, Margaret, I sometimes think of Arthur,' she said wistfully.

Margaret's face hardened. 'Do you?'

'Yes, he had the same lightness of being as George.'

Margaret sniffed. 'I suppose he did.'

'He used to make you laugh.'

'Yes, he did. Quite how he managed it, I'm not sure.'

'I remember that the most.'

'Probably because I don't laugh much any more.' She leaned towards Antoinette conspiratorially. 'You know, I feel a fraud sometimes, when I laugh.'

273

'Do you? Why?'

'Because I've forgotten how to do it. It no longer comes naturally. It feels contrived and out of character.' She shook her shoulders to show how uncomfortable she felt.

'But you are entitled to laugh just as much as anyone else.'

'I'm a terrible old sourpuss.'

Antoinette smiled; if ever there was a time to laugh, it was now. 'You don't *have* to be a sourpuss.'

'I was very gay when I was young. I was jolly and gay.' She looked put out, as if turning into a sourpuss had been forced upon her.

'You can't use that word these days, Margaret.'

'Rubbish! Now you can see what I mean when I say young people are selfish. That was a perfectly good word for happy before they came along and stole it.' The corners of her mouth quivered. She sucked in her cheeks. 'You see, Antoinette. I *am* a terrible old sourpuss!'

Suddenly, without warning, Margaret laughed. It bubbled up from her belly, through her chest, into her throat and out in a cheerful, frothy chortle. Antoinette laughed too. She couldn't remember the last time they had laughed together like that, if ever. She stared at Margaret in astonishment because she seemed to have transformed before her very eyes. She didn't look a fraud at all. On the contrary, she looked very relaxed in her mirth.

Once Margaret had gone Antoinette and Harris helped settle Rosamunde into the little sitting room by the fire. She sat on the sofa with her legs up and a blanket draped over her, watching television and sewing. Harris placed a plate of Mrs

Gunice's shortbread biscuits on the coffee table along with a pot of tea. Rosamunde had taken two of Dr Heyworth's painkillers and was now feeling much improved. In fact, as she put a biscuit into her mouth and took a bite, she decided things really couldn't be better.

Antoinette went outside to find Barry. She squinted as the sun shone bright and warm. Birdsong resounded across the park, a sugary breeze swept across her face, and her heart inflated with happiness.

Her gaze was drawn up to the hill where the folly stood distant and detached, passively surveying the estate with a quiet knowing. It was as if its windows could see—and there was a strange compassion in the way it watched, as if it were waiting for something, or someone, and in time its patience would pay off. She frowned. How odd to give a building human characteristics, she thought. She turned away and walked across the grass, but still she felt those gentle eyes upon her.

Chapter 19

David, Tom and Phaedra arrived back at Heathrow late on Sunday afternoon. The short break in the mountains had been idyllic, but now they were back in England they felt they were stepping out of an enchanted bubble into a world of concrete and stone. Tom had to return to his nightclub, David to the farm and Phaedra to her photography and Julius's persistent calls. They had paid their respects at the place where George had died, and they'd said goodbye. Now they had to get on with their lives without him. The thought was daunting. But what was even more daunting for David and Phaedra was the thought of having to go through the rest of their lives pretending to love each other as brother and sister, when they were both consumed with a very different kind of love.

The last couple of days had been testing. They had skied together all day and dined together in the evenings, growing close as they chatted on chairlifts and shared the tranquil beauty of the mountain's hidden glades and couloirs. Tom had joined them, oblivious of the growing attraction between them. In fact, so distracted was Tom by his own flowering friendship with Phaedra, he had failed to realize that the often cool formality between Phaedra and his brother was simply their way of concealing the truth—that they were beginning to find each other irresistible.

Phaedra knew it was unwise to spend time with David and resolved to distance herself once she returned to London. David was determined to see as much of her as possible, certain that being with her as a brother was better than not being with her at all.

They parted at the airport. Phaedra and Tom shared a cab into London while David had left his car in the long-term car park. He had embraced Phaedra and savoured the rare moment when they were pressed together, body to body, cheek to cheek. Only when he pulled away did he feel the terrible strain of his hopeless infatuation.

He drove down the M3, wondering how he was going to navigate his way through the minefield he had now laid out for himself. It would have been so much easier if he hadn't felt that she reciprocated his feelings. But she did. There was no doubt in his mind. He could tell. It was too strong for either of them to hide.

He drove to his house first because he was anxious to see Rufus. When he opened the front door the dog bounded out in a flurry of dust and fur, jumping up and straining his neck in an attempt to lick his master's face. David stroked him happily, tickling him behind the ears where he liked it best, and Rufus wagged his tail so excitedly his whole bottom moved as if it had a life of its own.

David dumped his bag in the hall then drove over to see his mother, with Rufus staring at him lovingly from the well of the passenger seat. As he turned off the farm track onto the drive he pulled onto the verge to let another car pass. He didn't recognize the navy-blue Volvo. The man waved and David was surprised to see that it was Dr Heyworth. Surprise turned to anxiety. Was his mother unwell? He hastily drove up to the house and ascended the steps two at a time. He was relieved to find her in perfect health in the little sitting room with Rosamunde and his grandmother.

'David!' Antoinette exclaimed happily. 'You're back.'

'And in one piece,' said Rosamunde. 'Sadly, I can't say the same about myself.'

David bent down to kiss his grandmother. She smiled up at him. 'Now tell us everything. How's that charming girl?'

'What was Dr Heyworth doing here?' he asked, pulling out one of the dining chairs since his aunt

277

was taking up the whole sofa as if it were a recliner.

'Rosamunde fell down the stairs,' Margaret informed him.

'Very silly of me,' Rosamunde cut in, clearly relishing the attention. 'Dr Heyworth's been a wonder. I'm feeling much better but he insists that I rest all week. So here I am, glued to the sofa while your mother spends all day in the garden getting her hands dirty.'

He looked at Antoinette incredulously. 'Really?'

'Yes, I have so much to tell you, so many plans afoot. But first, how did it go? Is Tom all right?'

David sat down. Harris appeared in the doorway with a tumbler of whisky on a tray. He greeted Harris warmly and thanked him.

'Will you stay for dinner, darling?' his mother asked.

'Love to,' David replied.

'So, we'll be four,' Antoinette told Harris.

'Very good, ma'am,' said Harris and left the room with a little nod.

David took a deep breath and stared a moment into his whisky glass. Those four days in Murenburg should have been about his father, but they'd been all about Phaedra. He couldn't get her out of his head. His father was gone, and he missed him terribly, Phaedra was here but forever out of his reach—he missed her more.

'It was cathartic to see where Dad died and to pay our respects there,' he said gravely. 'Tom found it hard, but it was good that he came. We can all move on now.'

'Was it a very big avalanche?' Antoinette asked fearfully.

278

'Big enough,' Margaret interrupted.

'It was quite big,' David replied. 'But the mountain was very peaceful and it was a beautiful day.' Then his face broke into a smile and he lowered his eyes. 'Phaedra was amazing. She made us all hold hands and say goodbye. It sounds cheesy, and it should have been, but somehow the way she did it made it feel very natural. It enabled us to have closure.'

'How lovely that she went with you,' Margaret enthused. Antoinette's gaze lingered on her son's beaming face, and as he continued to talk about Phaedra she noticed, to her horror, the glow of love in his skin. He radiated infatuation as if he were lit up from the inside like a Chinese lantern.

'She was wonderful with Tom, too,' David went on. 'He's very calm when he's around her and they talk and talk. He calls her his "guru" because she's so wise. I think she's just compassionate and non-judgemental.'

'When is she coming down?' Margaret asked.

'I haven't asked her.'

'Well, you must,' Margaret insisted. 'Ask her to come for the weekend. This is her home now.'

Margaret sniffed as if to seal the arrangement. 'Now, your mother and I think you should be getting out more. You spend all your time with that dog of yours, deep in the countryside. You're not going to find a wife on your tractor, so we've been thinking: wouldn't it be nice, now you have a sister, to ask her to introduce you to her friends? She must have lots of nice girls for you to meet. Birds of a feather flock together. Phaedra's very pretty and quite delightful; I'm sure her friends are just like her.'

279

David chuckled at the absurdity of the idea. The very fact that his mother and grandmother had been plotting together was in itself unimaginable. 'I have no intention of doing anything of the sort.'

'But why not?' Rosamunde asked. 'I think it's a wonderful idea.'

'I hate London, for a start.'

'Then she can ask her friends down here. The house is big enough and it's about time Antoinette filled it with people again. That's the way George always liked it, teeming with chums,' said Margaret.

'Phaedra would be embarrassed,' David explained. 'She doesn't feel this is her home. She's only just getting used to the fact that we're her family. She still calls Dad George and refers to him as "your father" to Tom and me. The last thing she's going to do is start organizing house parties for her friends.'

'I'll talk to her when she's down this weekend,' said Margaret, as if Phaedra had already accepted the invitation. 'We'll chat woman to woman. Leave it to me.'

'Please don't, Grandma.'

Margaret grinned and there was a mischievous twinkle in her eye. 'Sometimes, my dear boy, you have to trust those older and wiser than yourself. We do know what we're doing.'

Antoinette had never seen her son so electrified as when he spoke about Phaedra. He had enjoyed his fair share of romances in the past and on occasion brought girlfriends home, but now she knew that he had never really cared for any of them. Phaedra had enflamed his heart, and as his mother she feared for him. Out of all the girls in

280

the world, why had he taken a shine to the only one he couldn't have? It was so unfair. As much as she wanted his happiness, she didn't want *this*. It was simply wrong. But what could she do? She couldn't let on that she knew. He'd only deny it anyway. As she watched him eat his dinner she felt desperately sorry for him—and strangely fearful for herself. If David and Phaedra fell out, how would that affect *her*?

Love seemed to be blossoming at Fairfield. In addition to David, Rosamunde could speak of nothing but how kind and gentle William was. He'd been to see her that afternoon as promised and the three of them had had tea in the little sitting room. Mrs Gunice had made fresh shortbreads and Rosamunde had merrily eaten half of them, while Dr Heyworth had made his way through the other half. Antoinette had been sensitive and left them alone together. She'd also been keen to get back to the garden and Barry, who was busy planting down by the lake the vast quantity of shrubs she had bought at the garden centre. For the first time in her life she had a vision of what she wanted the place to look like. It was thrilling to see it materialize.

Dr Heyworth had found her later with her arms deep in mud. They had sat by the lake and chatted, mostly about Rosamunde. Antoinette was eager to encourage their friendship for her sister's sake. Rosamunde hadn't been lucky in love as a young woman; perhaps now, in her autumn years, she'd finally find happiness with William. He'd informed Antoinette that he would come every day until the patient was better, and Antoinette had smiled because she knew her sister was recovering nicely and that there was no longer any real need for a doctor. But if he wanted to come, using Rosamunde's accident as an excuse to visit her, Antoinette wasn't going to put him off.

After dinner, David drove his grandmother back to her house. Rosamunde retired to bed and Antoinette was left alone in the drawing room, suddenly feeling a little lost. It would take months for her to grow accustomed to George's absence. As Phaedra had wisely said, her children would move on in their lives, as all children do, but George had been her life and without him it felt as if there was nowhere to go.

She sat down at the piano and placed Mrs Heyworth's manuscript on the music stand. Tentatively she began to play. At first her fingers faltered and she hesitated over the more complicated chords. But soon she grew more confident and little by little her hands remembered what it felt like to move deftly over the keys and settled back into the comfortable flow of rising and falling notes. Her spirit lightened as the music lifted her high until she felt very far away from her worries and no longer alone.

David lay in bed reading. Rufus was snoring in his basket in the corner of the room; otherwise the night was quiet. He'd walked around the lake, all the time thinking of Phaedra and wondering whether she'd come down for the weekend. Somehow he doubted it. He had glimpsed fear in her eyes as they had embraced at the airport. If she pulled away now it was because she knew the dangers of getting too close.

He put down his book and stared into space. He longed to talk to her. The clock on his bedside table said midnight. It was too late to telephone. He picked up his iPhone and stared at it for a long while, deliberating what to do. Would she be asleep? Was she thinking of him?

He typed a text: *Just sitting here with Rufus. He's badgering me about asking you for the weekend. He won't let up until I do ... so—will you come? David*

He deliberated a long while before pressing *send*. It went with a whoosh. There, gone. Nothing he could do about it now. He stared at it, hoping for a reply, but none came. Finally he lay down and switched off the light. Sleep took a long time coming, but when it came it was deep and heavy, his dreams full of longing.

*   *   *

Phaedra awoke to see David's message on her telephone and her heart gave a sudden leap. She had been so tired the evening before, she'd ignored a call from Julius and turned her light out at nine. She lay in bed and smiled at the way David had used his dog to invite her for the weekend. That was very typical of his humour. She wanted more than anything to go down to the country, but she was aware of the risks. At least right now she had the strength to walk away. She wasn't in so deep that she couldn't extricate herself. Spending more time with David would only take her beyond the threshold of no return and cause her unbearable suffering, because it was an impossible situation. She'd already loved once before—her heart couldn't take another disappointment.

She showered and dressed, then went to have breakfast and read the papers at Caffè Nero on

283

the King's Road. It was a gloriously sunny morning. She couldn't help but wish she was at Fairfield where there were no concrete pavements, just rolling fields and thick woodland.

She sat on one of the sofas and gazed out of the window at the people passing by. Everyone seemed to have put away their winter clothes and walked with a bounce in their step. She, too, had a bounce in hers. She chuckled every time she thought of Rufus asking her to stay the weekend. But she had made up her mind. She had to say 'no'. It was the right thing to do.

She looked down at her mobile telephone and hesitated before replying to David. She didn't want to hurt his feelings. She wished she could explain. Biting her bottom lip, she knew that she could *never* explain—not ever.

At that moment it rang, displaying a number she recognized only because of the area code. It was Fairfield. With a stab of anxiety she answered it.

'Is that Phaedra?'

Phaedra recognized Margaret's voice immediately. 'Yes, it is.'

'Good. It's Margaret Frampton. I'm calling about this coming weekend.'

'Oh.'

'I know you stayed with David last time, but I really don't like to think of you languishing in his funny little cottage. I'd like you to stay with me.'

'Oh, well ... I ...' Phaedra didn't know what to say. Margaret's invitation was totally unexpected.

'Good, that's settled, then. I know Antoinette might not be happy, but she's got her hands full with poor old Rosamunde who's had the most ghastly accident.'

'What happened?'

'She fell all the way down the stairs and has a bruise the colour of a butcher's display.'

'Is she OK?'

'Well, nothing's broken, thank the Lord. But she's been told to rest for a whole week and Dr Heyworth is coming daily to check on her. So it must be serious. I think it would be too much for Antoinette to have you in the house.'

'Do you think?'

'Yes, my dear. I know I'm right. You stay with me and give Antoinette a little space.'

Whether she liked it or not, Phaedra was going to Fairfield for the weekend. 'OK, that would be lovely, thank you, Margaret.'

'No thank you necessary. It's a pleasure. Come down on Friday night if you can, then you can enjoy the whole weekend. You and I have some serious talking to do.'

'Oh? Do we?'

But before Phaedra could dwell on the sudden pang of anxiety that had cramped her stomach, Margaret explained. 'Yes, I have a favour to ask you—but it can wait for now. See you Friday.'

'Yes, see you Friday.'

Margaret hung up and Phaedra was left bewildered but excited. Margaret hadn't even tried to persuade her to go for the weekend. As far as she was concerned Phaedra was part of the family and belonged at Fairfield; there was no question of her not going.

With her heart aflutter she sent a text to David. *Dear Rufus, how can I refuse such an irresistible invitation? I'd love to come for the weekend, but I'm afraid David's grandmother has insisted I stay with*

285

her. Can I come over and make you pancakes nonetheless? Phaedra

She had barely pressed the *send* button when a reply alighted on her screen. *Woof woof! But you're not staying with Margaret!*

Phaedra laughed out loud. A pair of Chelsea Pensioners peered over their glasses and grinned at her.

Phaedra: *I'm too scared to decline.*

David: *Leave it to me, my bite is mightier than my bark...*

Phaedra: *You look more like a big, soppy dog, Rufus.*

David: *Don't you believe it! I'm only soppy in the company of pretty girls.*

Phaedra: *Is that a compliment, coming from a dog?*

David: *My boss agrees with me, but he's too shy to tell you...*

Phaedra: *Then it'll be our secret...*

David: *I'm not very good at keeping secrets from him, but I'll do my best... oh, here he comes now...*

Phaedra: *You'd better go, Rufus, and so must I. I have to work on my book...*

David: *Woof woof...*

Phaedra laughed all the way down the road. George had had a good sense of humour, but he hadn't had a *playful* sense of humour like David.

So she was going to stay another weekend at Fairfield. The thought of returning to that beautiful place made her spirits soar. She'd just have to keep her feelings in check. Surely it could be done. It *must* be done. Keeping her distance from David would inevitably cut her off from Fairfield and the rest of his family—which would

286

be devastating because she was drawn down there like a world-weary traveller to a warm, homely hearth. There was something irresistibly alluring about it, and as much as her head shouted at her not to go, her heart begged her to—and Phaedra was a girl who always put her heart before her head.

Chapter 20

Antoinette stood in front of the stone folly in a boiler suit and cap she'd bought from the agricultural store in Winchester, wielding a thick garden broom. 'I'll start on the inside,' she told Barry. 'You see what you can do on the outside.'

'Cutting back,' he said, scratching his chin.

'I think we should plant some pretty things here. Clematis that will climb up the walls and sweet-smelling shrubs where all these nettles have taken over. What do you think?'

He looked up at the sun. 'I think clematis would thrive here.'

'Good.'

'I know a man who can restore those chairs,' he said, pointing to a pair of pretty iron chairs set at a matching table beneath the pediment.

'Do you know who built it?'

He shook his head. 'No idea.'

'It's very romantic. There's bound to be a story behind it, don't you think?'

'Oh yes, there's sure to be,' said Barry. He began to pull out the nettles and toss them into the cart he'd pulled up behind one of the farm tractors.

'It's a mystery, ma'am.'

Antoinette disappeared inside and set about sweeping away the dust and the tangled spiders' webs that hung down from the corners of the folly like dirty pieces of gauze. There were dead moths on the windowsills and the rotting carcass of a bird on the floor. She noticed one of the window panes was broken, giving the poor bird an entrance into his tomb, but not an exit. Piled up against the back wall was a heap of furniture stored beneath a big white dust sheet. She'd need Barry's help to take it all outside.

Dr Heyworth had said he'd come at five. Although she didn't want to intrude on his flowering friendship with her sister, she was keen to tell him how she had played his mother's piece of music and been transported into a beautiful sunset. She wanted to show him the folly, too, since they had come up with the idea together of restoring it. She looked at her watch and wished she'd asked Mrs Gunice to make them sandwiches for lunch. It seemed a waste of time to return to the house to eat.

Little by little the folly was freed from the forest's tentacles. There was much to do, but by lunchtime Barry had pulled out all the nettles and cut back some of the shrubs that had begun to lay claim to the building. Plants had seeded themselves and hazel bushes had grown into each other, creating a thick tangle of wood and foliage. They stood and appraised their work, wiping sweaty brows with dirty hands. 'This is a good start,' said Antoinette.

'You don't realize how much there is to do until you get going,' Barry replied.

288

'I'll get David to help me at the weekend.'

'He can do the heavy work. All that furniture will need to come out so you can clean properly.'

'I'm so pleased we're resurrecting it, Barry. I never had time to do this sort of thing while George was alive.' She brushed a fly off her face. 'Life goes on, doesn't it? I mean, you think it won't. You can't imagine how it can. But it does.'

'It's like a river, Lady Frampton. If it comes up against an obstacle it will always find a way around it and continue on its path.'

'It's carrying me with it.'

'You have to keep looking ahead. Not down. Like a tightrope walker.'

'I know.' She smiled at him. 'Are you hungry?'

'Very.'

'Then let's go and get something to eat. We workers need fortification.'

'I have my sandwiches in the greenhouse.'

'Does your wife make them for you?'

'She's made them for me for forty years.'

'Have you really been married that long?'

'It'll be forty-three this autumn.'

'That's quite something, Barry.'

He gave a heavy sigh and grinned mischievously. 'It's a lifetime, Lady Frampton.'

They walked down the hill together, leaving the tractor by the folly for later. As Antoinette walked across the lawn David was striding towards her. 'I need to talk to you,' he said gravely.

Antoinette waved Barry off and the old man left the two of them alone. 'What's happened?' Her thoughts immediately turned to Tom and she felt the familiar sinking of her spirits.

'It's Grandma.'

'Oh.' She sighed with relief.

'She's invited Phaedra to stay the weekend.'

'Good.'

'With *her*.'

'Oh, not so good, then. Have you spoken to Phaedra?'

'She can't do anything about it. She won't be rude. But over my dead body is she going to stay with Grandma. She might never wake up in the morning.'

'I do see. You're not expecting *me* to say anything, are you?'

'Someone's got to say something.'

'It has to be you, David.'

'What's my reason?' He shrugged helplessly.

'That Josh and Tom are coming and so it'll be more fun for her in the house.'

'They'd better come, then.'

'I'm sure once they know Phaedra's coming, they'll all be down like a shot!'

'And Roberta!' He pulled a face.

'Roberta's just being overprotective. She'll come round in the end.'

He grinned. 'I hope you're right. I'll go and see Grandma right away.'

Antoinette hurried into the house to tell Rosamunde. The thought of Phaedra in Margaret's steely clutches was more than she could bear. She found her sister in the sitting room, doing her needlepoint while listening to a story on the radio. 'Can I talk?' she asked, aware that she was interrupting.

'It's not a very good story,' said Rosamunde. 'I'd rather watch the golf. Would you see if it's on?'

Antoinette pressed the switch on the television,

mildly irritated that Rosamunde couldn't do it herself. Her sister picked up the control. 'Now, remind me how to use Sky?'

'Really, Rosamunde, it's not rocket science.'

'It is to me. Do you think lunch is ready? I'm famished.'

'No point watching Sky, then, if you're going to have lunch.'

'I thought I might get up and sit at the table today.'

'Good.'

'Yes, I'm feeling a little better.'

'Has the bruising gone down?'

'Considerably, but I think Dr Heyworth should still come and have a look at it.'

'I don't think he's coming to check out your bruising, Rosamunde.'

Her sister's face flushed. 'You don't think . . . ?'

'I do.' Antoinette switched off the television and sat down. 'I think he's using it as an excuse to come and see you.'

'What will he do when I'm better?'

'Declare himself, I suppose, otherwise how is he going to see you?'

Rosamunde shivered with anxiety. 'Oh, really? I don't know . . . gosh, that makes me a little nervous. It really is too ridiculous!'

Antoinette smiled. 'He's coming for tea, isn't he?'

'Oh yes, I think he said five.'

'Then I shall leave you alone.'

'Oh no. Don't do that!' Rosamunde looked a little alarmed.

'I insist. I have so much to do up at the folly. In fact, let me go and wash my hands. I'm covered in dust.'

'Should I change my blouse for tea?'

'Yes, I think you should wear the blue one. Blue suits you, and why don't you wear your hair down for a change?'

'I haven't worn it down in thirty years!'

'Then now's a good time to start. By the way, we have a little problem.'

'Oh? What's that, then?'

'Margaret has asked Phaedra to stay with her this weekend.'

'Oh dear.'

'David's gone to talk to her, but I suspect she'll be storming over to see me as soon as he has gone.'

Rosamunde got up from the sofa with care. Her thigh was still tender but she was able to walk without pain. At least the horrid red colour had subsided somewhat. It reminded her of a hunting accident she had had in her twenties, except that the recovery had been so much quicker then.

She was getting old, that was the trouble. Was it very silly to be flirting at her age? Was she making a fool of herself? Wasn't she too set in her ways to embark on a relationship? Was she *ready* for one? She made her way over to the table and sat down gently. It *was* fun receiving the attentions of an attractive man. She couldn't remember the last time a man had made her feel special. It was hard to believe it, but there it was, so she might as well enjoy it instead of questioning whether or not she was ready. If she wasn't ready at her great age, she never would be. She'd take her sister's advice and wear her hair down. She wasn't pretty like Antoinette, but she could certainly improve on what God had given her. She sighed mournfully: God hadn't been very generous in that department.

*　　　*　　　*

David drew up outside the dower house. It was a pretty, harmoniously proportioned Queen Anne building with a steep tiled roof upon which four tall chimneys stood to attention like rigid sentries. Purple wisteria crept up the red-brick façade, breaking into leaf and surreptitiously stealing in through the open windows, only to be thwarted by Margaret and her secateurs. Pigeons roosted in the tangle of branches and frolicked among the leaves, and in May the flowers hung like grapes, giving off a sweet scent that filled all the rooms in the house.

David had always admired his grandmother's home. He didn't remember having been born there, nor the first few years of his life before his parents had moved into the big house. But he had happy memories of playing there as a young boy. His grandmother had had a game called 'The Milkman', with tiny white milk bottles and miniature slabs of butter and cheese. He had disappeared into that world for hours, spreading it out on the carpet behind the sofa in the sitting room. And her house had two staircases, one at the front and one at the back, which made it the perfect place for 'Cocky Ollie'—a game of hide-and-seek which the whole family would play together after Sunday lunch. Sometimes, when his parents had travelled together, he and his brothers had stayed at the dower house and stolen biscuits from the larder to eat beneath their beds in the middle of the night. Once, their grandfather had caught them. Unlike his wife, who was short-tempered and impatient, their grandfather had been a soft-hearted man with a readiness to laugh. He had tried to be cross, pursing his lips and putting his hands on his hips, but Tom had giggled and that small act of defiance had set the old man off into hearty guffaws. He had made them clear up the crumbs and promise never to steal again or their grandmother would give them a good tongue-lashing. They were well acquainted with her scolding and were grateful to their grandfather for his protection.

As he pulled up in front of the house David remembered that, in spite of her temper, Margaret had laughed a lot with Arthur. He was the only one who could really make her laugh; without his lightness, life had grown very heavy for his grandmother.

David noticed that his wasn't the only car parked on the gravel. An old Morris Minor sat in the shade of the yew hedge. David wondered to whom it belonged. He let Rufus out and watched him trot over to the strange car and immediately cock a leg against the front tyre. David wandered into the house through the front door. He didn't bother to knock, because he never had. His grandmother's house was as familiar as his own and she would have found it very strange had he rung the bell.

As he stepped into the hall he heard voices coming from the sitting room. At first the words were a low hum, like a big bee, but as he got nearer he could make out a man's voice—and that it was talking about love. He stopped at the door, which had been left ajar, and deliberated whether

294

or not to go in. He hadn't imagined his grandmother would have a suitor. He had rather assumed she'd be too old for that sort of thing—and too irritable. But here she was, in her sitting room, listening to a man speaking about love. His blood froze and he backed away, suddenly aware that he might be walking into a secret tryst. But as he crept back towards the front door, Basil scampered out of the sitting room, making loud snorting noises. David was left no option but to plunge in and hope he'd be forgiven for interrupting.

Margaret was startled to see him and withdrew her hand from Reverend Morley's. David was sure that she was blushing. 'Hi, Grandma,' he said in his most jovial tone, trying to pretend that he wasn't shocked by the sight of his grandmother with the vicar. 'Hello, Reverend Morley.'

'Hello, David.' Reverend Morley didn't look at all embarrassed.

'David, what are you doing here?' Margaret demanded.

'I just came to pay you a visit.'

'Nonsense. No one ever comes "just to pay me a visit".' She smiled at the vicar. 'They always want something!' she added dryly.

'I can come back another time.' He began to back away.

'Now is as good as any,' she insisted.

'I really should be leaving,' Reverend Morley began.

'No, you shouldn't,' Margaret retorted, putting a hand on his arm to stop him getting up. 'Why don't you sit down, David. Now you're here, you might as well stay.'

'All right.' He sat in his grandfather's old armchair and remembered the green bucket of cheddar biscuits that always used to sit on the side table, replenished daily by Moira, their Irish cook.

'You've come to speak to me about Phaedra, haven't you?' said Margaret.

There was no point in pretending otherwise. 'Among other things,' he replied airily.

'She's staying with *me* this weekend.'

'You don't think it'll be more fun for her at Mother's house?'

'Certainly not! I want to give her her inheritance, for a start, and we have a lot to talk about, she and I.' She turned to the vicar. 'She's a delightful girl.' Reverend Morley nodded, not knowing who they were talking about. 'You can't have her all to yourself, David. You have to share her. Besides, she was perfectly happy when I extended the invitation. I've never known anyone leap at an offer like she did.'

David knew there was no point arguing with her. Margaret always got her way. 'Well, that's settled, then.'

'Good.'

There was a long pause. Reverend Morley tried to loosen his dog collar. It was hot in Margaret's sitting room. 'Might I suggest you include some of us for dinner?' David said at last.

Margaret sucked in her cheeks. 'If you're very good I might have you all over for dinner on Saturday night.' David wondered anxiously about Friday. 'I'm asking her in order to get to know her, you see. If I have to fight for her attention with the rest of my family, I'll never get a look-in.'

'I can't imagine that's true,' said Reverend

Morley.

'Oh, you'd be surprised, Reverend. We Framptons are a pretty feisty lot.'

A little later David managed to leave with the excuse of having to get back to the farm. He stepped into the sunshine, dazed and a little angry. Rufus and Basil were charging around the garden, falling over each other on the grass. He whistled and Rufus bounded into the front seat while Basil yapped in annoyance. David was tempted to drive straight to his mother's to tell her about Margaret and the vicar, but he was more concerned about having failed Phaedra. She was stuck with his grandmother—*their* grandmother—and there was nothing he could do about it. He felt angry that Margaret had stepped in and asked Phaedra before either he or his mother had had a chance. Couldn't she see that a weekend with *her* would be torture for poor Phaedra? He couldn't bear to text her to tell her the bad news. Perhaps his grandmother would see sense by the end of the week.

He telephoned Tom instead, who was so appalled that he called Joshua. Joshua managed to get hold of his mother as she was on the point of returning to the folly after lunch. Antoinette felt as if her own daughter had been snatched from her arms and rushed into the little sitting room to tell Rosamunde. Rosamunde, in turn, was suitably outraged and confided in Dr Heyworth when he visited at five for Mrs Gunice's shortbread and tea.

'The arrogance of the woman to think that a young girl like Phaedra is going to enjoy staying the weekend with an old lady. I mean, it's preposterous!' She took a sip of Earl Grey.

297

'Is Lady Frampton very upset?' Dr Heyworth asked.

'She's up at the folly, taking her mind off it.'

'Ah, the folly.' He smiled. 'It's a very good thing that she's bringing that lovely building back to life. I feel it's symbolic of a new start for her.'

'She's certainly busy. I haven't seen anything of her. Really, I should be getting home, but now I'm stuck here on the sofa, unable to go anywhere.'

Dr Heyworth's attention was brought back to Rosamunde's hip. 'Is it still giving you pain?'

'Not so much, to be honest. It hurts a little when I walk, though, which I suppose is natural. I'm not as young as I once was. Things take longer to heal at our age, don't they?'

'I'm afraid they do.'

His eyes were so gentle Rosamunde's stomach gave a little flutter. She wondered whether he noticed that she wore her hair down. He hadn't said anything. 'I'd like to be helping my sister in the garden. She's full of enthusiasm all of a sudden. I even heard her playing the piano last night.'

A smile spread across Dr Heyworth's face. 'She was playing the piano?'

'Yes. She hasn't played for years. It didn't sound too good for the first half an hour but then she got it and the piece she played was utterly delightful. Sad, but delightful.' She bit off a piece of shortbread, pleased that William was taking such an interest in what she was saying. 'I think she's slowly realizing that there is life after George. Phaedra has given her a *raison d'être*, you know. I think she's the daughter Antoinette never had but longed for—and now Margaret has gone and been

298

underhand. Really, that woman is the limit!'

'Is there nothing that can be done?'

'I very much doubt it. Margaret is extremely headstrong, as you well know.'

'I think I'll go and see Lady Frampton after tea, just to make sure that she's all right.'

'Really? All the way up to the folly?'

'It's only a short walk. She took me there the other day.'

Rosamunde felt put out. She had rather hoped he would stay for another pot of tea. 'I wonder whether I could come with you?'

'Do you feel up to it?'

She sighed, defeated. 'Not really.'

'You must rest up, I'm afraid, and let nature get you well.'

'You will come tomorrow, won't you? I'm so enjoying our teas. Antoinette is going to disappear into her garden and I'll have no one to talk to. I'm meant to be looking after her and here I am, stuck, like a beached whale.'

'Not a whale, Rosamunde, surely,' said Dr Heyworth politely.

Rosamunde's heart recovered a little at the sight of the twinkle in his eyes. 'Not a whale, then. But I do feel useless. Such a silly thing to fall down the stairs.'

'It could happen to any one of us. There's nothing to be ashamed of, and I'm sure Lady Frampton enjoys having you here when she comes back in the evening. It's a big house and she must feel lonely on her own. Much better that you're here keeping her company and preventing her from dwelling on her loss.'

'You're so right, William. So I'm not overstaying

my welcome?'

'I'm sure you're not. Anyway, you must remain here recuperating for the rest of the week, at least.'

'And you'll come and have tea—perhaps not as a doctor, I can't pretend there's much for you to do in that capacity—but as a friend.'

'Agreed.' His smile was broad and Rosamunde was sure that she had taken their relationship one step further. His visits would no longer be on a professional basis but a social one. She brushed her hair off her shoulder. He still didn't say anything. Maybe he felt it was too intimate to comment on a lady's hair. She watched him leave then took the last biscuit. She'd have another pot of tea on her own.

* * *

Dr Heyworth found Antoinette at the folly. She was up a ladder brushing moss off the roof. 'Hello there!' she shouted down when she saw him approach.

'Hello, Lady Frampton. I thought I'd come and check on your progress.'

'I was hoping you might. There's so much to do, I'm a little overwhelmed.'

'Are you on your own?'

'Yes, Barry's gone back to the garden. I can't expect him to stay up here all day when there's so much to do down at the house. I'm perfectly happy up here, you know. It's so beautiful, I lose myself.'

'I can see why.'

'The boys will help me this weekend.'

'If you ever need a spare pair of hands, I'd be

300

very happy to help.'

Antoinette stopped her work for a moment. 'Do you really mean that?'

'Of course. I spend weekends in my garden; I'd be happy to spend a weekend in someone else's for a change.'

'You're booked in, then. Wonderful.' Her voice rose in excitement. 'We can get going on the inside. I have to take all the furniture out and give the floor and walls a good scrub. Then it needs painting ...'

'If I may boast, I'm a rather good painter.' He grinned and Antoinette laughed as he pulled a self-satisfied smile. His playfulness surprised her. He'd always been very formal.

'Well, I need a good painter, Dr Heyworth.'

He frowned, watching her carefully come down the ladder. What he was about to ask her suddenly didn't feel right, so he stopped himself. 'I even have overalls,' he said instead.

'Very important. You don't want to get paint over your nice clothes.'

'Exactly.'

'It's a lovely little place, isn't it?'

'It's going to be even more lovely once you've finished with it.'

'And what then?'

'Then?' He shrugged. 'We'll have tea in it!'

Chapter 21

David stepped into his mother's house at seven to find her in a state of mounting anguish at the prospect of sending Phaedra off to spend the weekend with her mother-in-law. 'It's like sending a virgin in to be devoured by the Minotaur,' she said, pacing up and down the kitchen floor, glass of wine in hand. She was still in her boiler suit and cap, mud caked into her fingernails and smeared across one cheek.

'At least the whole family will be down to whisk her off,' Rosamunde added helpfully. 'Are they all coming?' David asked, brightening.

'It's a full house,' said Antoinette. 'As soon as word got out they all "booked in" to lend their support. Phaedra's got a lot of fans in this family. George would be so happy.' She didn't mention Roberta. She was sure Phaedra would win her over in the end.

'Can't you all form up to Margaret and just tell her?' Rosamunde suggested.

'She won't budge,' said David. 'I subtly tried to suggest that Phaedra might be happier here with all of us ...'

'That was your mistake.' Antoinette swung around. 'You mustn't ever be subtle with Margaret.'

'Too late now, Mum.'

'What are we going to do?'

'We'll think of something,' said David. 'In the meantime I have to break the news to Phaedra.'

'If she wasn't so polite I think she'd pull out,'

302

said Antoinette.

'Might I remind you both that Phaedra seemed to like Margaret,' Rosamunde interjected. 'I know you all think she's the Wicked Witch of the West, but Phaedra, if I remember rightly, thought she was perfectly charming.'

David chuckled cynically. 'She won't by the end of the weekend!'

*   *   *

After having avoided Julius's calls for a week, Phaedra finally spoke to him. 'You're very hard to get hold of,' he said resentfully. 'Why haven't you returned my calls?'

'I'm sorry, I've been busy since I got back from Switzerland. I've been booked solid.'

'Well, that's a good thing. Not that you need to work nowadays.'

'I work because I love it, Julius. A woman without an interest is a very dull one.'

'So, how was it?'

'How was what?'

'Murenburg.'

'Oh, it was really magical.'

'Did you get closure as you hoped?'

'Oh yes. I feel I can now get on with the rest of my life.'

'Good. So how about dinner?'

She laughed at his persistence, but inside she felt a sense of claustrophobia, as if the walls were closing in around her, leaving her barely enough space to breathe. 'I'm very tired.'

'Nonsense. I'll take you somewhere cosy. We can eat early. How does eight o'clock sound?'

'You know, I've got so much work to do if I want to get this book finished.'

'Tomorrow, then?'

'Julius . . .'

His voice hardened. 'Come on. I've moved heaven and earth for you. The least you can do is have dinner with me. I'm not Jack the Ripper!'

'Wednesday.'

'Great. I'll pick you up at eight.' Then he chuckled. 'You and I are a great team, Phaedra.'

'I'm not sure I know what you mean.'

'Don't go all coy on me now, darling. I'll take you somewhere highly fashionable.'

'Anywhere will do.'

'I'll get my secretary to book at Le Caprice. That's usually a good place to people-watch.'

'Great,' she said, trying to inject some enthusiasm into her voice. The walls were closing in further. 'I must go, Julius.'

'See you Wednesday, darling.' She wondered why he had suddenly started calling her 'darling'. She didn't like it.

In a state of distress she flopped onto the sofa and wondered what she was going to do. If George were alive none of this would be happening. Julius wouldn't ever have asked her out on a date. He wouldn't have dared. But now George was no longer there to protect her she felt exposed, like a fish in a glass bowl within reach of a very greedy cat; a cat to whom she owed a great deal.

She picked up her telephone and sent a text to David. *Rufus, if you're there, would you call me . . . I need to talk to a nice, friendly dog. Phaedra*

*   *   *

David had just returned home from having dinner with his mother and aunt when his iPhone beeped with an incoming message. When he saw that it was Phaedra, his heart leaped. He switched on the lights and walked into the kitchen, then dialled her number. She answered after a single ring.

'Is that Rufus?' she asked.

'Woof!' said David.

She laughed. 'Oh, it's good to hear you.'

'Are you all right?'

She sighed. 'Just some man who's wearing me down.'

David's blood froze. 'Some man?' he croaked.

'He's creeping me out.'

'Who is he?'

'Oh, he's no one important. He just keeps asking me out.'

'Can't you say no?'

'I owe him.'

'You owe him what?' David was alarmed. 'Money?'

'No, not money. He's been very good to me, that's all. I feel it's rude to turn him down. It's only dinner.'

'Phaedra, you don't have to go out with a man just because he's been good to you. He's probably been good to you just so that you'll go out with him.'

Now it was Phaedra's turn to feel alarmed. 'I hadn't thought of that.' She sighed and changed the subject.

'I'm looking forward to the weekend,' she said.

'Ah,' said David slowly. 'We have a slight hitch.'

Phaedra's heart sank. 'I can't come?'

305

'No, of course you can come. The trouble is we're all fighting over you and I'm afraid Grandma has won.'

Phaedra was so relieved that the invitation hadn't been withdrawn, she would have thrown her arms around David if he hadn't been at the other end of the line. 'I'm delighted to be staying with Margaret.'

'You are?'

'Of course. I don't mind. She's very sweet.'

David nearly choked. 'Sweet? You can't really think she's sweet.'

'Look, I'd rather be staying with you but a weekend with your grandmother is not going to kill me. I'm very happy to be coming at all.'

'You can come whenever you like.'

'Then can I come on Thursday?' Fairfield was a safe haven to run to. She envisaged herself driving through those big gates and felt a stab of longing.

'Of course. Come and stay with me on Thursday and then I'll take you to Grandma's on Friday. She doesn't even have to know about it.'

She let out a relieved breath. 'That's wonderful.' Then in a small voice she added, 'I wish I could come now.'

'Any reason why you can't?'

For a moment she almost weakened. It would be so easy to jump in the car and drive down to Fairfield. But inside, her head shouted caution, and for once she obeyed. 'I have work commitments ...' She changed the subject. 'What's Rufus doing?'

'Lying on his beanbag in the kitchen.'

'Where are you?'

'On a stool in the kitchen.'

306

'How's the farm?'

'We need rain.'

'I'll do a rain dance then.'

'Yes, please.'

She laughed. 'Give that darling dog a big kiss from me.'

'I certainly will.' He wished she'd spare one for *him*.

'I'll see you on Thursday, then.'

Sensing her unease, he added: 'Listen, if you're worried about anything, you must call me.'

'I will, thank you.'

'And don't let this man take advantage of you.'

'I won't.'

'Whatever happens, just say no.'

'Oh, don't worry about that. I will,' she said firmly.

'I mean, what's the worst he can do?'

Phaedra's stomach churned with nausea. 'I know, you're right.' But when she put the telephone down she dropped her head into her hands; she knew very well the worst he could do.

The next couple of days dragged for Phaedra. She missed David and couldn't wait for Thursday to come. She prayed for rain and was delighted when, in the middle of the night, she was awoken to loud drops against her windows. It made her smile to think of David's farm getting a much-needed watering.

She went about her work, writing the editorial to go with the photographs. It wasn't easy, as she was a far better photographer than she was writer and the words didn't come naturally. Besides, she wasn't able to give it her full attention. Going through the photographs reminded her of George.

He had been with her during the taking of so many of them. Those pictures inspired memories, which in turn aroused emotions from sorrow to regret to finally fear, as every thought led back to Julius Beecher.

She missed the countryside. The weather was now very warm. Blossom had given way to thick green leaves and the parks were ablaze with flowers. Once, the traffic and bustle of the city had made her feel part of something; now it made her feel isolated and adrift. She longed to return to Fairfield where it was quiet and lush—and she longed for David.

Wednesday arrived and she keenly packed her weekend bag for the following day. Inside she was a tangle of nerves, excited to be leaving, yet anxious about her impending date with Julius. He was like an obstacle she had to overcome before she could flee to the safety of Fairfield.

That evening he appeared at her door at eight o'clock on the dot. She hadn't bothered to dress up, frightened that she'd give him the wrong impression were she to wear a dress again. Instead, she wore white jeans and a floral shirt, her hair up and barely any make-up. Julius was very pleased to see her. He *had* dressed up in a smart black jacket, crisp white shirt and crimson Hermès tie. His shoes were so shiny she could practically see the reflection of the street in the toes. He smelt strongly of cologne.

He kissed her, leaving a whiff of perfume on her cheek, and opened the car door. With a heavy sigh she climbed in, wishing the night were over and she was climbing *out* instead. He drove her to Piccadilly and parked the car in Arlington Street.

Le Caprice was full of fashionable people as Julius had promised, but Phaedra didn't bother to look around and chose the chair with its back to the room so Julius could sit in the corner and smile at those he knew.

To her surprise he didn't bully her, nor did he try to force his friendship upon her. Instead he entertained her with amusing stories about George, and she loosened up and began to enjoy herself. She felt foolish that she had allowed herself to panic over nothing.

At a table at the other end of the room Roberta had watched them walk in. Immediately fascinated, she ignored the anecdote her husband was telling the rest of the table, and narrowed her eyes to take in every detail. So, she thought with satisfaction, Phaedra and Julius were a couple after all. Her suspicions had been right. Then, just to confirm her hypothesis, Julius tenderly touched Phaedra's hand. Roberta was triumphant. She didn't need further proof, but the very fact that Phaedra had come in a pair of jeans without having done her hair or make-up suggested that they had been a couple for a very long time. They were at ease in each other's company. Goodness knows what they were plotting. When the waiter brought them two glasses of champagne, Roberta's heart hardened with loathing. Were they perhaps celebrating the success of their scam? Well, their party was a little premature, she thought resentfully. They might have managed to deceive the rest of her family, but they hadn't deceived *her*. She'd expose Phaedra for the liar she was if it was the last thing she did.

After dinner Julius drove Phaedra home. He

didn't ask to accompany her inside and he didn't request another date. He simply kissed her innocently on the cheek, made sure she got into the house safely, then returned to his car. She asked herself, as she tossed her handbag onto the kitchen table, whether her fears were born out of a guilty conscience. Julius was right, she owed him her friendship; it cost her nothing to give it.

*   *   *

'We need to conduct another DNA test,' Roberta insisted to Joshua as they changed for bed.

'Just because they were having dinner together, darling, doesn't mean they are a couple.'

'God, what more evidence of foul play do you need?' She threaded a hanger through her dress and hung it up in the wardrobe. 'Really, Joshua, doesn't it seem a little odd to you that George's lawyer and supposed daughter are having dinner together, just the two of them?'

'You read too many thrillers,' he replied, tossing his jacket over the back of the chair and unbuttoning his shirt. 'You know, I don't believe a girl like Phaedra is going to fancy a man like Julius. It just doesn't add up.'

'Powerful men are very attractive, Josh. If he's just masterminded her coming into hundreds of thousands of pounds, not to mention the Frampton Sapphires, don't you think she might find him just a teeny-weeny bit attractive?'

'Are you saying that Julius falsified Dad's will?' He looked at her gravely.

'I don't know. Could he do that?'

Joshua shook his head. 'Not easily.'

310

'But he could have falsified a DNA test, couldn't he? I mean, have any of us seen the results?'

'No, we just took Julius at his word.'

'Big mistake.' Roberta squeezed toothpaste onto her electric brush and began to work away at her teeth, staring thoughtfully at her reflection in the mirror. At length she spat out into the sink. 'Let's do another one, then,' she suggested.

Joshua climbed into bed. 'How are you going to do that? Mum will never let you, neither will David or Tom. They think she's marvellous.'

'I'll steal a bit of hair or something.'

'That'll be amusing to watch.'

'I'll take some off her hairbrush.'

'That means creeping into her room at Grandma's. Rather you than me,' he chuckled.

'You're not taking this very seriously,' she fumed, climbing in beside him.

He rolled over and kissed her taut cheek. 'I think you'll find she is who she says she is and that Julius is trying to get his leg over, which, let me add, he won't manage. Phaedra's just being polite. He's her ally in all of this, being Dad's right-hand man. He's probably been her friend from the very beginning. Don't forget that she's in mourning, too. Julius is probably a good shoulder to cry on.'

'Don't you believe it, Joshua. She's up to no good!'

'All right, Roberta PI. I'll leave you to expose the truth.' He kissed her again, but Roberta didn't notice. She was busy planning how she was going to do it.

*　　　*　　　*

The following morning Phaedra set off for Fairfield in a buoyant mood. She listened to the radio and sang along to the songs she knew as loudly as she could. With the windows down and the roof open she felt a rising sense of excitement as she drove along the motorway. Any anxiety about Julius was blown away by the wind and she looked forward to four days with David. She turned off the motorway and navigated down the winding lanes towards the town of Fairfield. The hedgerows were fluffy with cow parsley and the white-flowered blackthorn. It had rained in the night and the grasses shone with moisture. Birds frolicked in the sky, lambs gambolled in the fields and ponies flicked their tails to shoo away the flies. She passed pretty thatched cottages and motored over a quaint stone bridge that straddled a gently meandering stream. It was all so pretty she wished that she could live in the countryside where every day she was surrounded by such beauty. The London parks were nothing compared to this.

As she drove past the church she noticed David's grandmother in the sunshine, talking to the vicar. They were deep in conversation and Margaret was holding a posy of yellow flowers. Phaedra put her head down and drove on, but Margaret was far too engrossed with Reverend Morley to notice the little Fiat Uno.

At last she motored through the gates of Fairfield Park with a rising sense of excitement. She knew the way to David's cottage and turned right up the farm track. She drove around the woods that seemed to float in a sea of blue. The sight of the bluebells was so stunning that she stopped the car. As she got out a Land Rover motored around the corner. She half expected it to be one of David's employees, coming to tell her not to trespass, but as it got closer she saw that it was David.

'Phaedra!' he exclaimed happily, climbing out. 'What a nice surprise. I didn't think you'd be here so early.' Rufus clambered out and bounded up to her, greeting her like an old friend. She patted his soft head.

'I had to leave the city as soon as possible. It's becoming unbearable.'

'That I understand. I could never live in London.'

'And I missed Rufus.' She tickled him behind the ears.

'He missed you, too.' David watched her crouch down. She wore a floral sundress and a short denim jacket. Her blonde hair was unkempt and falling over her shoulders and down her back in thick tendrils. Every time he saw her he was struck by her beauty, as if seeing it for the first time. 'Were you stopping to see the bluebells?'

'I couldn't help myself. They're amazing.'

'If you like we can walk in them now. I'm in no hurry to go anywhere.'

'Farm life is good.'

He grinned. 'It is today. Thank you for the rain!'

'It worked, didn't it?'

'Certainly did.'

She swept her eyes over the fields of wheat. 'It all looks pretty healthy to me.'

'We needed rain for the fertilizer. The ground's very chalky so there's plenty of water stored underneath; it was overground that I was worried about.'

313

'Farmers always worry about something, don't they? Too much rain, too little, not enough sunshine, too much sunshine.'

He shrugged. 'I'm philosophical. There's nothing I can do about it, so I just take it as it comes. Let's walk through the woods. You're seeing them at their best.'

They strolled up the track that cut through the trees. The grass was lush and damp, the air sweet with the scent of bluebells. 'Shall I pick some for your kitchen?' she asked.

'No point, I'm afraid. They die very quickly if you take them out of the soil. Better to admire them here.' Ahead was a copse of large rhododendron bushes in pink, red and white. 'You can pick some of those, if you want.' He handed her his penknife.

'You're a good boy scout.'

'I think there's a boy scout in the heart of every farmer.' He watched her examining the flowers. He wanted to pick one and put it in her hair, but he knew that would be inappropriate. Instead, he sat on a pile of logs chopped from a tree that had fallen during a winter storm.

'I saw your grandmother outside the church, talking to the vicar,' she said.

'There's something very fishy going on,' he mused, rubbing his chin.

'How do you mean?'

'Well, I interrupted them having a rendezvous in her sitting room the other day. They were holding hands and he was talking about love.'

She cut a big pink flower. 'Are you suggesting she's having a romance?'

He screwed up his nose. 'I don't know what to think. If she is, it's very out of character.'

'Good for her.'

'Not so good for the vicar.'

She laughed. 'I think he'd just given her a bunch of flowers. Maybe he's wooing her.'

'Don't you think that's rather like wooing a scorpion?'

'You know, you're very mean, David,' she teased. 'I like Margaret.'

'And she likes you. She wants to give you the Sapphires.'

Phaedra walked over with her flowers and sat beside him on the logs. 'I don't want them, David.'

'Why not?'

She dropped her eyes into the trumpet of a red rhododendron where a large bumblebee was noisily sucking nectar. 'I don't wear jewellery. Whenever am I going to wear those? And I don't think they *should* be mine.'

'Dad wanted you to have them.'

'I know, but that doesn't mean that I *should* have them. I mean, I'm not a Frampton. Not really.'

'By blood you are.'

'I'll marry and become something else and then those beautiful jewels will be lost to your family forever. I don't think that's what your great-great-grandfather intended.'

David tried to ignore the idea of her marrying. 'My great-great-grandfather is dead and no longer cares,' he said.

'So is George, David,' she added softly. 'It's much more important to take care of the living.'

At that moment the bee flew out of the flower and landed unsteadily on Phaedra's arm. David made to shoo it away, but she stopped him. 'Don't, he's a friend,' she insisted. They watched the

315

insect, drunk on sugar, make its way down her arm to her hand. 'He's not going to hurt me. He's far too sensible for that.'

'Or too sleepy,' David replied. They watched it a while. 'You know, Grandma will be offended if you don't accept the jewels. She's very excited about giving them to you.'

'I'll accept them on loan, then. Perhaps I can leave them in your safe. I don't have one in London and I'd be so scared about losing them.'

He smiled. 'Do you know how much they're worth?'

'Not a clue.'

'Well over a million now.'

Her jaw dropped. 'Over a million pounds? Oh my God!'

'Are you sure you don't want them?'

She shook her head, flustered. 'I'm even surer now!'

She got up and handed David her bunch of flowers. 'I'll put this little bee somewhere safe so he can sleep it off.' Gently she put her finger in the insect's path and watched it heave its round body up onto it. Then she encouraged it to enter another trumpet. After a moment's hesitation, the smell of nectar was too great a temptation and it toddled in.

They returned to the vehicles and Phaedra followed David's Land Rover back to his house. Once he had taken her case upstairs they sat on his terrace with cups of tea and biscuits. Phaedra felt a soothing sense of peace wash over her as the sunshine warmed her skin and the birdsong lifted her spirits. London and Julius Beecher seemed a million miles away now. At Fairfield she felt safe.

316

She gazed across at David. His navy eyes were made more intense by the blue shirt he was wearing and his skin was tanned and weathered from his life in the outdoors. His rolled-up sleeves exposed strong brown forearms and big, capable hands. She found him desperately attractive. He returned her gaze and for a long moment neither withdrew their eyes. Phaedra knew she should look away, it wasn't prudent to encourage him; but while her head cried caution, her heart ignored the warning. It was so comfortable in the warmth of his stare and as familiar as if she had always been there.

Chapter 22

That night David and Phaedra dined alone in his kitchen. Phaedra had cooked a mushroom risotto and David opened a fine Burgundy. It pleased David that he had managed to smuggle her onto the estate without his mother or grandmother finding out. He had her all to himself.

They had spent the afternoon together, driving round the farm in his Land Rover with Rufus on the back seat. She had delighted in accompanying him as he went about his work and didn't mind at all that by the time they returned home she was hot and dusty.

After dinner they went outside to see the stars. Unlike the stars in London which were dimmed by the smog, they were as bright and twinkling as the most exquisitely cut diamonds. They decided to walk around the lake with Rufus. The darkness added an element of excitement to their midnight stroll and David had to put his hands in his pocket to stop himself from reaching out and taking hers. He kept reminding himself that they were siblings but the words seemed empty and meaningless. She didn't *feel* like his sister. Saying it was so didn't change the way he felt about her and the way those feelings were growing stronger and more unmanageable by the minute. If he could be convinced that she didn't feel the same he would somehow smother those feelings—but she laid her heart open every time she locked eyes with him.

They reached the lake, where the moon was reflected on the water like mercury. Bulrushes were silhouetted against it, their heavy heads gently swaying in the wind, and a fat moorhen sat sleeping on her nest in the middle, out of reach of foxes. As they walked around it they began to hear the dulcet tones of the piano, carried on the breeze from the big house. 'Who's playing at this hour?' David asked.

'Does your mother play?'

'She used to. But she hasn't touched the piano in years.'

They diverted their course and wandered up the lawn. 'You're not going to spy on her, are you?' Phaedra whispered.

'Why not?' he replied, setting off over the recently cut grass.

'You don't think Rufus will give the game away?' she hissed.

He watched his dog bound up to the window, where a single light shone from the drawing room. 'As long as Mother's dogs are shut away, we'll be OK.'

The music grew louder as they neared the window. It was a sad tune played fluidly.

'Is your aunt still here?' Phaedra asked.

'Yes. I think she's here for good.'

'Doesn't she have a home of her own?'

David chuckled quietly. 'You wouldn't think so, would you? She came to comfort Mum but now Mum's comforting her. She fell down the stairs.'

'Yes, Margaret told me. Poor thing.'

'She had drunk too much, apparently.'

'Oh dear.'

'At least it's given her the excuse to stay another week. Dr Heyworth has insisted she rest.'

'It's probably nice for your mother to have the company.'

'I think she's getting a little tired of her, actually. She spends all day out in the garden or up at the folly, restoring it, probably to get some time alone.'

'Oh, the folly,' exclaimed Phaedra in a loud hiss. 'I'm so pleased she's taking care of it.'

'She's requested that we all help her this weekend. At least it'll get you out of Grandma's clutches.' He stopped by the window and peered in. 'It's Mother,' he whispered.

'She plays beautifully.'

'She's in her dressing gown and she's lit a candle on the piano.'

'Is she by herself?'

He pulled a startled face. 'What are you suggesting?'

'I'm just thinking of your grandmother and the vicar. Maybe there's something in the water.'

He smacked her playfully on the arm. 'You're a wicked girl! Let's get out of here before she sees us.' Suddenly the music stopped. He grabbed Phaedra's hand and they ran off down the lawn.

Antoinette stood at the window and watched them disappear into the darkness. Rufus trotted up to the window and cocked his leg on the hellebores, not at all surprised to see her there. She frowned and wondered who the girl was with David. She'd looked suspiciously like Phaedra. That blonde curly hair was unmistakable. But would David be holding her hand? Surely not.

She returned to the piano with an uneasy feeling in the pit of her stomach. It had been niggling there since David had got back from Switzerland, set off by the way his face had lit up when he spoke about Phaedra. Now it niggled with more vigour as she deduced that the two people running down the lawn together holding hands were undoubtedly David and Phaedra. She knew her son was sensible. Had it been Tom she would have been seriously worried. The niggle, however, wasn't fear that David might embark on a relationship with his half-sister. On the contrary, she trusted he never would. The niggle was born out of sadness that if David had at last found his soulmate, he could never have her.

She blew out the candle and closed the piano lid. That piece of music soothed her spirits and lifted her higher, to somewhere beyond her senses where she felt flooded with peace: the same sense of peace she had felt in the church. There, too, she had perceived a presence that reassured her she wasn't alone. It was comforting to know that she could tap into that feeling simply by playing the piano.

She turned out the light and climbed the stairs to

her bedroom. She still hadn't finished clearing out George's room. It didn't frighten her as it had, but a part of her still wanted to hold onto his things because they connected her to him. If she shut them all away in boxes, wouldn't she be shutting him away, too? Surely his room, as he had left it, kept his memory alive.

She climbed into bed and switched off the light. Closing her eyes, she thought of George. Then, just as her grief rose in a wave of sadness, she turned her thoughts to the garden and the folly and to all the exciting things she planned to do. The window was open. The wind blew through the trees and an owl hooted to his mate. She listened to the familiar sounds of the night and was gently lulled to sleep.

David and Phaedra walked back round the lake. David dropped her hand, not because he wanted to, but because the longer he held it the greater the temptation to pull her towards him and kiss her. It was better not to have any physical contact at all. Phaedra folded her arms and continued walking, as if holding hands with him had been the most innocent thing in the world. In reality, her skin still tingled from his touch. If they hadn't been siblings she would have let him lead her to some secret spot by the lake and take her in his arms. She wished that things were different. But there was no changing them now.

That night they both lay in their separate beds, acutely aware of each other a few doors away. Phaedra tried to listen to the night's sounds, but David was everywhere. He was in the wind, in the mournful hooting of the owl and in the occasional cry of an animal set upon by a fox. His face shone through the darkness as she closed her eyes and willed herself to sleep, and when she did finally drift away, David was there in her dreams and George was gone.

The following day they breakfasted on Phaedra's pancakes then set off in the Land Rover to find Antoinette up at the folly. It was a bright, sunny morning but a cold easterly wind blew over the fields and swept the cotton wool clouds swiftly across the sky. Phaedra wore a sweater on top of her sundress but still she could see the goosebumps ripple across her naked legs. She wished she'd put on jeans instead, but the urge to look pretty for David had been greater than her sense.

They drove up the track. A family of swallows swooped and dived and a fat partridge with six young hurried across the grass to seek shelter in the undergrowth. Phaedra smiled at David and he grinned back, pleased that she took pleasure in the natural world as he did.

At last they reached the folly. As they stepped out of the Land Rover they could hear Antoinette singing contentedly inside. 'Mother,' David shouted. The singing stopped and Antoinette emerged in blue overalls, her hair tied back with an elastic band.

'Hello Phaedra,' she said happily, trying not to think about the vision of the two of them running down the lawn holding hands. 'When did you get here?'

'Yesterday,' Phaedra replied. 'I'd just had it with London. I couldn't bear it another minute. It's incredibly beautiful here, you're so lucky to live in the countryside every day of the week.'

So it had been Phaedra, after all, Antoinette thought, quelling the uneasiness before it rose again. 'When George was alive I spent most of the week in London. Now, looking back, I can't imagine how I managed it. After he died I had an impulsive plan to spend more time there, but then I discovered the garden, and now the thought of going back to the city fills me with horror. It's peaceful here.'

'What are you up to?'

'Ah, my new project. Come and have a look.'

'David says you need help.'

'I'd love some help. Dr Heyworth is coming tomorrow and Tom and Joshua will be here tonight.'

'How lovely. The whole family.'

Antoinette grinned; she couldn't tell the girl that they were all coming down to save her from Margaret. 'More hands, lighter work. You can all get stuck in tomorrow morning.'

'Who built it?'

'I have no idea,' Antoinette replied, leading her inside. 'It's very romantic, isn't it? Someone must know, surely. But I don't know who to ask.'

'I love a mystery,' said Phaedra.

'I fear this will always remain mysterious. At least we can restore it to its former glory.' She sighed. 'Shame walls can't talk.'

They all had lunch together at the big house. Phaedra noticed Rosamunde's new hairstyle immediately. She looked softer with it down. When she complimented her, Rosamunde looked bashful. 'I've worn it off my face for most of my life. I feel now is a little late to start something new.'

323

'It certainly isn't too late. You're young,' said Phaedra.

'You're very kind, my dear.'

'Age is irrelevant. I feel character is much more important. A person can be a young eighty-year-old or an old twenty-year-old. It's all about what's on the inside.'

'I agree,' said David.

Rosamunde wriggled with pleasure. 'In which case, Phaedra, you're a very old and wise thirty-two-year-old, although you don't look a day over twenty.' David caught Phaedra's eye and smiled covertly as her cheeks caught fire. Antoinette couldn't help but notice. Now she had been alerted to their closeness, she saw every secret glance and grin that passed between them. She didn't want to. Their growing affection for one another was beyond the normal behaviour of siblings and made her feel distinctly uncomfortable. It was just as well that Phaedra was going to spend the rest of the weekend with Margaret. *In future, she must stay here*, Antoinette thought to herself. It wasn't healthy for them to spend so much time alone together. Nothing good could come of it.

That afternoon when Dr Heyworth came for tea, Rosamunde was up at the folly, sitting on a chair beneath a blanket, while Antoinette, Phaedra and David were tearing down the ivy that covered the outside walls. Mrs Gunice had given him a Tupperware box of shortbread and a basket filled with cake, sandwiches and a couple of thermos flasks of tea, cups, plates and cutlery, to take up in his car. Dr Heyworth's heart swelled at the thought of spending all afternoon with the woman he loved and he accelerated up the hill to get there as

324

quickly as possible.

'Ah, William,' said Rosamunde excitedly when his car pulled up beside the blackthorn bushes. She waved and he waved back, his mouth extending into a wide smile. 'What have you got there?' she asked, watching him lift a big basket off the back seat.

'Tea,' he replied.

As he strode up the track to join her a gust of wind whipped his panama clean off his head. 'Oh dear!' he exclaimed.

'It's jolly windy up here and chilly when the sun goes behind a cloud,' said Rosamunde. He put the basket down at her feet and hurried off to catch his hat before it was picked up and carried off again.

'Ah, lovely, Mrs Gunice's shortbread,' she muttered, poking around in the basket.

'You're doing a terrific job, Lady Frampton,' he called out as a long tentacle of ivy fell onto the ground like a dead octopus.

'I've got a couple of helpers,' she replied.

'Many hands make light work,' said Rosamunde. 'I'd like to help myself.'

'But you mustn't,' said Dr Heyworth kindly. 'How is the patient feeling today?'

'I'm so much better. I walked up here very gently and now I'm nice and snug under this rug.'

'Can I pour you a cup of tea?'

'That would be very nice, thank you.'

He lifted the thermos flask out of the basket. 'Tomorrow I shall come prepared to get my hands dirty,' he said.

'Maybe I can help, too.'

'I'm sure your sister can find you something to

do that isn't too strenuous, don't you think, Lady Frampton?'

'She can clean the windows,' Antoinette called down from the roof.

'Why don't you come and have a cup of tea, Lady Frampton, while I continue pulling down the ivy. You must be in need of a rest, surely?'

Antoinette smiled at him. 'Coming from a doctor, how can I refuse?' She laughed and carefully descended the ladder. As she got to the bottom Dr Heyworth was there to help her. She took his hand and jumped the last couple of rungs onto the grass. 'Thank you.'

Dr Heyworth rolled up his sleeves. 'I can't rest while you are doing all the work. It doesn't sit well with me.'

'Then I will have a cup of tea with Rosamunde and watch the three of you doing the job for me.'

She laid out the rug that Mrs Gunice had put on top of the basket and sat down. David and Phaedra were up ladders pulling the ivy off the pediment that rested above the portico. It was tough going, as the weed clung obstinately to the stone. They used trowels to ease it carefully away, mindful not to damage the building beneath. They chatted contentedly, laughing every now and then, and even Rosamunde felt the energy between them.

'It's like they've known each other all their lives,' she said to her sister.

'Yes,' Antoinette replied edgily.

Rosamunde narrowed her eyes at her sister's tone of voice. 'They're very keen on each other, aren't they?' she whispered, turning her attention back to the portico.

Antoinette winced. 'What are you thinking?'

'Nothing, just that there's a certain frisson between them. But maybe they are just great friends. They've certainly hit it off.'

'You think they fancy each other, don't you? Well, they can't do anything about it. They're related.'

Rosamunde could see that her sister was getting agitated. 'Oh, really, Antoinette, you have nothing to worry about. David is a sensible boy.'

'I know, but I can't bear him to be unhappy. Unrequited love is a horrible thing.'

They both sipped their tea and watched the group slowly bring down all the ivy. Suddenly David cried out in excitement. 'Look! There's writing in the stone!' Dr Heyworth climbed down his ladder to get a better view. Phaedra wiped the remaining bits of stem away. There, clearly carved into the stone, were the words: *Dum spiro ti amo.* Followed by a date.

Antoinette got up and put her hands on her hips, gazing up at the engraving in astonishment. 'I don't believe it,' she gasped. 'A clue to our mystery. What does it mean? I bet you know Latin, Dr Heyworth!'

'I certainly do. While I breathe, I love you,' he replied.

'Oh my, how romantic!' Phaedra exclaimed.

'And the date, Dr Heyworth?' Antoinette added.

'1954.'

'So not as old as we thought.'

'When things are ravaged by nature, they look much older than they are. Buildings can be weathered in a matter of years,' said Dr Heyworth knowledgably.

'Well, who do we think built it?' Rosamunde

327

asked.

'I imagine a man built it for the woman he loved,' said David. 'Who lived here in 1954 but Grandpa?'

'He would have been in his twenties ... you don't think he built it for Margaret?' said Antoinette in amazement.

'Why would she have let it go to ruin like this if it had been built especially for her?' said David.

'I can't imagine,' Antoinette replied, pondering. 'I mean, it can't have been built by anyone else but Arthur.'

'And he wouldn't have built it for anyone else but Margaret.'

'Her family came from Bath, if I'm not mistaken,' Antoinette added. 'Hence the Bath stone.'

'That would make sense,' said Dr Heyworth.

'Phaedra, you have a mission this weekend,' said Antoinette excitedly. 'You're the only one who might be able to get the story out of her.'

'I'll do my best,' Phaedra replied, climbing down.

'Let's all have a cup of tea to celebrate,' David suggested heartily.

'There's cake, biscuits and egg sandwiches,' Rosamunde informed them. 'Mrs Gunice has once again prepared a feast!'

*   *   *

That evening David escorted Phaedra to his grandmother's house at the other side of the estate. Phaedra had visited the last time she was at Fairfield but now the clematis was out and the house looked even more beautiful in the pink light

328

of dusk. She parked her car by the hedge that separated the front of the house and the garden, while David pulled up on the gravel, leaving Rufus inside. He wasn't intending to stay long.

Margaret was overjoyed to see Phaedra. She hurried into the hall from her study with a wide smile and a warm embrace, which she threw enthusiastically around Phaedra. David didn't think he'd ever seen her in such a good mood. 'Thank you for bringing her, David. Before you go, can you put her case upstairs in the yellow room.' David did as he was told and carried the case upstairs. It wasn't very heavy. She hadn't brought much.

He tried to ascertain from her face whether Phaedra was happy or anxious at being left alone with Margaret. She grinned at him playfully and he couldn't tell whether she was putting on a brave face or was genuinely pleased to be there. As he left he felt bereft, like a boy who'd just let all the party balloons go. He returned to his car and to Rufus, who thumped his tail with pleasure at the sight of his master, but the thought of returning home alone made David's heart heavy with regret.

'Now, my dear, what can I get you to drink? I have a particularly good Sauvignon if you'd like wine. I'll have a glass of sherry,' said Margaret, leading her into the sitting room.

Phaedra ran her eyes over the pretty room. It was harmoniously square, with high ceilings, tall windows and a wide honey-coloured marble fireplace above which hung a portrait of Margaret as a young woman. She had been quite a beauty. Decorated with flair in pale yellows and blues, with antique wooden furniture and big, soft sofas and

329

armchairs, the room had a warmth that had more to do with the positive energy than the central heating. 'What a stunning room,' she exclaimed truthfully, settling into the sofa.

'I can't take credit for the decoration,' Margaret replied. 'Antoinette did it up when she lived here. I've done very little to it since. It's lasted rather well, hasn't it?'

'I think it's really lovely.'

'Good, I'm glad you like it. Antoinette has a thing for yellow.'

'It's a happy colour.'

'I agree, it is a happy colour. Now, let me call my girl.' She pressed a button that sat in a silver holder on the sofa table. A few moments later a cheerful young woman appeared at the door in a blue-and-white striped apron, her brown hair scraped back to reveal a round, freckly face with big blue eyes. 'Ah, Jenny, this is Phaedra. What did you say you wanted to drink, dear?'

'I'll have a glass of white wine, please,' Phaedra replied.

'Lovely, and a sherry for you, ma'am?' Jenny said to Margaret.

'As always,' Margaret retorted briskly.

'Lovely, back in a tick.' Jenny disappeared.

'I think she's had too much yellow,' said Margaret with a grin. 'Much too merry.'

'Is she always like that?'

'Always.'

'Lucky girl.'

'I suppose it's better than having someone who mopes about in a sulk all the time. And she's a very good cook.' Margaret sat down next to Phaedra. 'Isn't this nice,' she said with a sigh. 'I

330

have you all to myself. You know, they're all fighting for you over at the big house.'

'I'm sure they're not,' Phaedra replied modestly.

'Oh, they are. You've brought something magical into the family. I can't put my finger on it. But you have a special light, Phaedra, and we all want to bask in it.'

'Oh really, I don't deserve such a compliment. You've all been so kind to me, I feel so welcome.'

'I think Antoinette rather wished she had a daughter, and as for me, well, I only had George. I'd love to have had a little girl.' Her face darkened a moment. 'But that was never going to happen.'

'I'm sorry.'

'Oh, don't be. I have a granddaughter now and it's just lovely. Ah, Jenny, come in.'

The girl handed Margaret her sherry and she took a sip. Phaedra tasted the wine; it was perfectly chilled.

'David told me about your visit to Murenburg,' Margaret said.

'It was very healing, I think, for all of us.'

'The boys were lucky that you went with them.'

'I was pleased to go. I needed to see the place where George was taken and to let him go. I feel at peace now. I mean, I miss him and I think of him a great deal, but I don't feel that terrible ache. I think it's because I accept his death now. It's happened, there's nothing I can do to bring him back. What I can do now is cherish his memory and continue with my life, all the better for having crossed paths with him for a while.'

Margaret's face glowed with admiration. 'You're an old soul, Phaedra. I've been talking to

331

Reverend Morley about you and he agrees. You're wise beyond your years. You know, when you spoke to me up in Antoinette's spare room something magical happened. No one had ever spoken to me like that before. You see, I hadn't visited George's grave. I hadn't wanted to accept that he was dead. It was too much. Then, that day, I went with Joshua and something frightening happened. I stumbled across George's grave and I was suddenly so ashamed, because I didn't even know where it was. My son, I didn't even know which gravestone was his. I haven't even had anything to do with what's written on the official one. I've left it all to Antoinette. But I *should* have had a say. And then I felt a rush of sorrow. I thought I was having a heart attack, but you made it all so clear when you spoke to me. I hadn't grieved. I mean, how could I have grieved when I hadn't even accepted his death? With you I was able to talk about him and how I felt. It was such a release. I felt a different person afterwards.' Her smile wobbled. 'I put a bouquet of yellow flowers on his grave yesterday. I thought yellow, being a happy colour, would be nice. Reverend Morley has been so kind.'

So the flowers weren't a bouquet from the vicar, after all, thought Phaedra. 'Oh Margaret, I'm so pleased you feel better,' she said.

The old woman patted Phaedra's hand. 'You showed me the way, my dear.'

'Did I?'

'Oh yes, you were a light showing me the way to God. Reverend Morley has been my teacher and my guide. I can't imagine how I've got to my great age without having known that sense of God. It's wonderful and I have you to thank.'

'I really can't take credit for that.' Phaedra felt inadequate in the light of such high praise.

'You can, my dear, and you must. Now, I have something for you.' She picked up a red velvet box from the sofa table. 'George wanted you to have them and I think you're wholly deserving. At first I was against it, I'll be honest with you. They're Frampton jewels and I believed that they should remain in the family. But now I know you, I can't think of a better woman to give them to, even though you'll marry and send them off down another family line.' Phaedra's heart began to thump. She took the box with a sinking feeling. 'Go on, open it.'

Phaedra lifted the lid. There, sparkling as nothing in her entire experience had ever sparkled, lay the Frampton Sapphires. She gasped. Then she closed the lid quite suddenly. 'Margaret, I can't accept them.'

Margaret's face fell. 'Why ever not?'

'George was impulsive, as you know. He wished me to have them. But I'm sure had he lived he would have changed his mind.'

'You don't know that.'

'Oh, I do.' She laughed bitterly. 'His death has put me in a very awkward position, you have no idea. It would be wrong of me to take them. Your instincts were right. They should remain in the family.'

'But you *are* family!'

'As you said, I'll marry one day and take them away forever. They'll never belong to the Framptons again. That isn't right. Surely, in your heart, you know that isn't right.'

'It's what my son wanted.'

'It was a whim, Margaret. Really, I feel very bad ...'

'I insist.' Margaret patted her hand again. 'Sleep on it. You'll think differently in the morning.'

Phaedra sighed. She didn't want to offend her hostess. 'All right, I'll sleep on it.'

'Good. Now, let's go and eat. I'm sure you're hungry.' Phaedra followed her into the dining room. 'And you can tell me what's going on up at the folly. I'm sure David's told you, Antoinette is supposedly restoring it. Do you know why? I can't think what's got into the woman.'

Chapter 23

Margaret placed herself at the head of the table and Phaedra sat on her right. Jenny served dinner, which was asparagus soup to start, followed by rack of lamb, new potatoes and vegetables fresh from the garden. 'So, why's Antoinette restoring the folly? It was perfectly fine just the way it was,' said Margaret as Jenny disappeared into the kitchen.

'I think she's happy to have a project that takes her out of herself,' Phaedra replied.

'I thought she was doing that in the garden. Barry told me she'd taken him off to the garden centre and bought a whole heap of things to plant. Fiddling about in the garden is a very good thing. But the folly, I mean, it's up a hill for goodness sake. What's the point?'

'Curiosity, perhaps.'

Margaret looked bewildered. 'She's curious about the folly?'

'Oh, I am too. It's won me over.'

'Really, why?'

'Because it's so charming and so neglected. There's something mysterious about it, and romantic, don't you think?'

'Well, if she'd only asked, I would have told her. There's no mystery at all, and believe me, even less romance.'

'Oh, I'm disappointed.'

Margaret lifted her chin. 'It was built for me, by my husband.'

'That's romantic,' Phaedra said brightly.

'The reason for such a grand gesture was not entirely romantic, I'm afraid.' She put down her spoon and hesitated, as if deliberating how best to tell the story. 'You see, Arthur had an eye for the ladies. Or rather, one lady in particular. She was called Leonora and was rather pretty in a common sort of way, although I assure you she was very aristocratic, the daughter of an earl. Well, he had an affair, as many men do. His crime wasn't dallying with another woman, but getting caught. He always used to say the eleventh commandment is "Don't get caught", and what did the silly man go and do? Get caught. Ironic, don't you think?' Phaedra had gone pale. 'Oh, don't be alarmed, my dear. I took it in my stride. I'm stronger than I look.'

'What did you do?'

'I told him in no uncertain terms that I would leave him if he didn't leave *her*, preferably in the middle of a desert somewhere very far away.' She chuckled. 'Of course he gave her up immediately.

Men usually do when they have to choose between their lovers and their wives. They go scuttling back like beaten dogs, with their tails between their legs.'

'So, he built you the folly by way of an apology?'

Margaret smiled. 'Oh, you are a romantic girl, aren't you? Yes, very silly. He didn't need to go to all that trouble to get the stones from my birthplace and lug them all the way up to Hampshire. I never cared for the building.'

'But he loved you,' said Phaedra simply.

'In his way.'

'Men are very good at compartmentalizing. He probably loved you both in totally different ways.'

'Perhaps.'

'But his greatest love and loyalty was to you.'

'And he didn't want the scandal, don't forget. In those days it was a definite no-no.'

'It's quite a gesture to build a little house in a place where you can sit and enjoy the sunset. The location is the best on the entire estate, I'll bet.'

'Yes, it's a very pretty place.'

'The view is stunning. You can see the lake and the house, and the sky is so big. I'd like to sit up there and watch the sun rise and set. You get them both.'

'Well, I never sit there,' said Margaret briskly. She began to spoon her soup again.

'Did you forgive him in the end?' Phaedra asked.

'I think we just lived through it and came out the other end, a little stronger, a little warier, but never the same. These things change you. You're too young to know, but I can tell you from my experience, you shed a skin and emerge a little altered. In my case I became an old sourpuss.'

'Oh, Margaret, I don't think so.'

'I did. Oh, I still laughed. Arthur could make me laugh like no one else and I sort of begrudged him that. I didn't feel he deserved the reward of my happiness. So I became difficult just to punish him.' She took a sip of wine. 'Perhaps I didn't forgive him, not completely.'

'What would Reverend Morley think of that?'

'Very little. I know it's not very Christian. Forgiveness is one of Jesus's most enduring messages. But Arthur is long dead—and I'm still an old sourpuss.'

Phaedra felt her heart swell with compassion. 'I don't think you're a sourpuss, Margaret.'

Margaret's eyes twinkled with pleasure. 'That's because I like you. You can tell Antoinette that you've solved the mystery. She'll be very grateful, I'm sure.'

'It says "while I breathe, I love you", in Latin.'

Margaret looked surprised. 'Do you speak Latin?'

'Dr Heyworth.'

The old woman raised her eyebrows. 'Oh yes, he's sniffing around Antoinette, isn't he?'

'I thought he came to see Rosamunde.'

Margaret tutted. 'Have you had a good look at Rosamunde lately? No, I thought not. She's a perfectly nice human being but she's not attractive like Antoinette. Dear Dr Heyworth. I think he's been in love with her for thirty years. I could have told her that.'

'Antoinette doesn't know?'

'Of course not. Antoinette's very unassuming, and besides, she's still grieving for George.'

'Do you think he'll declare himself?'

337

'He won't if he's got any sense. Really, it would be very presumptuous. I suspect Rosamunde will return home and Dr Heyworth will retreat to his surgery and everything will go back to normal.'

They finished the lamb and ate a bowl of strawberries and blackberries from the supermarket for pudding. 'Now, I have a job for you.' Margaret changed the subject.

'I'm happy to help.'

'Good. Because I need you. It's regarding David.'

'Oh?'

'It's about time he found a nice girl to settle down with.' Margaret was too busy enjoying the strawberries to notice the blush that put the colour back into Phaedra's cheeks. 'He's getting on and it's been a very long time since he's had a girlfriend of any significance.'

'How can I help?'

'You're his half-sister and you're jolly pretty. You must have girlfriends like you in London you can introduce him to.'

'He hates London.'

'Then bring them down. I'm sure Antoinette would be happy to fill her spare rooms with your nice chums.'

'I don't have any girlfriends in London,' Phaedra protested, trying to get out of the obligation. 'They're all in Paris.'

'Surely you can find *one*.'

'He's very choosy.'

'That's his mistake. His standards are impossibly high. After all, he doesn't have a very exciting life, so it's not like he's got a great deal to offer a girl.'

'He lives on one of the most beautiful estates in

338

the country.'

'Yes, but how many girls want to live in the middle of a field? They all want to paint the town red. He should lower his standards, find a nice comely girl who'll be happy to live down here and have lots of children. One day he'll inherit the big house. I can't imagine anything worse than moving in as a bachelor; he'll rattle around in there like a pea in a shoebox. No, he has to find a wife and have a big family, and you, my dear, are going to help him find her.'

Phaedra sighed and lowered her eyes to her empty bowl. 'I'll do my best.'

'Good.' Then Margaret added with a smile, 'Such a shame you're blood, because you'd be perfect.'

After dinner she showed Phaedra to her room. It was cosy, with yellow floral wallpaper, matching curtains and a high iron bed. There was a jug of water and a glass on her bedside table along with a copy of the King James Bible. Phaedra wondered whether that was something Margaret had put there since her long chats with the Reverend.

'It might get too warm, in which case open the window,' Margaret told her, drawing the curtains.

'It's fine.'

'I like a warm house. At my age one feels the cold dreadfully.'

'That bed looks very comfortable.'

'It is, so sleep in. Breakfast will be in the conservatory when you're ready. No rush. If Basil comes in to wake you, ignore him and he'll soon go away. If you give him the slightest attention you won't be rid of him. You can't say you haven't been warned.'

'Don't worry, I love dogs,' Phaedra laughed.

'That's a very good thing. Goodnight, dear.'

Phaedra bathed and changed into her pyjamas. She turned off the lights and stood a while by the window, gazing out at the stars. She wondered whether David was taking Rufus around the lake and looking at the same stars. Her room looked onto the garden and sweet scents pervaded the room. She inhaled with pleasure as the familiar hooting of the owl resounded through the darkness. She remembered Boris the barn owl and wondered whether he was screeching outside David's house.

She missed him. It was pleasant enough in Margaret's house and in spite of what David thought of his grandmother, Phaedra liked her a great deal, but she would have preferred to be with him.

She climbed into bed and closed her eyes. She'd happily live in the middle of a field, married to a man who drove a tractor. She rolled over and sighed heavily. How could this situation ever resolve itself? The very thing which would enable her to have him would surely drive him away forever. She had no choice but to bite her tongue and lock her heart—and she might as well throw away the key, she thought forlornly.

She had loved before and suffered terribly. If she allowed herself to grow to love David with the same intensity she would only suffer again. She remembered her mother telling her as a child not to stare at the moon or it would drive her mad. But the moon had been so beautiful she couldn't tear her eyes away. It was like that now with David. She knew she would be driven crazy but she was unable to resist being with him. In the short term, at least, the pleasure was worth the pain.

She thought of Arthur and his affair with Leonora. Her stomach turned just to think of it. Poor Margaret, suffering as she did and trying so hard to be strong. It was no wonder that the woman had grown bitter. A person simply couldn't come back after such a cruel betrayal. She squeezed her eyes shut. A teardrop seeped through her lashes. She frowned and wiped it on the pillow. It was better not to think of sad things. She tried to think happy thoughts instead.

The ticking of the large clock on the mantelpiece kept her awake. She hadn't noticed the noise when she was getting ready for bed, but now, in the silence, it sounded like gunfire. She got up and switched the light on. It was a magnificent antique clock, presumably of great value. She thought a moment, then decided to wrap it in her jumper, place it in her suitcase, then lock the suitcase in the cupboard. She closed the door and listened. The ticking was now muted sufficiently for her to sleep.

The following morning she awoke to the patter of little feet scampering into her bedroom. She knew it was Basil, but instead of heeding Margaret's warning she rolled over and looked at him. He wagged his stumpy little tail and barked. There was no point in trying to go back to sleep after that, and besides, she was excited at the prospect of seeing David.

Margaret was in the conservatory, sipping coffee and reading the newspapers, when Phaedra came down. Sunlight streamed in through the glass and turned the room into a furnace. Margaret had opened the windows to cool it down. 'Good morning, my dear,' she said, smiling. 'Did you sleep well?'

'Like the dead.'

'Good. Now, what would you like for breakfast? Jenny can make you eggs if you like.'

Phaedra sat down. 'Eggs would be lovely. What a treat!'

She had just dipped her spoon into her boiled egg when three familiar faces appeared at the window. Margaret raised an eyebrow, but didn't seem in the least surprised. 'Ah, your rescue party. I was wondering when they were going to turn up.'

Phaedra stared at David, Joshua and Tom and grinned. 'I really don't need rescuing,' she laughed.

'We've come recruiting, actually,' said Tom, leading the way in. He kissed her cheek then took the chair beside her. 'Croissants, Grandma, do you mind? Phaedra won't eat them, will you, Phaedra?'

'I bought extra,' said Margaret. 'You don't think I didn't anticipate your visit? Mind you, I didn't expect all *three* of you. What have you done with Roberta and Amber?'

'They're having breakfast,' Joshua replied. He, too, kissed Phaedra. 'We thought you'd like to come and help Mum at the folly. We could do with an extra pair of hands.'

'Lucky I asked you to come for dinner last night,' said Margaret. 'I knew the boys wouldn't leave us alone for long.' But she didn't look put out. The sourpuss was finding it hard to sustain her tang. Joshua sat beside his grandmother and helped himself to a piece of toast. 'You might as well sit down and join us,' she added. 'I suppose everybody wants coffee and cooked breakfast?'

'You read my mind, Grandma,' said Tom.

'Don't they feed you up at the big house?'

'Never enough,' Tom added, shaking his head dolefully. 'I'm *always* hungry!'

David caught Phaedra's eye and smiled. 'I have a penchant for home-made pancakes,' he said, and Phaedra smiled back.

'I'm not a restaurant,' Margaret snapped. 'Eggs and bacon, take it or leave it.'

'I'll take it,' said David. He sat on Phaedra's other side.

'Did you take Rufus for a walk around the lake?' she asked quietly.

'Yes, how did you guess?'

'I wondered. Did you hear the owl?'

'Yes, but it wasn't Boris. Boris screeches.'

She laughed. 'Do you think they're friends?'

'I don't think they share dinner, if that's what you mean.'

She lowered her voice further. 'I know who built the folly and why. I'll tell you later.'

He glanced at his grandmother. She was in conversation with Joshua and Tom. 'When we're alone,' he replied.

Margaret did not want to go up to the folly, but she was happy to let Phaedra go. She reminded them that they were all invited for dinner. She had arranged treacle pudding especially for Tom, knowing it was one of his favourites.

Phaedra collected her camera from her car and then the four of them set off in David's Land Rover. Rufus sat in the well of the passenger seat with his head on Phaedra's knee. David noticed that his dog was growing as fond of her as he was. She seemed to electrify them all, for Joshua and

Tom bantered in the back as Phaedra laughed at their double act. They seemed to rise to their attractive new audience, and even David was unable to resist and laughed along with them.

They arrived at the folly to find Dr Heyworth, Rosamunde, Antoinette, Roberta and little Amber in her pram, watched over by the stout nanny, Kathy. They were greeted cheerfully by all except Roberta, who said a cold 'hello' to Phaedra, then proceeded to watch her suspiciously from the top of the ladder without uttering another word. The boys helped Dr Heyworth lift all the furniture out onto the grass while Phaedra removed the rest of the ivy from the far side of the folly, and Antoinette and Rosamunde, now much more mobile, swept and dusted where the furniture had been. They then scrubbed the floor and walls and cleaned the windows until they gleamed. It was more like a party than a chore. The air was filled with mirth as they chatted and joked while the sun rose in the sky and beat down upon them.

David and Phaedra simply enjoyed being together. They locked eyes when the others were too occupied with their tasks to see, and shared secret jokes and asides that only they understood. Antoinette was too absorbed in her jobs to worry about her son and stepdaughter, and Rosamunde was so busy watching the doctor that a family of ducks could have flown in through the window and she wouldn't have noticed.

Roberta was in a merry mood in spite of her doubts about Phaedra, or perhaps *because* of them. Her quest gave her a secret thrill, one that only she and Joshua knew about. This weekend she was determined to sneak into Phaedra's bedroom and extract some hair from her brush. She wasn't sure how to go about conducting a DNA test, but she knew people she could ask. It gave her pleasure to watch Phaedra as a hunter watches an ignorant stag. The girl had no idea that she was onto her. As far as Phaedra was concerned, she had got away with it.

As Roberta was scrubbing the wall, Joshua came up behind her and kissed her neck where the skin was exposed because she had put her hair up in a band. She smiled and turned to him, surprised. 'Hello there,' she said softly. 'What was that for?'

'I don't know. I just felt like kissing you.'

She giggled. 'That's nice.'

'This is fun, isn't it?' he said, putting an arm around her waist and squeezing her.

'Yes, we're a secret team, like undercover policemen.'

'Are you going to be *very* disappointed when you're wrong?' he laughed.

Roberta laughed with him. 'No, *you're* going to be very disappointed when I'm right!'

They picnicked in the shade. Phaedra retrieved her camera from the Land Rover and set about taking lots of photographs. She tried to disguise the fact that for every one she took of Dr Heyworth and David's family, she took three of David. She shot the folly too, from all directions, then checked the screen to examine her work.

Tom disappeared for a while, returning a little later with an old stereo he'd dug out of his bedroom cupboard. He put on a tape of Eighties dance tunes, much to the amusement of his siblings. Then he grabbed Phaedra and pulled her to her feet. Ignoring her protests, he proceeded to dance with her. Joshua roared with laughter and took Roberta by the hand. The four of them danced exuberantly in the sunshine until Rufus began to bark in confusion. Dr Heyworth, inspired by the young and encouraged by Antoinette's obvious enjoyment, asked Rosamunde to dance. Rosamunde looked mortified and declined, blaming her ailing hip. Undeterred, he approached Antoinette. 'Lady Frampton,' he began. 'May I have this dance?' She smiled at him shyly, half pleased, half embarrassed. 'I will be gentle with you,' he reassured her and held out his hand.

Rosamunde looked on uneasily as the object of her desire put his arm around her sister's waist and led her across the grass. While they danced, they laughed, locked their heads to be heard and moved in sync to the beat. Rosamunde told herself that he had only asked Antoinette out of politeness. Had *she* not declined, he'd be pressing himself against *her* instead.

David poured himself another glass of wine. He lay back on the rug and commented loudly on the extraordinary spectacle before him, but his eyes never left Phaedra, not for a moment.

The festive mood carried them all through the rest of the afternoon. Roberta left at teatime to take Amber and Kathy home, but the others remained at the folly. 'Tomorrow we paint,' Antoinette announced. 'So no Sunday best, please.'

'Does anyone know yet who built it?' Dr Heyworth asked.

Antoinette looked hopefully at Phaedra. 'Did you get anything out of her?'

'Arthur built it soon after they married,' she

replied lightly. 'A romantic gift, don't you think?'

'Very,' Antoinette replied, wondering why she had never been told.

Phaedra glanced at David. He knew she wasn't telling the whole truth. She looked back at Antoinette. 'She says she'd have told you had you ever asked.'

'Oh, so there's no mystery?' Antoinette was disappointed.

'No mystery.'

'Why doesn't she ever come up here, then?'

'You'll have to ask her that yourself. I forgot.'

'Perhaps it's too painful,' she mused.

'Perhaps,' Phaedra replied. Again she caught David's eye. It wasn't a story she'd relish telling him.

That evening they all dined at Margaret's. She had gone to great trouble to choose a menu they all liked. Arthur's cellar had been opened and David had chosen the finest wine. It was as if they had something important to celebrate. After dinner they played charades and even Margaret joined in, performing a very convincing Cruella De Vil to riotous applause from her astonished audience.

Antoinette watched her family unite in the most unlikely way, in the most unlikely place. Margaret's house had always been a place of rigid formality and few laughs. Now it was the centre of the revelry. She looked at Phaedra, in the middle of it all. She seemed to glow with a particularly golden light that drew everyone into her orbit, like a beautiful star—everyone except Roberta. Antoinette wished she'd make more of an effort to get to know her. She was sure Roberta would like her, if she gave the girl a chance.

Later, Tom went outside to smoke, taking Joshua with him. Rosamunde and Antoinette returned home and Margaret retired to bed. David seized the opportunity to speak to Phaedra alone. They went into the drinks room under the pretence of replenishing their glasses. Roberta seized her opportunity and hurried up the stairs to the yellow room.

'So, what's the real story?' David asked. Phaedra was reluctant to tell him, but even Margaret had said Arthur's affair was no secret, so she repeated what his grandmother had told her. He looked appalled. 'That explains a lot,' he said finally. 'Poor Grandma. I can't believe Grandpa could have done that to her, so soon after they married, too. He didn't look the type. I remember him as a very decent, respectable man.'

'He must have learned his lesson.'

'The folly is one hell of an apology. He must have felt really bad.'

'It's no surprise that she never goes up there. I don't suppose she ever got over the hurt.'

'You'd never have guessed, seeing them together.' He looked down at her solemnly. 'Are you going to tell Mother?'

'It's not for me to tell her.'

'I will,' said David after a moment's thought. 'It explains a great deal about Margaret.'

'We are all the sum of our experience,' said Phaedra gravely.

'Don't look so sad. What's your experience?' He grinned playfully.

She shook her head. 'Not for now.'

He frowned. 'Are you ever going to tell me?'

348

'There's little to tell.'

But he didn't believe her. 'I get the feeling you're keeping things from me.'

'We're all allowed a few skeletons.'

'I can't imagine you have many.'

'One or two.' She gazed up at him. For a fleeting moment she thought he was about to kiss her. He grew suddenly very serious and bent his head slightly. She caught her breath. She wanted him to so much. The moment seemed to last for an age, giving her time to see the last eighteen months flashing before her eyes. Just as his lips were about to brush hers, Tom shouted from behind the door.

'What's going on in there?'

He opened it and burst in. 'What are you two plotting?'

'The truth about the folly,' said David. 'Come in and we'll tell you.'

'Oh good, I love a scandal,' he exclaimed, rubbing his hands.

'I'll leave you to it,' Phaedra said. 'I think I'm going to go to bed.' And she left, ignoring the silent plea in David's eyes.

She escaped to her room and closed the door. Her heart was beating wildly, throwing itself against her ribcage like a frustrated parrot. She closed her eyes and took a deep, relieved breath. That had been close. If Tom hadn't disturbed them David would most certainly have kissed her, and then what? 'Oh God!' she sighed out loud, retreating into the bathroom to change for bed.

She washed her face and stared at her reflection in the mirror. What was she thinking? She should just walk away, but she was in far too deep now to turn her back on the Framptons—and she liked

349

them too much.

She pulled on her pyjamas and climbed into bed. She took a swig of water then switched off the light. The sound of creaking floorboards alerted her to the possibility that David might come up to find her. She stiffened, but all she could hear was her breathing—and the loud tick-tock of the clock.

She gasped in horror. Who had put it back? Margaret? Jenny? She slid beneath the sheet, wanting the mattress to swallow her up. Would they have thought she intended to steal it?

*　　　*　　　*

'I've got it!' Roberta hissed to Joshua, finding him in the sitting room.

'That was quick,' he replied.

'Doesn't take long. Her hairbrush was in the bathroom. I just pulled a bit out.' She patted her trouser pocket. 'Safe in here.'

'Lucky she didn't catch you in her room.'

'I'm far too clever for that. I saw her in the hall and dived into the next-door bedroom. Once she'd gone into her room, I ran downstairs. Simple.'

'You'd make such a good detective,' he flattered her.

'I know. I'm rather loving it, actually. I'm closing in. Soon it will all be over. You wait and see.'

Chapter 24

The following morning Margaret and Phaedra breakfasted together again in the conservatory. Grey clouds gathered in the sky. It looked as if it might rain. But Margaret was in an exuberant mood, sitting in her best dress and pearls ready for church. She took great pleasure reviewing the evening before and pronounced it an unprecedented success. 'It's been a very long time since the whole family got together like that. I'm not sure we've ever had such fun, even at Christmas,' she gushed, buttering a piece of wholemeal toast. Phaedra could not share her enthusiasm. She felt heavy-hearted; David had almost kissed her—and she had wanted him to. She poured herself a strong coffee and tried to look animated.

Margaret didn't mention the clock, so Phaedra didn't bring it up. Perhaps Jenny had found it and replaced it on the mantelpiece. Surely she would have worked out why Phaedra had hidden it. There was no reason for the guilty conscience—but right now, Phaedra felt guilty about everything.

After breakfast Margaret went to church with Joshua and Roberta, leaving Kathy in the house with Amber. Phaedra had made sure she was dressed in jeans and T-shirt in anticipation of spending the day painting, and waited nervously in the hall for David. She was disappointed when Tom arrived instead. She knew then that an invisible line had been crossed in the drinks room the night before.

351

Up at the folly Antoinette, Dr Heyworth, Rosamunde and David were already rolling up their sleeves and opening paintpots. Tom marched in and announced their arrival with gusto, as if he were an actor stepping onto the stage. They all greeted Phaedra warmly, except David who avoided meeting her eye. Antoinette gave Phaedra an overall and paintbrush. 'You can help Rosamunde with the woodwork,' she instructed. 'Make sure you use the eggshell.' She noticed the coolness between her son and Phaedra immediately and wondered what had happened to make them so awkward together. They had been getting along so well.

Tom put on the radio and they worked away to pop music that Rosamunde likened to savages let loose on drums. Dr Heyworth was full of joy and chatted happily to Antoinette as they painted the back wall with big rollers. Phaedra and Rosamunde tackled the woodwork together but Phaedra didn't feel like talking. She was too aware of David, who was up a ladder quietly painting the ceiling. Rosamunde talked for both of them, giving her opinion on modern music and lamenting the lack of talented singer-songwriters like the ones she had admired in her day. 'Music is far too overproduced these days,' she complained. 'You see, in my youth we had the Beatles and Marianne Faithfull—nothing can compare to them.'

Once or twice Phaedra caught David looking at her, but he quickly turned back to his task. She missed his banter and the laughs they shared, and suffered a terrible sense of loss. His presence filled the whole room and as much as she tried to concentrate on her brush and Rosamunde's dull

352

chit-chat, she couldn't forget that he was ignoring her, and feeling hurt by it.

Rufus lay on the grass outside with Basil and the Great Danes, who'd been brought up to join in the fun. The sky brightened and the rain never came. Joshua and Roberta appeared late morning and while Roberta helped Phaedra and Rosamunde with the woodwork, Joshua helped David and Dr Heyworth lift all the furniture back into the middle of the room. Phaedra was aware of Roberta's coldness towards her, but she didn't care. She only cared about David and whether or not their friendship had been irretrievably broken.

They finished the first coat by lunchtime. Antoinette had arranged for everyone to eat at her house, including Margaret, and they all threw off their overalls and piled into the drawing room for refreshments.

The celebratory atmosphere continued for all but Phaedra and David, who moved about the room, careful to avoid one another. Margaret asked how their project was going, but when Roberta suggested she come up and have a look, she shook her head and pursed her lips. 'I have no wish to see what memories you've disinterred, thank you very much. They were fine as they were, buried beneath years of dust and debris. It hasn't belonged to me for decades.' Then, aware she was sounding like an old sourpuss again, she smiled tightly. 'But you must all enjoy it. Arthur would be tickled pink to see it restored to its former glory.'

'He'd be more tickled to see *you* up there,' Antoinette ventured.

Margaret stiffened. 'Well, I'm not going to give him the satisfaction and that's that.' Antoinette was confused: surely his romantic gesture had been a *good* thing?

She thought it best to place David and Phaedra at opposite ends of the dining table. They had said nothing to each other all morning. For Phaedra, the situation was getting desperate. She knew she'd be leaving for London after lunch. If they didn't talk before she left it would be very awkward coming back again. She ate her roast beef and tried to pretend that she was as jolly as the rest of them. She was a good actress but this stretched her ability to the limit.

After lunch she hastily retreated to the upstairs bathroom. She remained in there for a while, sitting on the side of the bath, head in hands, feeling miserable. But she knew she couldn't hide all afternoon. As she walked back across the landing she saw George's room at the end of the corridor. His door was ajar, beckoning her to enter. She wondered whether Antoinette had done any more clearing out since she had last been there. Slowly she walked towards it, her heart thumping because she knew already that if she found herself alone, she'd begin to look for things—incriminating things that she didn't want Antoinette to find.

Gingerly she pushed open the door. The room was empty. She could hear the low rumble of voices from the drawing room downstairs and knew that she was quite safe for a while. She inhaled the smell of George and for a moment her heart stalled. Once again she was faced with all his belongings and the false hope that he might suddenly appear from the bathroom, as if he had never gone at all.

She began to snoop about the various trinket boxes that sat on the table at the end of the bed. She didn't know what she was looking for, and perhaps there was nothing that would make him look bad, but George had been a man who didn't like to throw things away. He had kept everything: letters, mementoes, memories ... lots of memories, and it was those that she wanted to erase.

Suddenly she felt the presence of someone at the door. She spun round and jumped when she saw Roberta, arms folded, leaning against the door frame. 'Sorry, did I startle you?' she asked.

'Not at all.' Phaedra felt the blood rush to her cheeks, making her look instantly guilty.

'Going through his things, are you?'

'Just remembering. Antoinette and I began a couple of weeks ago ...'

Roberta sighed. 'You don't have to pretend in front of me,' she said coldly. 'I already know you're lying.'

Phaedra was stunned. 'What are you talking about?'

'You're not George's daughter, are you?'

'Of course I am.'

'I know you and Julius cooked the whole thing up. Trouble is, no one else believes me. That's because they like you. But if you think for one minute that you're going to ....'

She was cut off mid sentence by David. He registered Phaedra's pale face and jumped to the conclusion that Roberta was being unkind. 'What's going on?' he demanded.

'Phaedra and I are just having a little chat,' said Roberta silkily. 'I found her in here going through

George's things.'

'Nothing wrong with that, Roberta,' he said in Phaedra's defence.

'I know. She's being very helpful.' She turned to go, then paused and turned round again. 'Did you have a good dinner with Julius the other night at Le Caprice?' Phaedra didn't know what to say. She stood there looking guilty, wishing she could flee. 'Josh and I were there with friends. You obviously didn't see us. Well, it was busy, wasn't it?' She gave an insincere smile, followed by a little sniff. 'I could see how close you and Julius are. Very touching.'

When Roberta disappeared, Phaedra began to cry. 'I feel sick,' she wept. 'I came in here for no reason at all. The door was ajar and I wanted to feel close … Roberta thinks Julius and I have concocted a plan to steal money. It's dreadful.'

David's heart buckled at the sight of her tears and he went over to wrap his arms around her. 'I'm sorry, she's got it into her head that you're an impostor. Nothing we can say will change her mind. Give her time, she'll get over it.' He pulled her close. 'The main thing is that none of us believe her.'

'She was so mean. So I had dinner with Julius. Where's the malice in that?'

'Was he the one you said was harassing you?'

'Yes.'

'You said you owed him.'

'He's been so kind. Ever since George's death he's taken me by the hand, explaining the will and advising me what to do. I wanted to go back to Paris, but he told me to stay and get to know you all. I'm glad I did. He's very persistent but I don't

356

want to be rude.'

'Look, let's go back downstairs and forget all about Roberta.'

She pulled away and wiped her face with her sleeve. 'Are *we* friends again, David?' she asked solemnly.

He smiled, relieved there was no longer any awkwardness between them. 'Of course we are,' he replied.

They returned to the drawing room separately. Dr Heyworth was at the piano, his fingers moving deftly over the keys, while Margaret held court in the armchair, her eyes misty as the music transported her, and the rest of the party, including Roberta, crowded around the piano, listening with admiration.

Phaedra sat on the sofa next to Margaret, who mouthed 'Isn't this lovely,' and patted her hand fondly. Harris brought in a tray of tea and coffee and Phaedra deliberately ignored David when he sauntered into the room a few minutes later. Had Antoinette been less enthralled by Dr Heyworth's music she might have noticed the rosy hue on Phaedra's cheeks and the contented grin that curled David's lips at the corners, even though the music was sad and up until this moment he'd had nothing to smile about.

'You're so talented,' Rosamunde gushed when Dr Heyworth finished playing.

He looked pleased. 'I had no choice but to learn piano. It's my mother's greatest passion.'

'You know Mother has taken up playing again,' David said, lifting the *Sunday Times* off the coffee table and flopping onto the sofa opposite Phaedra.

'Have you played the piece I gave you?' Dr

357

Heyworth asked Antoinette.

She blushed, anticipating the horror of being made to perform in front of everyone. 'Yes, it's really lovely. I've been practising, but I'm not very good at it yet.'

'Go on, Mum. Give it a go,' said Tom.

'Don't feel you have to play for me,' said Dr Heyworth tactfully. 'I didn't give you *Sunset* to embarrass you.'

'Quite,' said Rosamunde, who suddenly didn't want her sister showing off her talent. She had heard her play at night and knew how accomplished she was, even though she modestly denied any skill. 'Why don't you play something lively, William?' Rosamunde suggested.

'Righty-ho,' said the doctor. His eyes flicked across to see Antoinette's relief and he smiled, pleased that she hadn't been made to feel uncomfortable. 'I'll play a little jazz.'

'Great, I love jazz,' enthused Roberta. Joshua put his arm around her waist and she leaned against him contentedly. No one would have guessed that she had only just terrorized Phaedra in George's bedroom.

'Do you remember that jazz bar I took you to in New York?' he whispered.

'That was our fourth date. How could I forget?'

He laughed incredulously. 'You were counting?'

She elbowed him. 'Of course I was counting. I didn't let you kiss me until the fifth.'

David hid his face behind the newspaper but he could sense Phaedra the other side of it, watching him. He could feel her eyes burning through the paper. Even though their relationship was as hopeless as a bird with clipped wings, he couldn't

358

help but feel lifted by the fact that they were friends again. Right now nothing else mattered. The bird that cannot fly finds contentment on the ground. It is only when he gazes at the sky and reflects on the limitations of his clipped wings that his soul yearns for freedom.

Phaedra did not want to leave. The thought of returning to London gave her an aching homesickness in the pit of her stomach. Dr Heyworth drove off after tea, promising to help Antoinette finish the second coat of paint. Kathy climbed into the back of the BMW with Amber strapped into her baby seat, and Joshua and Roberta waved as they motored off down the drive. 'You can take me and Phaedra home,' said Margaret to David. 'Such a shame you have to leave, Phaedra. I've loved having you. I forgot how nice it was to have company. One gets used to living on one's own.'

Antoinette embraced Phaedra warmly. 'You must make this your home,' she said. 'You're a Frampton.'

Phaedra felt David's eyes upon her as his mother articulated the only reason why they couldn't be together. 'I'd love to make this my home,' she replied.

'But you can stay with *me* next weekend. Or am I going to have to fight a duel with Margaret?' She smiled at her mother-in-law.

Margaret huffed. 'I suppose I have to share you too.'

'I'm flattered you all want me,' said Phaedra, embarrassed by the attention. In the back of her mind Roberta rose up like a gargoyle and Phaedra shuddered to think of what she might do.

359

'Well, my dear, you're rather good company,' Margaret rejoined. 'You only have yourself to blame!'

Rosamunde kissed Phaedra. 'Well done painting today. We were a fine team.'

'Yes, we were. Still, you're going to have to finish off on your own.'

'I have Antoinette and William and of course David, when he's not on his tractor.'

'We might be able to have tea in it next weekend,' David suggested.

Margaret rolled her eyes. 'Come on, David. Stop dallying.' She whistled for Basil, who scampered round the corner so fast he looked like he was on wheels. 'Where have you been? I hope you're not dirty, I'm not in the mood for giving you a bath tonight.' She climbed into the front seat of David's Land Rover. Phaedra climbed in the back and waved cheerfully as they drove away. Inside she felt sadness gather around her like fog.

Upstairs she packed her bag. She noticed the clock on the mantelpiece and cringed. The weekend had started off so well, but ended in accusation and fear. She didn't know whether she'd come back here. She wasn't sure she dared see Roberta again. Always there remained the thought of Paris, like a bright lighthouse winking at her from afar, signalling safety.

When she came down the stairs David stepped forward to take her bag. Margaret handed her the red box containing the Frampton Sapphires. 'You must take this, I insist,' she said, pressing it into Phaedra's hands. 'Don't argue with me. I'll see you next weekend. Drive safely.' The day had exhausted her. She walked stiffly across the hall into the sitting room and closed the door.

'I can't take them,' Phaedra told David.

'She'll be upset if you don't.'

'Then you look after them for me. It'll be our secret.'

He grinned down at her. 'Another one!'

'Yes, we're collecting quite a few.'

He took the box and opened it. 'I'd like to see you wear them.'

'I'd look like a child trying on her mother's jewellery.'

'You'd look stunning, I promise you.'

'Only in your eyes.'

He closed the box and gazed at her fondly. 'Mine are the only ones that count.'

'David ...' she began, but her voice trailed off. They walked to the car, still parked in the shadow of the hedge.

'I don't want to go,' she said.

'You don't have to go. You know you can stay here for as long as you like. Fairfield is your home now.'

'I have work to do,' she sighed.

'Give up and come down here. You can finish your book in the peace of the countryside.'

'It's a tempting thought. But if I lived here, I wouldn't put together photographic books.'

He smiled playfully. 'Tell me, what would you do?'

She smiled back. 'Oh, I don't know ... I've never thought ...'

'You don't know? Come now, Phaedra, I know you better than that. Since when have you *not* had an opinion about everything?'

'All right, if you insist. I'd open the grounds to

361

the public and have a farm shop.'

'Would you?'

'Yes. The park and gardens are beautiful. People could picnic on the grass and enjoy the countryside. And I've always wanted to be a shopkeeper.'

He laughed. 'You're better than that, Phaedra.'

She frowned at him. 'You're contented driving your tractor, some would say you're better than *that*.'

'I stand corrected. You're right. I love being a farmer.'

'So, I'd love to be a shopkeeper.'

He nodded his approval. 'Then we'll do it.'

'I'm sure your mother would object.'

'I think you'd be surprised. Mother is longing for something to do.'

She pushed him playfully. 'I'd better go.' She climbed into the car and rolled down the window. 'Thank you, David.'

'What for?'

She smiled sheepishly. 'You know, *everything*.'

'I promised I'd look after you, didn't I?'

'And you've been true to your word.'

She turned the key and he patted the top of the car. 'Go carefully.'

'I will,' she replied and put the car into gear.

As she drove off she could see him waving in her rear-view mirror until she turned the corner. Then he was gone, replaced by the hedge and the drive as she motored down it. She shook her head in despair. *Oh Phaedra, what a mess!* she thought. *What on earth am I going to do now?*

There was heavy traffic as she drove into London. She sat daydreaming about David, listening to Sarah McLachlan, which made her even sadder. Then she thought of George and what he'd make of it all. If he was watching her in Heaven, she hoped he'd appreciate the tangle he'd got her into and do all in his power to do something about it. *Oh George, you got me into this, now you get me out of it!*

*   *   *

Rosamunde and Antoinette walked around the garden. The evening light was a soft pink as the sun sank in the western sky, catching the clouds and turning them into candyfloss. There was a chill in the wind and Antoinette wrapped her cardigan tightly around her and sighed with pleasure at the sight of growing shrubs and bulbs, and the sweet smell of viburnum and philadelphus that hung in the damp air. It had been the most delightful weekend. She felt blessed that Phaedra had been dropped into her life and silently thanked George for his parting gift.

Rosamunde thrust her hands into her jacket pockets. 'I think I should go home,' she ventured.

Antoinette looked surprised and stopped walking. 'Home as in *your* home?'

'Yes, I can't leave the dogs with Marjorie forever. It's time I got back to my life.'

'If you're sure.'

'I can pop back at the weekend if you're lonely, but I can't use my hip as an excuse any more.'

'Do you need an excuse?'

'No, of course not, but you don't need me now. You're busy in the garden and up at the folly. You're back on your feet again. David's just down

363

the road and you seem to be getting along much better with Margaret.'

'It's not a question of me "needing" you, Rosamunde. The truth is that I like having you around. We're sisters.' Rosamunde smiled gratefully. 'What about Dr Heyworth?' Antoinette added with a grin.

Rosamunde shook her head dolefully. 'I don't think he's coming up every day to visit *me*.'

'Well, of course he is,' Antoinette laughed, but she sensed what Rosamunde was going to say by the look on her face.

'No, my dear, I think he's using me as an excuse to see *you*.'

Antoinette was embarrassed. 'What nonsense!' she exclaimed.

'Don't panic. I'm sure he's got the sense not to leap on you. But he likes you. That's plain enough to see.'

'Oh Rosamunde, are you sure? You two were getting on so well.'

'I noticed when he danced with you. He didn't look at me once.'

'I'm sure you're wrong.' But she couldn't pretend she hadn't noticed too, although she had dismissed the notion as soon as it had come.

'Usually I am. I'm not very sensitive in these matters, as you know. But a woman knows when a man's not interested. At least, I do. It's something I've been used to all my life. I don't think I'm suited to romance, Antoinette. I'm too old, too set in my ways, and as much as I like the idea of it, the reality is, well, inconvenient. I mean, I couldn't possibly share my house with someone. A man would drive me up the wall with all his foibles and funny habits. No, I'm not cut out for it. I liked the attention but that's as far as it went. Truthfully, it's a relief. Really, it is. I'm relieved.' Antoinette listened to her sister and the more she listened the more she realized that her sister was in fact a little hurt by the doctor's rejection. Quite apart from perhaps liking *her*, Dr Heyworth had certainly led Rosamunde to believe that *she* was the object of his affection.

'I think he's behaved rather badly,' Antoinette said, walking on.

'No, he's behaved like a gentleman at all times. He came up to see my hip. It is I who misinterpreted his intentions. I've behaved like a teenager.'

'Don't be silly. You've done nothing of the sort.'

'I had a crush. I should know better at my age.'

'You keep mentioning your age. You're not yet sixty. That's not old.'

Rosamunde heaved a sigh. 'Oh, it's too old for romance.'

'Only if you think it is.'

'He didn't notice my hair down.' She laughed at that silly act of flirtation. 'I should have guessed at that point.'

'Your pride is intact.'

'Perhaps.'

Rosamunde decided to leave the following morning after breakfast. Antoinette went to bed that night pondering on what her sister had told her. Could Dr Heyworth *really* have developed feelings for her after so many years of treating her as a patient? Was Rosamunde imagining it? He had sought her out at the folly, for sure, and given her the music to play on the piano. She

365

remembered the dance and flushed. It had felt good to be in the arms of a man. But George had been gone such a short time, she wasn't ready to start thinking of someone else. It felt like a betrayal of George and she wanted more than anything to honour his memory. If Dr Heyworth liked her then they would remain friends and nothing more. She was flattered but not willing.

However, the thought of being on her own without Rosamunde just down the corridor filled her with dread. She didn't know if she was ready for that, either.

Chapter 25

Phaedra returned to London with a heavy heart. Cheyne Row wasn't home. She didn't *belong* there. As she drove up the Embankment she reflected on a life of stepping stones and the lonely sense of always stopping over, never belonging—constantly hopping to the next stone in the hope that it might feel right. Just like her mother. In fact, she mused, all her adult life she had been propelled by the— usually subconscious—yearning to belong.

She wondered whether her marriage had simply been a manifestation of that yearning. She had certainly never felt at home in Geneva: only in Paris, but now even Paris, the one city she had ever truly loved, was beginning to feel remote and out of reach. Fairfield was special. It didn't wave her off like a hotel at the end of a vacation, it didn't make her feel like a guest; it gave her a taste of permanence.

She thought of Antoinette and the sweet way she was beginning to mother her. She pictured Margaret and smiled at the thought of having a grandmother for the very first time. She was beginning to love them as they loved her. Then her mind turned to David and her heart filled with dread. He was so determined to live in the moment and not think about the future, but Phaedra now stared right into it. After all, she understood it better than he did. She knew what secret lay in its kinks and how to untangle it. And yet, were she to untangle it, she'd risk losing David, Antoinette, Margaret and Fairfield forever. There would be no going back.

She parked her car outside the Catholic church and gazed up at the impressive façade. 'My fate is in Your hands now,' she said quietly, her spirits sinking lower than ever because she feared that a knot as tightly twisted as hers could never be undone.

She stepped into her little hall and dropped her weekend bag on the tiled floor. The kitchen was stuffy, for the windows had been closed all weekend, so she wandered across the sitting room and slid open the glass door that led onto the patio. She could hear the distant rumble of traffic on the King's Road and imagined people going out for dinner with their lovers and friends, and the loneliness pinched her heart with cold fingers. She was a fool to imagine that she could ever be with David. She looked across at her big suitcase that was still in the middle of the sitting room. She'd been living out of it now for weeks. It was time she decided where she wanted to be.

At that moment her thoughts were disturbed by

the ringing of the doorbell. She wondered who could be calling at this time on a Sunday evening. Expecting someone from a charity requesting money, she was pleasantly surprised to see Julius. He was almost as surprised to see her.

'Julius! What are you doing here?' she asked.

'I was driving home from Gloucestershire and I thought to myself, I wonder if Phaedra's home yet and whether she'd like to come out for dinner.'

She smiled, grateful for his friendship. 'I've just got back, actually.'

'What luck. We can go somewhere local.'

'Why don't we walk to Daphne's? I like it there.'

'Good idea. It's a lovely evening.'

'Come in. I'll just change out of these clothes. I was painting a house this morning.'

'Whose house?' he called out as she made her way up the spiral staircase with her weekend bag.

'It's a little folly on top of the hill,' she shouted down.

'Really. I've never noticed a folly.'

'It's been hidden away for years. Antoinette is restoring it and we were all helping her.' She felt a pang of homesickness as she thought of the day before, when they'd all been dancing to Tom's stereo. 'It was such fun being part of it,' she said, but her voice trailed off and Julius didn't hear.

A few minutes later they were striding up Glebe Place. Phaedra had slipped on a floral sundress and short denim jacket. In her plimsolls she was only marginally taller than him. Her hair was loose and curly, bouncing over her shoulders as she walked, but she didn't notice the admiring looks from both men and women as she passed. Julius did, and he was proud to be walking alongside her.

He sensed tonight was the night it was all going to come together.

They chatted the entire way to Draycott Avenue without pause. It was a balmy evening. The sun was still hot, the streets full of people making the most of the last few hours of their weekend. There was a sense of celebration in the air, for spring had finally come after a long, cold winter. The trees were woolly, the skies blue, the air warm, and it was still light at half past eight. People spilled onto the pavements outside pubs and laughed together as their spirits thawed and their limbs loosened in the sunshine. Their mirth was infectious and it seemed the whole city vibrated with a sense of summer.

Julius was welcomed in the restaurant with the same respect he'd been accorded at the Ivy and Le Caprice. They were shown to their table, a round one in the corner by the window. A pleasant breeze swept in and Phaedra sat back in her chair, grateful that her loneliness had been plugged for a while. Julius wasted no time in ordering a bottle of chilled Sauvignon Blanc and a plate of *zucchini fritti* while they decided what they wanted to eat.

'This is very nice,' said Phaedra, taking a sip of wine.

'A good way to finish the weekend,' Julius laughed. 'When you've grown tired of Fairfield you must come and stay with me in Gloucestershire. I have a big house near Tetbury. You could say I'm a neighbour of the Prince of Wales.'

'Very grand,' she replied, indulgently. 'Do you ever ask him over for dinner?'

'Sadly, we're not yet acquainted. Still, the house was on for three million and I got it for two point seven-five. Bargain, considering the location and the size of it.'

'You live there all alone?'

He looked at her steadily. 'At the moment, yes. I go down at weekends. One day I hope to marry and fill it with kids. It's got a tennis court and a pool. Great for children.'

'Sounds ideal.'

'I'm a good catch, you know, Phaedra. I can offer a woman a comfortable life.'

'I'm sure you can.'

He watched her take another sip of wine. 'I'm glad you're relaxing tonight. You've been tense lately.'

'Have I?'

'Yes, but it's OK. I understand. Let me get a waiter, I'm ready to eat.' He clicked his fingers.

Phaedra chose from the menu and Julius ordered for her. The *zucchini fritti* were placed in the middle of the table and Phaedra tucked in hungrily. Julius helped himself to a handful and added a heap of salt. He watched her eat. He liked a woman with a hearty appetite; it meant she was hearty in bed, too. Women who picked at their food picked at life. He couldn't bear skinny women who ate only lettuce.

Phaedra ate properly and enjoyed it: now *that* was a woman worthy of his admiration. He liked her tumbling curly hair and her thick golden skin and pink cheeks. She looked wholesome, as if she'd been conceived in a haystack. Yet she had a mischievous curl to her lips when she smiled, which he found encouraging. Despite her angelic appearance, he imagined she was capable of all sorts of naughtiness. And now she was a rich woman too. She had it all.

'Tell me, have they given you the Frampton Sapphires yet?'

Phaedra finished her mouthful, suddenly feeling uncomfortable. 'I accepted them but I gave them to David to look after.'

'You did what?' Julius looked horrified.

'They're not mine, Julius. Not really. You know that.'

'Of course they're yours.'

'Look, I can't just turn up and take a suite of sapphires that's been in the family for generations. It's not right.'

'Don't be ridiculous. George wanted you to have them.'

'On a whim. He might have changed his mind further down the line.' She lowered her eyes. 'In fact, I know he would.'

'You know nothing of the sort. I knew George far better than you, don't forget. I was privy to his deepest thoughts. I know how he felt about you. He didn't change his will on a whim, as you suggest. Sure, he felt guilty; he should have come clean, but he gave them to you to prove that his love was there to stay.'

'Don't, Julius. I can't bear to talk about it any more.'

'You deserve those jewels even if you never wear them. You will hand them down to your children. Think of the inheritance.' His stare was bullying. 'Think of your children.'

The conversation was halted by the waiters bringing their first course. Phaedra gulped her wine and took the opportunity to change the subject. She didn't like discussing George with

371

Julius. It made her feel beleaguered, as if she were complicit in a crime she had no wish to be part of. So she asked him about himself, and he was content to rattle on about his success and to share his opinions without noticing her disinterest.

She thought of David and wished she were back in the secure embrace of Fairfield. Suddenly Julius represented everything that was distasteful about the city. He was full of greed, materialism and self-interest. She didn't imagine he had ever walked around his gardens in Gloucestershire and admired the flowers for their simple beauty. For Julius everything was about worth. The flowers were appreciated only for the value they added to the property as a whole. She began to wonder whether he was interested in her only because of the money she had inherited. Why else would he go on about the Frampton Sapphires? Surely anyone with Julius's knowledge would encourage her to do the right thing and give them back? She stared at him with new eyes. He wasn't advising her for her own good, but for his. She felt an unpleasant sensation creep over her body as she suddenly realized his intention.

Julius ordered coffee to prolong the evening. Phaedra longed to go home and close the door, leaving Julius safely on the other side. She watched him unwrap an amaretto. 'Have you seen one of these go up in flames?' he asked. She shook her head. He summoned a waiter with a brisk click of his fingers and asked for a box of matches.

Assuming the matches were for cigarettes, the waiter flushed and began to explain. Julius growled at him impatiently. 'They're not for cigarettes, you fool. I'm going to impress my lady friend here with a trick.'

'I do apologize,' said the waiter, blushing scarlet. Phaedra felt sorry for him and smiled sympathetically; Julius had no manners. A second later a different waiter appeared with matches and Julius lit the diaphanous Amaretto wrapper. They all watched it rise into the air, consumed in flames. A moment later it dropped onto the table in a puff of smoke. Phaedra felt uneasy. There was something sinister about Julius. She wished he didn't know so much about her—and she wished she'd never turned to him for help.

*   *   *

They walked to Cheyne Row beneath the street lamps. It was almost midnight. Julius was very pleased with himself and strode with a bounce in his step as if he had won the greatest prize. He told jokes and laughed vigorously while Phaedra walked beside him, barely uttering a word. She cheered up when she saw her front door. A few minutes more and she'd be inside.

Julius stopped as she searched for the key in her handbag. 'Phaedra,' he said. There was a silky tone to his voice. Her heart accelerated. She knew what was coming. 'Listen ...' he began.

'I've had a lovely evening, Julius,' she interjected hastily. 'Thank you so much. You're a dear friend.' She hoped the emphasis on the word 'friend' might deter him. But he seemed not to hear it. He came closer and she knew that he was going to kiss her. 'Julius, I like you so much, but ...' He wound his hand about her neck and pulled her towards his face. She could see the intention in his eyes, as if he were staring into a pot of gold. She resisted. 'Julius, please. I don't like you in that way.'

He released her. 'What are you playing at?' he demanded, the silky tone replaced by a cold metal timbre. 'You little tease!'

'I'm not teasing you. I've only ever been honest with you.'

'I don't think you know the meaning of the word "honest".'

She desperately wanted to get behind her door, where she was safe. The street was quiet. She was frightened of what he might do. 'Julius, I'm not ready for a relationship.'

'Don't fob me off with that crap.' He wiped his mouth with his sleeve as if the idea of kissing her now repulsed him. 'It's fine. I get it. I get what you're all about.'

'I thought we could be friends.'

'You *need* me. That's the only reason you've been seeing me, right? I'm no fool. In fact, I'm one of the best. You don't think I got to where I am today by being naïve, do you? Well, I'm not going to be there for you any more.' He snorted. 'There, see how you like it now? Cut loose and drifting.'

Phaedra blanched. 'Julius, come on. Don't be like that. I really like you.'

'You're not going to use me any more.' He walked off down the pavement. 'Have a nice life, Phaedra Chancellor!'

She watched, horrified, as he climbed into his car and roared away. Her legs felt numb with fear. Julius was now her enemy. She wondered how far he'd go to ruin her.

She retreated inside and locked the door behind her. Her big suitcase still lay on the floor in the sitting room, reminding her of everything she had to lose. With a leaden heart she climbed the stairs to her bedroom where her small weekend bag was lying open on the bed. She began to unpack it. Everything seemed to smell of Fairfield. She pressed her T-shirt to her nose, remembering the scenes at the folly and the moment when David had almost kissed her in the drinks room. Tears welled in her eyes so she could barely see what she was doing.

She ran a bath and soaked in bubbles, trying to convince herself that Julius wasn't as bad as she presumed. Perhaps he'd still harbour hope and therefore not betray her. She was tempted to call him, but he had turned so cold she was frightened of making it worse. She thought of telephoning David, but what would she say? When she later looked at her iPhone she had two missed calls and a text from David: *Phaedra, where are you ...?*

*　　　*　　　*

Julius put down his whisky and opened his safe. With an unsteady hand he pulled out a brown envelope. He chuckled to himself bitterly. Why were the most dangerous of documents always kept in brown envelopes? He pulled out a DVD and stared at it drunkenly. He had meant to send this to Lady Frampton a while ago but it wasn't until he had watched it again that he realized the devastating information it contained. To think he might have sent it unaware, had he not been compelled to watch it again to remember George.

George had been everything to him. Without George he was nothing. For all his bravado and boasting he was back right down at the bottom of the pile again because he had given the best part of twenty years to George alone. Now George had gone, leaving him without a job, but worse, without a friend. He'd have to start again. He didn't want to work for anyone else.

Julius felt the resentment burning in his heart like tar. If it wasn't for Phaedra George wouldn't have been so distracted on that fateful March afternoon. If it wasn't for Phaedra George might still be alive today. He tapped the DVD on his hand and picked up his glass. He took a swig. Now he was going to punish Phaedra for the part she had played in George's death, and for her rejection. Together they could have had it all. Nothing mattered any more because George was dead.

*   *   *

The following morning Rosamunde said goodbye to her sister. Barry carried her suitcase to the car and heaved it into the boot. Antoinette wrung her hands apprehensively. She had taken comfort from her sister's presence around the house. She had been good company. Now Antoinette would be alone.

'I'm not far away, should you need me,' said Rosamunde.

'Thank you for staying so long.'

'Don't be silly. You needed me. Now you're back on your feet again ... and the dogs must be missing me.' She embraced Antoinette and held her a little longer than was necessary. 'Life goes on, doesn't it?' she continued, pulling away. 'I can't sit in a lay-by for the rest of my life. I have to get back on the motorway!'

'Oh Rosamunde, I'm going to miss you. I've got used to you now.'

'Then it's good that I'm going. You can't depend on me forever. You have to get your life back, too.'

Antoinette's eyes glistened. 'I'm not sure what I'll do without you.'

Rosamunde felt the warm sense of being needed spread over her like rays of sunshine. 'You have your garden and the folly. I'm sure William will help you put on that final coat of paint.' Antoinette pulled a sympathetic face. 'Come now, I'm not to be pitied. It was a flirtation and nothing more. Fancy me falling in love at my age! Unthinkable.'

'Will you come again soon?'

'You only have to call.'

'I'll be rather lonely in this big old house without George.'

'You have Margaret.'

Antoinette grinned. 'Yes, Margaret. She's lightened up recently for some reason, hasn't she? Do you think it's Reverend Morley?'

'I pity the man, whoever he is.'

'Well, nothing would surprise me now.'

'Let's hope it lasts. I must go. Don't watch me drive off. I hate goodbyes. Off you go and do something in the garden. I'm sure Barry could do with help weeding. They'll all start coming up now, you know. You want to get them while they're small.'

Antoinette's heart flooded with compassion as Rosamunde climbed briskly into the front seat and put the key in the ignition. 'Drive carefully,' she said.

Rosamunde waved and took her spectacles out of their case. Antoinette walked up the steps then turned at the door. She saw her sister peering through the windscreen like a mole, her glasses perched on her nose, a frown on her forehead. She looked old like that and a little bewildered. Antoinette wondered what she had to get home for, besides her dogs. At least *she* had David.

Rosamunde's car disappeared round the hedge and out of sight. Antoinette took the dogs into the garden to find Barry. A menacing wall of cloud moved in over the horizon, as purple as a bruise. It would certainly rain. She tried not to think of being alone. After all, she had been alone on many occasions when George had been away on his adventures. It hadn't bothered her then. But now there was a permanence about her solitude that made her feel lonely. At least when George was alive there was always an end to it.

Barry was in the greenhouse, bustling about the potted plants. 'Ah, there you are, Barry. I thought I might do some weeding.'

'It's going to rain, ma'am.'

'I don't mind a bit of rain.'

'I think it'll be more than a bit.'

She was disappointed. 'So you think I should give it a miss today?'

'You can certainly start in the herbaceous border if you like. Lots of little nasties coming up already.'

'I'll start,' she said, brightening. 'Then if it rains I'll go back inside.'

'Righty-ho, ma'am. Just fill the wheelbarrow and I'll empty it for you when it's full.'

Antoinette managed to do an hour on her knees

378

in the border before the first drop of rain fell from the sky like a wet pebble. She looked up at the dark mass above her, amused that she had been so busy with her task that she hadn't noticed it creeping up on her. Hastily she took off her gloves and ran for the house, Wooster and Bertie trotting along behind her.

Harris was ready to make her a cup of tea. His presence was reassuring, as was the fire he'd lit in the little sitting room. But she had the whole day before her. What was she going to do without Rosamunde to talk to? She couldn't go outside, it was now raining hard—big, heavy drops like tropical rain. She could sit and do a crossword, or read a book. It didn't feel right to watch television in the middle of the day.

The room felt empty in spite of the cosy fire. Rosamunde had spent so much time lying on the sofa it now reverberated with her absence, like the loud ticking of the grandfather clock in the hall that seemed so much noisier than normal.

Harris brought in a tray of tea and Mrs Gunice's biscuits, which only served to remind her even more of her sister's departure. 'I'll take it upstairs, I think, Harris,' she said. 'As it's raining, I might as well go through George's room. I've been putting it off, but I can't put it off forever.' She wished Phaedra were there to help her. Her spirits lifted at the thought of that delightful girl and she felt a little happier as she climbed the stairs. Perhaps she'd come down at the weekend and help her finish what they'd started together.

George's room was silent. Harris put the tray on the table at the end of his bed. 'Would you like me to help you, ma'am?' he offered.

379

'Oh, would you, Harris? That would be very kind.'

He smiled at her and his sympathy made her eyes fill with tears. 'I'll go and get some more bin liners and boxes. I can see you've already made a good start.'

'There's an awful lot to throw away. Though I hate to destroy anything that might be of sentimental value.'

'It's only for you, ma'am,' Harris said gently. 'Lord Frampton doesn't need any of it now.'

'You're right. Let's just do it, Harris.' She took a shortbread biscuit and bit off the end. Rosamunde was right, they were extremely good biscuits.

That evening David and Margaret came for dinner. They ate one of Mrs Gunice's lasagnes in the kitchen. 'I've been going through George's room, Margaret,' Antoinette said once they'd helped themselves. 'If there's anything you'd like to keep, you must say. I'm being rather ruthless.'

Margaret thought about it a moment. 'I don't really need anything. I have photographs and a very good memory.'

'And you, David? I don't want to throw things away that you might like to have to remember him. Obviously I'm putting aside his cufflinks for Tom and nice clothes and things, just in case. But there are so many medals and trophies and boxes of knick-knacks. I don't know what to do with them.'

'I'd put his medals and trophies in boxes, Mum, and we can store them in the attic.'

'Joshua and Tom are more his size so they can choose which of his suits and jackets they'd like to have. I must say, it's not an enviable task.' She sighed beneath the weight of it. 'Margaret, what

380

did you do when Arthur died?'

Margaret looked solemn for a moment, then she lifted her chin. 'I gave most of it to charity.'

'Even the really good things?'

'I gave George his precious things, but sentimental things, I'm afraid I did away with them. I'm not a sentimental woman.' Then her expression softened and she added, almost wistfully: 'I rather wish I hadn't, now. Don't be rash in your sorting, Antoinette. Better to have things in boxes upstairs than in the bin where you can't ever get them back.'

'I'll get Phaedra to help me when she comes down this weekend. You *have* asked her, haven't you, David?'

David's face suddenly opened into a smile. 'I haven't, Mum, but I will.'

Margaret also smiled. 'What an uplifting girl she is. I must say, she's like a window, letting in the sunshine. She certainly pepped me up this weekend. She's tremendously good company.'

'I don't think we've ever had such an enjoyable weekend all together, do you?' said Antoinette. 'I think Phaedra's infected us all.'

'We must thank George, wherever he is, for bringing her into our lives,' Margaret suggested, raising her glass. Antoinette and David raised their glasses, too, but David raised his higher than anyone.

Chapter 26

After dinner David returned home and called Phaedra. He had tried to call her during the day, but she hadn't answered. He hoped she wasn't still worrying about Roberta.

Now it was dark and the park was silent but for the hooting of the owls in the wood and Boris screeching to his young in the tree outside David's window. He gave Rufus a biscuit and watched him settle on his beanbag, then he lay on the bed and called Phaedra. It was half past eleven, but she answered.

'Did I wake you?' he asked.

'No, I can't sleep anyway.'

'Why?'

'Because I'm fighting a terrible battle between my heart and my head.' David's own heart lurched. Was she about to articulate what had been simmering beneath the surface since they had first met? She hesitated.

'Go on.'

'I want to be a part of your family, David. I love your mother and Margaret, Tom's adorable and you and I are very close.'

'I sense there's a but,' he said uneasily, barely daring to breathe.

'Roberta's right. I'm not trying to inveigle my way into your family in order to steal the money, but I shouldn't be there at all.'

'Roberta's wrong.'

'She's trying to scare me off, I know that.'

'Phaedra, she's way out of line. You have to

382

ignore her.'

'I just don't think I should come down to Fairfield for a while.' David's spirits sank. 'It's been very intense over the last few weeks. I feel uncomfortable about the money your father left me and the Frampton Sapphires. It's all wrong. I'm sorry.'

'I won't accept that,' he replied firmly. 'You're a Frampton whether you like it or not.'

'Oh David, I lied . . .' The rest of the sentence got stuck in her throat.

'Listen,' he interrupted. 'I don't care that you lied. I know you did it to protect Mum and that's admirable.'

'I really did lie to protect her. I didn't know what else to do. I was put in such an awkward position. It wasn't my fault.'

'Don't get upset, Phaedra. I'm right here beside you.'

There was a long pause. For a moment he thought she might have cut off. Then she replied in a quiet voice. 'I wish you were.'

David's heart began to race. She sounded so near, she could almost have been lying beside him. 'Why don't you come down?' he suggested. 'Don't tell me you've got too much work to do. Come to Fairfield and open your farm shop. Forget Roberta and her hollow accusations. She's irrelevant. No one believes her and her opinions don't count anyway.'

She laughed regretfully. 'I'd love to do that more than anything in the world. Could we have pigs? I've always loved pigs, and piglets are so adorable.'

'You can have as many pigs as you like.'

'And a few chickens?'

'I can cope with chickens.'

'I love the blue ones.'

'There are blue chickens?'

'Yes, they're called Cochin chickens.'

'All right. We'll have some Cochin chickens, too.' The indulgent way he laughed made her smile.

'You're a good man, David.'

'What sort of farmer would I be if I said no to a few pigs and chickens?'

'There's enough space in Antoinette's vegetable garden to feed an entire town.'

'Do you want to tell her our plans, or shall I?'

'Won't she think it terribly presumptuous?'

'I bet she'll think it's a brilliant idea, and she'd love to go into business with you. Of that I'm certain.'

'It's a lovely dream.'

'That you have the power to turn into reality. You only have to get into your car and drive down the motorway. You can come and live here at Fairfield with me.'

At that suggestion she chuckled. 'Oh David ... you know that's impossible.'

'Nothing's impossible. I'm sure we can find you a cottage on the estate.'

'And kick some poor tenant out?'

'I'm the landlord.'

'But you're a kind landlord. You've cheered me up, anyhow.'

'You'll come this weekend, then?'

'Maybe.'

Phaedra felt a warm glimmer of hope in her heart as she turned off the light and laid her head on the pillow. Perhaps she didn't have to give it all up. There might be a future in England after all.

She pushed Roberta and Julius out of her mind and let it wander freely through fields of dreams.

She closed her eyes and imagined her farm shop. She saw herself in a white apron chatting to customers from behind the counter of pâtés, cold meats and pies. There would be fresh eggs from their hens and fruit and vegetables from their garden. All the produce would be seasonal and delicious and people would come from far and wide to buy from the shop and walk around the glorious park. The magic of Fairfield would infect all who saw it. She, David and Antoinette would work happily together. Perhaps Tom would get involved, too, and Rosamunde; maybe even Margaret would approve. It would be a *family* business. George would be so proud—and *she* would have made good. With those light, whimsical thoughts, she drifted off to sleep.

*   *   *

Antoinette couldn't sleep. She listened to the wind rustling through the trees and the creaking of the house, which sounded like the creaking of old bones, and was too frightened to sleep. So she got up and turned on the lights. She threw on her dressing gown and stepped into her slippers. Then she walked downstairs to the drawing room. It was cold in that big room, but she didn't mind. She went straight to the piano and opened the lid. She knew *Sunset* by heart now but she placed the music on the stand just in case. Then she sat down and rested her fingers on the keys. They felt at home there, hovering above the ivories. Slowly she began to play. She smiled as the music filled the room

385

and silenced the creaking, as if the old bones of the house were soothed into slumber.

It felt good to release her fears that way. Now her fingers knew the keys as feet know a well-trodden path. They danced as if they had a mind of their own and she was able to sit back and listen to the sad rise and fall of the melody. She thought of George, but soon it was Dr Heyworth's kind face leaning over the piano and applauding her efforts. She wanted to show him what she had learned and how well she now played. George had never cared much for music, but Dr Heyworth was very accomplished. It was *his* approval she wanted.

She stopped playing and pulled her hands off the keys. She rubbed her fingers. That was all she wanted from Dr Heyworth, she thought anxiously, his approval and his admiration as a pianist. There was nothing unseemly about that. She missed George, she missed him terribly—and with that thought she began to play again, but somehow now the magic was gone.

She closed the piano and stood up. Perhaps she'd sleep now. She looked at her watch; it was one in the morning. Soon the birds would begin to twitter and the sun would inch its way up from Australia and flood the fields with that clean dawn light.

The night was nearly over. She felt heartened to think of the approaching day. She hurried upstairs and climbed into bed. The house was now still, the owls had gone quiet, the wind had dropped. She closed her eyes and allowed herself to sink slowly into sleep at last.

The following morning a package arrived in the post from Julius Beecher. It was a DVD. The letter stated that he had meant to give it to her before but hadn't wanted to distress her. It was footage of George skiing in Murenburg a week before he died. *Watch it when you're ready, Lady Frampton. I wanted you to have it so that you are reassured that he was killed doing what he loved. My warmest regards to you and your family, Julius Beecher.*

Antoinette stared at the silver disc and felt a chill ripple across her skin. This was footage she had never seen of George, only days before he was gone forever. It was upsetting just to think of it— like watching him speaking from the grave. She was curious, of course, but frightened to see it alone. So she took it into her study and placed it in the top right-hand drawer of her desk where she kept important things like her passport and keys. She'd wait until she was surrounded by her family and they could watch it all together. Perhaps Rosamunde could be persuaded to come back for the weekend. *She* could watch it, too—and Phaedra. Yes, that's what she'd do. They'd watch it all together as a *family*, and their unity would give her strength.

*   *   *

David couldn't wait for the weekend. Phaedra had agreed to come and stay with him in his farmhouse. He drove his tractor up and down the fields, spraying fertilizer over the crops, imagining what life would be like married to her, avoiding the painful fact that marriage was impossible. The DNA test rose between them like an immovable mountain, but David kept his eyes firmly on his feet or the sky and pretended not to see it.

Phaedra tried to concentrate on her work. She

managed to write a few pages, then flicked through the pictures from the weekend on her laptop. She sat for hours mooning over photographs of David, trying to figure a way out of the mess George had got her into. She knew it was risky staying alone with him in his house, considering how they had so nearly kissed in the drinks room at Margaret's, but she couldn't bear to be near Roberta. Although her head begged her to return to Paris, her heart was drawn to David like a mouse to cheese in a trap.

She was aware that Julius Beecher hadn't called to apologize. It was strange not to hear from him—he had been so dogged in his pursuit of her. She hoped he had let her go and moved on to someone else. She didn't believe she'd broken his heart, for a man had to have a heart in the first place for it to break.

Julius was cold and calculating, a man who only wanted her for the bounty she brought with her. He must have tasted the high life with George and desired it for himself. She knew him to be devious. She wondered whether he had ever stolen from his boss. It was perfectly feasible. George had given him access to all his affairs and trusted him with his businesses. Julius had been more than a lawyer, he'd been his right hand. Thanks to Julius, George had been able to take off whenever he wanted. He'd been free, but at what cost? Phaedra wondered whether he was still stealing from George; after all, he continued to be in control of most of George's assets, while Joshua tried to navigate his way through his father's affairs.

*   *   *

388

Antoinette was delighted when Dr Heyworth telephoned to suggest they paint the second coat while the weather was good. She was flattered that he should offer to help. It was a hard task, for the room was large, but he insisted it was nothing but a pleasure for him. He didn't want to think of her tackling it on her own. Antoinette was relieved not only to have his company, but to have something to occupy her. The thought of spending another day going through George's room filled her with dread. Harris had been very helpful but she'd rather have Phaedra's moral support, or her children's, for Harris couldn't advise her about what to keep and what to throw away, in spite of his efforts.

Dr Heyworth arrived on Tuesday morning and they set off up the hill together in David's Land Rover. David was busy on his tractor and had no need for it. The dogs lay outside in the shade of a gnarled oak tree while Dr Heyworth and Antoinette laboured inside. They chatted merrily and laughed at each other's jokes and witty asides. Dr Heyworth's sense of humour suited Antoinette's perfectly and they both found the same things amusing. When they looked at their watches and realized it was already half past one, they were both equally surprised, for the morning had slipped away unnoticed as time tends to do when one is enjoying oneself.

They drove down to the house and lunched outside on the terrace for the first time that year. Barry had begun to put out the potted plants, now there was no fear of frost, and fat bees buzzed around the lilac and lavender bushes. A cuckoo

389

called out from the top of the garden and pigeons cooed on the roof of the house. Swallows dived and thrushes ate from the feeders Barry kept full for them. Dr Heyworth and Antoinette sat in the shade of the umbrella and enjoyed the sounds of summer. 'May is my favourite month,' said Antoinette. 'Everything looks so lush but so tidy. By August it's a losing battle in the garden.'

'Especially if we get a lot of rain,' Dr Heyworth agreed.

'Have you always loved gardening? You're very good at it.'

'My wife was the gardener, not me.'

Antoinette was stunned and almost dropped her fork. 'Your wife?'

Dr Heyworth smiled at her reaction. 'Yes, I had a wife once. She died young.'

'I'm so sorry.' She stared at him for signs of grief but he simply looked resigned. 'How long were you married?'

'Eight years.'

'How did she die? If you don't mind me asking,' she added quickly.

'Breast cancer. Nowadays women have a better chance.'

'What was her name?'

'June. She was a very sweet girl.'

'You didn't have children?'

'No, sadly not. Some things aren't meant to be.'

She gazed at him steadily, her heart flooding with sympathy. 'So, when you advised me to talk about my loss, you were speaking from experience?'

'Yes, I know what happens when you bottle things up. I bottled June up for twenty years until

390

it made me sick. I only began to get better when I started to talk about her.'

'Who did you talk to?'

'I paid a professional,' he replied sheepishly.

'There's no shame in that, Dr Heyworth.'

He frowned and put down his knife and fork. 'Lady Frampton, might I be presumptuous in supposing us friends?'

'Of course,' she answered.

'Then might I ask that you call me William?'

Antoinette felt the colour rush to her cheeks. 'William it is, then; you must call me Antoinette.' It seemed silly that he should have to ask, but she'd never thought of calling him anything but Dr Heyworth. 'You know you can't be my doctor now, don't you?'

'Why not?'

'Because I can't call my doctor by his Christian name, it doesn't feel right.'

'Then I will find you another doctor. I'm too old, and anyway, I'd much rather I was your friend.'

Antoinette laughed and noticed a little flutter in her stomach, as if she'd swallowed one of those fat bumblebees by mistake. 'So would I,' she replied and her blush deepened.

'By the way, I haven't seen your sister today,' Dr Heyworth said, picking up his knife and fork again and tucking into the leg of cold chicken.

'She went home. I'm afraid she had to get back to her dogs and her life. I'd asked a great deal of her: it was only fair that I let her go.'

'Are you all right on your own?' he asked, concerned.

'Of course. I'm fine. David's just down the track and Margaret is always close by. Rosamunde will

391

come and stay the odd weekend.'

'Good. I trust her hip is better.'

'Yes, I think she's well now. Well enough to take her dogs walking over the hills, in any case. I spoke to her last night. I've asked her to stay this weekend. She says she might have to bring her dogs, all four of them. Imagine!' She sighed and a shadow passed across her face.

'George's lawyer sent me a DVD of footage taken in Switzerland the week before he died. I haven't watched it yet. I thought I'd wait until the whole family were down and we can watch it together. There's strength in numbers and I think I'll need it.'

'I'm glad you're waiting. It would be tough to watch that on your own.'

She smiled. It felt good to share her anxieties. 'I'm afraid it'll set me back. I'm beginning to find myself again and feel better about my life.'

'The trouble is, Antoinette, it's now in your possession. It's unrealistic to think you can keep it but not watch it. You're only human.'

'You don't think it'll set me back?'

'It might be a good thing. If you see him enjoying himself, it might reassure you that he died doing what he loved. It might be good to see that his last days were happy ones.'

'You're right. It might help me move on.' She allowed her eyes to seek comfort in his. 'You moved on in the end, didn't you?'

'Everyone does, in their own time. It's not healthy to hold onto the past. In my experience, it's best to remember the good times and consider them a blessing. But you have years ahead of you; it's your choice how you live them. I chose to live mine without allowing the past to cast a shadow over them. It all happened long ago now. I'm grateful that I have those wonderful memories, and I accept the eight years we had together as part of the bigger plan. So was George's death. Now you must look after yourself. To do that you have to let him go when you feel ready, and look to the future.' His smile was encouraging. 'You have such a full life, Antoinette. And you're a deep and sensitive woman. You're already flowering as you take pleasure in your family, the garden and the folly. Allow those simple things to sustain you. We don't really need a great deal more.'

'You're so right, William.' She blushed again at the sound of his name. She thought of Rosamunde and how bravely she had fought her disappointment. 'Thank you for being a friend.'

'I have always been your friend, Antoinette. You just didn't know it.'

That night, Antoinette played classical music in the small sitting room. Harris had lit a fire before going home to his cottage at the end of the drive by the gate. It was heartening to think of him there. She put a box of George's letters on the coffee table and began to go through them slowly, taking care to read every one, for she hadn't had the time before, when she'd been busy sorting. There were postcards from friends and old letters from the boys at school. He had kept notes on speeches he had to write and the odd diary he had begun but never finished. George was good at beginning things, but not so good at seeing them through. He had always been keen to start the next project.

She remained on the sofa until well after

midnight. The DVD beckoned seductively to her from the desk in her study, but she knew it would be a mistake to watch it alone. She pulled out the photographs instead and carefully flicked through them. Shortly she came upon the ones she'd found with Phaedra, of the ruined castle in Jordan. She gazed into her husband's smiling face. He was striking a playful pose, showing off to whoever was taking the photograph. Then she noticed a shadow on the sand at the bottom of the picture. She hadn't seen it before. Now she stared at it more closely. It was a woman, clearly, her skirt blowing in the desert wind, standing on a dune to take his picture. Her shadow was long, so it must have been evening. She frowned uneasily and wondered who she was. Antoinette hadn't even known he'd gone to Jordan, let alone that he'd gone with a woman.

She hastily reassured herself that he probably went with a group, so naturally there'd be women present. However, the jokey pose made her skin go cold. There was something intimate about it and something carefree and informal about his smile— *it was the sort of smile a man would give to someone he loved.*

She put the photograph down as if it had grown too hot to hold. What if, while she was at home being a trusting wife and mother, George was gallivanting across the globe with another woman? She took a deep breath. It was unthinkable. It was totally out of character. He loved his family and his home; she was certain he'd never have done anything to jeopardize them. But as logical as her arguments sounded, her intuition told her different. He had gone away so much, it would have been easy to have led a double life.

She thought of the shadow on the sand and her imagination did the rest, until the shadow had materialized into a beautiful temptress, snaking her way into her husband's heart and turning it black.

Chapter 27

On Friday morning Phaedra drove down to Hampshire with a sick feeling in the pit of her stomach. She was excited at the prospect of seeing David, but afraid of getting herself into deeper trouble. She hadn't heard a word from Julius, which should have been a relief, but his silence made her uneasy. She sensed he was plotting some terrible revenge on her for rebuffing him and feared what he might do. She had found a family at last; the thought of losing it was unbearable.

She kept her eyes on the road as she motored past the church. She didn't want to think of George. It was because of him that she was denied his son. She was ashamed of the little nugget of resentment that had begun to grow in her heart so soon after his death. He could not have foreseen this. He wasn't entirely to blame. But still her heart turned hard when she thought of him now.

She motored through the iron gates and up the track to David's house. The blood began to throb in her temple as she approached. Sunshine bathed the countryside in a bright, uplifting light, and yet she sensed a barrage of grey cloud edging in over the horizon to steal her light away.

She drew up outside David's house and Rufus

bounded out, barking. David's Land Rover was parked by the hedge, the windows down, the windscreen covered in dust, suggesting that he'd just driven back from the farm. She glanced at her watch. It was midday: she was right on time.

A second later he was striding through the door in faded jeans and a blue shirt, sleeves rolled up to the elbows. The sight of his wide smile was enough to loosen the knot in her stomach and quieten her thumping heart. He walked up to the car as she parked it next to his and switched off the engine. He threw open the door and almost pulled her out. She laughed as he enfolded her in his arms and gave her a big hug. 'You smell good.'

'Your bluebells inspired me to buy a new scent,' she replied.

'I'm glad you came.'

'So am I.'

'Don't worry, I'll stand between you and Roberta like a loyal dog!'

She wrapped her arms around his middle and relaxed against him, sighing contentedly. It felt like home in his embrace, as if she had always been there. 'I want to show you the folly,' he said, releasing her. 'Mother's finished it, with the help of Dr Heyworth, who she now calls William.' He raised an eyebrow suggestively.

Phaedra laughed. 'It's nice they've become friends.'

'I think Mum likes him a bit more than that.'

'She deserves to have someone in her life.'

'It's a bit soon, isn't it?'

'I'm sure she wouldn't rush into anything. But don't you think it's nice that she has a suitor? Dr Heyworth is a real gentleman.'

396

David drew up in front of the folly and turned off the engine. The little building gleamed in the sunshine. It no longer looked neglected. Antoinette had planted clematis to grow up one side in place of the ivy, and big terracotta pots of topiary balls stood either side of the door. It looked inviting and David and Phaedra wandered in curiously. 'She's put all the furniture back,' said Phaedra, sweeping her eyes over the armchairs, tables and the big Persian rug that almost covered the entire floor. 'It looks like a home now.' David flopped down onto the sofa, stretching out his long legs. 'Very comfortable.'

Phaedra sat in the armchair beside the fireplace. 'Imagine, your grandfather built this for your grandmother in a bid to win her forgiveness, which she never gave him. It's so sad.'

He looked at her awry. 'And Mother and Dr Heyworth have lovingly restored it. What do you make of that?'

She laughed. 'Interesting.'

'It should be called Love's Folly.'

'That's a good double entendre. Love is madness.' She lowered her eyes, knowing he was gazing at her meaningfully.

'Don't you have work to do, Lord Frampton?' she said, changing the subject.

'I have loads of work to do, but you're a little distracting, Phaedra.'

She laughed and stood up. 'Come on. Show me what you get up to while I'm in London.'

So they left the folly and drove up to the farm, where David exchanged the Land Rover for his red tractor. Phaedra sat behind him in the cab and David turned on the engine. The tractor rattled noisily. Slowly but contentedly, David drove back to the fields.

*   *   *

That evening Tom, Joshua and Roberta arrived for the weekend. Antoinette had managed to put her fears aside and welcomed them excitedly, taking little Amber in her arms and carrying her into the drawing room.

Rosamunde drove up a little later, having persuaded Marjorie to look after the beagles for the weekend, agreeing in return to sign up to the WI and join the cookery course which was commencing the following week. Rosamunde couldn't think of anything worse than joining the WI, but Marjorie was too shy to go on her own and had long wanted to learn how to cook. It was a small price to pay for the pleasure of another weekend at Fairfield. Rosamunde would have agreed to anything.

It was a warm evening but Harris had lit a fire because the room was large and prone to feeling chilly, even in summer. David and Phaedra drove over for dinner and the party atmosphere that had prevailed the weekend before now continued in the same spirit. Roberta had arranged for a DNA test to be conducted on Phaedra's hair, comparing it with a strand of Joshua's. The results were due the following week. She smiled genially, like a wily crocodile, but neither Phaedra nor David was taken in by her saccharine sweetness. Margaret was unable to come, which surprised everyone. 'I think she's being courted by the vicar,' said David, grinning mischievously.

'Or rather, she's courting the vicar,' Tom added with a guffaw.

'Really, boys, you're so bad,' Antoinette chided, but she laughed, too. A romance between Margaret and the vicar had crossed her mind as well.

'I'm afraid to disappoint you all,' Phaedra cut in. 'She's being courted by God.'

They all stared at her in astonishment. 'God?' Joshua repeated. 'What do you mean?'

'I didn't think Margaret had much time for Him,' said Rosamunde.

'She's been seeing a lot of Reverend Morley, not because she's in love with him, but because she's in love with God. She's just discovered Him and He's making her happy,' Phaedra explained.

'Ah,' said Antoinette. 'That makes sense.'

David looked disappointed. 'So when I saw her alone with Reverend Morley in her sitting room, holding his hand and listening to him talking about love, it was God's love and not *his* that he was speaking of?'

'I'm sorry,' Phaedra replied. 'I know you were hoping for a big love story.' She looked away, embarrassed, for those words were too close to the truth.

'I don't think Margaret would ever allow herself to fall for a vicar,' said Roberta. 'I mean, you know how snobbish she is.'

David would once have commented, *'Takes one to know one,'* but he didn't feel like provoking her as he once had. 'I don't think anyone would ever be good enough for Grandma,' he said instead.

'She's typical of her generation,' said Antoinette. 'Personally, I don't think it matters where a person

399

comes from so long as they're kind. Kindness is the most important quality, I think.'

'You're absolutely right,' Rosamunde agreed, settling down with her sherry as if she had never left. 'You see, in Margaret's day it was all about class and one could never be courted by a man who wasn't on the same social level or, even better, above. Thankfully life has changed. Besides, one is never too old to fall in love, surely.'

Antoinette looked at her sister sympathetically and thought of Dr Heyworth. She wondered whether Rosamunde was destined to be alone forever, or whether there was someone out there for her.

They ate in the dining room and the chatter was loud and vibrant. David sat at the head of the table with Phaedra on his right. Antoinette observed how seamlessly life goes on. Now her eldest was Lord Frampton and seated in her husband's old chair. The family was still there; they had simply moved around a place. One day their children would sit in *their* seats and life would go on in the same way. She never thought that the hole George left could be filled, but it had, and they were now building upon it as upon the ruins of an old civilization. And so the generations would continue to come and go as they always had. George was simply one small brick in the ever expanding metropolis of life, as were they.

She noticed the frisson between David and Phaedra as they laughed and whispered to each other, their heads inclining, almost touching; their gazes heavy and full of significance. She recognized love when she saw it and now there was no doubt in her mind that Phaedra and David had strong feelings for each other. She knew it was an impossible relationship and wished that Phaedra was not George's daughter but a girl David had met and brought home for the weekend. As it was, there was no way the two of them could ever love each other freely. They were imprisoned forever by George's DNA. *What a waste*, she thought and glanced around the room at the rest of her family. She wondered whether she was the only one to notice.

At the end of dinner she stood up to make an announcement. The room fell silent. 'I'm glad you're all here this weekend, because I have something I'd like to share with you. Will you come into the sitting room with me?'

Everyone exchanged baffled looks but did as she requested. Harris had already placed a tray of tea and coffee on the table in the corner. The family settled on the sofas and chairs and Tom switched on the television. Antoinette gave him the disc. 'I received this on Tuesday, but didn't want to watch it alone. It's the last footage of George before he was killed. Julius Beecher sent it to me as he was skiing with him the week before.' She wrung her hands anxiously. 'I'm not sure whether it's a good idea or a bad idea, but now I have it, I feel compelled to watch it. Perhaps it will reassure us all that George was taken doing something he loved.'

Phaedra suddenly felt nauseous. Anything to do with Julius Beecher now made her intensely suspicious. She folded her arms to dull the noise of her thumping heart and hoped her fears were wrong. As the DVD came on she felt her hands begin to sweat, and the knot in the pit of her

401

stomach grew tight again. No one said a word. They watched as George's jovial face materialized on the TV screen—rugged, handsome and happy. Antoinette put a tissue to her eye and sniffed.

'Julius, will you switch that thing off!' George said, then laughed, his teeth white against the black of his helmet and the deep tan of his skin. He then turned and skied off down a narrow couloir, where David, Tom and Phaedra had skied a few weeks before. His style was strong and effortless, as if skiing were as easy as walking. The slope was extremely steep but George hopped down, his powerful body moving through the snow like a young athlete. He reached the bottom and whooped with joy, pushing his goggles up onto his helmet, taking deep breaths. He waved at Julius and shouted something inaudible. Andy, his regular guide, followed after, as adept as George, his red ski suit bright in the glare of the snow.

Julius then turned the camera on himself. 'So, here we are again, me, George and Andy, doing what we do best. It's a warm four degrees but the snow is great on the north slopes and there's a lot to be had. It's not for the faint-hearted, but that's what George likes best. Better get on, the boss is shouting at me.' He gave a cheesy grin, his round face pink and shiny. The screen went black only to come to life again a moment later on another part of the mountain.

The family watched, mesmerized, as George teased Julius playfully, spoke to the camera and larked about. No one dared look at anyone else for fear of catching tears that might be infectious. There was a great deal of footage—of them climbing and drinking sloe gin at the top from

402

George's silver hip flask, descending formidable slopes and skiing over smooth meadows into the village of Serneus. Antoinette bit her fingernails as she watched her husband enjoying himself, unaware that as little as a week later he'd be dead.

Tom took his mother's hand. She smiled at him gratefully, then turned her glistening eyes back to the TV screen. Phaedra felt like crying as well but she was too scared. Her jaw was so stiff it had begun to ache. She had a horrid feeling that those clouds she had sensed earlier were now closing in.

Once again Julius turned the camera on himself. 'Here we are now at the top of the Gameinde Boden. It's been a long climb but worth every step, for there below us are miles of virgin slopes. Oh, it's going to be good!' he exclaimed excitedly. Then in the background George's voice could be heard on the telephone.

At first it didn't sound significant. His voice was muffled against the wind and Julius's cheerful chatter. But then the wind dropped and Julius got distracted by something Andy was pointing at. 'Darling, I love you,' George was saying. Once again Julius's voice spoke over George's so it was impossible to hear what he said next. Tom grinned at his mother, assuming he was speaking to *her*, but Antoinette had frozen as if she were made of ice. 'It's as simple as that ...' George continued. 'No, my darling, I told you, I was going to tell you but I didn't want to spoil what we have ... I was going to tell you, I promise. Nothing changes the way I feel about you ... no, you're wrong, you are more than that ... you have to forgive me ...' He was begging, clearly distressed. 'Please, darling, forgive me ...'

403

The room suddenly turned cold and everyone sat petrified with shock, unable to tear their eyes off the screen. Rosamunde looked at her sister, whose face was as pale as uncooked dough.

'I told you, I never lied, I just didn't tell you the truth ...' George continued. Julius had stopped talking as if he, too, wanted to hear George's conversation. He turned the camera around and began to film Andy. Their conversation then smothered George's. The screen went black again. It ended there, leaving everyone dazed and bewildered and very embarrassed.

'Whom was Dad speaking to?' Joshua demanded. They all looked at each other blankly. Tom shrugged. Antoinette began to cry. Rosamunde's face had darkened with indignation.

Phaedra squeezed David's hand, then let it go. Julius had got his revenge, as she knew he would. She stood up. 'He was speaking to me,' she replied steadily. The eyes that turned on her were fierce in their condemnation. David went grey, as if he had aged ten years in a single moment.

'You, Phaedra?' Antoinette gasped.

Phaedra dropped her gaze onto Roberta's smug face. 'You were right, Roberta. I'm not a Frampton,' she stated simply.

'What did I tell you?' Roberta exclaimed triumphantly. She shot her husband a reproachful look. He was too appalled to respond.

'But you're wrong in that I never wanted any money from George and certainly not those beautiful sapphires. I never wanted anything but George's love.'

'God, Phaedra! How could you?' Tom cried out as his mother began to sob. 'We trusted you!'

404

'Let her speak,' said David. His composure was chilling. Phaedra didn't know whether she could continue. She had now lost everyone dear.

'I'm not George's daughter,' she went on, clenching her jaw to restrain her despair. 'I was his lover.' There was a collective gasp, but Phaedra continued bravely. She wanted to come clean and tell them the whole story. Since they all looked too traumatized to speak, she had the floor to herself. 'We met a year and a half ago when I was photographing in the Himalayas. I didn't realize he was married because he never told me. I was living in Paris and he came over from time to time. I never had any reason to mistrust him. I moved to London a month before he was killed, to be close to him. There I found out he was married. Not because someone told me, but because I was researching my book on the Internet and his name came up in connection with an article about British climbers. I went mad. I loved him, but I couldn't be with another woman's husband. So I finished it, but George wouldn't hear of it. He tried to win me back. He told me he was going to include me in his will and give me those family sapphires. It was a gut reaction and one I'm sure he would have reversed, had he lived. I now realize what an impulsive, fickle man he could be. I told him I didn't want anything from him, just the one thing he couldn't give me. But George went off skiing with Julius. He thought I'd come round, given a bit of time to reflect. He called me constantly, but my answer was always the same.' She took a deep breath. A small part of her felt relieved not to have to lie any more. 'When he died I was left no alternative but to invent a story.

You were going to find out the truth unless I hid it, and I couldn't bear for his family to be hurt. If he hadn't changed his will none of you would ever have known.' She looked at Antoinette's streaming eyes and her heart faltered. She swallowed hard to contain her own tears. 'Julius came up with the idea for me to pose as George's daughter. On our second trek a man at base camp assumed we were father and daughter, so I called George "Dad" as a joke. That gave Julius the idea. It was the only way. I meant to come down only once and meet you all. I never expected to return. I certainly never expected to love you the way I do. Perhaps I should have gone straight back to Paris. You'd never have met me and you would have discovered that George had been unfaithful only when the will was read. I did what I thought was right at the time—I never imagined I'd live to regret it so much.' She wiped her face with the back of her hand. She couldn't look at David. His silence said more than words ever could.

'So, who's your real father?' Joshua asked, his face hard and unforgiving.

'Jack was my father. He left when I was ten and I never saw him again. He died a few years back, in New Zealand.' The cold weight of their stares was too much to carry. 'I think I'd better go,' she said quietly. No one stopped her. They watched her leave and close the door behind her.

Phaedra ran across the fields to David's house, her heart shattered into a thousand pieces. She looked back every few minutes and searched the darkness for David, hoping that he might come running after her. But he didn't appear, and through her tears she saw the place she loved

406

disappear into a watery blur. She had gambled and lost everything.

Back at the house the sitting room was frozen in stunned silence. David put his head in his hands. He had never felt such despair. Phaedra was not his blood after all, but she had been his father's mistress. He didn't know which was worse. Either way, he could never have her. Once again fate had given with one hand and taken with the other.

Antoinette stared at the blank television screen and felt the peace she had worked so hard to find turn into a fiery ball of devastation. Her world was reduced to ruins and the girl she had grown to love was at the very centre of it. She knew she'd never forgive her.

Rosamunde was the first to speak. 'How dare she come into your home, accept your hospitality and the warmth of your embrace, knowing all the time that ...' She couldn't articulate the words. It was so horrendous as to be rendered unspeakable.

'I'm so sorry, Mum,' said Tom, putting his arm around her. 'I loved Dad, but frankly, what a shit.'

'How could he do that?' Joshua mumbled.

'How could Phaedra ...' Antoinette sniffed, then broke down in tears again.

'She lied to us,' said David, only now understanding her relief when the only lie he had discovered in Switzerland was the age on her passport.

'I thought she was such a good thing,' said Tom. 'What a bitch!'

'Oh dear, I do so hate being right,' said Roberta, standing up and switching off the television. 'I smelled a rat right from the start. But now I wish I'd been wrong.'

'Darling,' said Joshua, trying to silence her before she said something she'd regret.

'Let me speak, Josh. I'm not going to gloat. God, I'm a member of this family, too, and I hate to see you all so devastated. I suspected that she and Julius had concocted a plan, but I never in a million years thought that she would be George's mistress. I don't believe she's lying, in which case she was wronged as well. George tried to have both wife and lover and hoped neither one would find out about the other. What a mess! I thought she was after the Frampton Sapphires.'

'She never wanted them,' David interjected. 'She gave them to me to keep.'

'Thank God she's come clean and those valuable jewels will remain in the family,' Roberta exclaimed with a satisfied sniff.

'What on earth possessed Dad to be so rash?' Joshua questioned.

'I suspected George was having an affair,' said Antoinette, to everyone's surprise. 'I sensed it intuitively, as women do. But I never expected the woman to be Phaedra.' She began to cry again. 'I feel so let down.'

'I think you need a stiff drink,' Rosamunde suggested.

'No, I want to go to bed. I'm suddenly very tired.' Tom helped her up. 'What will Margaret say? She'll be devastated. She loved Phaedra, too.'

'I'll tell her,' David suggested.

'No, I'll tell her tomorrow. I think it's better coming from me,' Antoinette insisted.

Rosamunde felt a strong sense of déjà vu as she tucked her sister into bed. 'You were doing so well,' she said regretfully.

408

'I'm back to square one. Only worse than I was before.' Antoinette wiped her eyes on the pillow. 'Do you think George loved me at all?'

'Oh, Antoinette, of course he did. You know what men are like. Phaedra was a short fling. Nothing more.'

'But he was saying how much he loved Phaedra. I think she was everything that I was not. Perhaps if I'd skied and been braver ...'

'It's got nothing to do with that. You were a good wife to George and he loved you dearly.'

'I feel worthless, Rosamunde.'

'I know you do. But married men have had affairs since time immemorial. Love and sex are two very different things. He had a crush, as simple as that, the same as he had a crush on lots of things. Do you remember how he'd become infatuated with a new project then toss it to Julius to take on? He always lost interest after a while, didn't he? Well, Phaedra was just like that, a crush. Had he lived he would probably have binned her already and changed back his will.' Rosamunde sighed heavily. 'I must say, I'm disappointed in George. I never expected this of him.'

'I feel like going to his grave and taking away all the flowers I've ever put there. I *hate* him.'

'No, you don't.'

'Yes, I do. I hate him, Rosamunde. I hate him and I don't ever want to see Phaedra again.'

Chapter 28

The following morning Antoinette awoke at dawn. Her initial sense of happiness at the sight of the pale light breaking through the gaps in the curtains and the promise of another day in the garden was robbed by the sudden onslaught of memories from the night before. She lay in bed and stiffened as they surfaced one by one like corpses from beneath a green and vibrant pasture, stealing all that was familiar and tender, until she had to clamber out of bed and retch into the lavatory next door.

Had her marriage been a sham? Had George lied when he said he loved her? Had she been a naïve idiot for trusting him? She had never before felt so wretched. Last night George had died for her all over again, yet one question lingered that would never be answered: had she ever truly known him?

She showered and dressed. It was 6 a.m.; the rest of the family were fast asleep. Only David would be up because she knew that he would be as broken as she was. The mother in her wanted to rush to him and wrap her arms around him, to take the burden of loss away, but the woman in her knew that she hadn't the strength to carry anyone else's pain but her own, and even that was too great for her fragile shoulders.

Her heart yearned for solace. She paced the room, finding the memories of George too searing now. She'd throw all his old things into a bag and burn them. Reduce them and all their secrets to

410

ash. They were tarnished with the dye of his duplicitous life and she wanted nothing more to do with them. No wonder Phaedra had known about the ruins in Jordan—she had been there. *She* was the shadow in the photograph. George was posing for *her*. She remembered sitting on the floor of his bedroom with Phaedra and sharing her innermost thoughts, believing she had a daughter she could trust. At those memories her whole body began to shake with fury and hurt. She had to get out. She had to be anywhere but here.

It was cool in the garden. The grass was wet with dew, the sky a clear, watery blue. She walked swiftly across it in the direction of the folly, yearning for the quiet solitude of that little house on the hill.

As she left the garden and mansion behind she began to feel a little better. The wind swept through her hair and dried her damp cheeks. She could breathe again and took in great gulps of air. The patchwork of woolly fields and frothy hedgerows stretched out into the valley below her. From where she now walked, Fairfield looked small and insignificant.

At last she reached the folly. The sight of the warm yellow stone and the pots of topiary raised her spirits and she reached for the door with a sense of relief. She opened it and stepped inside. To her surprise, Margaret was already in there, seated in the armchair, a blanket arranged over her knees, Basil lying bored across her lap.

The old woman looked up in surprise. 'Oh, Antoinette, it's you. I didn't expect anyone to come up at this time of the morning.'

'What are you doing?' Antoinette asked,

disappointed that she was not alone.

'I could ask *you* the same question.'

'I couldn't sleep,' Antoinette replied.

'Me neither. I've been up for hours,' Margaret complained.

'Are you all right?'

'I thought it was time I forgave Arthur. I can't be a good Christian if I am unable to do that. But it's proving much harder than I thought. I imagined here would be a good place to start. I must say, Antoinette, you've done a splendid job. It's very comfortable.'

'Thank you.' Antoinette sank onto the sofa. 'I've got some bad news for you, I'm afraid.'

'Oh no, not someone else to forgive, I hope.'

'I'm afraid so.'

Margaret sighed. 'Oh dear. Well, I suppose I could do a job lot. Who is it this time?' Antoinette hesitated, not wanting to upset her mother-in-law. 'Well, don't dither! Tell me while I'm in good heart.'

'It's Phaedra.'

Margaret blanched. 'Is she all right?'

'She's not George's daughter.'

'She's not?'

'I'm afraid she's not a Frampton.'

'Not a Frampton! Then who the devil is she?'

Antoinette lowered her eyes. It was almost too painful to verbalize the truth. She dropped her head into her hand. 'George's mistress.'

Margaret's face went from pale grey to bright red and her mouth thinned into a furious line. She inhaled through dilated nostrils like a dragon. 'It's not true!' she gasped.

'I'm afraid it is. She confessed to us last night.'

412

'How?'

'Julius Beecher sent a DVD of George's last days skiing before the avalanche. It contained footage of him talking to Phaedra on his mobile telephone.'

'What was he saying?'

Antoinette's eyes filled with tears. 'That he loved her.'

'Good Lord. Are you sure he wasn't talking to you, dear?'

'Absolutely sure. He was asking forgiveness.'

'Whatever for?'

'For not telling Phaedra that he was married. You see, she pretended to be his daughter after he died because he had included her in his will. She said it was the only way to protect me from finding out that he'd been unfaithful.'

'How devious! I suppose she's run off with the Frampton Sapphires?'

'No, she gave them to David. She said she didn't want them.'

'Guilty conscience,' said Margaret darkly.

'Yes, probably.'

Margaret narrowed her eyes. 'So Julius lied about the DNA test?'

'Yes.'

'I never liked Julius Beecher. Not one little bit. He's a horrible worm of a man. I was right not to trust him. Wasn't I the one who needed convincing at the very beginning? I should have followed my instincts, but the girl was very charming.' She shook her head. 'A convincing liar. I must say, I'm very disappointed.'

'Me too,' said Antoinette. 'I'm shocked and saddened.'

413

Margaret's eyes widened as she suddenly seized upon vital evidence to incriminate Phaedra further. 'You know she tried to steal my clock.'

'Your clock?'

'Yes, the one on the mantelpiece in the yellow room. Jenny found it wrapped in clothes, hidden in her suitcase at the back of the cupboard. At the time I thought she must have been bothered by the loud ticking, but now I realize she must have intended to steal it. What a snake in the grass!'

They sat in silence for a while, digesting the terrible facts. The trees rustled in the wind outside and sunshine tumbled in through the glass Rosamunde had cleaned so thoroughly, yet neither felt uplifted. 'Why do you need to forgive Arthur?' Antoinette asked at last. 'What did *he* do?'

'And I poured my heart out to Phaedra,' Margaret continued, enraged. 'I trusted her.' She wrung her hands. 'I don't know who is worse, George or Arthur. Or maybe they're the same. Like father like son.' She laughed bitterly but there was no joy in her eyes, which remained hooded with sorrow. 'Arthur had an affair when George was a little boy. I found out and he came racing back.' She looked at Antoinette steadily. 'Men always return to their wives, my dear.'

Antoinette was astonished. 'Not you as well!'

'I'm afraid we're in the same boat.'

'Did Arthur love this other woman?'

'I suppose in his way he did. Men's hearts aren't like women's.'

'Rosamunde says it's very common for married men to have affairs. Is that true?'

'No, I don't think that's true. I suspect most are faithful all their lives. Perhaps all *Frampton* men

414

have affairs. However, I do believe that men have different needs from women. I realize now that there are many ways to love. Arthur loved me *and* his mistress, just as George probably loved both you *and* Phaedra, in different ways. But I also feel sure he'd have come scuttling back to you had you found out about it, just like Arthur did. Goodness knows, he might have built *you* a folly like this one.' Margaret watched a fat tear roll down Antoinette's cheek. Instead of finding her tears irritating, she was moved by them. 'My dear girl, you have a jolly good cry, you'll feel so much better. Let it all out.' She lowered her eyes ponderously. 'That's what Phaedra said and she was right. I let it all out and felt a great deal better. Still, I'm just as hard-hearted about Arthur as you must be about George. Who would have thought we'd have *that* in common?' Antoinette snivelled and Margaret smiled kindly. 'You know, the sensible side of me would advise you to work towards forgiveness. Even if you never quite get there, try to keep your eye on it and make it your goal, because I have spent decades feeling resentful and you don't want to end up an old sourpuss like me, do you?'

'You're not a sourpuss, Margaret. You're a very kind person,' Antoinette replied, wiping her eyes with a white handkerchief.

Margaret's eyes glistened. 'That's very nicc of you to say. I've been called many things, but kind has never been one of them.'

'Shall I light a fire?' Antoinette suggested, getting up.

'Good idea. It's jolly chilly in here.'

'Well, it's very early. I don't suppose anyone is

awake yet.'

Margaret grew serious. 'How is David?'

Antoinette turned to her, log in hand. 'You *know*, I suppose?'

'I wondered.'

'I think he's broken-hearted.' Antoinette threw the log into the grate.

'He'll mend,' said Margaret, but neither of them believed it.

'We *all* will,' Antoinette agreed. She placed a few more logs in the fireplace and lit it with a lighter. It soon roared boisterously.

'I don't suppose you have coffee up here, do you?' Margaret asked, running her eyes over the immaculate room.

'I'm afraid not,' Antoinette replied.

'Then we'll put in an order.' The Dowager Lady Frampton grinned and pulled out her mobile telephone.

Antoinette was amazed. 'I forgot you had one of those.'

'Tom got it for me, in case I fell and couldn't get up. Really, he thinks I'm an old cripple.'

'He's very thoughtful.'

'I shall call the house and get Harris to bring us some breakfast. I don't know about you but all this emotion has made me hungry.'

'Me too.' Antoinette smiled at Margaret and the old lady smiled back.

'Let's see if he can do it without letting the rest of the family know. I'm rather enjoying being up here with you, Antoinette. Just the two of us.' She dialled the number. A moment later Harris answered. 'Ah Harris, I wonder whether you might do me and Lady Frampton a small favour ...'

416

*   *   *

David was inconsolable. He hadn't slept all night. Everything reminded him of Phaedra, from Boris screeching in the tree outside his window to the Aga that brought back memories of pancakes and cosy suppers at the kitchen table. He replayed conversations over and over in his head and now understood the deeper significance of her words: *I'm not a Frampton, David ... I don't feel comfortable accepting hospitality from your mother... I'm not sure I can live without George ... I've been desperately, deliriously and overwhelmingly in love ... I didn't know. I swear I didn't know ... Thank you for your forgiveness ... Oh David, I lied ...* Her voice was carried from the past on waves of memory, a sentence at a time, and he dissected each one and made sense of it from the vantage point of what he now knew.

He felt a fool for not having worked it out. She never declared that she was a Frampton, except when she originally told the lie in the library with Julius Beecher. She felt guilty about accepting the Frampton Sapphires, insisting that they stay within the family. She never called George 'Dad' and always referred to him as 'your father', and the more he thought about it, the more he realized that her mourning for his death was more like the grief of a lover than the sorrow of a child. It was all so clear in retrospect. How he had prayed for the DNA test to disappear—and now it had, she had been propelled even further away than before.

He hadn't bothered to shave. His face was dark with bristles and restless shadows beneath his eyes.

417

He had never loved a woman as much as he loved Phaedra. He had invested every fibre of his heart into her. Now it felt as if those fibres had been ripped from his chest and hung torn and bleeding. Her betrayal was total and devastating, he didn't think he'd ever recover, and yet at the very bottom of his battered heart was the faint hope that somehow there might be a way for her to redeem herself: a small window of light through which he could leap to forgive her.

He made himself a strong cup of coffee. Rufus lay on the floor, watching him with sad eyes. Once or twice he sighed, as if he knew the situation and felt as sorry as his master. David's thoughts moved from Phaedra to Julius Beecher. Was it possible that he sent the DVD without having watched it? Or had he seen it and exposed Phaedra on purpose? Either way, *he* was now ruined for having lied about the DNA test. Why would he ruin himself, unless the satisfaction of ruining *her* was greater than his will to survive? Why would he wish her such misfortune—unless perhaps they were in it together and she had betrayed him in some way?

David remembered Roberta saying that she had seen them having dinner together at Le Caprice, and how much like a couple they had looked. His body stiffened with fury. As far as he was concerned, they were welcome to each other.

*   *   *

When Antoinette returned to the house with Margaret and Basil, Dr Heyworth's car was parked on the gravel. 'You have a visitor,' said Margaret.

418

'A *surprise* visitor, unless I'm losing my mind.' Antoinette looked at her watch. 'It's 8 a.m., I can't imagine what's brought him here so early.'

'Brought who, my dear?'

'Dr Heyworth. That's his car.'

'Really, Dr Heyworth.' She smiled slyly. 'Well well well, I wonder why he's come calling.'

They stepped into the hall to find the whole family in a huddle, explaining the details of the night before to Dr Heyworth, who was patiently trying to listen to four people all speaking at the same time. When they saw Antoinette, they rushed at her like a herd of cattle.

'What's going on?' she enquired, alarmed.

'I was so worried when you weren't in your bed that I called Dr Heyworth,' said Rosamunde importantly. 'I thought you might have done something silly.'

'What, like go and throw myself off the roof or something? Really, Rosamunde, you know me better than that.'

'I think everyone should calm down and stop making a mountain out of a molehill,' said Margaret, pushing through the throng. 'Nice to see you, Dr Heyworth. While you're here you can write me out a prescription for sleeping pills.'

'I didn't think you took them,' said Antoinette, following her into the drawing room.

'I've surprised myself a lot recently. This is just another surprise. No reason to panic. I am quite myself, I assure you.'

Joshua, Roberta, Tom, Rosamunde and Dr Heyworth settled themselves on the sofas and chairs. 'Where did you go, Mum?' asked Tom, who was still in his pyjamas, dressing gown and slippers, his hair sticking up in tufts.

'I went to the folly,' she replied.

'Where she found *me*,' Margaret added.

'What were *you* doing there so early?' Roberta asked, holding Amber tightly in her arms so she didn't wriggle away.

'Goodness me, it's the Fairfield Inquisition. I was trying to forgive Arthur,' she stated with a sigh.

'For what?' Roberta enquired.

Margaret rolled her eyes. 'Really, Phaedra was far too good at keeping secrets for her own good. I was rather hoping she'd tell David, who'd tell Antoinette, who'd tell the rest of you, then I wouldn't have to expend my breath.' Harris appeared in the doorway. 'Ah, you're a paragon of discretion, Harris.'

'Thank you, ma'am,' he replied gravely.

'We've left the remains of breakfast up at the folly. I hope you don't mind.'

'Not at all, ma'am. I'll go and fetch it later.'

'So all the while we've been panicking, Harris knew where you were?' said Joshua wearily.

'I told him not to tell you. Your mother and I needed time to talk.' Margaret addressed Harris. 'I think strong coffee for everyone.'

'Yes, ma'am,' he replied and left the room.

'Well, you worried the hell out of us,' Joshua said crossly.

'How nice to know you care,' said Margaret with a grin. 'No one would have sent a search party out for me, I don't imagine.'

'We would if we knew you'd gone missing,' said Roberta kindly.

'Thank you, Roberta. You've always batted on my side.'

420

They remained in the drawing room and Harris brought in tea and coffee on a tray. Margaret told the story of Arthur's affair and the strangest thing happened. The more she talked about it, the less it caused her pain. In fact, by the third recounting of the story, it seemed a rather silly thing to have got all worked up about. 'So, *dear* Arthur built the folly for me and I never bothered to go up and look at it,' she continued nonchalantly. 'I mean, I did, of course, once or twice, but I didn't want to let him off the hook. It gave me satisfaction to dangle my forgiveness in front of him like a carrot on a string. Poor Arthur was always on the back foot and he did love me. I know he did. I just never let him know how much I loved him.'

'That's a very sad story,' said Roberta.

'Indeed,' Dr Heyworth agreed.

'Well, I don't suppose he cares very much about my forgiveness now, but I need to do it for my soul. I doubt I'll get to Heaven without it.' She turned to Antoinette. 'And we do all want to get to Heaven, don't we?'

'I'm not sure, if George is there,' Antoinette muttered.

'After the way he's behaved I imagine he's still rattling those pearly gates,' commented Tom loyally.

'It's *your* soul you want to concentrate on now,' Margaret advised. 'Now, Dr Heyworth, how about that prescription?'

At the end of the weekend Joshua, Roberta and Tom returned to London and Rosamunde drove reluctantly back to Dorset and the frightful prospect of joining the WI. Margaret wandered into the yellow spare room where Phaedra had

421

stayed, and ran her hands over the ornamental clock on the mantelpiece, ashamed that she had ever accused the girl of trying to steal it. She knew in her heart that Phaedra was a good person; only a good person could have seen off the sourpuss.

Antoinette was alone once more and lonelier than ever. She felt bereft all over again, as if Phaedra had died. The girl had lightened the burden of George's death and brought sunshine into the shadowy corners of Antoinette's heart, but now she'd discovered that the sunshine was phoney and George hadn't been the man she thought he was. It was as if she had woken up to find that everything she believed to be real was, in fact, made of ether. She felt angry and let down but above all humiliated. They had taken advantage of her trusting nature and stolen her joy. She wondered whether she'd ever feel joy again or whether, as she rather suspected, it would be lost forever.

She played the piano to ease the hurt and during those moments she did feel some relief. The music took the pressure off her heart and gave her the means to vent her misery. Dr Heyworth's *Sunset* was especially helpful because it reached the part where her pain was greatest and alleviated it a little, like balm to a wound.

Chapter 29

Phaedra sat on the Eurostar on her way to Paris. There was nothing left for her now in England. She'd spent all night pacing the floor and packing her suitcase, then left the house on Cheyne Row forever. It had never felt like home anyway.

She sat numbly and watched the countryside rush past her window. She wanted to put as much distance between Fairfield and herself as possible. Every thought of the Framptons was like a knife to her heart. Her conscience twisted with guilt and she hated herself for what she had done to David. She should have walked away at the very beginning when she'd had the chance. She could have been the illegitimate daughter they met once and never saw again, but she had allowed herself to be seduced by the family—and to fall in love with David.

She tore the blade from her heart and tried to think of her future. She'd return to Paris and the life she had lived before she met George. It must still be there, somewhere, beneath the wreckage. She'd dig it up and rebuild. The pain would drive her deeper, she told herself. It would make her a better person, a more compassionate person—a *stronger* person.

She alighted onto the platform and stood a moment, forlorn, as the other passengers hurried past her to their husbands and wives, their jobs and their lives. She had no one. She was more alone than she had ever been because she had known what it was like to be part of a family.

Slowly she dragged her suitcases up the platform, through the busy station hall to the taxi rank beyond. She'd return to her flat and finish her book and let time heal. Perhaps time would even help her forget. Right now she hated George for the devastation he had caused. He had broken her heart all over again—through his son.

It began to rain. She stood in her summer dress and denim jacket and let it wash over her. Then she began to cry. The other people in the queue pretended they hadn't noticed. A child pulled his mother's hand and pointed. When she finally reached the front she was wet through to her skin. A kindly taxi driver put her cases in the boot of his car and opened the door for her. He smiled at her sympathetically. 'Are you all right, Miss?' he asked in French.

'Homesick,' she replied, then cried even harder at the thought of what she had left behind.

* * *

The week following the revelation was the bleakest of David's life. The hours empty, the nights soulless, the countryside rendered powerless because his heart was too heavy to glory in its beauty. He churned memories of Phaedra around and around in his head and they fluctuated from rose-coloured to jet black as each one led back to her deception.

He wondered whether she was still in London, or whether she had fled to Paris. He had thought about texting her many times and found himself staring at his telephone in the hope that she might contact him, but she never did. In spite of his

424

anger he missed her dreadfully, so much so that he was unable to concentrate on anything else but his own unhappiness. The more he thought about her, the lower he sank. He loved her—how he wished he could turn love off like a tap.

What maddened him the most was the part that Julius Beecher had played in the scam. Were they a couple as Roberta had suggested, or had Phaedra been the victim of Julius's selfish plotting? He *had* to know, and finally, after days of no contact, he realized that there was only one way to put an end to his miserable conjecture. He'd have to call her and ask.

As he expected, Phaedra's telephone number was no longer in service. She had probably thrown her iPhone into the Thames. So he drove up to London. He knew there was a chance that she wouldn't be at home. That she'd have fled to Paris, or further, back to Canada. He gripped the steering wheel and turned off the Embankment into Oakley Street. At last he drew into Cheyne Row and parked outside her small house. He peered at the windows. It didn't look as if anyone was in. The panes were dark. A pile of letters was wedged into the letter box, too big to make it through. His heart lurched at the realization that she hadn't been there for a while, days perhaps. He climbed out of the car and pulled the letters from the letter box, then looked through the gap. The hall was dim. There was nothing on the round table by the spiral staircase. More correspondence lay on the mat. She had gone.

For the first time since he was a boy, David cried. He slumped down on the pavement and put his head in his hands. His sobs didn't get stuck in his

425

throat, as he no longer had the strength to suppress them. He relaxed his chest and gave vent to his misery with abandon. Judging by the mail, she hadn't left a forwarding address. He felt helpless. She could have gone anywhere—Geneva, Paris, America, Canada ... Tibet ... the possibilities were endless. She had no roots for him to trace.

Suddenly, his quest wasn't about finding out whether or not Julius and Phaedra had been lovers, but about finding Phaedra. There on the pavement outside her house, a small window of light materialized for him to leap through and forgive her. He simply couldn't live without her— that was all there was to it. However grave her crime, he couldn't remain angry with her forever. She had been deceived, the same as his mother. If anyone was to blame, it was his father.

But how could David find her when she had left no trail? There was only one person who might know. He lifted his head out of his hands and his face hardened: Julius Beecher.

* * *

Julius's office was in an elegant Georgian building off Berkeley Square in London's smart West End. When David announced his name, the receptionist paled. 'I'm very sorry for your loss, Lord Frampton. I'll let Mr Beecher know you're here,' she said, and picked up her telephone. A moment later Julius was in the hall, his arms outstretched, a disingenuous smile broadening his pink face. David noticed that his eyes remained as cold as concrete. He had never liked his father's lawyer.

426

Now he liked him even less.

'My dear David. What a nice surprise.' He extended his hand and David shook it without returning his smile. 'Come into my office. Mrs Carrington will get you a cup of tea, or would you prefer coffee?'

'Nothing, thank you,' David replied. 'This won't take long.' He followed Julius down the carpeted corridor into an airy room on the left. The windows faced directly onto the little garden in the centre of Berkeley Square. Julius's desk was vast, piled high with neatly organized papers in leather trays and two computer screens. There was a sofa and a pair of armchairs arranged around a coffee table laden with Christie's catalogues and glossy volumes on English country houses. The mahogany bookcase was full of antiquarian books and the latest history and biography prize-winners in hardback. A few silver trophies took pride of place in the middle, above the flat-screen television. David wondered what they were for. He doubted the portly little man had ever won anything. Perhaps they had belonged to his father.

As he swept his eyes around the room he noticed the large collage of photographs that took up an entire wall. They were all of George—every single one—either Julius with George, or Julius with George and some dignitary. David felt uneasy seeing his father's face smiling out like that from so many frames; it reeked of obsession. He had always known Julius had admired his boss, he had just never known how much. 'Ah, you've noticed my wall of fame,' Julius laughed. 'I thought very highly of your father, as you know. He was a great man. It was a tragedy, that's all I can say. A

427

tragedy that has changed my life forever. There'll never be another George Frampton.'

He took the chair behind his desk and knitted his fingers expectantly. 'So what brings you up to the Big Smoke?'

David bristled at his sarcastic tone. 'You lied about the DNA test,' he replied, sitting down opposite.

Julius's face darkened, the smile gone as quickly as if he had pulled off a mask. 'So you know.' He shrugged. 'It was bound to come out sometime.'

'No, it only came out because you let it. You knew full well what was on that DVD.'

Julius picked up a pen and began to twirl it between his stumpy fingers. He sighed insincerely. 'Oh dear, that must be very distressing for your mother. I'm so sorry.'

'Spare me your sympathy, Julius.'

A small smile curled the corners of his lips. 'I don't suppose Phaedra's so welcome now at Fairfield. Such a pity. The road to Hell is paved with good intentions.'

David watched him gloat at Phaedra's demise and suddenly it all became very clear. 'She rebuffed you, didn't she?' he said, heart racing.

'I don't know what you mean.'

'You thought you'd take revenge by sending my mother the DVD because Phaedra had hurt your pride. After all you did for her, plotting and scheming, she didn't want you.'

'David, you're barking up the wrong tree.'

'You not only betrayed Phaedra, you betrayed my father.' He swept his eyes over the wall of photographs. 'You profess to care about him and yet you destroy his memory and all those he loved.'

'You don't know what you're talking about,' Julius growled. 'I'd have given my life for George. Your father was a better man than any of his sons.'

'He had a lapse of judgement when he chose you as his man Friday. Or perhaps he chose you *because* you were underhand. I always considered my father an honourable man. Now I'm not so sure.'

Julius was visibly rattled. 'Your father was a brilliant man. Phaedra seduced him and because of her he took his eye off the ball. She pulled him down. He might not have died if she hadn't made him miserable. He became reckless after she refused to see him any more. He threw himself down that mountain as if he had a death wish.'

'You mean he took his eye off *you*, Julius? Admit it, you were jealous. They went trekking, what, twice?—long treks in the Himalayas, something he never did with you. You weren't jealous of Mum because she never got in the way. But Phaedra did. He was crazy about her, wasn't he? Suddenly you were relegated to the shadows, excluded from all the fun.'

'It wasn't going to last,' Julius snapped. 'It was an obsession. You know your father: he was the obsessive type, but his fixations never lasted long. He'd have changed his will back in the end.'

'Was it your idea to pretend she was his daughter?'

'She came to me in a panic once she knew she'd been included in his will. She didn't want to hurt his family. So I concocted the scam to protect George. You know, he would never have left Antoinette. It was nothing more than an infatuation and it wouldn't have lasted. Now

429

Phaedra's where she would have been had he not died: out in the cold. As I said, he would have tired of her in the end.'

'She really rattled you, didn't she?' said David. 'But your plan hasn't worked. I'm going to ask her to come back, once I find her.'

Julius recovered his composure a little once he realized he still had the upper hand. 'Ah, she's run off, has she?'

'As you intended, she was shocked and hurt by the revelation in the DVD. But I'm going to find her.'

'Well, if you've come here in the hope of discovering where she is, I have no idea.' He shrugged carelessly. 'And if I did know, why on earth do you think I'd tell you?'

David wanted to reach over and punch him. It wouldn't have been difficult; the man was half his size and as soft as jelly, but he held back. There was no point either in taunting him about the obvious fact that he would no longer be employed to run George's estate. David kept his dignity and stood up, thrusting his hands in his pockets to prevent himself doing something stupid. 'I wish you luck, Julius. Once it's made public that you falsified the DNA test, I don't imagine you'll find much work in this town. I'm surprised: for a man as meticulous as you, your actions were extremely clumsy.'

Julius smiled like a snake. 'And I wish you luck, David. You'll need it to find Phaedra. I imagine by now she's losing herself in the deepest depths of America. A girl like Phaedra is easy to lose. No roots, no ties, nothing.' He clicked his fingers. 'Gone, like a flame in the wind. You can see

430

yourself to the door.'

David's veneer of calmness crumbled once he reached the pavement. He began to shake and staggered to his car where he remained for a long while, taking deep breaths and fighting the rising nausea. His head swam so that he was unable to organize his thoughts. Where was he to look now? Who did he know who knew her? No one.

He left London defeated. All he could do now was hope that she'd have the courage to contact *him*.

When he reached Fairfield Park he found his mother and Margaret up at the folly with Dr Heyworth. The three sat talking in front of the fire like refugees from a terrible tornado, seeking shelter in the little house on the hill. Of course, the subject was Phaedra—a subject they were wearing thin with their incessant discussion.

When David burst in they were shocked by his unkempt appearance. It was as if he hadn't slept or bathed for days. Antoinette was wrenched out of herself at the sight of her son's despair, and suddenly hers paled into insignificance. 'David, are you all right?' she asked. He looked like a man who had lost everything.

'Dear boy, come and sit down,' said Margaret gently. 'She's gone, hasn't she?'

David flopped onto the sofa beside his mother and put his head in his hands. He didn't feel at all embarrassed to show his unhappiness. They might as well know the truth. 'She's left and taken everything with her,' he said. 'She's not coming back.'

Antoinette put a hand on his shoulder. 'You love her very much, don't you?' He couldn't answer and

431

Antoinette didn't know what else to say. She could offer no words of comfort.

'I don't know where's she's gone. She could be anywhere. I suspect she's tossed her phone into the Thames, because she doesn't return my calls or texts. That bloody Julius Beecher wasn't any help either.'

'You went to see Beecher?' Margaret was appalled.

David lifted his head out of his hands. 'What a sick man he is.'

'In what way is he sick?' Dr Heyworth asked.

'He's got a massive wall of photos of Dad, like he was obsessed with him. It's weird. I think he was jealous of Phaedra because she came between them. You know how close Dad and Julius were. Julius was like his shadow, always one step behind, but always there. Then after Dad died, he tried to have Phaedra for himself, as if he wanted to step into Dad's shoes. Suddenly there was the chance, through her, of becoming Dad, with a big fat bank balance and the Frampton Sapphires. It was too good an opportunity to miss. But she rejected him, as any girl of good sense and taste would, so he betrayed her.'

'You mean he sent the DVD on purpose, knowing it would expose Phaedra?' Antoinette exclaimed, looking at Dr Heyworth. 'I'm so naïve.'

'There's nothing wrong in believing the best of everyone. It's an admirable quality, Antoinette,' said Dr Heyworth gently.

'I'm not so sure,' she replied, lowering her eyes. 'I've been much too trusting recently.'

'It doesn't surprise me at all that that odious man sent the DVD on purpose, and it worked,' said

Margaret. 'What a weasel.'

'Well, he's lost everything now, too. I don't imagine anyone will employ him when they find out what he's done.'

'He had already lost everything, that's why he was so ready to bring Phaedra down with him,' said Margaret wisely. 'A man only commits professional suicide when he's got nothing more to lose.'

David shook his head regretfully. 'I should have gone after her when she left. What an idiot I am! She was as much to be pitied as you, Mum. Really, I know I shouldn't say that, and you won't want to hear it, but I believe it's true. She loved Dad and he lied to her, as he lied to you. You both have more in common than you realize.' Antoinette listened but said nothing. She wasn't ready to be so forgiving.

'I think we all need time to let the dust settle,' Margaret suggested diplomatically. 'It's been a terrible shock and we all feel bitterly deceived. We can't control what will happen in the future, and right now, I don't think we're ready to project. *Que será, será*, isn't that what the Spanish say? What will be, will be. We all need something to do. We can't mope about aimlessly like lost dogs.'

'This folly was my hobby,' said Antoinette mournfully. 'But now it's finished.'

'There's always plenty to do in the gardens,' Dr Heyworth suggested.

David rubbed his chin thoughtfully. 'What about opening a farm shop?'

The suggestion appeared to come out of nowhere. Margaret and Antoinette looked at him in surprise. 'I think that's an inspired idea,' said Margaret. 'I can't imagine why we didn't think of it

433

before.'

'Where would we put it?' Antoinette asked.

'In one of the farm buildings. We've plenty of barns to choose from,' said David.

'There's nothing like it anywhere near Fairfield,' Dr Heyworth added enthusiastically. 'It would be very popular.'

'We could have animals,' Antoinette suggested with mounting excitement. 'Hens ... and cows ...'

'And pigs,' David added, thinking of Phaedra. 'Piglets are very cute.'

Margaret narrowed her eyes. Cute wasn't an English word or one that David would normally use. 'I sense someone else's fingerprints all over this idea,' she said.

'It's Phaedra's,' David confessed bashfully.

'It's a good one,' said Dr Heyworth. 'At least I think so.'

'What else did she suggest?' Margaret asked.

'To open the park to the public.' David imagined that was one step too far for his grandmother, but she put her head on one side as if weighing up the pros and cons.

'It's not such a bad idea. Fairfield is built to be admired and enjoyed.'

'We could open it during the summer only, for perhaps a couple of weeks or so,' said Antoinette brightly. 'It would give Barry and me an incentive to make the gardens as wonderful as possible. There's a lot more I'd like to do around the lake. I'd like to have ducks, for a start.'

'Ducks, Antoinette? I think you should have geese and swans,' Margaret remarked.

'Don't swans belong to the Queen?' said Dr Heyworth.

434

'I'm sure Her Majesty would lend us a few if we asked her nicely,' Margaret grinned. 'So, how about it? Are we all agreed? *This* will be our project. No more wallowing, let's put ourselves to work.'

Antoinette glanced anxiously at David. 'I'm in,' she said.

'Me too,' he answered flatly, but he knew his heart wouldn't be.

'Then that's settled.' Margaret turned her hawkish gaze on Dr Heyworth. 'Any good with animals, Dr Heyworth?'

'I'm sure I could put my hand to anything,' he replied with a smile.

'Then you're in too.'

'It would be a pleasure to help.'

'Good.' Margaret looked at her watch. 'I say, it's sherry time. Shall I give Harris a call?'

Chapter 30

The idea, born with a roar, petered out into a squeak. Antoinette talked a lot about the farm shop and bought a book in which she wrote down endless lists of ideas, but she never actually *did* anything about them. David helped her choose the barn and planned the car park, piggery and henhouse, but nothing came of those decisions. Dr Heyworth found a suitable manager who had been a patient of his. He was aptly named Toby Lemon and used to run a chain of grocery stores before he had left to start up on his own. The recession had put a stop to his plans and now he worked for the

435

local supermarket, which he hated. But while there was no business, there was no job to offer him. Margaret tried to fire Antoinette with enthusiasm but she was aware that only one person could restore her spirit. It was going to be impossible to replace Phaedra.

The summer days lengthened, the crops grew tall and yellow, the weather got warmer, yet David's heart was as bleak as midwinter. He kept his pain to himself, although everyone knew the cause. Joshua, Roberta and Tom continued to come down at weekends but the atmosphere was heavy. Every now and then they'd get all excited about the farm shop and Tom would threaten to leave his job in London and come down to run it, but then they'd leave and a few more weeks would pass before they discussed the topic again.

David didn't join in the family gatherings as he used to. He remained in his house, reading his books, or on the farm, working. At harvest time he drove his tractor well into the night, carting grain from the combines to the barns. On rainy days he swept the floors and heaped the corn. He took solace from being busy. If he was busy he didn't have time to think of Phaedra and wonder what she was doing and whether she ever thought of him.

Often he gazed up at the moon as he walked Rufus around the lake at night and imagined her staring up at it too, remembering the time they spied on Antoinette playing the piano; the first time he had held her hand; the sudden realization that he loved her. He wondered whether she still cared for him, or whether she'd moved on as easily as she'd moved away. After all, they had enjoyed a

436

mild flirtation. There had been nothing in her behaviour to suggest that she'd been 'desperately, deliriously and overwhelmingly' in love with him as she'd been with his father.

Since she had made no effort to get in touch with him, she obviously had no desire to see him. He vowed to let her go.

At the beginning of September Antoinette found she was feeling less resentful towards Phaedra. She couldn't pretend that she didn't miss her. The girl had brought sunshine into the house. Since her departure Fairfield Park had been cast in shadow and no one laughed any more. Even Roberta, at first triumphant that her suspicions had been right, seemed ashamed, as if embarrassed to have been so dogged in her determination to expose her. The truth was that Antoinette wished Phaedra was George's daughter after all, and that she would come back and things would return to the way they were before everything had gone so terribly wrong. She wanted Phaedra back, untarnished.

It was a dull, rainy afternoon when she suddenly felt the urge to visit George's grave. She hadn't been there since the dreadful DVD exposure in the spring, and up until that moment hadn't wanted to. She had felt nothing but resentment and fury, but now, due to the passing of time, she just felt sad. George had taken so much and he didn't even know it.

She drove into Fairfield, parked her car on the verge, and hurried through the drizzle to the church beneath a large golfing umbrella. The building looked grey and austere in the rain. The windows were dark, the big door shut, but there, leaning against George's shiny new headstone, was a bunch of yellow roses. They glowed out of the gloom like a beacon of hope and her heart leapt at the thought that Phaedra might have come back. She stared at the flowers, her spirit injected with a shot of optimism. Was it possible that all the while she'd been missing her, Phaedra was right here in Fairfield? She looked around in a fever of anticipation but the graveyard was empty except for a few mean-looking crows. She dropped her shoulders in disappointment. If it wasn't Phaedra it could only be Margaret. *She* was the person in the family who came regularly to church. She bent down and picked up the flowers. They were fresh and sweet-smelling and covered in little drops of rain.

'Oh George, do you realize the trouble you're in?' she said quietly. 'Do you have any idea of the wreckage you've left behind? You've jumped ship and left us all to crash on the rocks.' It felt strangely good to unburden her thoughts to the man who had inspired them. 'I now realize that perhaps you *did* love me and that you loved Phaedra, too. You probably loved us both in different ways, as Margaret suggested. Perhaps together we completed the woman you wanted to be with. I one half, Phaedra the other. It's odd, because I feel incomplete without her, as if we really are two halves of a whole. I miss her, George. I miss her very much. She brought joy into our home and now it's gone. It's going to take me a while to forgive you—it's taken years for your mother to forgive your father for the same transgression, so imagine, I'm not there yet. But I *am* trying. Wherever you are, if you can hear me, know that I am doing my best—and if you have

438

any power at all, bring her back.' Her eyes welled with tears as she replaced the roses against the headstone. Instead of returning to her car, she walked through the churchyard to the wooden gate in the hedge that led into Dr Heyworth's house.

A moment later she stood at his conservatory door and knocked on the glass. The lights were on so she knew he must be at home. She tried the door; it opened easily. 'Hello!' she called out. 'It's me, Antoinette!' She sniffed. Wasn't that the smell of burning? Seized with a sudden panic she hurried through the conservatory and down the corridor to the kitchen. 'William! William! Are you all right? It's me, Antoinette! William!'

The kitchen was full of smoke and Dr Heyworth was hastily opening windows to let it out. When he saw Antoinette he looked embarrassed. 'Oh dear, you've caught me burning cake.'

'Cake?' she exclaimed. 'Is that what it is?'

'I was making you a lemon cake. But I got distracted.'

'Good Lord, it looks like the place is on fire.'

He bent down and pulled out of the oven a round tin of what looked like charcoal. 'Here it is. Not very appetizing, is it?'

'Not your best,' she said with a smile. 'I'm sorry I barged in.'

'You came through the church gate, I assume.'

'Yes. It's become a habit.'

'It's a habit I like. I tell you what. Fancy going out for tea?'

She laughed. 'I haven't been out for tea since I was at school and my parents used to take me out on Sundays.'

'Then let's make a new habit. Let's go and have a

cup of tea and a slice of cake in Oliver's.'

'I've always walked past Oliver's but never been in.'

'How little you know your own town, Lady Frampton.' He grinned at her. 'What shall I do with this?' He held up the smoking cake.

'Oh, it's a shame to throw it away,' Antoinette joked. 'I'd save it for a special occasion.'

'Good idea.' He placed it on the counter. 'Now, let me go and change my shirt.'

Oliver's was steamy, the tables full of damp people who had sought refuge from the rain. They chose a table at the back and ordered. Antoinette found the smell of freshly baked bread and ground coffee comforting. She looked across at Dr Heyworth and found him comforting too.

'I went to visit George's grave,' she told him. 'I hadn't been since the spring. I felt it was time I had a word with him.'

Dr Heyworth smiled at her kindly. 'Do you feel better?'

'Yes, I do. I don't know whether he heard anything of what I said to him, but at least I got it off my chest.'

'That's good.'

'You see, Margaret held onto her resentment for so long it made her sour. I don't want to turn out like that.'

'You won't, Antoinette, because you'll forgive George. There's nothing else you can do. Resenting him won't change what he did, nor will it make you feel better; it will just fester and make you miserable. So accept the past, let it go and move on. That way you won't allow it to ruin your future.'

440

'And what of Phaedra, William? What about her?'

Dr Heyworth registered the anguish in her eyes, anguish that hadn't been there when she had spoken about George. 'You miss her, don't you?' he said.

'Very much—and I feel bad for having loathed her like I did. It was unfair of me.'

'You had to go through that process in order to get here. Only time could allow you the perspective.'

'But she's gone forever.'

'Perhaps.'

'It's just so unfair. Everyone's been pulled down by her absence. She was with us for such a short time and yet she made a big impression. Fairfield was such a happy place. Now we all mope about like children at a party once the entertainer's gone. Tom sleeps all day, Joshua sulks in the drawing room reading the papers, Roberta just looks guilty all the time as if it's her fault Phaedra left. I just want things to go back to the way they were.'

'They will, in time.'

'I hope you're right.' She grinned at him guiltily. 'I can't even get my act together to start the farm shop. It's such a good idea, but I don't have the incentive without Phaedra. I know we'd have had such fun doing it together, like when we restored the folly. Do you remember when we danced? How we laughed, all of us together. That's a lost afternoon we'll never get back.'

'But there will be more afternoons like it, perhaps better. Don't dwell in the past, Antoinette. Live in the Now.'

She grinned at him as the waitress placed tea and

cake on the table. 'I think this might taste a little better than your cake,' she said with a chuckle. 'What do you think?'

* * *

The following day as she knelt on the bank of the lake, placing the weeping willow into the hole Barry had dug, she thought of William. She smiled at the memory of him burning the cake, the sheepish expression on his face when he had seen her standing in the doorway, and their tea at Oliver's. She looked forward to his visits. He had been a great source of comfort during the last six months and the only person who managed to make her feel light inside.

She loved the way he now turned up without calling first. Sometimes he brought another score of music for her to learn, other times they'd walk up to the folly and chat in front of the fire—they never ran out of things to say. He was a wise counsel and a sympathetic listener but he was also witty, and the more she got to know him the more she appreciated his humour. He had a very dry sense of humour, transmuting sorrow into laughter, and little by little Antoinette found that with him she could shake off her melancholy and feel joy again.

She patted the earth around the weeping willow and stood up to admire it. 'This will be beautiful once it's big,' she said to Barry.

'Willows grow quite quickly.'

'Good. What next?' She turned to the row of plants and shrubs neatly placed on the grass behind her and thought how beautiful it was going to look. Without Phaedra her plans of opening the garden to the public in the summer and starting the farm shop seemed like a pipe dream—she didn't feel brave enough to do those things on her own. She wiped her brow and glanced up at the house, half expecting to see William striding down the lawn towards her, but instead Basil scurried into view to herald the arrival of Margaret.

The old lady marched down to the lake in her long green coat and wellington boots. Once, that sight would have struck fear into Antoinette's heart, but now her heart warmed in anticipation of her mother-in-law's good company and irreverent humour. 'Come and see what we're doing down here,' she said as Margaret reached her.

'Gosh, haven't you been busy at the garden centre.' Margaret's cheeks were rosy from her walk. She wore a green headscarf tied at the chin and a pair of designer sunglasses Tom had given her. They looked comical teamed with her Barbour coat and rubber boots.

'It's keeping me very busy.'

'That's the spirit. The gardens are so big, you start at one end and by the time you reach the other it's time to go back to the beginning again.'

'Do you want to come in for a cup of tea? I could do with a break.'

'That would be lovely.' They set off up the lawn towards the house. 'You know, I've just had Roberta on the telephone. She and Joshua have been asked to a very grand charity dinner-dance at Battersea Power Station. Do you think David would lend her the Frampton Sapphires? By rights they belong to him now, being the eldest son. It's just the occasion and it would be nice for them to get a little wear.'

'You know what he thinks of Roberta,' said Antoinette.

'It's about time he buried the hatchet! Really, it's no help at all having those two at each other's throats.'

'Let me ask him. You never know …'

'It would be nice. We all have to make up and move on.'

Antoinette shook her head. 'I'm not sure David can.'

'Really, is it that bad?'

'Yes, it's bad, Margaret. His heart is well and truly broken.'

'Good gracious, I never realized. Well, something must be done.'

'He won't go looking for her. He thinks she doesn't want him. In any case, he wouldn't know where to start looking.'

Margaret narrowed her eyes. 'Are *you* ready to forgive her, Antoinette?'

'I think I am,' Antoinette replied, a little anxiously. She realized now that in spite of the charade, the girl's extraordinary gift of transforming lives had been very real. 'At least, if I suddenly found myself face to face, I don't think I'd be able to resist her.' She sighed and pulled off her boots. 'I'm not sure she'd want to see us, though. I have a dreadful feeling she's gone, never to be found.'

That evening, when Antoinette broached the subject of lending Roberta the Frampton Sapphires, David shrugged noncommittally and changed the subject. His face was so dark and serious these days, falling into a scowl as if it were

444

his natural repose, that she didn't think it wise to persist. They dined together in the little sitting room, just the two of them, and Antoinette tried to draw him out of himself. She'd lost George and then Phaedra; with every day that passed misery took David a little further from her, too. Soon he'd be but the shell of a man. She was determined not to let that happen. But save finding Phaedra and bringing her back, there was nothing she could do. He didn't want to go out and meet people; he had even withdrawn from his friends. His life was reduced to the farm and Rufus and he seemed to have given up on joy. A long, bleak winter stretched out before them.

The second weekend in September Rosamunde came to stay along with Joshua, Roberta and Tom. Antoinette had asked Margaret for dinner and the atmosphere, although more subdued than when Phaedra had been a part of the family, was lighter than before. Antoinette didn't know why it was so. Perhaps it was simply time putting some distance between the horrendous events of spring and the beginning of autumn: a new season, a new chapter, a new beginning. She thought of the leaves on the trees turning brown and falling to the ground, and wondered whether they, as a family, could shed their pain and grow afresh again.

'How's the Women's Institute?' Margaret asked Rosamunde.

'Well, I didn't really want to join, but you know Marjorie, my neighbour who looks after the dogs when I'm away, was very keen to take the cookery course. I couldn't let her down and I owed her a great debt of thanks. So I'm keeping her company. She needs me, you see. I couldn't say no.'

Antoinette noticed the excited light in her sister's eyes. 'Of course you couldn't, Rosamunde. You're very generous, considering how reluctant you were to join.'

'Well, it's not really my sort of thing, but they need people like me on the charity side,' Rosamunde continued, fooling no one. 'I'm tireless when it comes to raising money and I'm very good at organizing people.'

'Sounds just your thing,' said Tom, stuffing his mouth with a roast potato.

'I do like to be busy,' Rosamunde replied. 'There's nothing worse than being bored. The WI takes up all of my time, which is more than I intended, but they need me, and I'm not one to let people down.' Antoinette caught Margaret's eye and noticed the old woman's mouth twitching at the corners. She looked away in case Rosamunde saw them making fun of her.

'Roberta, do tell us about the dance you're going to. Sounds frightfully grand,' said Margaret.

'Oh it is, very grand. We went last year and everyone who is anyone will be there!' she said excitedly.

'Then I can't imagine why I haven't been invited,' said Tom.

'That's because you're not anyone,' Joshua joked, not unkindly.

'There's a lot of talk of the Duke and Duchess of Cambridge attending, but no one knows for sure. It's very hush-hush,' Roberta informed them.

'Sounds very jolly,' Margaret enthused. 'In my day I went to all the best parties and my dance card was always full.'

'Grandma, we don't have dance cards nowadays,'

Tom laughed.

'Girls don't play hard to get and men don't open doors, either,' Margaret sighed. 'I wouldn't think I was so clever if I were you.'

Tom rolled his eyes melodramatically. 'I hate girls who play hard to get.'

'The girl who wins you in the end will be the one you always felt was out of your reach, mark my words, Those are the girls with quality,' Margaret told him firmly. 'Play around with sluts by all means, but marry a girl of quality, wouldn't you agree, Antoinette?'

'Of course,' she replied, distracted suddenly by the sound of the front door.

A moment later David stood in the doorway with Rufus. 'David!' Antoinette exclaimed in surprise. 'I wasn't expecting you for dinner.'

'I'm not staying,' he replied. He looked awkward. In his hands he held a red box. Roberta recognized it immediately and her heart gave a little skip.

'Oh, do,' his mother pleaded. 'It's been so long since we've all been together.'

'Your mother's right. Do stay,' Rosamunde echoed.

Margaret interrupted in a tone which demanded to be obeyed. 'You're not going anywhere before you've had a good dinner, David. You look like a lean and hungry wolf. Joshua, bring one of those chairs to the table.' She waved her hand in the direction of the spare Chippendale chairs, resting tidily against the wall.

'I've come to give Roberta the Frampton Sapphires for her party,' David said.

Roberta's face shone with excitement. 'Oh, David, I don't know what to say.' But she knew

447

what to do. Propelled by gratitude and over five months of self-reproach, she pushed out her chair and rushed round the table to thank him. David was astonished when she threw her arms around his neck and pressed her lips to his bristly cheek. 'Thank you!' she said earnestly. 'This means a great deal to me.'

Her genuine appreciation warmed David's frozen heart and the stern expression on his face softened. The beginnings of a small smile twitched the corners of his mouth. He handed her the box. 'Come and join us,' she said. 'Please.' The meaningful look in her eyes told him that she wanted his forgiveness.

'All right, I'll stay,' he replied with a resigned sigh, but Antoinette could tell that he was pleased to have been persuaded.

He helped himself to a large plate of dinner and sat down between Rosamunde and his grandmother. Roberta watched him from across the table. She knew he was devastated about Phaedra, but she hadn't realized how badly broken he was. It was as if he had stopped caring about himself. He was unshaven, purple around the eyes and sullen—a shadow of the witty, charismatic man he had once been. It was as if Phaedra had sucked the life out of him and left a dark husk in his place. Her heart buckled at the sight, and even though she knew she wasn't to blame for Phaedra's lies, she had played a big part in hunting her down. What if she could play a part in putting it right?

Chapter 31

Three days later Margaret collapsed. She managed to get to the telephone and call David, who happened to be at home having his breakfast. 'David, thank the Lord, I've taken a turn. You have to come over right now. It might be a heart attack!' David thought she sounded a little too lively for someone suffering a heart attack, but he hurried into his Land Rover and drove over at once.

He found Margaret lying on the sofa with her eyes closed, hands folded across her body as if she were already dead. He tiptoed in fearfully, but as soon as his foot touched the carpet she opened her eyes with a start. 'Oh, it's you,' she said in a feeble voice. 'You gave me a fright.'

'Sorry, Grandma.' He approached the sofa, relieved. 'How are you feeling?'

'Weak.' She took a laboured breath. 'Very weak.'

'I'll call Dr Heyworth.'

'No, don't call anyone. I need to talk to you quickly. If I'm going to die I want to be given time to say my piece.'

David looked appalled. 'You're not going to die.'

'We're all going to go sometime. Now listen.' He sat down beside her on the armchair and shuffled it closer. 'It's about Phaedra.'

'Grandma, are you sure I shouldn't call Dr Heyworth? If it's a heart attack ...'

'It's not a heart attack. I don't know what it is. Death, probably. Now listen. It's important. I have a dying wish. Indulge me!'

449

'OK, what is it?'

'You must go to Paris and bring Phaedra back.' David opened his mouth to object, but Margaret closed her eyes again and for a terrifying moment she seemed to be drifting away.

'Go on,' he urged her softly.

She inhaled and opened her eyes. 'It is my dying wish that Phaedra is brought back into the family so that we can all be happy again.'

'But Grandma, I wouldn't know where to find her.' Then he frowned. 'Did you just say Paris?'

'Yes, Paris. I have her address.'

'How on earth do you have her address?'

'Don't ask, long story, I don't have time.' She took his hand and gripped it hard. 'It's written on a piece of paper on my desk. You have to be quick. I might not last . . .'

David strode over to the desk and found the paper lying on the blotter. He stared at the words, heart racing. So Phaedra was in Paris, after all. But what if she had moved on and no longer wished to see him? Margaret read his thoughts. 'This isn't about you, David,' she continued from the sofa. 'This is about me and my dying wish. I want to forgive her before I meet my maker.'

'Grandma!'

'You have to do it for *me*.'

'Why don't you send someone else?'

'Who else could I send, David? Really, you're being very difficult. I'm dying!'

David wasn't so sure. 'How do you know she's there?'

'I don't. It's a gamble, but it's all I have.'

'What do I say to her? She's not going to be very happy to see me after . . .'

'Goodness, David, if you don't get going I'll be dead before you leave the country!'

'OK, I'll go, but I'm calling Mother and Dr Heyworth whether you like it or not.'

'Fine, I suppose you can't leave me here to peg out on my own.'

David waited for his mother to arrive then left in a hurry to make arrangements to set off immediately. He wondered how his grandmother had got the address and how long she'd had it. The whole thing was very perplexing. He wasn't sure Phaedra would be there: after all, she seemed to spend a lot of time travelling. She could be up a mountain for all he knew, the other side of the world. But his grandmother had insisted, so he had no choice. If she really *was* dying, he had to do his duty and bring Phaedra back. He suddenly felt sick with nerves. What was he going to say to her? So much time had passed, they'd be strangers.

Antoinette was distraught to find Margaret languishing on the sofa. She rushed to her side and took her hand tearfully. 'Oh, Margaret, don't leave me now we've just become friends.'

Margaret opened her hooded eyes like a wily iguana. 'Where's Dr Heyworth?'

'He's on his way. David called him, too. He shouldn't be long. Can I get you anything?'

'No, I'll just stay here where I'm comfortable.' She knitted her fingers and sighed contentedly.

'How are you feeling?'

'Numb.'

Antoinette was seized with panic. 'Numb? Where?'

'Everywhere. I feel like I'm slipping away.'

'Please don't. Hang in there: William will be here

any minute.'

Margaret raised an eyebrow. 'You like Dr Heyworth, don't you?'

'Yes, I do.'

'He might not be top drawer, but he'd be good for you.'

'Oh, Margaret, how can you think of something like that at a time like this!'

The old lady scrutinized her daughter-in-law and detected two pink stains on the balls of her cheeks. 'Because if I'm going to pop off, I'd like to feel everyone was settled.'

'You're not going to pop off.'

'Well, I'm very old.'

'You're very strong.'

'I'm rather looking forward to seeing Arthur, you know.'

'He can wait.'

Margaret smiled. 'So, what are you going to do about Dr Heyworth? You said you liked him.'

'Not in that way!'

'Why not in that way? What's wrong with him?'

'Nothing. It's just that George ...'

'George is gone, my dear, and he's not coming back. You have the rest of your life to live and it's not so much fun being on your own. Trust me, I know. William, as you call him, likes you very much, any fool can see that. Give him a little encouragement, Antoinette.'

'I'm not sure how.'

Margaret sighed impatiently. 'Really, no one seems very capable of doing anything by themselves in the love department.'

Suddenly they heard the hall door open and close with a bang. Heavy footsteps could be heard

452

striding towards them. A moment later Dr Heyworth appeared in the sitting room, and just behind him a very grim-faced Reverend Morley. 'Oh good, you're *both* here,' Margaret exclaimed. 'Reverend, you can give me the last rites.'

The vicar looked horrified. Dr Heyworth grinned. 'So the patient has recovered a little, I see.'

'William, you must see to her at once!' Antoinette commanded. 'Reverend Morley and I will wait in the hall.' She stood up and rushed over. 'You have to get her better, William,' she hissed. 'It's very important that she doesn't die. I can't cope without her.'

'I'll do my best,' he replied.

Antoinette and the vicar sat in the hall while Dr Heyworth closed the sitting-room door and went over to examine the patient. After a brief inspection he sat in the armchair and gave her a stern look. 'Well, as I suspected, Lady Frampton, you are in the very best of health.'

'Oh good,' she replied, sitting up and swinging her legs down. 'What a relief.'

'Certainly for Lady Frampton.'

'Call her Antoinette,' said Margaret. 'It's confusing having two of us.'

'I'm very glad that Reverend Morley is no longer needed. He can go home without the grim prospect of another funeral.'

'I think I gave him quite a fright. Did you see his face? It was as white as a sheet!'

'You gave Antoinette a fright, too.'

'That wasn't my intention,' she was quick to reply.

'Then if I may be so bold, what was?'

She smiled at him a little sheepishly. 'I'm afraid I concocted the plan with Roberta. You see, David's falling apart and I can't bear to watch it. His heart is broken and shows no signs of mending. Roberta remembered that Phaedra was house-sitting in London for a friend. So she went round and asked for Phaedra's address in Paris. It was really very simple. The girl was happy to give it.'

'Why the "heart attack"?'

'Because wild horses wouldn't drag David to Paris. He thinks Phaedra has moved on and wants nothing more to do with him. So I thought that, if it's my dying wish, he'd *have* to go.'

'Surely there was an easier way, without having to scare the living daylights out of everyone.'

'You tell me, Dr Heyworth. Roberta and I couldn't think of one.' She grinned wickedly. 'I must say, it's rather nice to know that people care.'

'More than you realize.'

'Don't let me down, Doctor. Antoinette will be furious if she realizes I've lied.'

He sighed, reluctant to be involved in her plotting. 'All right, just this once. But please don't do it again.'

'I promise. You'd better go and tell them the good news.'

When Dr Heyworth opened the sitting-room door, Antoinette and Reverend Morley leapt to their feet. 'How is she?' Antoinette asked.

'She's going to be fine,' Dr Heyworth replied. 'She just needs to rest.'

Antoinette was so relieved she threw her arms around his neck. 'Oh, thank you!' she breathed. 'I knew you'd save her.'

Dr Heyworth was caught off guard. 'I had

454

nothing to do with it,' he said, embarrassed. 'She's very robust.'

Antoinette pulled away, blushing. 'I was so worried. I couldn't bear to lose another person I love.'

'It's all right, you've got her for a while yet.'

'That's exceedingly good news,' said Reverend Morley, walking past them into the sitting room.

'I'm afraid you've come over for nothing,' said Margaret.

'To the contrary, I've discovered that you're well. I shall return home full of joy.'

'I'm afraid I can't offer you a cup of tea, I gave Jenny the day off.'

'What bad luck you had to fall ill on the one day Jenny wasn't here.'

'I know, Sod's Law! But I can certainly pour you a sherry.'

'What would the doctor say?'

'I don't think it really matters. He's got other things on his mind,' she replied, a mischievous twinkle in her eyes.

Dr Heyworth and Antoinette left the vicar and Margaret in the sitting room and walked outside to their cars. 'You don't think I should invite her to stay at my house for a while, just until she recovers?' Antoinette asked.

'She's fine where she is, I assure you,' Dr Heyworth replied.

'What if she takes another turn?'

'I don't think she will. The sort of turn she took was a one-off.'

Antoinette smiled. 'I'm so pleased. David told me she was dying. I was terribly worried.'

'*She* told David she was dying. Old people tend

455

to think the worst.'

'I don't know where David disappeared to in such a hurry.'

Dr Heyworth decided not to enlighten her. If David had wanted his mother to know, he would have told her himself. 'I'm not sure. But he'll be relieved to know that his grandmother is alive and kicking!' He opened the back door of his Volvo and placed his doctor's bag on the seat.

'William,' Antoinette ventured, her heart suddenly beating wildly.

'Yes?'

'I think I've mastered *Sunset*.'

He smiled, pleased. 'I'd love to hear you play it.'

'Would you?'

'Very much.'

'I'd be happy to play it for you. I've played it a lot recently. I think I know it quite well.'

At that moment Reverend Morley opened the front door of the house and stepped out. 'The gates of Heaven are not ready to open for the Dowager Lady Frampton,' he said heartily, making for his car.

'She might outlive us all,' said Dr Heyworth.

'Now *that* would be a miracle,' Antoinette added, feeling her pulse slow down. Her attempt to encourage Dr Heyworth had stalled before it had begun. Maybe it was too soon after George's death. Perhaps she wasn't ready. Of course there was the possibility that Dr Heyworth did not reciprocate her feelings and that he had only ever wanted friendship—a possibility that left her feeling a little foolish. She watched him climb into his car and waved him off. Then she went back into the house to check on Margaret, her heart surprisingly heavy.

*   *   *

David took a train to London and from there the Eurostar to Paris. He carried a small overnight bag with the bare essentials. He did not expect to stay long. If Phaedra wasn't at home, he'd come back and tell his grandmother that he had done his best.

He sat in the first-class carriage and watched the English countryside rush past the window; then, as the train whizzed into the tunnel and the glass went black, he suddenly realized that he was no longer staring outside but at his own anguished reflection. He gazed at it in horror. He hadn't noticed how dishevelled he had become. His gaunt face and hollow eyes looked as if they belonged to someone else, and he ran a hand pensively over the thick stubble on his chin. What would Phaedra think? Would she recognize him? She certainly wouldn't find him attractive—perhaps she never had. He wished he had taken more care of himself. At the very least he could have shaved.

As the train neared Paris he began to get nervous. He hadn't managed to read more than a few pages of his book, for his thoughts kept interrupting and replaying scenes from the past like a broken DVD stuck on a favourite movie scene. He should have worn out his memories considering the amount of times he had rerun them in his head, but they still shone bright with the same power to hurt.

He cast his eyes around the carriage at the businessmen and women in suits and an elegantly dressed mother with young children. None of them

457

seemed to have a worry in the world as they sat reading magazines or newspapers and the children played quietly on their computer games. It felt surreal, as if David were the only man in the world to nurse a broken heart.

At last the train drew into the station and he descended. He moved through the throng in a daze, eyes on the ground, going through every possible scenario again.

He climbed into a taxi and asked to be taken to rue de Longchamps. The car pulled out onto the road and his stomach knotted into a tight ball. He wasn't sure whether the nausea rising in his stomach was due to his nerves or to the taxi jerking to a stop at a red traffic light. It was early evening. Paris was bathed in a soft amber light as the sun sank slowly in the sky, painting the water of the Seine with bright strokes of red and gold. Electric lights glowed in shop windows and street lamps lit up a cascade of brown leaves as they were carried on the wind before collecting in clusters on the damp pavements and gutters. He let his gaze wander over the town houses with their elegantly curved grey roofs, peeping dormer windows and pretty iron balconies, and knew why Phaedra loved Paris so much. It still had the charm of a bygone age.

Phaedra's apartment was in the centre of the city. He hadn't expected to arrive so quickly. He didn't feel he was prepared. So he paid the cabbie and found a nearby café where he could have a cup of coffee and work out what he was going to say. He sat by the window at a small table and stared into the street, half hoping, half terrified that Phaedra might pass by.

458

The wind picked up, people came and went, but David remained with his empty coffee cup, gazing anxiously out into the dark street. He tried to devise a dialogue, but nothing sounded natural. He started by explaining that Margaret had suffered a stroke, but ended up babbling and sounding confused—and it was only a rehearsal played out in his head. Finally he realized he'd just have to face Phaedra and see what happened. There was always the chance the words would come to him in the heat of the moment. There was always the chance she wouldn't be there at all. He paid the bill, leaving a tip, even though the waiter had been typically grumpy.

He stood up to leave. The café was crowded now. He hadn't noticed. He began to push past the tables and the people standing, waiting to be seated. Then his eyes were drawn to the other end of the room where a weary-looking blonde woman was staring at him, unblinking, her pale-grey eyes large and fearful. He stopped and looked more intently. At first he didn't recognize her. She was thinner now, her skin white against the black of her shirt, her hair pulled into a tight ponytail. A waiter obscured his view for a moment and David tried to see round him. Was it or wasn't it? The waiter moved on; she was still there against the wall, gazing back at him.

David caught his breath. It was Phaedra. He felt his chest grow tight as he began to make his way towards her, but the people in his path made his struggle all the more difficult, like wading through a rough sea: one step forward, one step back. She stood up, and for a terrible moment she disappeared behind a trio of grungy teenagers.

David searched the crowd for her, his eyes frantically jumping from face to face, until at last she came steadily towards him, like a gull propelled on a wave.

It no longer mattered what he was going to say, because the longing in her eyes confirmed that she felt as wretched as he did. His heart quickened, his spirits soared and the knot in his stomach unravelled as she held out her hand and he took it, pulling her the final few steps towards him until they were reunited at last, body to body, chest to chest, saying more in that kiss than they could ever say in words.

*   *   *

Back at Fairfield Park Antoinette sat at the piano, fingers moving deftly over the keys because by now she knew the piece by heart. The dogs lay on the rugs, the fire smouldered in the grate, the house was still. She thought of Dr Heyworth and cringed when she recalled her clumsy attempt to give him encouragement, as Margaret had advised her to do. She wished she hadn't said it because it had sounded unnatural. She hoped Dr Heyworth hadn't been put off by it. How presumptuous to have thought he might be attracted to her. She began to play the piece more vigorously.

The telephone interrupted her playing. She sighed and got up to answer it. 'Hello,' she said.

'It's William,' he replied.

'Oh, William.' Her voice brightened. 'What a surprise.'

'I was wondering whether I could come over and listen to you playing the piano.'

460

'Now?'

'Well, if it's not too late.'

'No, of course not.'

'Good. I'll ring the bell.'

No sooner had Antoinette put the telephone down than the doorbell rang. She frowned. He couldn't possibly have got there that quickly. Her heartbeat quickened with fear. Who would come calling so late? Suddenly she wished she wasn't alone in such a big house. Harris was in the cottage at the bottom of the drive, David across the lake; if she screamed no one would hear her. For a moment she froze, unable to move. The bell rang again, this time more insistently. The dogs awoke from their sleep and jumped to their feet.

Accompanied by the Danes she found the courage to walk across the room to the hall, then stood wringing her hands. 'Who is it?' she called out.

'Me!'

Bertie began to bark.

'William?' She wanted to cry with relief. 'What are you doing there?'

'I said I'd ring the bell.'

She hurried forward to open the door. 'But you got here so quickly.'

His smiling face appeared on the doorstep. 'I was already here,' he replied. Then his face fell at the sight of her. 'Did I frighten you?'

'A little,' she confessed.

'My darling Antoinette, I'm so sorry.' Then he gazed at her solemnly. 'All right, I'll come clean. I didn't come here to listen to your piano-playing.'

'You didn't?'

He shook his head. 'No. I came here ...' He

hesitated. For a second he looked embarrassed. Antoinette smiled softly, which was all the encouragement he needed. He cupped her face in his hands and bent down and kissed her.

Chapter 32

The following morning Antoinette walked around the gardens with a lighter heart than she had had since George died. Dr Heyworth had driven off well after midnight and she had remained alone in the house, but without the ache of loneliness. She had gone to bed and lain awake, replaying the kiss and the subsequent few hours they had enjoyed together in the drawing room. He had listened to her playing the piano, leaning on the top, gazing lovingly into her face as if the music came from her lips and not from her fingers. Then they had sat side by side and played a spontaneous duet, laughing as their improvization declined into tuneless chords and clashing disharmony.

Her love for William was different from her love for George. In spite of her husband's infidelity, she still loved him. She didn't condone his betrayal, but she had found a way to forgive him by trying to understand why. In Phaedra he had encountered a companion who shared his passion for adventure. She was a free spirit, as happy in remote places as he was, with the courage that Antoinette lacked. Phaedra skied, climbed and was undoubtedly just as much at home in a tent on the mountainside as in a warm hotel bed. Antoinette had fulfilled his domestic need, but had left a gaping breach in the

462

other part of his life—the part which was almost more important to him. He had spent so much time alone in the mountains it was easy to understand how he should fall for a beautiful young woman who was willing to share his enthusiasm for nature's wildest places. But during the time he was infatuated with Phaedra, he had never treated Antoinette any differently. He had been just as affectionate, just as attentive. Their life together hadn't changed in any way and she was reassured that his heart had remained constant, even though his infatuation had for a time clouded his judgement. Antoinette chose to believe that, as with all of George's crushes, he would eventually have tired of Phaedra.

Where George had craved adventure, William was content just to be. With him she felt safe, but also valuable. There were no mountains to lure him away and no panoramas to steal his heart. Antoinette was his passion and she was sure of it. With George she had shared the children, Fairfield and his deepest thoughts. With William she shared the gardens, music and *her* deepest thoughts. He gave her his time and his full attention and she never felt his focus pulled in another direction. There was something very steady about her love for William; it was as warm and gentle as a summer meadow.

With these thoughts she wandered through the orchard. Fat, rosy apples caused the branches of the apple trees to droop; a few of the fruit lay on the grass, nibbled by wasps. The trees she had planted with Barry were thriving, their leaves beginning to turn brown as autumn blew in on an easterly wind. She looked at those dying leaves and realized that human beings were a little like trees; that in spite of such loss, their spirits had the strength to live through winter and find happiness again in the spring of new opportunities. She believed that in William she had found spring after a winter of grief. Perhaps now she'd accept the loss of Phaedra, too.

When she went inside she telephoned Margaret to see how she was. Jenny answered and informed her that her mother-in-law was resting. When Antoinette suggested she come over, Jenny was quick to tell her that Margaret was in fact asleep and that it would be best not to wake her. She reassured her that, apart from a little tiredness, Margaret was quite well. Antoinette hung up, feeling a little uneasy. Something wasn't right, but she couldn't work out what it was.

At midday Dr Heyworth arrived with his car boot full of shrubs. 'I thought we could plant these down by the lake,' he said, kissing her tenderly. 'What do you think?'

'You're so thoughtful, thank you,' she replied happily. 'How lovely that we have the whole afternoon ahead of us.'

'I've been thinking: we should go away together.'

'Where to?'

'I don't know.' He shrugged. 'Anywhere but here. Paris, Vienna, Rome, wherever you like. When was the last time you went away?'

'Gosh,' she sighed; it was a long way back. 'A year ago at least.'

'Then it's about time you left Fairfield.' His face brightened. 'Have you ever been to India?'

'No.'

'Neither have I. We can discover it together.'

464

She hesitated. 'But what about Margaret?'

'She'll be all right on her own. David's here.'

'You know, I called this morning and Jenny said she was resting. Then she said she was asleep. She sounded nervous to me, as if she was lying.'

'Why would she lie?'

'Because Margaret will have asked her to.'

'Oh. Would you like to go and see her?'

'I'm not sure. I don't want to disturb her if she *is* sleeping . . .'

At that moment Harris appeared on the porch. 'Lady Frampton, the Dowager Lady Frampton has just called.'

'You see, I knew something was wrong!' Antoinette exclaimed, hurrying back into the house. 'What did she say, Harris?'

'She wants you to meet her at the folly right away.'

'The folly? What's she doing up there? I thought she was resting!'

'She says it's important,' said Harris.

Antoinette turned to Dr Heyworth. 'You have to come with me, William. I sense something's going on, but I don't know what. Yesterday she was dying and today she's up at the folly, demanding that I go and join her. What's it all about?'

Dr Heyworth smiled knowingly, remembering what Margaret had told him the day before. 'Let's go and find out.'

They set off at a pace with Bertie and Wooster trotting ahead into the garden. Light-grey clouds hung heavily in the sky, but every now and then the heavens glowed as the sun tried to burn through. As they reached the top of the hill they spotted David's Land Rover parked on the track. 'Oh dear,

465

it looks like she called David, too.' Antoinette turned to Dr Heyworth in panic. 'You don't think she's getting us all up here to say goodbye, do you? Oh God, I hope she's OK.'

'She's as strong as an ox,' said Dr Heyworth confidently.

'No, she isn't. She just pretends she is. Inside, she's as soft as the rest of us. I know it sounds odd, considering our troubled relationship, but since George died I've grown to like her. No, more than that, I'm fond of her, terribly fond of her.' She accelerated her pace.

Dr Heyworth took her hand and squeezed it. 'She's fine, Antoinette. Trust me, she has many years left in her.'

At last they reached the folly. Antoinette took a deep breath and pushed open the door. There, sitting on the sofas and chairs around the fire, were Margaret, Reverend Morley, David and Phaedra.

Antoinette put her hand to her heart. 'You're all right, Margaret!' she sighed, wanting to cry with relief.

'Of course I'm all right,' Margaret retorted from the armchair. 'But you're not. Come and sit down, dear, and let me explain.'

Antoinette stared in bewilderment at David and Phaedra, sitting together on the sofa. David had shaved, but that wasn't the only thing that made him look different. He was happy. Very, very happy. Reverend Morley stood up at once and offered Antoinette the armchair beside the fire. She sat down gratefully and watched Dr Heyworth find a chair and pull it up between the sofa and Margaret. Reverend Morley perched on the club

466

fender.

'Yesterday you were dying, Margaret. Now here you are with David and Phaedra. What's going on?' Antoinette noticed that Phaedra looked smaller than before, her narrow shoulders as thin as coat hangers in her olive-green cardigan. But her face was radiant and her cheeks as pink as crab apples; only her eyes betrayed a certain apprehension. She glanced at Antoinette then hastily looked away.

'Well, frankly, I'm bored of watching my family mope around as if the sun has packed up and gone away. I missed Phaedra too, and being a selfish woman, I wanted her back as much for myself as for everyone else. Roberta was my partner in crime. She remembered that Phaedra had been house-sitting for a friend and took it upon herself, without any encouragement from me, to go round and ask for a forwarding address. It was very simple. She then called me and gave me the address in rue de Longchamps. Well, we both knew that David can be stubborn. He didn't think Phaedra would want to see him, so I had to put on an act.'

Antoinette looked horrified. '*That* was an act?'

'Yes, I didn't realize quite how good I was. Perhaps I should have been an actress.' She glanced at Reverend Morley. 'I'm sorry I put you all through that, but I had no choice. Isn't it wonderful that I'm so well!'

'So, poor David thought you were dying, too?' Antoinette turned to her son, who shrugged carelessly, as if it had been nothing.

'Let's just say I wasn't totally convinced. She was a little too energetic for a dying person,' he reassured her.

'But off you went, dutifully, to bring Phaedra back.' Margaret smiled triumphantly. 'And that's exactly what you did. Now, I know this was very underhand, Antoinette, and you're probably very cross with me for going behind your back. But I'm old and wise and I know better than you do what's good for you. I know you missed Phaedra as much as the rest of us, and you're never going to do the farm shop on your own. I want to be alive to enjoy those piglets.'

Phaedra risked a glance at Antoinette. She wasn't sure George's wife would forgive her. David had promised her she would, explaining that time had allowed Antoinette to gain some perspective and consequently a little understanding. Phaedra still hadn't been certain, however, and David had had to work hard to persuade her to come home with him. Deep down Antoinette needed her, he had said, even if she hadn't the vision to see it yet. Now Phaedra looked at her fearfully.

If Antoinette had been asked the day before how she would feel were she suddenly faced with Phaedra, she would have declared that mentally she wasn't ready to forgive. However, it is one thing to think coldly from one's head and quite another to think warmly from one's heart. Now that the two women were together in the same room, Antoinette felt her heart swell with compassion. She stood up and walked over to Phaedra, propelled by an impulse that had little to do with thought. She reached out and drew her up from the sofa. Without hesitation, she enveloped her tightly. 'I'm glad you're home,' she said softly,

468

feeling Phaedra's childlike frame and the trembling that ran through it. Phaedra's tears seeped into Antoinette's shirt. She rested her head on her shoulder and closed her eyes. The two women embraced for a long moment. Antoinette didn't need to explain, because forgiveness was in her gesture and in the words she whispered for only Phaedra to hear.

'Right, well, I'm glad it's all worked out,' said Margaret. She narrowed her eyes and registered the tender expression on Dr Heyworth's face as he watched Antoinette. 'Looks like it's just you and me now, Reverend,' she added to the vicar, who momentarily looked a little nervous. 'I think a call to Harris for some supplies wouldn't go amiss,' she added, pulling her mobile telephone out of her pocket. 'What does everyone want?'

Epilogue

A year and a half later

Margaret sat with Reverend Morley at the round table beneath the folly's grand pediment. She gazed down at the gardens of Fairfield Park and watched with amazement as the estate slowly filled up with visitors. Since Antoinette had decided to open it to the public for the whole of June, the work in the borders, wild gardens and around the lake had increased so that now the place looked even more beautiful than when *she* had employed an army of gardeners. Margaret had always known that Antoinette had great flair but she had never imagined that those fingers, so deft at handling fabrics and furnishings, could turn their magic to garden design.

Margaret had enjoyed watching her redecorate the house. The silly woman had refrained from changing anything in all the years she had lived there with George, for fear of offending *her*. If Antoinette had ever asked her opinion she would have told her that the place had been in dire need of redecoration for decades—in fact, she would have done it herself if she'd had the will, which she hadn't. Decorating houses didn't interest her like it interested Antoinette. Now that she had married William Heyworth and moved into his house in the village, Antoinette was restoring the big house for David and Phaedra, and the result was as astonishing as the gardens.

'I do like a happy ending,' Margaret said, sighing

with satisfaction. Reverend Morley nodded thoughtfully, sipping his tea which Mrs Gunice had sent up in a thermos flask. 'Phaedra returned and everything shifted back into place again. She's a dear girl and very capable, though I do respect her for leaving the decoration of the house to Antoinette. It's important to be aware of one's limitations. I'm not sure I like so much pink in the bedroom, however. Fine for a little girl, but Phaedra's a woman. Of course, one can't interfere everywhere, so I bit my tongue; it's *her* bedroom, after all, and Antoinette insists the choice of colour had nothing to do with her. In fact, if I remember rightly, she said it was David's choice. Blue would have been more appropriate. Still, I have to say that Phaedra's jolly good at running the farm shop. I'm not sure Tom is a great contributor, though he's doing his best and it's nice to see him helping in the family business. That nightclub of his was never a good thing. Now all we need to do is find him a nice girl so that he can settle down too. You know, when George was around, although he kept the family together, he never managed to make us all like one another. Oh, those years were very tense. It was like walking on eggshells around Antoinette. The lovely thing is that since his death we've all become friends. I think that's got a lot to do with Phaedra. Don't ask me how she does it; I'm not a psychologist, but she has a wonderful magic. To think that we almost lost her.' She sighed again, this time with relish. 'I took it upon myself, you remember. Sometimes one has to simply take control when others are too stubborn or uncertain to do it for themselves. I knew that she'd come back if we asked her. Forgiveness is a wonderful thing, isn't it, Reverend Morley?'

Reverend Morley put down his teacup. 'Lady Frampton,' he began, a little hesitantly. 'Don't you think now, after all the years we've known each other, that you might call me Joseph?'

Margaret was appalled. 'Joseph? Good gracious, no. You're a man of God, Reverend Morley, calling you Joseph would diminish you. A man of your stature should have a title that reflects your distinction and gives your position a sense of gravitas and formality. I look up to you, Reverend, and I respect your opinion on everything. I couldn't possibly start calling you Joseph. What a ridiculous suggestion.'

Reverend Morley picked up his teacup again, cowed. It wasn't often that he could get a word in to offer his opinion these days.

'I must say that it was jolly good of Phaedra to lend the Frampton Sapphires to Roberta indefinitely,' Margaret continued. 'She insists she will never wear them and David has at last accepted her reasons. I can't say I mind terribly who has them as long as they stay in the family. One has to honour one's ancestors, don't you think?' But before the vicar could comment, she was off again. 'Ironic that after having masqueraded as a Frampton, Phaedra became onc. David wastcd no time in putting a ring on her finger, and I don't blame him. He'd suffered her running off once before; he wasn't going to let *that* happen again.' She smiled contentedly. 'I thought I'd be dead by now, but look at me: still here to enjoy all the goings-on. And there are an awful lot of goings-on at Fairfield, don't you agree?' She settled her imperious gaze on her companion. 'Reverend Morley, you haven't said a single word for a long time. Have you lost your tongue?' Then her eyes softened and she smiled at him fondly. 'Why do you put up with me?'

He smiled back and shook his head. 'Because you're never dull, Lady Frampton—and you have a good heart.'

'Ah, that's the bottom of it. Heart. Life would be jolly cold and unfriendly if there was no heart. Tell me, Reverend . . .'

'Yes?'

She sighed happily. 'Anything.'

'Anything?' The vicar, as was so often the case, found himself confounded by Margaret Frampton.

'Yes, tell me anything you like.' She sat back and folded her hands in her lap expectantly.

That evening David and Phaedra walked Rufus around the lake. The moon was big and fat like a glowing puffer fish, stars glimmered and glittered in the immense sky and somewhere in the middle of the woods a pair of owls hooted to one another in a haunting courtship. David and Phaedra held hands. In spite of the months that had passed they still felt blessed to be together. They remembered the pain of separation and knew that whatever happened in their marriage, they would never be parted like that again.

'I have an idea,' said David suddenly, gazing up at the hill where the folly could be seen by the light of the moon. 'You always said that you wanted to see the dawn from the folly.'

'Yes, I did. Are you about to suggest we go and spend the night up there?' She felt a frisson of excitement through her bones.

474

'The sofa's deep enough for two. Mother had it tailor-made especially big.'

'I'm not sure she had *that* in mind when she commissioned it.'

He swung her around. 'It's very romantic up there,' he said, and kissed her forehead.

'And I do have a wild and reckless streak,' she joked, pulling him closer.

He kissed her lips. 'There are blankets and a fire, Grandma's hidden stash of wine ...'

'Just you, me and Rufus and the sounds of the woods,' she murmured.

'Let's do it.'

She laughed. 'As you wish, milord.'

'Then come, milady, and let me show you *my* wild and reckless streak!'

They set off up the lawn side by side, hand in hand, full of excitement. The dew sparkled in the silvery light as they strode over the grass, and Rufus, thinking he was going for a long walk, disappeared into the undergrowth. When at last they reached the folly they stood a while and let their eyes wander over the mysterious beauty of the night. The valley below was lit up so that shafts of light illuminated the ground as brightly as if it were day.

Phaedra leaned against her husband. 'I'm very happy, David,' she said softly. 'I never thought I'd ever belong anywhere.'

He bent down and rested his cheek on top of her head. 'Your destiny was always here with me, and I thank the God that made it so.'

'You know, in the depth of my despair I asked George to put right his wrong; I think he did.'

'If he's watching now, I bet he's as happy as we

are—that is, if he's not still rattling those pearly gates.'

Phaedra turned round and gazed up at him anxiously. 'Darling, he's not rattling the pearly gates. He's walked right through them. Trust me. It's because of George that we're together. It's because of George that we're all of us happy. It's because of George that I love you.'

He brushed a tendril of hair off her face. 'You once said that you were "desperately, deliriously and overwhelmingly" in love with Dad. You also said you'd never love like that again.'

She smiled up at him, aware that the love she felt for David could never be put into words. 'I don't love you like that, my darling, and I'm glad I never will.'

476

Acknowledgements

I am incredibly fortunate to have two dynamic teams at Simon & Schuster, one in the UK and one in the USA, and I would like to thank them both wholeheartedly for working on my book with such enthusiasm and positivity: my UK editor Suzanne Baboneau and my USA editor Trish Todd, Kerr MacRae, Clare Hey, Katie McGowan, Hannah Corbett and Lizzie Gardiner. I am so grateful and thrilled that the books they produce so beautifully reflect my stories in perfect pitch.

I'd like to thank Sheila Crowley, my brilliant agent and dear friend, for being a formidable ally and strong support. She's always there when I need her and always fiercely optimistic and motivated.

I stayed with Ed and Maryam Eisler at their Jacobean house in Hampshire and felt so inspired I built this novel around it, with licence to add a hill or two and a folly! I thank them for inspiring me. I also want to thank Jane Yarrow, Samantha Heyworth, Amanda Newson, Fiona Sherriff, Eloise Goldstein and Sarah Vine for enhancing my life in so many ways and consequently adding to the pot of ideas that feed my imagination.

I'd like to thank my husband, Sebag, for his continuing patience and wisdom. He's always ready to help weave plots and give me advice when I need it. Most of all he makes me laugh like no one else in the world—and that's the recipe for good health and happiness! I really wouldn't have written all these novels without him.

My mother is always my first reader and her observations and ideas really matter and make a big difference to the final manuscript. I'm extremely grateful for her time and dedication—and for her generosity, because so many of her stories are sewn into the pages of my books and she's never said she minds!

My father is a deeply spiritual man and has taught me so much about what is important in Life and why we're all here, struggling to find meaning to it all. If my novels have some of his depth then I have achieved a wonderful thing.

I thank my children, Lily and Sasha, for filling my heart so full of love that it overflows.

478